Seeking Stars

A multicultural celebrity romance

Leonor Soliz

Leonor Soliz

Cover Art by Leonor Soliz

First edition

Paperback ISBN: 978-1-7782872-3-7
Ebook ISBN: 978-1-7782872-4-4

To my eight-year-old self, who wrote her first Meet Cute with so much joy in her heart.

Contents

Author's Note

M Y BOOKS ALWAYS END in a Happily Ever After. My stories are generally fluffy, with a good mix of humor and angst. Nevertheless, I believe it's important to give readers every chance to consent to reading my book. Although I write generally comforting romance, if you'd like to access a list of content warnings for this story, check the QR code below with your phone (paperback) , or visit leonorsoliz.com/books/seeking-stars.

Chapter 1

L IAM'S PERSONA MADE HIS living— a really good living, at that. Eight out of ten people recognized his face. Promotional posters featured him across tall buildings, all over the world. Movie trailers centered him as the hero, and his characters never failed to meet his brand of action and emotion, CGI optional. The lead actress always wanted him, and so did millions of fans across the world. Yet none of it would help him now.

His therapist arched her thin eyebrow at him, her eyes focused and bright on his face. It meant trouble; she'd heard something of note and would call him out on it. He closed his eyes to block her out for just one more second. A futile effort, and the only option he had.

"What did I say?" He went back on his words, but didn't find anything particularly incriminating. He'd said it all before.

I'm the vehicle of people's income and I end up as currency.

Dr. Linda's gesture didn't waver. "It's not what you said, but how you said it."

He reviewed his statement again, focusing on his tone.

"Oh." He scratched his eyebrow before he let his hand fall in his lap, listless.

"You're still bitter, Liam."

He sighed. "I guess I am. Can you blame me?"

"Of course not. You've worked hard to get here, to understand yourself... but your life still doesn't reflect those changes. And I think— tell me if I'm wrong— I think that you're exhausted by it all, in your soul."

His stomach dropped at Dr. Linda's words, despite the comfort of her understanding. Emptiness filled his chest now, a concave, vacant space.

"Bitterness, though..." she adjusted her glasses, her focus completely on him. "There's a certain hopelessness to it, isn't there? Powerlessness."

Liam opened his mouth to reply, to defend against something. He didn't even know what, really, but she lifted her hand to stop him.

"Don't just jump to talk back. Check in with how you feel, remember?"

He closed his mouth in a snap and pressed his lips together, as if to stop the words from escaping him. He brought his attention inwards; the heavy mass of a black hole still occupied his chest.

"That's right," Dr. Linda said. "What do you notice?"

"I'm empty. Drained. Heavy."

She nodded. Her eyes softened on him. He liked the constant reassurances that she offered, like saying, *I see you. You're doing well.*

"Yes. It's so tough, isn't it?" she asked.

"Yes. I'm... done. I need a change. I can't keep going like this."

"Perfect. That's right. Change is good. Let that fuel you to say no to them, Liam."

But his lips pressed together again, trapping his *no* inside with all the other words once more.

———

Of the thousand times Ana had to spell her name in her life, not once had she done it with trepidation swirling in her stomach. Nerves and hope lodged in her throat, and she struggled to speak with a clear voice into the phone.

"A - n - a. L - i - r - a," she dictated. Ana had just received her contract to finalize details with Diana, her brand new agent, and Diana's assistant, Tiwa, had called to go over the final edits.

"One *n* only, is that correct?" Tiwa asked.

Her question didn't alter Ana's feelings. Having a non-classical English name meant many things in this country, including a lifetime of spelling it out to people. It could be worse; had Ana been born in Ecuador like her parents, her full name would be Ana María Lira Gutiérrez. Not only would that triple the time she spent dictating her name, but she'd be forced to explain over and over again that, yes, she had two last names.

Having to confirm her first name had only one consonant seemed like a small problem, comparatively. "Yes, just the one *n*."

"All right, Ms. Lira. Everything seems to be in order. Diana is very excited to be signing you on."

"I'm really excited, too."

"You should have received your plane ticket information to your email inbox earlier today. Can you confirm for me that you got it? That your name is spelled out correctly there?"

She had received it and her name had been fine. Seeing the information in her inbox had sparked such excitement in her, that Ana had called her best friend Ely— Elena at birth, but no one called her that— and they'd spent ten minutes listing the ways in which it marked a before and after in Ana's career. Thanks to now having Diana as an agent, Ana's work teetered on the brink of reaching multitudes.

"I did, yeah," she said. "All good."

"Excellent. We'll see you next week to sign the documents and make it official with a nice champagne toast."

"Sounds great. I will see you then."

Ana ended the call with shaking fingers. Her goal summoned her, so close; just a few more days and her future would open up. She took several deep breaths, chanting the mantra Ely had made up for her in her mind: *you got it, it's yours. Nothing will ruin this. You'll rock it.*

You got it. You got it. You got it.

Her phone rang again, taking her out of her hard-earned peace. She glanced at the screen and rushed to answer. The agency's name flashed on the screen.

"Yes, hello? Is something amiss?"

The briefest of silences.

"Hello," the person on the phone said. "This is John Coulton's office at Total Creatives Agency. May I speak with Ms. Lira?"

"This is her."

"Good morning, Ms. Lira. My name is Magda, and I am Mr. Coulton's assistant. I would like to schedule a meeting with you to discuss an opportunity. Mr. Coulton would like to know if you have availability for this Friday morning?"

"Uhm... I'm sorry, I'm not sure— is this related to my signing with Diana?"

Diana worked for Total Creatives, too. Ana's brain tried to come up with reasons as to why another agent might want to talk to her, but it came up empty.

"No, Ms. Myers doesn't know about this yet." Magda didn't so much as clear her throat to say that. Like Diana was an after-thought. Her next words confirmed it. "Mr. Coulton wants to talk to you as soon as possible and he might not appreciate waiting until Diana can be involved. We'll arrange things with Ms. Myers, don't worry about it. Does Friday work?"

"I can do Monday," Ana decided. She needed to research this Coulton person; if they could decide things and not worry about Diana's opinion, then they were higher up than Diana. "I have a ticket for Sunday and I'll be in LA that same evening to finalize my contract with Ms. Myers."

"We'll arrange for a chartered flight for you and I'll reach out to Ms. Myers' office to clear things up. Is Friday a good day?"

Ana didn't miss the subtle change in Magda's voice. Polite words did nothing to hide the steel in her tone. "Yes."

"Excellent," the assistant said. "We'll email you the details. Thank you so much for accommodating; Mr. Coulton really appreciates it. We'll see you on Friday. Goodbye."

The call ended with a soft click. Ana hadn't even gotten a chance to say goodbye.

Why would Coulton be in a hurry to meet with Ana? She needed to be prepared for unpredictable things and she really, really needed to research this Mr. Coulton.

***

"You're nervous." Ely sat on Ana's bed, and from her spot pointed out the obvious.

Ana didn't immediately acknowledge her friend's words; she continued lining her toiletries on a shelf of her closet, mentally checking what she needed to take to her trip to LA. Three days had gone by since the mysterious call from TCA, and Ana had barely thought about anything else.

"Hard not to be," she replied, taking a couple of products and adding them to her carry-on suitcase. Reaching to it on her bed, her long hair slid down her shoulder, brushing her arm on its path.

"Mr. Coulton manages some of the biggest names in Hollywood and he wants to meet with me. For reasons no one has thought to share, I might add."

"Do you think he wants to sign you?"

Ana let out an incredulous chuckle. "I doubt it. I was in the middle of signing with Diana and, yeah, I had been contacted by a couple other people but, well, none of them were that important."

"Maybe Coulton is a fan, saw you were being signed in the same agency and he decided to scoop you up for himself?"

"Don't say that," Ana half-growled, disliking the way her stomach rolled in waves. "It's going to make me more nervous. Besides, there's like a 0.2% chance that that's the case. He represents people like Sam Russel, Liam McMillan, one of the Chrises even."

"Mhh, Liam," Ely sighed. "He's my favorite of the Chrises."

"That makes no sense."

"You know it does. We have many actors of that caliber called Chris and Liam is the best of them. Even if he doesn't have the right name."

Ana rolled her eyes at her friend. Taking two blazers out of her closet, she held them at shoulder height, considering which one might give the right vibe for her business look.

"Anyway," Ana continued, "there was an item in the itinerary they sent me that said I had a meeting with Diana to sign the documents. I'm pretty sure I'm still going to work with her. On the other hand, I have at least one meeting booked with Coulton, but there were no other details included. Also, it literally said at *least* one meeting with Coulton. No mention of a maximum number, or when those extra meetings might happen, if at all. It grates, honestly."

"Go with the navy one. The stripes still make it fun, and the blush one looks amazing on your skin but is less powerful looking." Ely stood up and placed the blush fabric against Ana's forearm. They both admired the way it made Ana's light brown skin come alive. She sighed in agreement with Ely, who continued saying, "People in high places, girl. They do what they want."

Ana nodded and packed her navy blazer in the small suitcase.

"But soon you'll be famous and you'll be one of those people in power," Ely added. "Your platform will be bigger and you'll use it to educate the masses."

At this, Ana laughed. "One can dream!"

"In any case, you'll have to keep me updated. I won't let go of my phone. I want all the details!"

Chapter 2

THREE TIMES LIAM HAD tried to convince his agent to give him a break. With two calls and one meeting under his belt, Liam decided not to take his car to the fourth scheduled attempt. While he typically enjoyed driving, doing so in LA required a specific mindset he didn't have that day. Aside from the terrible city traffic, on a day like this, it nauseated him to imagine someone might recognize him while at a red light, and cause an embarrassing ruckus. He needed to be in a good mood to cope with something like that. So, no. It was the wrong day for that.

Morgan, Liam's PA, organized for one of TCA's drivers to pick him up instead. They made it from home to the building in record time; he had ten minutes to spare. Despite that, when the elevator's door opened on the 23rd floor, Magda's assistant waited for him. Someone must have seen him in the building and announced his arrival; perhaps one of the guards saw him on a security camera. It could still creep him out, how someone always watched. Everywhere.

"Welcome, Mr. McMillan. Thank you so much for coming. Please follow me to the board room; Mr. Coulton will be with you shortly."

"Hello, Alexis." Liam followed her and sat in one of the elegant leather chairs in the room.

"Can I offer you something to drink?"

"I'm good, thanks."

"Let me know if you need anything."

She closed the door behind her. If everything went as usual, Coulton wouldn't make him wait too long. When Liam came to the office, they treated him like the top priority. Liam knew the deal; they treated him like this because of the money he brought them. The moment he didn't, they would stop.

Liam tried to be okay with the reality of it. At the very least, he hoped to use it for leverage. He'd need it, if Liam hoped to negotiate things with his agent and push, this time.

"Liam!" Coulton's voice greeted him, loud and excited. Liam got up and offered his hand. "It's so good to see you, my friend."

"You too." Liam shook the older man's hand. "You have news for me? I'm surprised that you called me back so quickly after our last conversation."

"That I do," Coulton said. They sat in front of each other across the glass meeting table. "I took what you said to heart, and I think I've found a solution we will all like."

"So you're going to give me a break? Let me take a long, restful vacation?"

"I pressed pause on your schedule, moved things around, even begged a few people— and was able to get you four weeks off."

Liam bit on the corner of his mouth to stop himself from complaining. He had asked for three months.

He let his hands curl into loose fists. "So you agree that it won't ruin my career."

"Oh, it would absolutely ruin things. Your trajectory would change from an upward curve to a flat one. You want to capitalize now. If you had an Oscar or two things would be different, but right now, just–"

"Just three years since my career truly began," Liam interrupted. "C'mon, man. You've got to freshen up your speech. It's getting old."

"Okay, then I'll tell you something I haven't told you before. You started late. You had no formal training. You knew nobody. If that random director hadn't cast you in the only good movie he ever made, no one would know you. You're hot right now and we definitely don't want to lose that, or you will be that actor that was very popular for three movies and then was gone. They'll make a *Where Are They Now* episode of you. Part of my job is to make sure that that doesn't happen."

Liam crossed his arms. He hid his tightening fists behind them. "It's been twelve movies and more interviews, promos, press tours, and networking events than I can count. I'm always doing more than one thing at a time— a main project, a promo of some sort, and starting something else. When we signed four years ago, you said you wanted to represent me because I have talent, not just good looks. That it'd help me build a strong career."

"What does that have to do with anything? That is still very much true. It's also true that that's not enough in Hollywood. Whatever your talent or muscle mass are, if you disappear from the collective minds, I won't be able to book you in anything."

Liam uncrossed his arms only so that he could rub his face in frustration, both hands scratching against his unshaven skin.

"Look," Coulton said this time, his tone significantly less boisterous. "All I'm trying to do is make you into a big name. One that people will remember and that directors fight over. Someone who is going to be making movies into his fifties and beyond. That's what you want, right?"

Air boiled in Liam's lungs. Again he had to ask himself why he did all of it— the acting, the promos, the traveling— and why it still felt like Coulton had it wrong. Why Liam couldn't tell his agent what he really wanted. What he needed. The answer lived somewhere inside him, chained to his breast bone, but Liam could put no words to it.

The fight deflated in his chest, leaving him in a deep sigh. His shoulders dropped under the weight of his doubt.

"Yes, that's what you want," Coulton answered for Liam. "So let me do my job."

Liam forced out a long, calming breath. "Okay, yeah. Okay. I'll take the month. How far can I go? Do you promise no PR calls?"

"I promise no PR calls."

Something in how he said it made Liam suspicious. "No PR calls, but...?"

"But you won't be alone."

Ana set her features in a confident and friendly look, and stepped into the tall, glass building in which TCA's offices resided. She introduced herself at the information desk, following the instructions she'd received. Not five minutes later, a neatly dressed woman welcomed her and, with quick steps, guided Ana to the elevators and up.

With the number 23 button alight on the chrome panel, Ana's stomach dropped under the pull of gravity. She focused on the changing numbers indicating the quick pace at which they climbed floors; reciting each new digit in her mind helped her keep her eyes away from the mirrors around her. She didn't want to check her looks again— she had done enough of that at the hotel and she liked the result: fitted pinstripe navy blazer over a rock band shirt, dark forest green skinny pantsuit, and bold, dark red lips hit the note just right.

You got it, you got it, you got it.

The elevator's doors opened and the woman ushered Ana forward and to someone else. The doors closed again behind her.

"Hi Ms. Lira, my name is Alexis, I'm Magda's assistant."

The assistant to the assistant. It meant high stakes.

"Hi, Alexis. It's nice to meet you."

The attractive woman didn't offer her hand. Her eyes surveyed Ana top to bottom. "I love your suit! So modern and refreshing." She offered a small smile, before turning around and walking away. Unsure of the sincerity in Alexis' comment, Ana followed, a single twist in her stomach. Alexis continued, "You will be called into the meeting soon. You can wait over here," she indicated with a light hand, pointing at a stylish sitting area. "Magda will come get you."

With a quick turn, she faced Ana and clasped her hands in front of her. Uncertain, Ana opted for sitting on the leather couch, looking up expectantly at Alexis.

"We have a variety of teas and coffees to offer. What would you prefer?"

"Coffee, black. Thanks," she added.

"What kind of coffee?"

"Whichever is strong and caffeinated and doesn't taste over-burnt."

The smallest of wrinkles marred Alexis's nose. Subtle, but not so subtle that Ana didn't notice. Ana straightened her back tall.

"You got it," Alexis said with a practiced smile. She lifted her wrist and peeked at her smart watch. "I have to answer this. I'll take your coffee to you once you're in the boardroom. I will check in on you as soon as I have a moment. Get comfortable!"

Alexis walked away, lifting a hand to her headset. "Good morning, this is Mr. Coulton's office. You're speaking with Alexis. How may I help you?"

She disappeared around a corner.

Ana crossed her legs and put her hands on her lap. She knew better than to get on her phone. Instead, she inspected the room, paying attention to the decor and willing herself to calm down. Not knowing the purpose of the meeting made things worse; she didn't even know if she'd meet with one or ten people. Being in the dark never failed to make her feel lost at sea. She hated it. But surely, focusing on the cool red vase with exotic flowers would help her rock the meeting.

"Ms. Lira, perfect timing." A new person stood at the edge of the sitting area. "I am Magda. They're ready for you. If you'll follow me," she said, and with a full-body movement— one side moving back three quarters, a sweeping hand casually indicating a sanded glass door— showed her which way to go.

Ana stood and followed. Hoping no one spied on her, she allowed herself one nervous gesture: she tugged at the hem of her blazer, straightening it down.

Magda opened the double glass doors and went into the boardroom. Ana put on her biggest, brightest smile, using her best feature as a shield, and went in after her.

"Ms. Ana Lira, Mr. Coulton," Magda announced.

Ana walked into the room and stood to the side of the conference table, between two men sitting opposite each other. She ignored the broad-shouldered man with his back still to her. She focused instead on the man facing her, noticing a few of his features in a flash: black hair with a high forehead, deep wrinkles marking an expressive face. Thick eyebrows, smart gray eyes.

Tanned skin, and a smile so friendly that it had to be practiced. He stood and shook her hand, strong but not crushing.

"It's a pleasure to meet you, Ms. Lira. I've heard some good things about you."

"The pleasure is mine, thank you, Mr. Coulton."

"Please call me Coulton, everyone does."

"I will, thank you."

Making herself acknowledge the second person in the room, she turned, focused, and froze, her smile still in place.

"This is Liam McMillan," Coulton said next to her. With a knowing chuckle, he added, "I'm confident you know who he is."

The world scratched to a halt. She stared at him for an indefinite amount of time— a tenth of a second? A full minute? Five?— her mind slow to pick up.

He slouched in his seat. A mix of casual and despondent, an elbow on the arm of his chair and his head heavy on his hand, only his eyes looked up at her. Big, green, intense eyes, bestowed with thick, long eyelashes. The most striking green eyes Hollywood had ever known, as she'd once seen them described in a magazine at a grocery store's till. The preferred color of so many romance novels, despite the implausibility of having every attractive man blessed with them. Perfect for the leading role he often occupied everywhere. Ideal to bring the best romantic heroes to the screen. He stood out, close up shots making those eyes shine and promise you the perfect happily ever after was possible for you, too. No matter the law of probabilities. He'd won the phenotypic lottery and it put her on guard. No one had a right to be that gorgeous.

Her awareness seemed to flip back on with a mental gasp, and a loud voice begging to the universe that this was all a mirage and she had not appeared shocked. Nor made it awkward.

His head pointed down and to the side, the corner of his mouth curling down. She welcomed his preemptive displeasure at... so mething... everything? It let her see through his Hollywood charm to the condescending man he clearly was. Her awareness narrowed, and the resolution to be unaffected by him came right after, grounding her in a second.

She shot her hand forward. "Hello," she said, pleased at how calm her voice sounded. "Nice to meet you."

There, perfectly polite. She gave herself a mental pat on the back.

He hesitated, she was sure of that, but finally extended a hand to shake hers.

"You too." He didn't mean it.

The hand holding hers was soft, his voice deep and clear in real life too; she had wondered, from the movies she'd watched of his. She tucked that annoying detail away in her brain to consider later; right now she needed to focus on being unmoved. His voice had also been full of annoyance and Ana didn't deserve that treatment.

"Sit down, please," Coulton said next to her, and she took the seat at the head of the table, between both men.

As if on cue, Alexis brought in a tray of drinks.

"Thank you, Alexis."

Soon the three of them sat alone again.

"All right, let's talk," Coulton said. "I suspect you don't know what you're doing here, Ms. Lira."

"Ana, please, and you're right. I wasn't informed about the purpose of this meeting, but I understand that I will be seeing Diana later today."

"You would know that better than me, really." Coulton dismissed Diana without a care. Ana could feel green lasers pointing at her from the other side of the table. "I just asked Magda to make sure you joined us for this meeting and she made it happen."

Ana said nothing about the casual show of power.

"You like Queen?" Liam asked, drawing her attention back to him. At her look of confusion, he gestured to the shirt she wore under her patterned blazer.

She glanced at the classic image of the group's lead singer on her chest, one arm extended up above his head, the other holding the mic close to his face.

"Oh, yes. Freddy is the best." She left it at that, limiting herself to facts.

"Agreed." A sudden grin appeared on Liam's perfect face. The same grin he flashed often for the cameras. "Though I have to say, I'm partial to Brian, myself."

"They were all amazing." She added a tiny upward slant to her lips for Coulton's benefit. Not responding to Liam's smile might make her look antagonistic and, if this was a work meeting, she needed to be careful. Polite. She also forced her eyes to remain focused on his, unwavering; as much as she would have liked to let them roam all over him and memorize every one of Liam McMillan's features, she couldn't afford to appear starstruck—both out of pride and professionalism.

"Glad to see you like her," Coulton said, mostly to Liam. The older man must have thought that if Liam smiled at Ana, then he must approve of her, somehow. Ana still had her doubts. "I had to scramble for a solution once you asked me for help and, well, I won't bore you with the details, but learning about Ms. Lira's talent was a lightbulb moment."

"Okay," Ana said. "I appreciate being of help, I do, but I could help a lot more if I knew what it is I'm supposed to be doing."

"Forgive me, Ana, you're right. Let me explain," he began, before taking a sip of his coffee.

Ana copied him. Liam didn't move. Clearly, he did not want to be a part of this meeting.

"Liam here is... extremely busy, as you can imagine. Everyone wants a piece of him right now. Any stress you assume comes with his job, well, triple it. Such a schedule is important yet exhausting. He wants to slow down for a short period of time and, as my wife continues to remind me, compromise is key to any good relationship. So, I've figured out a way to give Liam somewhat of a break without affecting his PR opportunities."

"Right," she said. "How do I fit into your compromise?"

"My wife figured that out, actually. I was... verbalizing, shall I say, some of my stresses of the day, and she noted that people don't typically know what it's like to be a celebrity. Or they can imagine, but they still want more. They all live in this contradicting place of thinking they know a celebrity like they know their spouse, and always craving more. They want to get close to the life of an A-Lister, get into their mind, see what they assume to be the splendor and glamor of fame. Or, they want to see them fail." Coulton added a chuckle here, as if this was all kind of a joke. Ana didn't find it in her to share in his amusement. "Thing is, my wife's a fan of your work, Ana. She gave me the idea."

Time slowed down again. All synapsis in her brain froze for one, two, three seconds. A tonne of bricks found a home in her lungs.

"A documentary?" Ana barely registered the skeptical tone to her question. Her mind had gone blank.

"A documentary," Liam confirmed, but his voice lacked the almost giddy excitement lacing Coulton's words.

"I saw some of your work, Ana," Coulton continued, ignoring Liam's evident displeasure. "The way you film— the way you study your story— it would be the perfect way to showcase Liam's most human side. I understand you do your own editing?"

A documentary? Of Liam McMillan?!

"Right, yes," she confirmed, still reeling. "I find that it helps me tell the story properly. I get to know the people I work with so closely during the filming process, that editing everything myself helps me figure out exactly what I want to keep and what can go. Also, no one gets to see the moments that don't make it into the movie. I find that the people I work with like that, for privacy."

It also helped her save a lot of money, but she didn't say that.

"Imagine my pleasure when I discovered we were signing you up at TCA," Coulton said. "We could keep it all in-house! So I had Magda call you. Diana is over the moon at the idea, of course. Now here you are."

"Here I am," Ana agreed, mostly to buy herself time.

A documentary. Of Liam McMillan.

Her brain short-circuited.

"I trust I don't have to say how big this would be for your career, Ana," Coulton started to say, before being interrupted by Liam.

"I don't think it's Ana that you need to convince here. This is the complete opposite of what I asked for. I asked for a break, time to rest. I didn't ask to become an object of study. No offense, Ana."

He dismissed her with a flick of his hand. She narrowed her eyes at him but didn't get to say anything. She'd become invisible to them as they faced each other.

Coulton's voice grew louder. "And I explained to you why I don't think an actual break is a good idea. I want to be able to tell the press that you're on an exciting project, something that hasn't been done before."

"And I explained that I want a vacation. If you tell me I need to wait six months, even a year for hell's sake, but I'll get an actual, alone to do whatever I please break—"

"Liam, I told you, this is not the time. It may not be the time for another year or two. These are going to be the most intense five years of your life, yes, but it's five years of investment for a lifetime of dreams... and you're halfway there."

"I hit the ground running when I signed with you and I haven't taken a single break yet. I've let you set the tone, and the pace, of everything I've done since signing with you. I think I deserve rest, four years in."

"You'll have time to rest when you make it, Liam. When you have the world at your feet. Don't forget it's keeping a steady pace that wins marathons. Don't quit on the final leg of the race! You'll leave this stage behind sooner than you'll realize and, I promise you— the results will last forever. Don't throw it all away now. You hired me to be your agent and your manager. Hell, I'd like to think I'm also your friend and mentor!"

"If I may," Ana interrupted, clearing her throat, "a documentary won't work if Mr. McMillan isn't on board. I like to get really close to the people I work with, which requires openness and vulnerability. If he's not willing, then the whole thing is destined to fail."

"You sound like my therapist," Liam grumbled. For a moment, Ana thought he'd continue, but he didn't.

"The work I do can sometimes feel like therapy because it's unguarded," Ana acknowledged. She added, "Only I don't help you find the answers. Whatever you come up with are the answers shared with the world. Nothing more, but definitely nothing less. I share *your* truth with the world." She gave her statement a second to sink in. "I think I need to leave you both to discuss. At this point

I half-expect to be made to sign an NDA," she joked, but neither man seemed to think it funny.

"I'm sure I don't need to explain how detrimental it would be to you, if people were to learn you don't know how to keep conversations private. Your professional reputation is all you have, and I suggest you're careful with it. Or would an NDA make you feel better?" Coulton asked, all friendliness gone.

Ana recognized the threat and the test. "I don't need an NDA. My brand is intimate, raw, honest people in film. I'm not about to jeopardize that."

Coulton gave her the tiniest smile. "I like you."

"That's good," she said. "But you need him—" she pointed at Liam— "to trust me. To want this."

"We'll reach out again soon. Can you arrange your schedule to stay in LA for a couple more days?"

Her original return date had been set for the next day but, hell yeah, she could rearrange her schedule. She had to do what she could to get this opportunity. Coulton didn't know that Ana had been racking her brain for ideas for her next project, or how she'd welcomed the relief of being offered to sign with Diana. Ana had made a little bit of a name for herself, but she still existed lightyears away from achieving her ultimate goal. Working with Liam McMillan could change everything.

Pausing for effect, she said, "I don't think I have anything significant back home until Monday." She didn't bother to add that the important thing was Ely's birthday. "I can stay for the weekend."

"Perfect," Coulton said. "We'll talk."

After storming out of Coulton's office, Liam went home, checked if his therapist could fit him in for a quick consult over the phone, and proceeded to look Ana up online.

He recognized her on the second link he clicked on his phone. He frowned, frozen for a second— he'd seen her work before. From what he remembered, he'd enjoyed it. He'd even subscribed to one of her profiles! But he hadn't realized it during their brief time together. Curious, he cast a couple of her trailers to the big screen in front of him, and soaked in the new piece of information.

He read a couple of articles and downloaded one of her films to watch later. With the TV off, he waited for his therapist's call in silence, the simmering in his veins persistent but low. The darkened screen reflected a slightly distorted version of him; the man in the black glass rested his arms on the back of the sofa, an ankle over the other knee. His shaking foot was the only part of him that betrayed his emotional state.

His therapist's name lit up his phone and he answered on the first ring.

He grabbed the phone in his hand. "Coulton fucking tricked me," he blurted.

"Okay, breathe." Dr. Linda said on the phone. "I'm glad I could fit you in for a quick call, Liam, because it sounds like you need to talk this through. Start from the beginning."

"Coulton called me in for a meeting this morning." Faint tremors echoed through his muscles, not quite there, but not far either. "He set me up. He agreed to push my contracts into the future, move things around, giving me a month... but not a break. He found a documentary filmmaker and he's trying to make me sign with her. To sell my private life for a reduced workload."

"Oh. I'd ask how you feel about it but I can hear it in your voice. You're angry."

"I'm pissed off, yeah. You know how much I need rest, and how much I want to have that... that personal space where I get to be me. Coulton wants to commodify my time off, pretending it's a break."

"I can see how that would push your buttons. How did you respond?"

Liam closed his eyes, hiding from her question and his own resulting frustration. "I didn't give him an answer."

"I see. Still having trouble asking him for what you want?"

"C'mon, Doctor. You know I don't have a grasp of what I want yet." He closed his lips into a thin line and waited for his therapist's answer. At least she wouldn't make him wait for what was coming.

She laughed on the phone. "Sorry for my reaction, Liam. It's that you call me Doctor when you're exasperated with me. I'm going to guess it's because you know I'll challenge you on this."

He had to chuckle. Having her accurately guess how he felt always made him feel better. "Yep. You got it right. Go ahead, challenge me."

"You know what you want. We've spent a lot of time exploring that. One thing is what you want from Coulton: for him to back off a little. We also know what you want from life— we've talked about it, right? You want to find your people. Your inner circle. Maybe someone you can love romantically and who loves you back. Am I correct about that? Do I remember that right?"

"...yeah." Liam's smile came reluctantly to his face. "You remember that right."

"Then you know what I'm going to say next. You're not trying to figure out what you want. You're trying to figure out how to ask for a break and get it, so you can rest from the pace of everything and invest time into relationships."

"Thanks, yeah. That's it." A slow, controlled sigh left his lungs. "But how do I do that, Doc?"

The silence in the line didn't last long. "By risking it, Liam. You have to ask for it and deal with what happens."

Dread settled heavy on his stomach, a clear *no* resounding in his mind. How could he still be so divided? How could he know so clearly what he wanted for himself, while rejecting the idea of asking for it at the same time?

"I'm not ready to risk it." He shook his head, even though Dr. Linda couldn't see him. "I don't know why."

"And that's okay. Just give yourself the chance to find out. To try again and again to reach your goals."

He opened his eyes but frowned. "Wait. You're not suggesting that I do the documentary, are you?"

She was silent on the line for a second, but she seemed to recover from the change in topic with ease.

"What makes you say that?" she asked, curiosity in her voice.

"Well, I..." he opened and closed his mouth a few times, and scratched the back of his neck with his free hand. "Do you know who Ana Lira is?"

"No."

"She's the documentary filmmaker Coulton is trying to contract me with. I didn't recognize her in the meeting, but I looked her up after I left the Agency and I've actually watched some of her stuff. Her films are really good; warm and friendly and... fuck. If she made a documentary like that of me then a project like that might not be so bad."

"Oh, that's interesting. Seems like you think it'd help you, somehow? You made this connection for a reason; when I said you should give yourself a chance to figure things out, you thought I meant you should do the documentary."

Liam took a deep breath, trying to organize his thoughts. "I'm not sure that it'd help with the Coulton thing but I realized... maybe it helps with my other goals. If her documentaries are as honest as they seem..." he shook his foot with renewed force. "She's all about getting to know people. So I wouldn't have a break to rest so much but I... could practice getting to know people again. Maybe I could show her parts of who I am and try to know her. See what happens."

"How do you feel about that? It has potential risks, but the fact that it's a contracted project— it could contain this little experiment to a finite time. Actually put some boundaries down for how this could work."

"I could add clauses to the contract to protect anything I don't want to share."

"And you could test how to open up to someone, figure out if you can trust them... that could move you closer to finding your inner circle. It's not friendship, necessarily, not in this scope, but I can see how you'd make the connection, if her films are personal like that."

"Shit. That's scary but... smart. She does seem to share a lot of herself in her films, too. So this is as close to real as I've had for a while."

"And it could give you time to find out how to stand up to Coulton, despite your arrangements with him and your contracts with producers and brands and PR people. With a lessened workload."

"Also, because it's a contract that benefits her, too, we'd both be getting something out of it. I don't want to use her."

"Liam, I really like this. But what I like matters very little. So think more about it. Weigh the pros and cons and make a decision that aligns with the work you're doing on yourself. I gotta go but I think you should really consider giving this a chance."

They scheduled a follow up appointment and said their good-byes. Liam dropped his phone onto the sofa on the pillow next to him, and stared into space for a while.

———

"Anyway," Ely said on the phone. "That happened. You met Liam McMillan."

Ana could still hear the echo of Ely's original scream, when she told her best friend about the meeting earlier in the call. At the time, Ely had shouted "LIAM FUCKING MCMILLAN?!" and proceeded to pick apart every word and gesture with intense interest.

"Yep, I did. Pity we decided he's such a Hollywood Man-diva."

"Sure, but his personality doesn't really change how he looks, does it? I mean, we just gawked at pictures of him. Some of Mother Nature's best work, right there."

Ana didn't open the pictures Ely had sent her again. "I didn't gawk." She had. "Personally, I'll focus on my newfound boss energy. I'm gonna need it if I end up working with him."

"Can you hear yourself saying that? You might work with him. Honestly. Wow."

"But I might not. Did you miss the part where Coulton was pushing this on him?"

"Don't tell me you wouldn't take the job if he agreed to it."

Ana pressed her lips together for a moment, but was forced to admit the truth. To Ely, at least. "No, you're right. I'd jump to do it. Can you imagine what it would do for my career?"

"Ugh, Ana. I hope it happens."

"We'll see. Now I'll let you go. It's late in Illinois."

They said their goodbyes and Ana tossed her phone on the hotel bed. She lay back, hands loose on her stomach as she stared at the ceiling. Her brain continued to revise her reaction to the shocking day and she didn't fight it; even if the project never came to be and Liam McMillan never became more than an anecdote to her, Ana's drive to make another documentary grew strong again inside of her. Maybe she could still make a film about Hollywood, somehow.

Despite her best judgment, Ana picked up her phone again and perused the pictures Ely had sent her earlier. Maybe she'd find inspiration in staring at the man.

She went back to the photo of him striding out of the ocean. He was undeniably, impossibly good looking. The swim shorts he wore hung low on his hips, leaving little to the imagination, showcasing that V that Ely had expertly referred to as his Adonis belt. Golden skin spoke of endless days under the California sun. Chiseled abs led into an expansive chest, and to broad shoulders that glistened as sunlight reflected off the water still coating them. Her body responded as if she were right there with him, her fingers tingling at the fantasy of touching those shoulders, running her nails down his chest. She bit her bottom lip; the image lighting up her phone was glorious. A wide, winning smile stretched across his perfect face, directed at the person next to him. His hair, mid-range brown in person, looked almost black just out of the water. Ana felt sorry for the guy standing next to Liam; on any given day, she'd say that he was attractive. When Liam stood next to him, no one could pay attention to anyone else.

She scrolled to the next one, a portrait of him at a red carpet event. He wore a suit cut to perfection, highlighting the triangle of his shape, drawing the eyes up to his handsome face.

She blushed. She should stop gawking over pictures of him—both out of pride and professionalism. That should be her new mantra. Yet she couldn't help herself; she moved to the next one.

A professional headshot filled her screen. His expression serious, it held a hint of inner steel in the corner of his lips, a whisper of a challenge in the shape of his eyes. It made it seem like he looked straight at her, daring her to deny that he could get everything he wanted. Her heart skipped a beat— looking at photos turned out to be dangerous.

"Fuck," she uttered, before locking her phone and tossing it away again.

No, she couldn't afford to spend any more time admiring his perfect looks. His looks didn't erase the fact he'd been rude to her. It didn't matter how attractive he was; she would feel only neutrality for him. She needed that, in case the documentary happened. If it didn't, then she'd give herself permission to have mixed feelings about him— appreciating his body but disliking him. Until she had a definitive answer, detachment was the name of the game.

Resolutely ignoring her phone and the pictures within, she opened her laptop and made herself work, instead.

It took Ana fifteen minutes to find her rhythm. She got lost in the process and worked for an hour, but an email from Diana distracted her. Ana let her cursor hover on the notification until it disappeared. What were the protocols? She'd signed with Diana just hours before, and didn't know if she was supposed to be on call for her messages.

She doubted it, but curiosity won. She opened her inbox and clicked on the email.

> Hi Ana, it was great meeting you in person earlier today.
> I'm excited to work with you! The road ahead is long but
> rewarding.

Mr. Coulton's office messaged me. You can expect a call or a text from Mr. McMillan sometime tonight. I expect you know how important it is that you act professionally and keep everything private. Mr. McMillan is, of course, an important client of ours and Mr. Coulton is one of the higher ups. If this deal goes through—"

Through the corner of her screen, a notification showed up with a text. An unknown number, followed by the intro lines: "Hi Ana, this is Liam McM. I got your num..."

With just a couple of rushed clicks, she opened the text from her computer.

Liam: Hi Ana, this is
Liam McM. I got your
number from Coulton
bc I wanted to talk a
bit more with you.
That ok?

Liam McMillan had her phone number, had sent her a message, and seemed to randomly choose words to abbreviate when texting.

Oh shit. Oh shit!

And what the hell happened to neutrality? A text from him and her heart sprinted to a gallop. She covered her mouth with her free hand and forced slow breathing into her chest. She gave herself a minute to mentally screech and think about her reply, before deciding to simply answer his question.

Ana: Sure. What would
you like to talk about?

The dots appeared on her screen right away, and so did the nerves in her stomach.

> **Liam**: First off, I'm sorry
> about this morning. I was
> in a mood bc Coulton was
> being obtuse and I was a
> bit of an ass to you. I realize
> I barely acknowledged you
> this morn but it had noth to
> do with you.

Stop the rollercoaster of a day. He apologized? Maybe he wasn't as vain as she'd thought, or maybe he was more self-aware than she'd given him credit for. Maybe she could give him the benefit of the doubt, regardless, for now. In any case, one point for impartiality.

Ana: That's good to know.

Had that been too sharp? She should have dropped the period!

> **Liam**: I was also wondering
> if you'd be open to meeting
> with me tmrw morn. I want
> to talk ab this documentary
> idea. Maybe you can bring

30

your camera and you can
show me how a docu would
work? There's a nice place
I know that's usually very
private.

Ana: Yes, I can do that

There. No period this time.

Liam: Does 10am work?
Where are you staying?
Send me your address and
I'll send someone to pick
you up. When you get there,
ask for the tropical garden.
I'll be at the center fountain.

Ana: Sounds good!
I look forward to it

After some deliberation, Ana saved his number simply as Liam.

Chapter 3

T HE TROPICAL AREA OF the Botanical Gardens was smaller than she'd imagined. Surrounded by the greenery of the conservatory at large, the greenhouse, inhabited by a tropical ecosystem, was a beautiful structure of wrought green iron and glass, not bigger than a medium, one-story house. Inside, the air hit her like a blanket had wrapped around her, warm and dense with humidity. Lush plants filled the place and flowers of intense colors popped among the deep green.

Ana found Liam standing with his back to her by the central fountain. Her eyes roamed his wide shoulders and narrow hips, her attention glued to the beautiful proportions of his body. Her steps slowed down, conflicting thoughts threatening to trip her up.

This is a standard consult meeting. Don't mention or think about the pictures you deleted from your phone last night. He's an equal, someone you're curious about. He's not a broody, unreachable famous person, nor a hot, dreamy actor.

She took a deep breath full of petrichor and tore her eyes away. In her line of work, professional behavior looked like this.

He turned when she approached, likely hearing the crunch of gravel under her feet.

"Hi," he said, his million-dollar smile holding more warmth than she'd expected. He was clean shaven today. "Thanks for agreeing to meet with me. I know I wasn't very friendly yesterday."

His eyes held a sheepish look. His hands were casually tucked in his jeans' front pockets, a simple white t-shirt stretching across his broad chest.

She kept her eyes above his neck and dismissed his apparent self-consciousness with a casual shrug. "I think we both know this benefits me more than you, so I should be thanking you."

He responded by lifting a corner of his mouth. He took a quick perusal of her. "Do you always carry all that equipment?"

"No, but you said you'd like to learn how this would work, so I came prepared."

"Right." He motioned to a point behind her with his chin, hands still in his pockets. "Do you want to sit? There's a bench overlooking the fountain."

"Sounds good."

He sat in the corner of the bench, at a three-quarters angle to her. One of his arms looped around the back of the bench, the other resting on his thigh. She folded a leg under her and sat with her back to the arm rest, facing him fully, and put her bag and the equipment she carried between them.

"Do you know where you'd like to start?" Ana asked to break the silence.

"Did you bring your camera?"

"Yep." She fished for it in her bag and held it in her hand, hesitant.

"Don't worry. I won't break it."

She stared at him; he studied her back. Forcing rich, humid air into her lungs, she gave the camera to him with a small smile. "I know. Sorry."

He took it in his big hand. "It's smaller than I imagined. Different from what I'm used to."

She looked at it in his palm, trying to see it through his eyes: a small device, a lot like an old photograph camera from the 90s, with a puff on top for the microphone and a preview screen. It looked nothing like the powerful devices filming him, on the high-budget sets common for him.

"It has to be unobtrusive," she explained. "I want it to be the least relevant thing in the room."

"That makes sense." He shifted the camera from hand to hand. "If you were recording this conversation for the documentary, what would you do?"

She extended her hand, asking for the camera back. She turned it on and placed it on her lap, angling the preview screen to check the frame. Her stomach settled as her hands moved assuredly over the camera, making small adjustments to the angle and focus.

"I'm not recording now," she said. "This one has that red dot here—" she showed him with a fingertip— "when it's filming. I either hold it with this strap in my hand or put it somewhere high and nearby, depending on how I'm trying to frame the person I'm working with. I tend to check the frame only a few times, or it takes spontaneity and, you know, that natural feeling out of it."

"Yeah." His quick grin shone with what she imagined amounted to half its potency. God, he was handsome. She refused to allow the unwelcome thought to show through.

"This one right now has a 500 gig memory card. I film everything into as many of those as I need to and then edit that content. That mostly happens after I'm done but sometimes I also do a bit of editing while I'm filming. It helps me come up with my questions."

He nodded, his eyes fixating on the camera lens. His smile softened until it disappeared, a thoughtful look now on his face. She let him search within himself, stretching time between them. Sitting in comfortable silence with her interviewees proved critical, time and time again, to create the atmosphere her fans enjoyed.

"I'll confess something." He lifted his eyes to hers. They sparkled. "I've seen your work. I discovered it last year and I really like what you do. I actually subscribe to your YouTube channel."

"What?!" She couldn't control the incredulous tone of her voice any more than she could believe he liked her films. So much for remaining unaffected.

"Yeah." He chuckled. He may have found her reaction amusing, but she did not. Heat flooded her face. "I use a pseudonym online, of course."

"Of course," she echoed, commanding her body to calm down.

"I happen to love what you do. You have this way of telling someone's story that's just... it makes you feel like you're being invited into this person's life, and allowed to see something intimate, and like you should be thankful for the gift. I first watched that one about dating you did? So good. And last night I watched the one with the Māori teacher."

Her face warmed again, but her body relaxed. She hadn't expected candor from a self-absorbed star. Perhaps she'd jumped to conclusions too quickly, when she met him the day before.

She cleared her throat, silently begging her face to return to its natural olive tone once more.

"I guess there's a difference between liking my work and wanting to be a part of it."

"Yes. Exactly."

She cast her eyes down to her lap and fiddled with her camera, looking for something to say. Silence didn't feel as comfortable now. She looked up to the fountain for inspiration.

"So... did you recognize me in the office? When I came in."

The sound that came out of him could have been a scoff or a strangled chuckle, and lived somewhere in the middle.

"No. I was too wound up to look at you properly. Now I see it, though."

"Except for noticing my Queen shirt."

He nodded and gave her a small smile. "I'd like to propose something. How about you record our meeting right now, and we pretend this is going to be in the documentary? If I end up agreeing to do it, you can use it."

"And if you don't?"

He shrugged. "You delete it."

She waited a moment. "Do you want me to sign something saying that?"

He stilled and his lips went rigid for an instant. "No, not for this. I'm not that fussy."

"Okay." She pressed the record button and decided to be more careful with the sass. She chose a lower angle which, although unflattering, could feel like a secret moment. "I'm recording."

"What happens next?" he asked. Curiosity drove him. He hadn't been lying when he told her he liked her films.

"We talk." After checking the camera's screen again, she met his gaze once more.

She had gorgeous brown eyes, a vivid burnt umber that stared deeply into him. Her dark hair fell straight down, almost to her waist. Her lips were unpainted today, yet they managed to distract from her big eyes, drawing his attention to their soft shape. She wore a casual outfit: another 80's rock band t-shirt, with the sleeves rolled up, and light-washed jeans that hinted at her generous curves.

Fuck. How studied was her look? Because it seemed unpretentious, but cynicism made him question her authenticity anyway. Plenty of people had fed this automatic doubt since arriving in Hollywood... but no. He'd take her at face value. If he was going to give this thing a chance and get to know her, he couldn't be so self-absorbed he assumed the worst of her.

"About?" He made himself ask.

"Anything."

He studied her. Her face remained open, neutral. Her body relaxed.

"Okay." He nodded once. "So, do you always announce that you've started recording?"

"No, it typically gets in the way. I just do it once or twice but, later, you can pretty much assume I'm recording if I'm around. You can always check for the recording light or ask me."

"Right. Well, ask me something."

She gave him an inquisitive look, as if she were trying to read him and his intentions. Maybe he wasn't the only one measuring, assessing.

It didn't take her long to speak. "To make this as real as possible, I'll simply ask what's on my mind. That's how this typically goes."

"Sure."

"What made you text me last night?"

His mind went blank.

"You can tell me you don't want to answer, if you like," she added.

"No, I mean..." He scratched the back of his head. Time to act as he said he wanted to act. He forced his words out. "After you left, Coulton continued to tell me how taking a break is a bad idea, and that letting you make a documentary about what's going on with me was a great one. That's the gist of it, anyway."

She pursed her lips and brought them to the side, as if wanting to chuckle but hiding it. "Did you ever tell him you knew my work?"

"No. I didn't want to give him the satisfaction."

She laughed, a full, hearty sound. A wave of pleasure went through him, surprising him. He liked that she hadn't held back this time. That he caused it.

"I imagine he said something good?" Her eyes were still crinkling at the corners. "Something to make you consider it?"

Ana gazed at the fountain. Her nose had a light bump, adding character to her face. Her attractive face.

"Yeah. He said to talk to my therapist," he explained without thinking, still lost in looking at her.

She responded to his comment by turning towards him. His eyes locked with hers, wide open.

Burnt umber. Brown ash left by a fire. Tantalizing. He licked his bottom lip.

"And did you talk to your therapist? Was that what convinced you to reach out?" She asked.

He nodded. "Dr. Linda— my therapist— she said that it might slow things down and that it was a good idea."

"And that was it?"

"No, that was only part of it." He considered for a moment, wondering how to proceed, stealing a look at the camera. "She also said that spending time answering your questions could make me think about things differently."

"Things? What things?"

"Things that I talk about in therapy. Personal things. She said I should try to think of what the documentary could do for me, before deciding whether I want to be a part of it."

She accepted that with one nod. "Okay. That makes sense."

She stared at the fountain again, and he did the same. It both excited and unsettled him that he'd been able to share that with her, after knowing her for such little time. That she'd taken his words without pushing.

"Coulton knew that I'd listen to my therapist," Liam added, unprompted. "He gambled that she'd like the idea and, lucky for him, she did."

"You know," she said after a while, "I started college thinking I wanted a major in film and a minor in psychology. I think that I make documentaries because it helps me understand people, get to the soul of a person, but it's way better than becoming a therapist, because you don't have to deal with as many years of training or all the responsibilities."

He grinned. "This is something I noticed. You also talk about yourself in your films."

"Yes, that's on purpose. For one, I'm social like that." She glanced back at him for a second with a brief smile, before turning back to the water. "Also, I think it's only fair. I ask for a lot of vulnerability from the people I work with, and I try to pay it back with some of my own."

"I also know that you try to answer a main, existential question in your films. Do you know what question you'd ask if we worked together?"

This time, she smiled without looking at him. "Nope." She laughed. "I'll tell you a secret. I typically don't know the question until after I've started. It's like... I get this deep curiosity about people. Then I want to learn more about them. When I take a step back I see themes, and that's where the question comes from."

"What's made other people do it? Because to me it feels so... exposing. I already feel exposed often. This possibility is unsettling because so much already is said about me, whether I approve of it or not. I'm hesitant to give them more."

"That makes sense," she said, turning again to peer at him. "Maybe you could see this as a chance to show the real you, outside of the same worn out questions you get. You do have some control with me, because you can always choose what you answer or don't. You can also tell me anything you think matters; that you'd like me and the audience to know. And I know this doesn't mean as much, but I would never want to be unfair to you. At the core of what I do, I try to make the process just for the people I work with— I want to make sure my people feel held, safe."

Wow. He hadn't needed to share what he wanted for her to offer it to him.

With a deep breath, he jumped into the abyss.

"Would you be open to going on a trip with me?"

She perked up. "Now? I guess I can—"

"No. For the documentary."

"I... what?! Does that mean... but then..."

"Hear me out." He leaned forward closer to her, tracking her face to read her reaction. "You come to LA and we get out of the city together. Go somewhere private, stay there for a few days then go to the next place. Have some adventures... or stay put, whatever we feel like. You ask me questions. We do this documentary. Coulton gets off my back. I still kinda get a break."

Her eyes searched his. He followed the train of her thoughts in the changing curve of her eyebrow, the way she pressed her lips together, and in the tiny smile that curled the corner of her lips.

He wished he could read her mind. Her expressive face was intriguing and not clear enough, at the same time. He wanted to know more.

His lips mirrored hers.

"It would be a lot of time together," she said after a few beats. "A lot. Are you sure you want me around that much?"

"No," he replied with a smirk, "but I do know I love road trips."

She smirked back and he laughed. He dismissed the comment with a wave of his hand. "I think you're not bad, I guess. First impressions, and all that."

She maintained her smirk and he grinned, pleased at himself.

"That's not the same as thinking I'm good," she finally replied. "Being together so much could easily get on our nerves. If we're not better than *not bad* as a team, a road trip would be terrible."

"Well, I don't know if we're a *good* team yet, do I? But perhaps I may still get a chance to make up my mind about you."

"As in, you'll do the documentary?"

He grinned, a tingling tease of hope behind his breast bone. He offered her his hand to close the deal.

"Let's do this, Ana Lira."

With a glorious smile lighting up the space between them, she shook his hand.

Chapter 4

AFTER RETURNING FROM THE garden, Ana'd gone out, taken public transit— the best way to really get a feel for a city, in her opinion— and walked. She'd visited Los Angeles before and had done some of the tourist stuff; this time she wanted to see more of everyday life. Even so, she took one of those tour buses that talked about celebrities, their movies, and homes, recording material for the documentary.

Holy crap, Liam McMillan had agreed to the documentary. He'd assured her he'd deal with Coulton, and that Coulton would talk to Diana and come up with the paperwork. All Ana had to do was go home, pack, and prepare.

She'd returned to her hotel room exhausted, happy to get room service and watch TV. She had just closed the door after giving back the trays, dishes, and cart, thinking she might call Ely and give her an update, when she got a new text from Liam.

Liam: if we text, will it
be included in the docu?

Ana: Maybe. I may mention
something about our texting
during one of my voiceovers.
Maybe comment on something
I learned about you through
texting

The smile that had appeared on her face in response to his "docu" stayed in place after pressing send. She could almost sigh in relief that Liam had these kinds of questions; most people she worked with had asked similar things in the past.

A new text came in while she still held her phone in her hands.

Liam: you're being
really patient

Ana: Gotta be if I want
to earn your trust :)

Liam: thing is, if you tell
me that's your purpose,
how am I going to trust you?
Then your patience is fake ;)

> **Ana**: Or I'm so honest that
> I tell you all about my
> ulterior motives directly?

Liam: still diffic to trust you
if I know it's what you want

> **Ana**: why wouldn't I want your
> trust? Of course I want it.
> What really matters is what
> I'm going to do with it

Liam: and what are you going
to do with it?

> **Ana**: a documentary ;)

They continued to text on and off until she lay in bed in the dark, willing herself to put away her phone but unable to.

She opened up her text chain with Liam, going over their conversation again. She chuckled at the budding banter between them, interspersed among his questions: would she move to LA temporarily? Would she basically be with him all the time? Book time for interviews? She didn't have all the answers, for a lot of it depended on what worked for him.

The more they talked, the more real he appeared, and the more it seemed to change her first opinion of him. Sometime that evening, he'd stopped being an unapproachable Hollywood actor and became someone she craved filming. She'd done more than find neutrality: she'd found curiosity.

With a sigh, she put her phone on her bedside table and pulled the covers to her shoulders. It was too late to call Ely, anyway.

She woke up the next morning half-expecting to have a new text from him, but there was nothing new until after she had taken a shower.

Liam: You up? Had breakfast?
If not, meet me for a bite.
If yes, meet me for coffee?

Ana chuckled. He texted weird but it always managed to put a smile on her face.

Ana: Awake, yes. Breakfast,
not yet. Meet, yes.

Liam: Efficient texting :)
Approved. Is half an hr ok
to send someone to
pick you up?

Ana: yep. They can come,
pick me up, and drop me

off at the mysterious
rendezvous place.

Liam: Funny. See
you soon.

A car picked her up promptly. After about twenty minutes of driving, Ana arrived at a fancy-looking restaurant. The driver informed her that Liam would be waiting inside.

"Hey," he said as she approached him. She sat across from him. "This place okay?"

"Yes, I think so. I don't know much about the restaurant options here in LA, so I'll trust you."

"This place should be fine. It's a snobby place, so the people that come here often don't care that I'm around."

She nodded. "Is the food good?"

"Yes, very good."

"Then it's perfect."

After ordering food and drinks and settling into it, she took her camera out. She set it up but let her finger hover on the record button, before looking at him. She pressed record after his nod.

"Just make sure it's only us on the frame. People here wouldn't want to be recorded without permission." He drunk some of his coffee.

"Of course. If anyone shows up in the frame, I can edit the image out."

A server came with their drinks; she sipped some of her coffee.

"So, what did you want to talk about?" she asked.

"I have an idea." He turned his cup on its plate, drawing out the moment. "I want to run it by you."

"Okay..."

"So now we know we'll go on a trip. I'm thinking of a few places I want to go to; there's a couple of locations by the ocean and one in the mountains we could go to as well. How does that sound?"

"Amazing. Honestly." She willed herself to keep her scream of excitement inside. The waiters aided her by bringing their food and distracting them.

"Anyway," Liam took a sip of coffee and continued once they were alone again, putting his cup down with a clink. "I was thinking I'd like to go on the trip next week, if that's okay with you? The first place I want to go to is available right away."

"It's really up to you. I don't know if you have a sister, but you can think of me as a pesky sister who has a lot of questions and is obsessed with cameras. You wouldn't ask that sister if she's okay with the plans surrounding a fun trip you're taking her to, right? You'd just tell her to get ready and then you'd be very patient with her about all the questions she will ask while you're driving."

"You don't know if I have a sister? You didn't look me up online?"

"I haven't, actually. I know you have a brother but that's all. Is it just the two of you? Are you six siblings? No idea, and I want to keep it that way. I'm trying really hard to get to know the real you, not what is shown on YouTube, magazines, and tabloids."

Ana said nothing about how while she hadn't read up on Liam, Ely had sent her a bunch of pictures they had lusted over, or how Ana had to constantly correct her own preconceptions about him. Biting the corner of her mouth, she told herself she spoke the truth: she aimed to know him for who he really was.

"I don't have a sister," he finally offered, stabbing a strawberry with his fork. "Only the one brother. I'd prefer a different example, though; I'd much rather not see you as my sibling."

She let out a small sigh of relief and smiled again. "Why is that?"

"My brother and I are not that patient with each other, let's say that. My experience of siblinghood is of tense undercurrents."

"Okay, then." She buttered a piece of bread. "New suggestion. Think of me as your shadow— but a shadow that interjects, has an opinion, and a thousand questions."

He laughed, the sound of it expansive and open. She didn't care that she could see a couple of people staring at them from the corner of her eye; he appeared relieved, as well. "Sounds good. You can be my shadow and ask me a thousand questions. I will say that it kind of falls in line with something else I was thinking. If you're going to be like my shadow, then my idea makes even more sense."

"Oh?" She took a bite of bread, barely registering the delicious piece of heaven. He drank some more coffee, something in the way he moved telling her he was stalling.

His eyes were cast on his plate. "During that road trip, we're gonna be all over each other. I mean, we're going to be together all the time. So I was thinking about it and realized it doesn't make sense to send you to a hotel for two nights before we go on the trip and spend the next few weeks with each other, every day and night. I have plenty of room at home and so maybe you should come stay at my place. In the guest room. You're supposed to get a close-up look at my life, right? It'd give you a chance to see me in the privacy of my own space. I think this makes sense."

Her eyes zeroed in on him. He had shared his idea in one long, quick breath, and she didn't know what to say to it. The possibility alone of what he proposed brought her thoughts to a halt.

"I don't know, I might be wrong," he offered, hands still in their place on the table. He released something like a frustrated huff. "My thought was that we can start getting comfortable around each other before being on the road. Is it a bad idea? I've never done this before so I could use your guidance if I'm off base."

She took another bite of heavenly bread to gain some time. He ate more of his food, too, not looking at her, letting her think.

On one hand, the director side of her loved the idea. Being with him all the time could only multiply her chances to really get to know him. And access to his home like that? Content gold. The kind of material she could film by spending all day with him glittered in her mind's eye. On the other hand, being with him so much could make him feel like she invaded his life completely—more than she already was. Who could be authentic under those circumstances? Not to say anything of the overwhelming notion that she, a small-time director and a hot-blooded woman, was in awe at the idea of spending so much time with him.

"Not necessarily off base." She spoke slowly, thinking fast. "If I stay at your place that would be different from what usually happens during filming because, typically, I just meet my people for a few hours at a time. Maybe a full day here and there. What you're saying is... risky. Don't you think it could get suffocating?"

"If it is suffocating in LA, it's going to be suffocating on the trip."

"You're right about that. And as a director I love the idea but, are you sure you want to sacrifice that part of your privacy, too?"

"If it's too much, we can always spend time in our own rooms, go out alone, whatever. Even if we're both in my house it doesn't mean we have to be next to each other all the time."

"And then, what? I'm guessing we'd just go out as needed together, if you're going somewhere?"

"Basically," he confirmed. "But I'm a homebody anyway. It'll save us time and hotel costs and such."

"Then... then I guess it'd be wonderful to get to see you at home, if you're okay with it."

He finally lifted his eyes to hers again, a small smile on his lips. "Let's agree we're both pushing our luck here."

She smiled in return, and they finished their brunch avoiding the topic and chatting about the city instead.

———

Ana flew back to Illinois that afternoon, after an awkward goodbye to Liam by the restaurant. She left her incessant mental review of the weekend on the plane, and called Ely to give her the news upon arriving at her place.

"Hey, Ely," Ana said to her phone. She lay on her bed, already relishing the opportunity to shock her friend with her news.

"Hey, Ana! I guess you're not too famous yet for your old neighborhood friends?"

"Not yet, but I can't make any promises for the future," Ana teased. "Hey, I know it's late, but what are we up to tomorrow? Happy pre-birthday!"

"Thank you! Well, I thought eating out with my besties would suffice. What time would work for you?"

"Sometime in the evening. After four, I'm guessing. I don't have to do a lot tomorrow, but I will be waiting for documents to sign for my new project." She stretched on the bed, an expectant smile taking over her face.

"Wait. Is it happening?! Are you working with Liam the Hottest Man Alive Friggin' McMillan?!"

"Yes!" Ana laughed. "We agreed to it this morning over breakfast."

"No, oh my God, seriously?! You're on having-casual-brunch-on-a-Sunday terms with Liam McFuckingMillan?!"

"I guess you could say that."

"I can't with this, Ana. From this moment onwards, be assured of my endless jealousy."

Ana turned to her side, grabbing a pillow for comfort. "I wish I could pack you in my suitcase."

"I'm short enough that we could possibly make it work."

"You're not that short. Then we have some small issues like food and pee breaks."

"Sure, keep him all to yourself, then. Unless he's coming to my birthday dinner tomorrow?"

"Ha ha, no."

"Bummer. Are you going to LA, then? How's it gonna work? Tell me everything."

Ana bit her lip, her grin still in place. "I'm flying to LA on Friday and then... well, you'll never guess," she started, but stopped in the middle of the sentence to make Ely suffer. She only continued once Ely had growled her displeasure on the phone. With a smirk, Ana added, "I'm going to stay at his place, Ely. In LA. Then we're going on a road trip, I don't even know where."

"What?! What?! I can't, I honestly can't. I can't breathe."

"I love you, Ely. This is making you sound like we're sixteen again."

"Maybe it's part of an early middle-age crisis...?" The question had ended on a high, long note, as if Ely herself had her doubts.

Ana laughed. "You're turning 27. This is not a mid-life crisis."

"Right. Also, not important. What's important is that you're going to be in close contact with Liam McMillan for what, three weeks? Four? And at least part of it will happen within the intimate, close-quarters confines of a car. Like, your elbows might touch. And I already know you'll refuse to send me pictures."

"I've never sent you pictures of my documentary people. Why would I send you one of Liam? At least not without his consent. I'm going to learn a lot of private stuff about him and it would be unprofessional if I—"

"Ugh, you're torturing me. *Liam*, she says, like they're best friends. When should I come to help you pack?"

"Help me pack? Why?"

"Because you need to plan what you're taking with you, of course. We've thirsted over him for years, and you're going to be spending plenty of quality time with him. There are going to be many opportunities for a wild night and—"

"No! No, no. No." Tension gripped her stomach even as she chuckled. "That's never gonna happen. I'm not there to seduce him, but to get to know him. I'm making a documentary about who this mega-star is in real life and what he's going through at this moment of his career. I definitely, most absolutely, will not risk how good this could be for me by appearing unprofessional because I couldn't keep it in my pants. A fling isn't worth what this could mean for me, Ely. We can go back to thirsting after the premiere. Deal?"

Chapter 5

E LY DROPPED ANA OFF at the small Central Illinois Regional Airport on Friday, pretending to cry in envy at Ana's amazing circumstances. With a final hug, she'd asked Ana to please behave like Ely would, were she ever to be given such an opportunity. Ana made no promises.

One of TCA's drivers picked her up at LAX in the early evening, and drove her to the address Liam had texted her the night before. Tall walls surrounded the face to his property, partially covered by greenery; a solid gate obscured the view. Once inside the front yard, she studied the modern one storey building, with its large wooden door and floor-to-ceiling tinted windows.

Nerves took hold of her stomach. She got out of the car just as Liam opened the door to his house; the driver stayed in the car, while Liam and Ana met next to the now-open trunk.

"Hey," Ana greeted him, struck again by his presence. His very real, still unexpected, solid presence. "Thanks for having me."

He gave her a sideways glance, standing still next to the back of the vehicle, not quite reaching for the bags. His eyes didn't stay on her. "Hey. Of course. If we're doing this, we might as well."

He wore black jeans and a black t-shirt. He had a light stubble going again, shadowing his face. He stared at her bags, frowning, and the corner of his mouth crimped in a tense angle.

"Honestly, if you'd rather I go somewhere else..." she offered.

He reached for her two bags and held both on one hand, reaching to close the trunk with the other. "No need. It was my idea to invite you here."

Liam signaled the driver he was free to leave. She stared at the closing gate for a moment, before turning back to Liam.

He finally faced her. He pointed to the door behind him with a small jerk of his head. "C'mon in. I'll show you to your room."

The lights in the house were a warm yellow, highlighting the many wooden details crafted among the stark, cool concrete. Colorful art hung on several of the walls; they seemed to be a couple distinct styles, as if he liked two very specific artists. All across the far side, a glass wall opened to a patio. A small pool broke the space as a center feature. More greenery around the patio provided privacy, except on the long edge: a view of the city below and the infinite ocean to its side.

"Your house is beautiful," she said.

He led her through a hallway. "Thanks. I spend a lot of time here so I made sure I loved it."

"Makes sense."

He opened the door to a bedroom.

"You can stay here." He entered the room and left her bags on the bed. Her stomach flipped. "There's a bathroom over there and, well. All the typical stuff."

She glanced around the room, the sweep ending on him. He put his hands in his pockets, as if he didn't know what to do with them now that he didn't carry her bags.

"This is perfect, thanks," she replied. They stood facing each other.

"How was the flight?"

"Fine. Packed tight."

He smiled. "Did they feed you?"

"Of course not."

He chuckled. "Okay, then I'm glad I ordered food. Take some time to freshen up, if that's still something you're supposed to say to a guest. I'll be in the kitchen or living room somewhere."

"Thank you."

He nodded. In the short, awkward silence that followed, they gave each other a small smile.

"Okay, then. Let me know if you need anything."

He closed the door on his way out. Making herself move, she opened her bags and took a couple of things out; not much, since they were leaving for the road in less than 48 hours. She put her toiletry bag in the bathroom and washed her face. She stared at herself in the mirror, completely out of place. What did anyone mean by freshening up? How long did that take?

And, shit, had there been a hint of tension between them? Hopefully she was overthinking it, because she needed them to be comfortable with each other if she hoped to pull this off.

Liam closed the door behind him, the click of it loud in the silent house. He stayed fixed on the spot, reminding himself that having Ana in his place did really make the most sense. It would be a real test to his growth and everything he'd been learning in therapy; proving it was okay to trust the process of getting to know someone. As long as he didn't come to regret it...

He walked away and sat on the sofa, turning on the TV in the hope to fill the space until she came out of her room. She did, half an hour later.

Ignoring the minor spike of adrenaline, he turned to her. "Are you hungry?"

Without waiting for a reply, Liam got up and went to the kitchen. He opened cupboards and drawers and took out glasses, plates, silverware, and napkins. He turned to leave it all on the kitchen island, which had an overhang to make it into a small, simple bar. Ana came closer and sat on a barstool on the other side of it, taking things and organizing them into two places.

He added the take out boxes next to her and she began adding food on her plate. There was no filming equipment around.

"You don't have the camera out." He filled up his own plate with his favorite Indian dish.

"Yeah, I thought I'd give it 'til tomorrow." She left one container on the stone surface and reached for another. She took a scoop out of it and added it to her plate. "Look," she added, her hands moving more slowly now. "I know that me being here and the whole documentary thing are not something you were craving in your life, precisely..."

He continued to put food on his plate, pressing his lips together not to smile at her choice of words. He said nothing.

"I just... is this too awkward?" she continued. "Tell me it's not too awkward."

"Maybe a little awkward."

"Can we work with *a little awkward*? You seem like a private person. I kinda have to invade that but... how can I make it better for you?"

He turned and put his plate in the microwave, buying himself time. He needed to find the right words.

"What do you want to drink?" he asked.

"Water's fine, a slice of lemon if you have it."

He went to the fridge and took out one of the yellow fruit. He ran the water and washed it, before reaching for a knife.

"I knew what I was getting myself into when I invited you here." Cutting up the lemon into slices, he dropped them onto a small plate and passed it to her. "I just need some time to adapt. I'm not used to having people around here."

"I see. Are there any parts of the house you don't want me to film? I don't see any photos around but I can make sure to avoid anything too personal. And don't worry— I'm not going to try to get into your bedroom."

His eyes shot to her. Hers widened as she realized the different potential interpretations of what she said.

This was a momentous time. Did he choose to show her his impish side, or not?

He went for it, unable to contain the teasing smile that took over his lips. "We're still talking about filming, right?"

"Yes! Oh my god, yes, Liam."

He grinned and licked his bottom lip.

"You wanna rethink the words you're using?"

"Oh god." She dropped her face to her hands, hiding behind them. "Let me rephrase. I want to be respectful of your privacy so please let me know what's out of bounds. I'm trying to take this seriously. You added those clauses to the contract for a reason."

She made room between her fingers and watched him through them. He abandoned playfulness and followed her train of thought instead, with half a grin still in place.

"You get why I added those things, right?"

She went back to setting up her place, eyes still shy. "I assumed it's because you want to keep control over what people learn about you. And I mean, I get that. Not that it was easy for me to accept; the idea that you get a veto on the final cut is scary for me."

"I don't get a veto on the whole thing, though," he countered, "just up to three scenes."

The microwave beeped. He took his plate out and put Ana's in. She squeezed lemon juice into a glass and threw the scrunched piece of fruit inside.

He reached for her glass and took it to the fridge's water dispenser. "Ice?"

"Yes, please."

He gave her back the glass and proceeded to repeat the process with his own.

"I didn't ask before," she said, "but are you open to discussion? I'll respect your wishes, of course, but can I poke first?"

"As a sign of my goodwill and generosity, I'll say yes."

Her shyness went away at his teasing, and a glint appeared in her eyes. "I appreciate that. Very magnanimous of you."

He laughed. "You're welcome."

"Okay then. Is the awkwardness gone? Have we ironed out details? Are we ready for this?"

He took her plate out of the microwave and gave it to her. He walked around the island and sat in front of his food.

"As ready as can be," he said.

"And are we ready for the trip?"

"Almost. My PA is coming tomorrow to help me finalize a few things, and I have a couple of calls scheduled. But on Sunday, I'm free."

"Can I hover around as you do these things tomorrow?"

He filled his fork with food, before stealing a glance at her. "I expected you to. That's what we signed up for, right? You can even ask questions."

Chapter 6

R OAD TRIPS GAVE ANA butterflies. Since this particular trip
was for work, she caged them in.

She came out of the guest bedroom with her two bags. Liam
wasn't out of his room yet, so she left them near the main door
and went back into the kitchen. She filled up her water bottle and
he came out of his room, big bag in hand.

"You ready?" His eyes sparkled.

With only a few words and gestures, they closed up the house
and got their things into Liam's car. They loaded the big, dark
green luxury SUV up with groceries, too, which to Ana only added
mystery to the trip.

She got comfortable on the passenger side as he closed the
main house door, admiring the tech signaling a relatively new,
very expensive model. He appeared by the driver's door and got
comfortable in the car, too.

"God, I love road trips," he said as the engine purred to life. He
put on an 80s mix playlist and, with it filling the car, drove out of
the property.

"Me too. Growing up, this is how we did family vacations. My
dad loves to drive and we'd go out and explore different cities
and states around our town. In a way, I think it helped him feel
more settled in this country. Getting to know the area made him

feel familiar with it which, in turn, made him feel more like he belonged."

"I can see that. My ancestors— a bunch of northern European folks— came here a while ago and I guess to them it was a lot of, let's see where we can find some land and make it ours."

"Right, that's what it probably was like back then, instead of visa applications and stuff. Let's just get this land, a king faraway said it's okay. Oh, you say it's inhabited already? I don't think that matters."

"Did you come here little, or were you born here?"

Ana's belly tightened. Questions like this often came with a load of emotional labor on Ana's part. She took a deep, fortifying breath and tried to find what to say.

He must have mistaken the meaning of her silence, for he apologized. "Sorry, you don't have to answer that. I assumed that if your dad wanted to feel settled in this country that he was an immigrant, but I think I shouldn't have assumed."

"Yes, he's an immigrant." She bit her lip. "Both my parents are. I was born here, though."

It was his turn to be silent. He drove them on the Ventura Freeway, following a steady pace.

She played with the loose threads of her distressed jeans. "You're right. What I told you suggested they immigrated here."

"I don't want to be insensitive."

"It matters that you know there's a wrong way to talk about it." She forced a sigh out, making up her mind. "Go on, say what you're thinking. I'll let you know if you cross a line."

"Okay, then." He cleared his throat. "How did they end up here?"

"My dad got a study visa for his graduate degree. My mom tagged along. I came into the picture after they'd gotten their green card, a couple of years after he finished his Masters."

"What does he do?"

"He's an engineer."

"Do you have siblings?"

"Nope. Unless you count Ely. We've known each other since we were five. She's the sister I never had."

"Is she who you talked to on the phone last night?"

Ana blinked twice in quick succession. She thought he hadn't noticed.

"Yes. I'm sorry if I was too loud."

"Nah, don't worry about that. I was just curious. I didn't eavesdrop, though, I swear."

"And I swear we didn't talk about you. This time." She grinned.

She took her camera out and, with help from a flexible tripod, set it up on the dashboard. She had to put the music very low for both copyright and filming reasons, which was a pity.

"Very funny." His words dripped with sarcasm.

This time, she chuckled. "No, really. We talk about whatever. We've been friends for so long that we practically share half our brain and could find something to say about seeing paint dry."

"Curious, I thought I didn't ask."

"I guess." She rolled her eyes. He must have known she did, despite not moving his eyes from the road, because he laughed.

Satisfied with the recording angle, she left it filming as they sat in a brief silence.

"Sounds like a great friendship," he added.

"Yeah. I can't imagine my life without her. She's amazing. She balances me out. Where I'm more toned down, she takes life by the horns. Do you have any friendships like that?"

"Not really," he said after a minute. "I do have people I consider friends; people I make sure I see when I go to visit my parents and stuff like that. There's also Logan. We were roommates for years and we're close. It's tough, though, with my schedule and all the traveling."

Ana stared out of the window. "Yeah? So what I saw yesterday— the meetings, the training, the calls— that's your life while in LA... but you also travel a lot."

"Yes. Sometimes it's about principal photography on location, sometimes it's promotional stuff. I fly out for anywhere from two days at a time to two months or more. The longer periods are rare, thanks to CGI, but travel like that is part of an actor's life."

"There was a time my dad was consulting for a company. They kept flying him out to their headquarters. For a year, he traveled back and forth every few weeks. After about six months of that, he said he never wanted to get on a plane ever again."

"It can be rough, yeah. On one hand it's about comfort; that's one of the things where being paid as well as I am is good, because it means I can make the airplane better, and the hotel better, to try to balance out the fact I am not at home, you know?"

Los Angeles shone under the sun, buildings and trees around them clear in the warm light. "Also, at least the way the internet talks about it, famous people are always traveling with a group."

"I often travel with people. Mo, or my PR team, plus stylists, sometimes a producer or two. So that part is true."

"What about taking your friends? Or a girlfriend— or a boyfriend— or someone there for you, not your public persona."

He didn't respond right away. She turned to study him; his eyes were still focused on the road, and a frown was evident on his profile.

"I haven't had a lot of luck with that."

"You want to tell me more?"

She hoped she'd hit the right note in her question. She really wanted him to open up and share every detail of his life, but knew she couldn't push. Vulnerability was better in drops than in a waterfall.

They were coming out of the city, the car making its way into the hills.

"Ever since coming to Hollywood— the first year with all that filming and prep work, then being dropped into fame three years ago— I've lived most of my life within the industry. There are amazing things about my life and also not so good ones. Which I know is true for everyone, whether they're actors or engineers. One thing about my life is that I've had a hard time adjusting to all the people around me who want to be known and crave fame. I don't want to be famous; I want to act and have freedom to choose the projects I want to get involved in. I also one hundred percent understand that I won't get that freedom unless people want to see me in any role. That is, I need fans. I need people to think of me and say, *yeah, I like that guy! I want to see what he's up to*, whether it's a rom com or a psychological thriller. So I do want fame, even though I don't enjoy it."

She took a deep breath. "That makes sense."

"To hop on a plane with me to go on a promo tour in Europe, people around me have to either do nothing but be happy keeping me company, or be able to drop things for weeks at a time, or do their job from a computer at random times from random places. Not a lot of people I care about can do that, and the people I've met in Hollywood that could travel like that, haven't been people I've really clicked with, yet."

"I see. Yeah, I think I get it. Ely wouldn't be able to hop on a plane like that, and making friends as an adult is such a pain. Sounds like it's been that way for you."

He sighed. "Plus the issue of knowing if people are your friends because they like you, or because you're a popular name right now, or they're hoping to jet about in chartered flights."

"Right. I don't know anything about that."

"I didn't, either, until I woke up one day and everyone knew who I was."

Ana's eyebrows shot up. Liam sat rigid on his side of the car, the only sign of movement the small adjustments his hands did on the wheel.

He shook his head as if to clear it. Ana was tempted to copy him.

"Let's press pause on all of that. I don't know about you but, to me, getting on the road means a stop for gas and the convenience store."

Swallowing the unfinished thoughts in her mind, she echoed the change in energy he brought to the space between them.

"Cheap, bad coffee and gross snacks for breakfast." She slapped her thigh. "Perfect."

"Exactly. Only I need to ask you a favor." He triggered the signal and turned into an exit to a gas station. "I need you to go into the convenience store for me. I'll stay out and fill up the tank."

"Sure. What do you want?"

"Just get me a hot breakfast sandwich and something crunchy. Even if my trainer kills me for it when I'm back."

"Got it."

He drove into the solitary gas station and parked by a pump. She hopped out of the car and, right before she closed the door, he called her name.

"Hey, Ana." As he talked, he reached for the glove compartment, took a baseball cap from it, and put it on. "Keep the receipt. I'm sending them all to TCA."

"It's fine, it's on me—" she started, distracted by the way his muscles and tendons shifted in his toned forearm.

He interrupted her. "No, really. Coulton did his best to make this into a work trip, so he's gonna have to pay. Literally."

She tore her eyes from his forearms and tried to look him in the eye, but the sunglasses got in the way. She saw herself reflected there instead, long hair floating in the breeze and an awkward line to her lips.

"Well... technically, the production company this is being filmed with is... me. He'll forward the receipts to me."

"Oh." He sat back, hand resting on top of the wheel.

"So... it really is fine. This is on me. I'm expensing it, too."

"That means you're my director, producer, and interviewer."

She cocked her head. "Yep."

"You're the boss."

"Am I, though?"

"You're right," he said, opening his door wide but not stepping down yet. He still faced her. "Neither of us is really running the show."

***

Ana balanced a tray with two large coffees in one hand, and carried a bag full of convenience store goodies in the other.

As she approached the car, she realized Liam didn't stand alone— a father-son duo chatted with him, the kid jumping up and down in his place. Liam took off his sunglasses and took a selfie with them. Not wanting to intrude, she silently opened her door and set the coffees in the console's cup holders, and the bag at the feet of her seat.

"Oh, you're here," Liam exclaimed, drawing her eyes to him. Ana noticed the strain in the slant of his shoulders but said nothing. "Shall we?"

"Yes, let's go." She hoped her smile looked friendly to father and son; she hid her perplexity behind it. Of course she'd known people might approach them if they were in public, but she hadn't thought to prepare for it at a lonely gas station. The whole situation seemed surreal, but her intuition told her that a friendly demeanor was the best way to support Liam.

She got in the car and buckled her seatbelt. She glanced at Liam's side window as he did the same. Together they waved at the two standing there next to the car; they hadn't moved away. The father gave Ana a curious look, before lifting his phone and taking another picture of them. With a slow roll of the car, they left the gas station.

"Fans?" she asked, trying for an overture a couple of minutes later.

Tension quirked the corner of his mouth; he wasn't fully back to his typical self, yet. She caught herself expecting him to be used to people asking for pictures in random places, and frowned at the thought. Could one ever get used to it?

"Yeah." His voice sounded gruff. He cleared his throat. "I hoped that staying out of the store would be enough to avoid recognition, but they parked right at the pump next to ours and the kid recognized me from *Space Bureau*."

Space Bureau was one of his top grossing films. The boy must have been into the franchise enough that a hat, sunglasses, and short beard weren't enough to disguise him.

"It probably didn't help that you had a bit of a beard in the second movie, when your character went rogue."

"So you watched that movie."

"Yep. I've watched a few of your films."

"Did you like them?" Liam inhaled deeply and let it out slowly; the tension in his shoulders went down somewhat.

One of her favorite scenes from one of his romcoms hijacked her mind: when he's fighting with the heroine and she could see the moment his anger turned to lust, the very green of his eyes appearing to burst into flames... and how he made his intentions clear by unbuttoning his shirt, white tan skin filling the screen.

"Yeah, they're good." She hoped she'd hidden the intensity of her reaction to the memory.

"Glad to know." His voice relaxed and a small smile appeared on his lips.

Ana remained quiet, unsure what to say.

They drove for a while in silence, the soft music playing low in the background. Liam was the first to speak again.

"Have you posted anything on social media about the documentary? There's the statement TCA made announcing the film but I haven't checked social media." His tone held a worried note, but Ana couldn't make out what the problem was.

"Not yet." She guessed at his line of thinking. Perhaps he worried about privacy. "I had been planning to talk to you about it. Diana gave me your PR guidelines and said she wants me to post every few days, but I can wait to post something if you'd prefer—"

"No, I think you should post something about it soon," Liam said, surprising her. "Did you see the way the dad looked at you? He'll likely post about meeting us on his profile somewhere and, if he says anything about you, some people might jump to conclusions. If he's private it'll be fine but, if he's not, the scary fans may decide to find you online and who knows what might happen after."

Ana's brain seemed to be having trouble processing his words. "Are you saying that some of your fans could target me online?"

"Yeah. I don't know if you thought about it when you agreed to the documentary, but it's a possibility."

"I didn't think..." She gulped and sorted through different scenarios filling her head: hateful private messages on her social media, mean comments on her videos. She didn't pale often, but her blood rushed away from her face all the same. "I expected some people to think I'm too small a director to be working with you, but— targeted?"

He stole a quick glance at her, his frown deepening. He went back to focusing on the road, but his eyebrows remained furrowed.

"Ana... I think you may not have realized this yet, but—"

"What?" she asked, a chill running down her back at the tone of his voice.

"Did you realize that... well, that many people will assume we're together? Romantically? And a bunch of them will hate you for it."

Her brain short circuited. "But... no, I mean—why would they think we're together? No one would believe that you and I—"

"It's not that unrealistic. And whether it's real or not, they won't care. Whether we deny it or not, some of them will believe we're lying. I hope you're prepared."

She shook her head. Her mouth opened as if to say something, but no words came out. Her mind was empty, except for confusing images of what people would assume was between them.

"If we post about the project," he added, "there'll be an official version out there."

"Okay. Yeah." She nodded, taking her phone out of her pocket and opening a social media app. Following his plan brought the intensity of her feelings down, some of which tempted her with images of her and Liam in compromising positions. "I could post a panning shot I took of your patio yesterday… I'll put that into a story. Make a highlight on my profile for this project. I'll also make a post of me arriving in LA. With those I can announce this documentary on Social Media and hopefully that'll help."

"Yeah. I probably should post something soon, too."

After adding some stickers to her post, "New Project", "So Excited", she wrote a quick caption about arriving in LA. She read it out loud to him.

"So happy to announce my new project. I hope you all enjoy this one. I'll be sharing some bits and pieces as I work on it but, for now, surprise! I'm in LA." She published the content she'd prepared.

"Let's hope this works."

"It should work," she added mostly for her own benefit.

Chapter 7

A COUPLE OF HOURS later, Liam took an exit that put them on a small side road. They followed it for a while; Ana watched out the window, enjoying the trees lining their way, the changing bits of land beyond. The longer they drove, the rougher the journey became. Pavement had given way to gravel, then to dirt.

"Are you going to tell me more about where we're going?" Ana asked. "All I know is the coordinates, which both Diana and Ely know, by the way, because apparently it doesn't have a proper address? Suspicious, Liam."

It had taken a bit of conversation for his stress to dissolve but, after eating snacks— he seemed to have a strong preference for chips, eating most of them by himself— and chit-chatting about adventures she had with Ely over the years, he was back to the casual personality Ana was learning to associate with him.

He laughed at her supposed worry. "I promise I'm not a dangerous man. We're going to an isolated beach house I like."

"*Isolated beach house* aren't necessarily reassuring words in this context, but I'm sure it's all so perfectly safe and lovely. Isn't it?"

"It is." He smiled. "You'll see. I haven't been here for a long time, probably three years or more. At least since before doing *Love, Never.*"

"Your first rom-com; first big movie for you."

"Yeah. You a fan?" He asked, his grin turning flirtatious. When he stole a glance at her, there was a twinkle in his eyes.

Ana's eyebrows shot up. She hadn't expected the change in tone, nor the return of flirty Liam so soon. She had been simply going over her short mental files of Liam's filmography, not fawning over him.

"I've seen it." She looked at him sideways, suppressing a smile, wrapping herself in nonchalant impartiality. She dismissed the idea of ever telling him that she and Ely had watched the movie a few times.

"What's your favorite part?"

She huffed a strangled laugh. She pursed her lips, trying to quiet it further. "When she's going to slap you but ends up punching you."

He tsked. "That wasn't me, it was the antagonist."

"Oh, really? Got confused."

His chuckle was a bit dark. "Fine, that's what I get for asking," he said, shaking his head in disapproval. Ana allowed herself a short snicker.

He'd barely finished saying that when, after taking one last turn, the road opened into a slice of paradise.

The house was a one story, wood cabin. Planters full of flowers lined one side. A deck surrounded the structure, except for the back where an extension of the roof covered two empty parking spots. The lot where the house lived seemed to be a small cove, rocky cliffs around it, green shrubbery on the top edge.

They parked in silence. Ana hopped out of the car, taking a deep breath full of brine. Without waiting for Liam, she turned slowly, taking the place in, before walking past the cabin to inspect the deck in front of the house. A couple of lounging chairs looked out to the ocean, which seemed just a few steps away. In admiration, she leaned on the wooden railing, taking a deep, contented sigh.

"I see you love it, too," Liam said behind her.

She'd twisted to look at him over her shoulder, wisps of her loose hair whipping around in the ocean breeze. She thought she'd gush about the cabin, the tall cliffs that surrounded it and gave it unparalleled privacy, the ocean... but the words died in her throat.

Instead, she stared at Liam standing there on the deck, hands casually resting on his hips. A gust of wind played with his shirt, revealing a strip of naked, tan skin right above the waistband of his jeans. His smile was bright and proud, his hair messy and windswept, his arms and chest solid. His eyes sparkled with what she imagined was delight, the sun shining on them like emeralds.

"Beautiful," she said without thinking. She tensed up and bit hard on the inside of her cheek, immediate regret for the word, but he didn't seem to notice. She closed it inside a lead vault in her mind and ran away from it as fast as she could.

"Yes," he agreed, facing the sea. One of his hands reached up to scratch his growing beard. "I say we get things out of the car and then, I don't know about you, but I'm going to jump right into the water."

She straightened and turned to him, digging her nails into the palm of her hands.

"Sounds good." If only her heart would stop its galloping.

As they took their bags and provisions out of the car, Ana kept the door of the vault in her mind sealed shut. She offered to put things away and organize the cabin and Liam, offering to make dinner to compensate for it, had run to a bedroom with his bag. He hadn't seemed to notice she avoided looking at him directly.

He came out in shorts and a shirt, wearing flip flops, with a towel in his hand. He waved and stepped outside, glee all over his face.

From the corner of her eye, she tracked him through one of the big windows facing the sea. He left the towel on the railing and, in a swift motion, took off his shirt. He hung it from the railing, too, next to the towel. He gave her his back, so she turned to him and watched him kick his flip flops off his feet and jump onto the sand. He jogged into the water; she remained still and lost in the middle of the small living room.

"That's inconvenient," she murmured into the empty cabin. She didn't dare open the lead door and fully inspect what was inside but it didn't matter— she knew what she'd hidden inside.

Developing a crush on Liam was ill-advised. Liam was one of the most handsome men she'd ever met so, sure, being charmed was to be expected. Letting that grow into something else? Allowing it to bubble up into a spark of unadulterated fixation screamed danger. She needed to keep that in check, stomp on the spark and suffocate it. Just because he flirted with her a couple of times it did not mean she could afford to go beyond general appreciation.

Professional. She could keep it professional. She didn't dare risk even imagining a universe where she took action on her attraction to him.

A few minutes later, she stepped out onto the deck and set the camera for a wide angle, to record him from afar swimming in the ocean. She left the camera there, before going back inside to set the place for their stay, and scold herself into line.

―――

Liam's favorite thing about spending time at the beach was the change in the pace of things. Hours stretched; even the sun seemed to slow down on its path. He'd worried that Ana's presence would get in the way of his relaxation, but if the past couple of days were any indication, the next few weeks would be fun. Only a few days since they'd started filming, and not only did he tend to forget she was recording; it was fun hanging out with her.

He had a call booked with Dr. Linda for the next day; she'd be happy that he'd found a way to get so much out of this project already. He certainly was.

After a good workout in the sand, he took a refreshing morning swim in the cool Pacific waters. With loose muscles and a pleased smile on his face, he approached the table on the deck where Ana had just finished setting up some food for breakfast.

"Thanks, Ana. I'll clean up after."

"No problem."

They sat and put food on their plates; she poured coffee for the both of them. They ate in silence for a few minutes and by the time he thought of something to say, she tried to talk as well. They both interrupted themselves and, realizing neither of them had continued, they chuckled.

"Go ahead," he said. "You first."

"You've shared that you're the kind of celebrity that doesn't enjoy fame. What did you mean? You said a few things but I don't think I really get it." She buttered some toast and took a bite.

He didn't respond right away. "I don't think you can. Not until you've been through it."

"Could you try? Maybe just... three things you don't like."

He took a sip of coffee. "Okay. In no particular order, the first thing I'll say, exercising and dieting. I like exercising but this is too much. And when I make an action movie or a rom-com with shirtless scenes, it's worse. Strict meal plans and dehydration. It's so unhealthy and yet, it's part of the job."

"All to look good to the masses."

"Yep. It's in the contracts, you know? That you'll have a certain look. Of course, everyone in the business encourages it because sex sells. People expect a body in a main role to look a certain way, in my case as a guy probably because of a skewed sense of what masculinity looks like. The people consuming these movies probably have no idea it's actually a bad thing to do to your body. There is such a thing as over-exercising and, of course, under-eating is a big deal, too. Insurance premiums for health are sky high because of it."

In rebellion to that fact, he reached for another slice of toast.

"Okay," she agreed, nodding. "I can totally see that. And I suppose the objectification that comes with it must be a lot, too."

He lifted a shoulder. "Sometimes. Not gonna lie, it's really cool to be seen as attractive and, if people are relatively respectful, I'm okay with someone being a fan just for the thirst factor. No big deal. What I don't like is when in order to get a job I have to push my body to the limit or I won't get a role, or when people around me can't see past that. Does that make sense?"

"Mmmh. That if people employing you or having a relationship with you only want you for the thirst factor."

"I guess clichés are clichés for a reason."

"Right. Because you don't want to be wanted just for your body."

He chuckled as his face scrunched up. "I guess that sounds..."

"Standard. I think everyone wants to know they're liked or wanted for who they are as a whole."

Liam pursed his lips. Yeah, it was as simple as that. He was another regular person, that way. The fact she could see that so clearly filled him with warmth that had nothing to do with the California sun shining on them.

"What else?" She asked.

"Another thing I dislike— paparazzi." He could hear the contempt in his voice and felt no remorse over it. "It's obscene how terrible they are. Everyone has a camera now so to stay in business they push every boundary. It's one thing to be recognized wherever you go, that creepy feeling that you're always being watched, or even the scary fans, but paps? They see you as an object that makes them money and nothing else."

"That sounds terrible. I think I'd hate it if people felt entitled to accost me, ask personal stuff, or to tell lies about my life. Paparazzi seem like my worst nightmare."

"They are a complete nightmare. They've accosted my brother, who wants nothing to do with the film industry. A couple of my exes have been approached as well. So it's not just about how they treat me and the people I care about. Anyone I spend time with gets attacked online, which is terrible in its own way, but for people to make a profession out of it? I have a hard time with it."

"Makes sense to me that you hate them." She put her hand on his forearm and squeezed, before snatching it away to drink some of her coffee. He zeroed in on the place her fingers had pressed on his skin, pretty sure it was the first time they touched. "And that you feel like there's no privacy. No freedom from watching eyes."

"It's one of the main reasons why I started therapy. Fame is a monster that demands to be fed with bits of my soul, and I don't want to give it all away."

"I'm sorry, Liam. I can see how this documentary is asking for pieces of your soul, too."

He lifted his eyes to hers and searched there for something, anything that would tell him she really meant that. That she really got what he shared. He thought he could see honesty there.

He smiled. "It is. I will say, though... if you keep letting me get to know you, too, at least I'll feel like I'm not the only one giving."

She mirrored his gesture. "I'd like that, yes."

"So tell me if things get hard, okay? I don't know how to explain this to you in a way that can prepare you for what you might see of fame, just by being around me."

She dismissed his concern with a one-shoulder shrug and he bit his tongue, afraid to burst her bubble so thoroughly.

"I'll be around you for this project and then I'll be gone," she said. "I don't think it'll get much worse than the couple of flames I've gotten on Social Media."

"You did get some, then, huh?"

"Yep. Telling me you're too good for me." She let out a nervous chuckle.

Liam opened his mouth to challenge that notion but thought better of it. What could he really say? That they could be a good fit if they wanted didn't sound quite right.

"What did you say? Did you say anything?" He finally got out. "To the people sending you stuff online."

"No. Like you said, I could say whatever and they would believe what they want."

"Does it bother you?" he asked, unsure of what he was looking to get from her.

She bit her lips as she thought, the action narrowing his attention to her full lips. He tore his gaze away.

She had left the crust of her toast aside, and busied herself making it into crumbs. "I... no, it doesn't bother me," she said after a while. "Beyond the fact that I have no control over it, that is. People will think what they will and that's uncomfortable. I do worry though, because it could impact my career negatively if people think that I... that we... if I appear in any way unprofessional."

He pressed his lips. She thought that if people assumed they were together it could play against her. What a novel concept.

He cleared his throat and glanced at the camera, filming them from the edge of the table. "Yeah, it's another difficult thing about fame. You have to work really hard on appearances; even if someone is rude to you, you can't answer at the same level. Still, you have no control over what people think about you."

"No one does, though, right? No one gets to decide what other people believe about you."

"That's true." He rested his head on one of his hands, palm open holding his temple. "But most people have to contend with a few circles of people: their family, their coworkers, the random person they bumped into at the grocery store. Being famous puts you in everyone's circle. A million people have an opinion about you. It takes a lot of resilience and self-assurance to cope with that, especially when they're forming opinions based on a lie someone made up of you. Or maybe it's just me. I have to keep myself in check to deal with all of that."

She nodded in understanding, leaving the crumbs aside. "It really sounds shitty, what you described."

He chuckled at her choice of words. "Yeah, it is. But I love my job— I don't want to discount all the good, either."

"Tell me about the good. Let's end this on a good note."

"I'm not sure that it says a lot of good about me... but I like to be recognized for what I can do with my acting. Feeling I can tell a story and do it right, with my body, with my voice. We as people— humanity— we're storytellers. Ever since we sat around a fire, we were telling stories. Maybe you can understand what I mean by that."

They smiled at each other, a glimmer of understanding and connection between them. They were both storytellers.

"I remember when you started to show up in movies." She pulled an elastic tie from her wrist and, raking her fingers through her long hair, she put it up into a high ponytail. There was comfort and grace in her movements, and watching her do it calmed his brain. "I only have a very basic, superficial knowledge of actors and actresses, but I remember people talking about how you had done a nice range of movies, showing how you could do different types of films and do well in all of them."

"Yes, and that feels good. So many people dream of being in the position I'm in; they spend years trying their best and they don't make it. So much of it is luck; I don't think I'm the only one who can do what I do. Yet, here I am, and I like that people see that I can actually act."

"That you're more than a pretty face?" she teased him.

Her comment pulled a half-grin from him. "You could say that." After a while, he continued. "It's also that being well-known gives me freedom. I don't mean financial freedom, though that of course is really nice, not gonna pretend it isn't. What I mean by freedom, though, is that I get to act and, if I keep going like this, I'll get to choose scripts I really love soon. I'll get access to projects I really want to do, exploring ideas and characters I can be passionate about. I like acting, I really do. So if I can work on things I'm in love with, well... I'd be living an incredible life."

Chapter 8

L IAM LEANED BACK AGAINST his chair. He and Ana sat in comfortable silence, having finished their food. He lifted his face to the sun and soaked its warmth, eyes closed.

"This is the life." He sighed. "What do you say I take care of all of this, then we get in the water?"

He opened his eyes and squinted at her when she didn't respond. She mirrored him in her chair, leaning back with arms crossed on her midriff. Her ponytail fell straight behind her back.

"Oh." Her only movement was her biting her lip. He did his best to suppress the pull that hooked in his gut at seeing her do that. She chuckled, but it sounded self-deprecating. "Truth is, I don't think that I want to. It makes me nervous."

He welcomed the distraction, his interest piqued at her confession. He stretched back in the chair, locking his hands behind his head. "How come?"

"I haven't been in the ocean enough, and never on a beach with waves like this."

Liam checked the tide. Waves were crashing, but they didn't seem particularly strong or high. He turned to her and leaned forward, resting his elbows on the table to support his torso.

"I'm already not a hundred percent comfortable in the water. There," she added as she pointed at the sea with her chin, "I'm afraid a wave will throw me down and tumble me around like a washing machine, to finally spit me out or swallow me in."

He laughed, the sound reverberating on the cliffs around them. A couple of birds took flight. "That's quite the image."

"I'm sure it's funny to you. You probably have the best sea legs around. No, you do have the best sea legs around, fact. Because I have none."

"Only thing is, sea legs are what you need when on a boat, not for swimming." His grin was so big he could feel it stretching his face.

"Proves my point." She shrugged. "I don't know enough."

"Okay, then," he said, standing and collecting the dishes. "I'll clean up, you'll put on your swimsuit, and we'll get in the water. I'll help you."

She froze up. "No, you're not."

He left the plates and cups in a makeshift tower on the table. He rested his weight on it on his hands, fingers splayed wide.

"You're right, I shouldn't have just said it, I should have asked. Ana, will you join me in the water? I can help you find your swimming sea legs."

"No, thank you." She grabbed the used napkins and some of the cutlery. "You go ahead, go swim, I'll clean up—"

"C'mon, Ana. I'll be there the whole time. We'll take it slow. You can't study how to swim in the ocean in books. You have to experience it, and I can be your lifeguard on duty."

He gave her a smile, turning on the charm with ease. She didn't say anything; her lips pressed together and her hands clutched the things they held.

"Okay, hey," he said, resting a hand on her shoulder. It was the first time he reached out to touch her. He looked at his hand on her warm brown skin as he continued talking. "I won't push, so if you tell me you don't want to then we don't have to... but I'd love it if you'd let me teach you how to swim in the waves."

She looked up and stared at him, frowning. He didn't take away his hand. He could almost see the thought click into place. He knew she'd agreed even before she said it out loud.

Ana went into her room and searched her things for her bikini. Her stomach rolled with nerves at the prospect of swimming in the waves with Liam, so much so that it took her until she was free of her bra to realize that she'd be half naked in front of him to do so.

Her movements jerked, body frozen for a heartbeat, two, before she resolutely finished the task. She prepared for the swim, finding her towel and slathering sunscreen all over, and filling in the cracks already weakening the structure of her mental safe. She was here for work, dammit. She had to control this. She would. His looks or whatever he'd think of hers would not be a factor in this.

She steeled her backbone and walked out of her room. She found Liam on the deck, wearing only his swim shorts, and applying sunscreen on his chest.

"Ready?" he asked.

She gulped and tore her eyes away from his defined muscles, bringing her attention to the camera set up. She placed it on the railing looking out into the water, framing a wide shot of the beach.

"I don't know about that, but let's do it anyway," she replied. Seemed he wouldn't make it easy on her to avoid thinking of how gorgeous he was, or how much her hormones wanted to delight in him.

They left their towels hanging next to the camera and made their way to the water. They stopped when soft waves reached below her knees.

The sound here seemed to be just as loud as when they were on the deck. Cold water rushed around her calves, and Liam stood next to her, within easy reach.

"How much further should we go?" She gazed at the water bathing her lower legs, then up to the horizon.

"We should go a bit further. Not much we can do until at least your knees are underwater. We'll probably practice breaking the waves with your hips first."

"Okay." She hoped he wouldn't keep talking about her body.

She tried to take a step forward; she knew her feet had sunk in the sand a bit as they stood there, but was unprepared for how it changed her balance. She stumbled.

He must have been paying attention; his hand shot forward to support her back. She glanced at him, trying to contain her irritation at herself. Ignoring the feel of his broad palm on her skin. Again.

She huffed. "From one to ten, how out of place do I look, and why is it ten?"

"You're fine," he lied. She raised an eyebrow. He let go of her back and offered her his hand. "Let me help?"

She looked at it, hesitating, and not only because they were in the water.

"C'mon. It'll be fine." He waved his hand between them and, with a flourish, offered it again. "I promise I know what I'm doing."

She let out a long-suffering breath and took his hand. "Promise you won't make fun of me if I fall."

"I'll try my hardest."

He led her deeper into the water. She gasped the first time white water crushed into her, cold mist raining on her skin.

He smiled at the sound. "You're okay. Always look at the waves. Prepare for what's coming. You can meet it with your side, jump over, or dive under."

"You make it sound like I'm playing a contact sport." She looked at the coming waves with suspicion. She barely registered that she grabbed Liam's hand more strongly.

"In a way you are, I guess. But it's fun and refreshing."

"I'm still waiting to see the fun part," she grumbled.

He laughed, a deep and happy sound, and something in her relaxed. "God, Ana. I didn't know you had this side to you. So grumpy."

"Just letting out some nerves."

"Okay, let me show you. I'll let go of your hand and jump over a wave, dive under another. Just keep lifting your feet so that they don't sink in the sand."

"What if a big wave comes?"

"Go back a little so that the water is lower but you can still see me clearly."

She let go of his hand and went back. She watched him diving over and under waves, like he and the ocean were on opposing teams. After a few minutes of that, he came back to her. He ran his fingers through his wet hair to pull it back; he had drops all over his shoulders, chest and abs. Her lower belly tingled. Her mouth watered.

She made herself look back up to his eyes. "It really did look like you were playing a game."

He gave her a knowing look. She ignored it. "It feels like that."

"Have you ever had a wave throw you down for a tumble?"

He grinned. "Many times."

She must have made a face because he laughed.

"Hasn't happened since I turned fifteen and was big enough to be a match for the waves, and had enough wisdom in me to know when not to risk it."

"I'll have to count on your body mass and brain, then," she said, asking for his hand. He gave it to her.

"That's fine. And your body mass will do just fine." He cast a barely concealed appreciative gaze down her curves.

They reached the spot where water mostly flowed around her hips. She gained basic confidence as she met the white water with her side, squeezing Liam's hand hard enough to crunch his bones together. He didn't complain once.

"Oh no," she exclaimed as a big wave swept towards them. It rolled in fast, white water threatening to reach up to her shoulders. Her brain deduced she should dive under it like she'd seen Liam do, but she wasn't ready for that. The small wall of white surf approached swiftly and, despite her best efforts to control her terror, a scream escaped her.

Instinctually, without letting go of his hand, she stepped into Liam's body and used her free hand to grab his neck. He chuckled; he gripped her waist and pulled her in close. He broke the wave for her, his wide shoulders taking most of its force. Salt water splashed all over them.

He didn't let go of her; water rushed around them and past them. Tendrils of her hair had gotten loose from her ponytail, and now stuck flatly on her temples. She lifted her face to him. His eyes sparkled as he focused on her, a wondrous grin on his face. Her heart skipped a beat and, as they continued to look at each other, his smile seemed to falter.

"My feet aren't touching the sand." Her eyes roamed over his face. His beard had some red to it when wet. Another wave broke against his back.

He held her hand between them, close to his shoulder. His other hand still held her securely against his broad chest. He stared into her eyes for another second but broke the connection, turning his sight to the horizon.

The spell broken, her brain offered an overwhelming catalog of just how much of her skin touched his, of the flutter in her heart, and the confusion in her mind. He might have looked at her lips but she wasn't sure; he had turned away so quickly.

"Okay, don't let go," he said without releasing her. He made his way further into the water, taking her with him. His hand remained firm on the flesh of her back, digging pleasurably into the softness of it. "Depending on how much the sand has changed since last night, we may be able to cross the breaking point, then you won't have to worry about the waves until you get more comfortable in the water."

He took them past the breaking point and she avoided looking at his face again, setting her eyes on the horizon and incoming waves. She had no control over her heartbeat, and she hoped he couldn't feel it drumming against him.

Right when she found her calm again, they went up a few feet as they rode a wave that hadn't broken.

"Oh!" she exclaimed, enjoying the sensation. "I liked that!"

"You did, huh?" He grinned at her.

"It's like a roller coaster drop!"

They stayed at that point, letting her get used to the ups and downs of the waves before they crested. He must have noticed she'd relaxed; he let go of her and, a little bit later, her hand as well.

———

Ana followed Liam out of the water. Her body grew heavier with each step, gravity suddenly strong after spending so much time in the weightless environment of the sea. Without discussing it, they each sat on one of the lounge chairs and let the warm air dry them up. After sunbathing for a while, Liam offered to get something to drink; Ana set up the camera from its spot on the railing, this time looking at the cabin and at them.

He gave her a glass and both sat back on the chairs. She brought her knees up and rested her temple on them, gazing at him.

"Got a question for me?" he asked, nodding in the camera's direction.

He took a sip of his drink, his hair still half-wet, curls brightening up as water evaporated, and his eyes bright as he looked at her. A corner of his mouth lifted in a slow, soft smile. Almost cheeky. She pursed her lips to contain a sigh, her lungs locking air inside as if it somehow would help contain her reaction to him.

Fuck. She said she would control it, but failure swept towards her like one of those big, scary waves.

Maybe the solution was to become academic about the whole thing. Acknowledge the reality of it but framing it as no more than a conceptual inquiry. Keeping it rational, instructional. Philosophical. He'd given her the perfect opportunity, after all.

"Yes. Let's talk about attractiveness. When did you realize just how striking you are?"

He seemed to come close to spitting some of his drink. "Excuse me?"

"When did you learn how handsome you are?"

She pushed her nerves into the safety box in her brain, closing its door quickly so nothing new would come out, and prayed it would do a better job at guarding her anxiety than it had her crush. This was a scholastic query, after all; a probe for documentary material. No need to worry.

She took a sip of her drink and added, "Unless the problem isn't in understanding the question, and it's more that you don't want to answer? You can tell me if that's what's going on."

He used the back of his hand to dry his lips, before running a fingertip over eyebrow. She tapped her fingers on the surface of her glass.

"I'm just shocked by the question, that's all," he said.

"Why?"

"I wasn't sure you thought of me as... handsome, to use your word."

Her eyes widened. "Of course I think so. I'm a straight woman with a body that wants other bodies. You must know that how you look is part of your success, and that most people like how you look."

"Yeah, I know, but no one is attractive to everyone, and everyone is attractive to someone. I thought maybe you were on the side of those who say, oh, I know people see him as attractive, but he doesn't do much for me."

"Oh, no, I really get it— I mean, why people see you that way... react that way..."

He rubbed the back of his neck, his lips tense. Crap, she'd indirectly admitted she was attracted to him. She hadn't meant to share *that*. She cringed.

"I'm sorry, I didn't mean to make you uncomfortable," she said. "We don't have to talk about it if you don't want to."

He left his glass on the deck next to his lounge chair and crossed his arms on his chest, quiet for several moments.

"No, it's fine, I get why you'd want to talk about it. It's been pretty key to my success," he conceded.

"Okay." She took a deep breath, imploring she could handle the conversation, and eternally grateful that she could edit all the awkwardness away. "When did you realize, then?"

"I guess in high school. Before that I had been told I was a pretty boy or that someone thought I'd grow up to be handsome, but it was after I noticed the attention I got from girls that I realized I was seen as desirable. That I understood what it meant and what it did for me."

He sighed; his face remained neutral, except for a hint of tension on his lips.

"Why do you sound resigned?" she asked.

"I guess... because high school was fun that way, but even then I realized that my looks don't guarantee a thing. I still got my heart broken by Sara in sophomore year, I still had to study to stay in the honors program, I still had to prove myself. Nowadays, the way I look is about expectations— about moving money from one pocket to the next."

"It's in the contracts, like you said."

"Yeah. Movies, sponsorships, conventions..."

"It's still helpful, though, isn't it? People make snap judgements of you in a much more positive light than of someone who isn't as attractive— that's science. But it probably helps to hold on to success in Hollywood, too, right?"

"All of that is true, yes. Given the choice, we would all want to be seen as attractive— or for it not to be a thing at all. I know I'm lucky and that I did nothing to earn this. And if someone likes it, that's good... but it's not the thing that helps me have fulfillment in life. At least, not in the way that I want. If my looks are all someone takes into consideration, I would lose value as soon as I don't look young and muscular."

"But by then you'll probably look dignified, like a hot professor. Men do get to age and are still seen as handsome."

"That's... probably right," he said with a smirk. "I guess, yes, I would still be able to find work, even if it's not as often as I do now. But work is only a part of my life. I really don't think how I look will do anything for my relationships. How attractive I am is a factor only for casual stuff, not for long term relationships."

"People who love you don't love you because of your looks, but for who you are."

"That's exactly my point. How attractive I am doesn't matter for the things that matter." Liam shrugged. "But I know it does work in my favor."

It took her a couple of minutes to let his words sink in. She straightened her legs on the lounge chair, crossing them at the ankles.

"I suppose that how attractive you are functions for you the same way it does for everyone. Privilege and objectification."

He nodded. "I think so. Is that how it's been for you too, then? How do you handle being attractive?"

She whipped her head to look at him. He stared back, dead serious.

"How I handle it?" she asked, her voice coming out thinner than before.

"Yes, you. I'm sure you've had to figure that stuff out, too."

She squinted her eyes at him and tried to joke. "Are you looking for payback?"

He lifted his hands defensively. "You told me I could ask questions."

He was clearly not letting her get away with misdirection.

She crossed her arms and leaned back, thinking it over. "I guess it's hard for me to think we can compare experiences. You're classically attractive. You're Hollywood Hot. You've probably been seen as attractive half your life. You're what, thirty?"

"Thirty one in a month."

"Right. So let's say you've known you're attractive since you were sixteen. That's practically half your life. I really didn't have much luck in that department until my early twenties." She shook one of her feet. "So only for the past five years or so, and not nearly to the same degree as you. Plenty of people think I'm unattractive, too."

"Okay," he said as if he found it hard to believe but was trying to. His eyes roamed her thighs, the same ones that had been called too big and too fat before. "And how do you feel when seen as attractive, over these past few years?"

She gazed at the horizon, pretending not to notice and not to care if he was checking her out. She didn't change her position to hide the rolls on her belly. "It has pros and cons. When I started being seen as... pretty, maybe; when that began— it felt different. People smiled at me more and sometimes I thought that people let me get away with things, like a traffic ticket or something. Or they suddenly saw my parent's background as romantic rather than controversial because they immigrated here. There may be more I didn't notice. At the same time... I don't like that it's harder to be invisible. So, yeah, I think I tend to avoid spending a lot of time on my looks, you know, in my everyday, because I don't want to add to that. I'd rather be comfortable living my life in the safety of being average looking unless I feel like making an effort—"

He scoffed. "You're not average looking."

Ana's words died in her throat.

He frowned, eyes glassy as if his words surprised him and need-ed to re-evaluate his thoughts.

His face relaxed a second later, a small grin accompanying the twinkle in his eyes. "I'm not going to pretend I didn't say that."

"Okay."

"You were saying that you try not to flaunt your hotness because you want to blend in."

"I don't think we need to exaggerate here," she tried. A smile forced its way on her face despite herself.

It seemed that flirty Liam had made yet another appearance. It was dangerous how often he moved them into that territory.

His grin widened. "That you have to work hard at hiding how good-looking you are."

"Stop." She chuckled, keeping her eyes off him.

"That being so fetching is hard."

He laughed when she scrunched up her face. She shouldn't care if he found her attractive. She was happy with herself, and that should be enough.

"I'm going to throw this drink at you," she threatened, but it only made him laugh harder.

"Fine, fine, I'll stop," he finally conceded. "But I think you kinda agree with me, then. A pleasing face and alluring body are nice to have, but it's not all good."

"Is this beauty fragility?" she asked.

His grin didn't waver. "Why don't I leave you to think it through? I'll go make us an early dinner."

"And another drink, please."

Chapter 9

L IAM WORKED OUT AFTER waking up, and spent the rest of the morning again teaching Ana how to swim safely in the ocean. He enjoyed helping her, seeing her growing comfort in the water, and catching glimpses of the stray drops running down her skin. He had to stop himself from studying the lines of her body too often, or how she moved. Even now, as they walked out of the ocean and onto the deck, his eyes kept wanting to trace the lush shape of her ass and those delicious, thick thighs of hers.

He tore his eyes away from her body for the hundredth time. He didn't feel bad about the growing lust in his blood— it made sense, there was plenty to enjoy in looking at Ana— but he didn't want to pay a lot of attention to it either. They were still getting to know each other and, whether they became friends or not after the filming was done, things would likely not go in a romantic direction for a long time... if ever. Many things would have to happen before anything like that could come to be. With that in mind, ogling just didn't feel right. Morally. Because his body certainly enjoyed it.

They went into the house and Liam opened the fridge, looking for food. "Want lunch? I can make something."

"Yes, please. Ugh, I'm so cold!"

He got sliced bread and the makings for a sandwich out of the fridge and put it all on the countertop next to it. He glanced at Ana, catching the moment she shivered. Noting the way it caused the flesh of her stomach and full breasts to jiggle.

Good God. Do not check if her nipples are hard.

He turned back to the fridge and took a controlled breath. He grabbed some mixed greens for a salad and by the time he turned back around, he was grateful to see she had wrapped a towel around herself.

Her phone lit up on the table between them. She reached out for it.

"Yes? Oh, hi, Diana." Ana sat on one of the table chairs. "I'm fine, thanks! What's up?"

Liam set up to make the food, pretending not to be listening.

"No, it should be fine. Everything is good," she continued, before a short silence filled the cabin. "Uhm… Yeah, sure. Of course."

She stood again and gave Liam a sheepish smile, pointing in the general direction of her room while mouthing, *be right back.*

He finished preparing the food and left it ready on the island, cleaning everything else up. Thinking that Ana would enjoy the sunny day, he moved plates and glasses outside. He had just returned to the kitchen when Ana came out of her room. Thankfully— regretfully— for the better, she'd put on a long shirt.

"C'mon, it's ready," he said, and she followed him out.

They sat and had a few bites and, by the time she gave him a third wary look, he was too curious to wait.

"Okay. Out with it," he said.

"What?"

He arched an eyebrow. "Looks like something happened in the call?"

She stared back at him, and let a quick puff of air out. "It's just that it's awkward."

"Is it something your agent said?"

"Yeah." She took a sip of water and, leaning against the chair, crossed her arms around her waist. "Diana had a few things she wanted to discuss with me."

"Such us? Or is it private? Sorry, it's just these looks you're giving me... but you don't have to tell me."

"I don't think it's private... she wanted me alone when discussing it but I think it was 'cause she wanted to give me time to digest things. She didn't say I couldn't talk to you about it... and, to be honest, even if she had I don't think I should keep you out of it."

"Is this something I'm going to have to discuss with Coulton?"

"I don't know. Maybe."

He leaned forward and rested his arms on the table. "Tell me, then. I'll decide about Coulton after."

"Okay. Well, Diana wanted to talk about two things. One, she wanted an update on the filming, if I thought I was getting the content I needed. She had some suggestions and stuff."

She looked up to the sky, and something about the gesture told Liam that Ana wasn't pleased with that part of it.

"Is that what's awkward?" he asked.

"No, that's just... pressure, I'd say. She had some suggestions on the angles I should be pursuing for the film." She dismissed it with a shake of her head. "I think she bought my reasons why I'm not pursuing an *angle* so that wasn't the problem. The awkward part is more to do with the other thing she wanted to discuss."

"Ana, just tell me."

She pursed her lips to the side. "She also wanted to let me know that there has been some conversation on social media about us.

That there are people who not only think we're together, but that are... campaigning, let's say, for our relationship to last."

"Oh." Relief pulled a chuckle out of him. "That's it? That we have shippers?"

"Shippers!" she exclaimed. Her eyes lit up with mirth. "Can you believe it?"

He smiled. "I can. It took longer than I thought, to be honest."

"It's ridiculous. There are like, two things out there about this project. How can they put those two together and go, wow, they're so into each other."

"They don't need to know much to see what they want to see."

She sighed. "I remember you saying that."

She added salad to her plate and he ate more of his sandwich.

"Anyway," she continued, "Diana wanted me to know. She instructed me to post more to social media about the project and to clarify that we're not involved; that this is all purely professional."

"Are you... in trouble with her?"

Her eyes shot to his and stayed for a beat, but she took them away a second later. "I don't think so. She said that she expected this to happen, too, and that she'd send me some guidelines about how to handle it later. She wanted to know if anything was happening between us and of course I said there's nothing romantic going on."

"Right." He drank water and hoped the cold liquid would quelch the small fire in his belly at her statement. "Do you want me to help with posting something?"

"What are you thinking?"

"We can both post some pictures online. Plan something together."

"Do you need to discuss it with Coulton? Or your PR team?"

He lifted a shoulder and took the last bite of his sandwich. "No. Coulton doesn't say much about social media— he thinks it's beneath him— unless my PR team is so frustrated with me 'cause of my constant rejection of them that they complain to him."

He gave her a quick grin and she laughed in response. "What could you do that makes them so angry they need to rat you out?"

"I don't post enough, according to them, and I won't let them take over either. I've also refused to do things like pretending I'm dating models and stuff."

"They've wanted you to fake relationships?"

"Oh yeah, it happens all the time, but I don't want to do it. They'd push more, but I fired the last team that got really pushy that way."

"Wow. I thought that stuff didn't happen."

"But it does."

Ana chewed and swallowed a big bite of bread before speaking again. "Well, if you don't need to ask for permission like us lowly talent, then it could be cool to post something we came up with together."

He shook his head at *lowly talent* but ignored it. "Okay. Give me your phone."

She arched an eyebrow but gave it to him.

"I'll take a picture of us," he explained. He double clicked it to open the photo app. "You can post it to social media, tag me, and say something about how fun it is to get to work with me. Only if it's true, of course. I wouldn't want you to fake anything."

His lips stretched into a teasing smile. Seemed he couldn't stop himself from flirting with her. He didn't even realize he was doing it, half the time, until warmth spread down from his navel at her reaction.

She rolled her eyes but her lips curled into a reluctant smile. "Oh, sure. I guess I can say working with you is fine."

He laughed and, lifting her cell, took a quick picture of them.

"There." He gave her the phone back.

Still with a grudging smile on her lips, she began typing. Taking out his phone, he opened Instagram and waited for the notification of her tag; she had written, "Liam is a really cool guy! It's awesome doing business with someone you could be friends with. So glad we're doing this documentary to show you all."

The warmth inside of him swept up into his chest and wrapped itself around his heart. It shocked him that he could react that way at reading her words.

"Nice, thank you," he said, reposting her photo and adding, *she's a cool one too.*

Not five seconds after posting, the app showed several reactions to his post. The same must have happened for her.

"Half of the comments say they don't believe this is business." Her voice seemed breathless. "Like what we said didn't matter."

He locked his phone and put it face down on the table. She did the same and turned to him, silently asking for an explanation.

"Yeah, that's how it happens sometimes. It's good to say what you want to say, if you really want to, but they may go wild with speculation anyway. So... maybe you let them go wild, next time."

"Next time?"

He nodded, and she sighed.

Chapter 10

ANA IGNORED HER PHONE for the next few hours. Liam told her more about Sara, who broke Liam's heart by ending their four-month relationship before Valentine's Day, and Ana told him about her unrequited crush on Germaine, a French exchange student.

After sharing a simple pasta salad dinner, Liam busied himself putting dishes in the dishwasher; Ana sat on the sofa to text with Ely.

"I can hear you snickering from here," he called from the kitchen nearby. "What's up?"

"Ely and I are texting. We're talking about the reaction on the internet to our posts earlier. She's sending me screenshots of the wildest things she finds." She chuckled. "There's a name for us, Liam. Apparently, our couple name is #mcana."

"You haven't asked, but I'd say don't get into that habit. It's like reading the comments section of the news." He started the dishwasher and washed the sink.

"No, I know, but Ely is having a field day over this. I'm not the one looking; I'm letting her decide what's worth sharing and then we laugh about it. It's nice to know she's looking and helping me make fun of it. It must mean it's not that bad, right? That it's happening."

He turned the tap off and dried his hands, before he came to stand behind the sofa. He leaned down and rested his hands on the back of it. She looked up at him; his eyes shone with playfulness.

"Mh. How good-natured is she?"

"She's the best, why?"

He lifted one of his hands to scratch his bearded chin. "What if you sent her a picture of my disapproving face?"

Ana grinned. "And what are you disapproving of?"

"Let's say I'm worried she's walking a fine line, going down that rabbit hole."

Still smiling, she framed him for a picture and he posed as if he were displeased at them. She sent it to Ely with the caption, *someone isn't happy we're having so much fun.*

"I told her I wouldn't send any pictures of you, so it'll shock her."

Silence broke right after her statement; Liam was quick to add more.

"Hey, how do you feel about sitting on the deck, drinking something alcoholic, and talking?"

Ana's eyes left her phone to stare at him. They were definitely comfortable spending time together, seemingly enjoying each other's company. If she were to risk the thought, she'd say they were growing close. A double-edged sword.

"Sounds great," she said, suppressing the heady blend of butterflies and nerves battling in her stomach. She could not let her mixed up feelings get in the way of their comfort with each other; it would ruin the intimacy and trust needed for the documentary. "What do we have?"

They got everything in place: Scotch for him, gin for her, the camera in place, even blankets in case it got cold. Once they'd gotten comfortable on their now-usual lounge chairs, he asked her about Ely.

"Did she say anything about the picture?"

Ana unlocked her phone and checked her texts. Ely had sent a picture of herself flipping her hair as if she didn't care about Liam's opinion. Ana laughed and showed it to Liam, who chuckled.

"I'm glad to see she's not a fan," he said. "Keeping things real."

"She is a fan, but it's not enough to impress her. She has a very strong sense of authenticity."

The sun was about to touch the horizon, its light casting the world in shades of gold.

"She sounds awesome, from the bits you've said. But why is she going into the fangirling black hole?" He drank from his tumbler and sighed with pleasure.

"That's not what she's doing," Ana argued, putting her phone away. "She's just enjoying the fact that her best friend, me, is being rumored to be on a sexcapade with Liam McMillan."

A cold breeze sliced through them, bringing with it change that stabbed the air. It had nothing to do with the weather.

Her senses sharpened as she stared at him. "I'm sorry, Liam. I get the feeling I said the wrong thing."

He stayed silent, making her nervous. A deep groove marked the space between his eyebrows, his eyes dark. His mouth betrayed a small rictus, stillness throughout his body.

"Actually, I know I said the wrong thing," she tried. The change made her feel unsettled, needing to make things better somehow. "Looking back, there are one or two things that I think may have upset you—"

"Ana, stop. Yes, I'm angry, but not at you. It's bigger than that, and I know it. I'm trying to buy myself some time so I don't lash out."

She could hear the tension in his voice; it traveled through her body and settled like a stone in her belly. Sensing she should give him the time he needed, she leaned back in her chair, shoulders inwards, hands between her thighs. Biting her lips, she made herself wait.

"Okay," he said a minute later. She thought she heard half a snickering laugh. "The problem was that there's a lot of irony in this for me; the conversation about being attractive, talking about relationships, a sexcapade on social media... and the fact we're not having sex."

"Of course we're not having sex," she exclaimed despite herself, more shock than apology in her tone. "We're working. As much as it doesn't feel like it, this is work. I couldn't possibly risk my professional reputation even if— at the end— I do hope we're forming some sort of friendship... but whatever happens, this is work."

He shook his head, his mouth curling down as if he'd had to swallow an unsavory bite. She pursed her lips, holding back the flood of questions and suggestions wanting to come out.

"I know you're recording, but can I be frank?" he finally asked.

"Please. Let's have this conversation. I don't want to talk because of the project, I want to talk to clear the air between us. We may be recording this but it might not make it into the film and that's fine. I'll probably keep like 10% of everything I have and I'm pretty good about cutting out stuff that's just too personal. So let's not let the camera stop this... please. If we can't talk openly, then the whole thing falls apart."

He bent a leg and rested his wrist on the lifted knee, the groove in his eyebrows still present. "Agreed."

"Good." She shifted toward him, and into a position that let her study him more clearly. "So, the irony made you angry."

"Yeah. Why does everyone have an opinion on my personal life? People want to know if I have a girlfriend or ten or, if I'm not seeing anyone, then they ask, *why?* Well, I want to ask, why does it matter? Why do people have an opinion on it? Is she pretty, or which gender am I really attracted to? Should I break up, should I stay— is she pregnant? No one is good enough for me, but being single is not allowed, either. They think I owe them my life."

Ana sighed. Just spending time with him had brought her into his vortex. She'd experienced so little of this and she already disliked it. He was surrounded by this every day and had been for years; of course it affected him.

He continued. "Whatever I do, people assume I'm having sex five times a day and they want to know. They look into it and make connections as if— as if my life is proprietary. They make it up if they don't find anything. It's like they believe that because I act and I make money for it, my personal life and my feelings belong to them. They feel free to talk about it. My love life and my sex life are for public consumption. Even when I'm having sex zero times a day. When the only person I'm spending time with is here because it's work."

Crap. In her attempt to manage her discomfort, she'd been a part of those people taking ownership of something that should belong to him. Making fun of the idea that people thought they were involved. Like it didn't affect her... but forgot to check if it could be affecting him.

His shoulders were heavy, his hands curled into fists. His frown seemed deeper but his eyes... his eyes were sad. Maybe because, when she'd explained what made this so funny, that people had gotten it so wrong, that she was only here for work— well, she'd made him feel alone.

Her stomach dropped. As much as she liked him, it was true: the documentary was the only reason they were in this place, for this long, talking like this. She couldn't deny the truth of her words and their meaning; she hadn't lied to him: her presence in this cabin was limited to the purposes of this project. She could still apologize for what it did to him, though.

Sobering up, she sighed and looked him in the eyes. "I'm sorry I was so flippant about what's going on in social media. Making fun of it helped, but I didn't think about how it might make you feel. You're right, I shouldn't make light of something that's so personal to you."

His furrowed eyebrows relaxed somewhat, his hands loosening up. The glow of the setting sun made him look like a bronze, sad star god.

"I'm sorry to ruin your fun," he said. "I should remember I was like that at the start, too. It used to be easy to laugh about it all in the beginning."

"What happened? What changed?" her own voice came out low now, matching his.

He didn't reply right away. His eyes jumped between hers, his lips in a tense line. So many little ticks and movements on his expressive face, making it clear he hesitated.

Wanting to comfort him and show him he could open up safely, she got up and sat on his chair, next to his knees. She watched him, her back to the sunset; his face softened as the seconds ticked by. With a small smile making an appearance, he looked away at the sun on its way into the ocean.

"It's fucking lonely sometimes in this industry," he said. "I have friends. I love them, and I do my best, but I can't keep up with their lives as much, because what they're going through is just so different from my life. I tried to make friends in the industry but... maybe I've just had bad luck and I haven't met the right people, or maybe I don't know how to find them. It's also simply having the time to invest in creating relationships, when I'm so busy. Anyway, the point is... most of what I've come across has been shitty."

"What do you mean, shitty?"

"Mostly, I mean fake. Or someone wanting something from me. I get that a lot in this business ends up being transactional, but is it too much to ask for people to be upfront about it?"

She could hear the hurt in his words, how he'd grown jilted as people lied and used him.

"For what it's worth," she said, not quite able to meet his eyes, turning her face to look at her hands on her lap. "I would actually like it if this grows to be more than about the documentary. I'd like to be your friend, too."

He nodded his acknowledgement, reaching out to her. His hand covered hers, warm and big, and he squeezed once before retreating.

"Want to tell me what happened?" she asked.

He seemed to think it over, his eyes shifting on the horizon.

"Early last year was rough. I was quite burnt out— about work and people, to be honest. I'd been getting more and more cynical, careless, even mean at times. I was on the road to becoming a really ugly person."

"Mmmh. I wouldn't say you're an ugly person, inside."

He glanced at her before his face turned down and to the side, as if he couldn't face her. She waited for him to make up his mind; he let his head drop, chin to the chest.

"Remember how I was becoming an asshole?"

"So you said."

"I was seeing someone. I wasn't nice to her. I could say I was like that because I knew she just wanted money and fame out of me, but that doesn't justify how much of a douche I was. One night we were having sex and I was self-absorbed, kind of angry. I knew I wasn't actually with her, but going through the motions. Meanwhile, she was moaning and screaming and saying stuff like, *you're the best I've ever had.* Such bullshit. I don't think I did a single thing that was for her that night. I knew she was performing and doing what she thought I'd like. Still, I kept at it, mechanical, uncaring."

Ana cringed at the bitterness in his story, recognizing the rancor he kept inside him somewhere.

"After, as I lay there with her next to me, I realized that in all our dates she hadn't asked me a single thing about who I am as a person, and I hadn't asked her a single thing either. Dates were mediocre, time together was mediocre, the sex was mediocre. The whole thing... fake and perfunctory. I felt so disgusted with myself. So, I broke up with her, took a week off from people except for work— I just showed up and left as soon as possible, no socializing. I focused on trying to figure out how to move forward. I was a part of the problem at that point, right? I needed to do better. So I vowed no more sex or relationships until I knew how to trust that they were real, and I found a therapist."

He hadn't met her eyes as he told her about this time in his life, and hers roamed his face, searching for him, learning the lines of pain on it. Heaviness in her chest for him— yes, he'd been selfish and maybe mean with that ex, and he also had done something about it.

She gave herself permission to reach to him, putting a hand on his knee and squeezing. Still not looking at her, he put his hand on hers again, a sad, tiny smile on his face.

"How long ago was that?"

"More than a year now."

Light faded around them, the space filling up with deep purples and grays. She squeezed his knee again and took her hand away, reaching for her glass.

She took a sip of her drink. "I'm sorry you've had such crappy experiences. I'd like to reassure you, but I can't say that I know it'll be different next time. I've been burnt, too, and sometimes I find it hard to believe myself. I'm still trying to find my feet again after my last relationship, so I'm not sure how any of that works. I do hope it'll happen for you, though. That you'll find someone you can trust loves you for who you are."

"Me, too." He reached for his glass as well. "Would you share your story with me?"

Ana drank more gin before putting the glass down next to the chair they still shared. She collected her thoughts, readying herself to open up to him. He'd trusted *her*, not Ana the director, and she wanted to reciprocate.

"I was in a long-term relationship. I thought he was the one, you know? That he was it for me. So I settled, planned my future with him. Imagine my shock when I learned he had cheated on me throughout our relationship. There wasn't a single time in our relationship when he was monogamous with me. By the time I uncovered everything, I'd learned about eight side relationships. Not even casual sex cheating only, he also had actual, long relationships. We had agreed to be only with one another. He looked me in the eye and told me he wanted that with me. Learning that it had all been a lie, well, it shook me."

"What an asshole," he exclaimed. Like he really meant it.

"That was almost two years ago. It really messed me up 'cause I'd trusted him completely. Going through the break up left me with a million questions and a tonne of mistrust. I don't know that I've fully recovered, to be honest."

"So you also have questions about how a good, true relationship happens?"

"Yeah. Especially the part about it being true. I thought it was true, but it wasn't. I don't know how to trust myself or the other person and if I don't know if it's real, how can I jump and risk the pain of being wrong again?"

"I don't think you're supposed to know people are lying to you, Ana. You had to trust him or how would it have worked?"

"I should have seen the signs. I should have known. We were so young when we got together. I was 21 and he was 22. Who meets their life-long partner that young?"

"Some people do. My parents are high school sweethearts. I think they're happy together."

"I guess that means we're not one of the lucky ones."

"I suppose we're not. Still, doesn't mean we won't be. I think the only way it'll even be a possibility is to risk it."

She gave him a reticent smile, one that pulled to the side. "Is that hope in your words, Liam?"

He laughed. "I'm just trying to argue with you."

She squinted her eyes at him, her half-suppressed grin still in place.

"Yeah, okay. I'm also trying to convince myself," he conceded.

He lifted both his knees and rested his arms on them, hands held together. He studied the horizon. His eyes were now forest green, rich and deep, and his skin looked dark gold in the light of the setting sun.

As she waited for more, she turned in her spot to look out to the ocean too. In the tone of his silence, she imagined she could hear the thoughts running through his brain. She let him make up his mind, admiring the fading sunset next to him. There were faint clouds of a deep red where the ocean seemed to end, fading into pinks and violets and, above them, deep blue. Some stars had shown up, twinkling and bright.

"I think," he finally said, "the alternative is to doubt everyone, and the kind of relationship I want can't exist within that."

Well— shoot. He was right. The truth of his statement was heavy and scary and accurate.

She leaned to the side to bump his legs with her shoulder. "Can't argue with that."

"I don't blame her— the woman I was with. She probably thought she had to be like that to be liked, because that's what society teaches people. And I was a big part of what got me in that mess. I'm sure there are plenty of people who feel the way I do, and plenty of people I could meet that would be the right person for me, be it for friendship or something different. I need to believe that I'll find them, that's all."

She turned to look out to the horizon, still sitting by his knees. She sighed. "I think this conversation is something I'm going to take with me, Liam. Thanks for trusting me with it."

"You make it easy, Ana."

―――

"Thanks for sharing your story, too," he said. She sat close to him yet not enough; from his place further back than her on the chair, he could see only part of her face.

"I meant the part about being friends, you know. A friend would share." She lifted her arms and casually braided her hair to the side. "I've stayed in contact with most people I worked with for my films. Getting to know someone like this makes me really care about them," she added, looking at him sideways and giving him a smile. He really liked her smile.

He moved forward on the chair, putting one leg down on the ground for balance. They were sharing the chair now, side by side, shoulder to shoulder.

"So you think you know me well enough yet?" he asked.

He didn't know what he was doing; whether he wanted to get reassurances that she enjoyed him as a person, or that she felt differently about him than the other people she had worked with in the past. Either way, he couldn't help himself.

"I think I'm still figuring you out," she replied, turning her head to look at him.

He turned his head to look at her, as well. "And?"

She pursed her lips, as if trying to determine the best course of action. "If you're curious, I can tell you what I think I've learned so far."

"Yes, please. Go ahead."

She nodded. "If someone had asked me what I'd feel if I ever met you, I'd have guessed starstruck. Instead, since Coulton's office, that's not what I've felt. Granted, it helped that you were moody that day, because my pride squelched any giddiness I might have felt."

He grinned. "That's good."

"Your hesitation at being seen through my camera helped me see past the glitter. Made you more real. It made me want to get to know *you*."

His chest softened, old gates creaking as they opened to receive her words. He thanked whatever had made him want to ask, because he craved having someone see him that way. Someone other than his therapist, anyway.

"Thank you. I appreciate that," he tried, knowing that such simple words couldn't express all he meant.

They were still looking at each other. Her eyes searched his face. He hoped his gaze remained open and that she found enough there to want to keep looking; he really wanted her to keep looking.

"I hope I can say this right," she added, leaning into him so that her shoulder pressed against his arm. "Spending all this time with you has helped me see that there's nothing special about you, Liam. You're not different. You're just like any other person doing their job, taking their talents and trying to use them well. The circumstances are strange and weird and overwhelming... but that says nothing about who you really are. Meanwhile, the glitter has made you invisible to most people, and it's caused you hurt."

His open chest flooded, the wave of it inundating him and seizing up his throat. He didn't know it could be like this, feeling understood by someone else.

She must have thought he'd misunderstood her meaning, for she put her hand on his thigh and squeezed, her forehead wrinkling with worry.

"I'm sorry, I don't mean anything bad by it. What I mean is—"

"I think I know what you meant," he managed, rawness in his voice. "And it means more than I can say."

"Good, because I also think you feel alone, and it makes me sad."

He reached and put his hand under hers. Her brown eyes called to him, pulling him in; he said nothing else, struck by them.

She shook her head. "It must be so fucking lonely, to have so many people surround you and seek you out, but none that'll bother going deeper than skin level."

He let himself interlock his fingers with hers, there where their hands rested on his leg. It was his way to say what he couldn't, that he hadn't felt alone since she'd been around.

Chapter 11

L IAM DIDN'T MEAN TO keep to himself after his conversation with Ana two nights before. The confusing feelings he harbored upon waking up the following morning disappeared after a strenuous workout and, since Ana seemed busy working on her computer, he'd gotten into a book for most of the day. He'd even relaxed enough to take his first nap in ages. They'd had dinner and gone to bed without much shared time

He had different plans for the hours ahead. The antsy feeling in his belly begged for a change.

The part of him that actually enjoyed exercising convinced him to do cardio and finish with a swim. He came out of the ocean and onto the deck, finding Ana on a lounge chair scrolling her phone.

"Morning." He sat on the other chair. "All caught up with work?"

Ana put her phone on a small table between the chairs. She turned her big camera on and placed it at the end of her chair, framing him mostly. "Morning. Yeah, done for now. Just Diana wanting a bit of a write up. How was your swim?"

"It was great. The current is a bit rough though, so if you want to go in, let me know."

"Thanks. I don't think I'll swim any time soon; I'm enjoying the sun."

"So, a write up? I've never had to write something for Coulton." He reached for the sunscreen bottle on the small table between them. He applied it with business-like precision, hands fast on his calves.

"Apparently the request came from Coulton's office. Diana didn't say as much, but if I read between the lines, I think they want to make sure I don't mess things up."

Liam frowned. "That's... shitty, isn't it? You're the director. They wanted you for a reason."

"Yeah, but also I'm super new and unknown. They probably don't want to give me free rein with their highest grossing star."

"But isn't it suppressing you as an artist? Your films are unscripted for a reason."

"Sure... but I don't have enough of a name to do as I please."

He finished putting sunblock on his legs and moved to his arms. "I used to feel the same way when I started with Coulton. He said I needed to sign with three movies, I did. He said I needed to go on a long promo tour, I did. And I guess it's what brought me here, so he was right... you could say I have the name now, but I still don't get to say no often. Hell, we're here because I couldn't say no."

"Is this how it is?" She lifted her legs and rested her arms on her knees. "Having an agent?"

"I don't know, to be honest. I've only worked with Coulton, but sometimes I wonder..."

He left the sentence hanging, thoughts disappearing into a corner of his mind. His hands stilled, falling to his lap.

Her eyes were gentle as he looked into them, as if he could find the damn answers there.

"I think," he said after a while, "that I'm afraid that if Coulton's guidance built me up, I owe him. I know I do. And I don't know how... or if..."

"Yeah? How much you can push back without being ungrateful?"

A small click marked a piece of him getting into place. A curl pulled at the corner of his lips. "That's... ridiculous, isn't it?"

She smiled. "I don't think so. I think it means you recognize you didn't build your level of fame alone."

A tingle appeared close to his heart at her words and he let them be, uninspected. He grinned at her, distracting them both from the moment. "Or I'm too proud to owe anyone anything."

She chuckled. "Yeah, I don't think that's it."

He shrugged and continued applying sunscreen. "Anyway, that's part of it, for sure. I know I need a change but how to ask for it and truly make it happen is a bit of a mystery."

"I'm sure you'll figure it out."

"I'd say maybe think of how much you let Diana control rather than manage and," he gave her an impish grin, "if you figure it out, let me know."

She laughed. "Deal. Good luck to us."

"Good luck to you editing this bit without vilifying our agents. But I wanted to ask you something. Are we ready to move on? Go to the next place?"

He glanced at her, catching the way her eyes roamed his chest. He looked away and hid a smile, ignoring the echo of attraction he felt in response. For now. Until he knew how far to take it.

Liam left the bottle on the table and took the spray to apply sunscreen on his back. He considered asking her for help, but that would push his luck even more than flirting.

Ana took the bottle he'd been using and applied sunblock to her legs. "Oh. Well, I love it here but... sure, of course."

Her legs tempted his eyes, calling him to study the soft flesh and the smatter of cute dimples on them. Her skin had gotten several shades darker during their time in the cabin.

He kept his eyes on her face. "C'mon. I'm asking you because I want to know what you think. I don't need you to just say yes to everything."

"That's sweet," she said, giving him a glorious smile. "But I'm honestly okay with whatever you prefer. This trip is your pseudo-vacation. Letting you choose is something I can do for you."

"This is another thing that's probably gonna mess up your editing, right? You'll have to keep it chronological."

"Your beard isn't helping either but you don't see me complaining."

Fuck it. He liked flirting with her.

He grinned. "That's probably because I look good with a beard. Don't you agree? Tell me the truth."

She laughed, the sound warming him up from the inside. "You're such a flirt. And so cocky. Guess you have to be that way to make it in your industry."

"The mistake you're making is thinking I flirt with everyone."

Her grin faltered. He would have asked about it, but she continued the conversation.

"I'll handle the editing situation. Don't worry about it. Let's do what'll make you happy."

"Okay." He pressed pause on his desire to ask, to push, to learn why it affected her to learn he enjoyed flirting with her. To have her confirm that she was aware of the attraction building between them, and question why she didn't like it. "Then tomorrow, we're going somewhere else."

And maybe, with a new place and more time, he'd find a way to test the line where they could acknowledge how they felt, and take their sweet time to choose if they ever wanted to do something about it.

———

Ana helped Liam pack the car the next day, saying quick goodbyes to the cabin.

"Are you going to tell me where we're going?" she asked, setting the camera on the dashboard once more. "Again, I have coordinates only."

He started the car and began driving. "I'd've hoped you'd trust me a bit by now."

"Maybe I do. Maybe I'd still rather know, you know?"

"But you do know. It just doesn't have an address, either."

"How do you even find these places?"

"There's a secret society of fancy California hideaway cabins I'm a part of."

She laughed. "That can't possibly be true but, if it is, you have enough money to be eccentric like that, I'm sure."

Two hours full of banter later, they stopped at a grocery store to stock up. Liam wore his hat and with it plus his beard, he decided to risk it and join her for shopping.

When someone stared at them for too long in the produce section, he pretended to shrink behind her. He grabbed the back of her Foreigner shirt, scrunching it in his hands as he used her like a shield.

She laughed and twisted at the waist to hiss in his direction. "You know you're too big to do that, right? You're calling more attention to yourself."

He straightened and relaxed his hands on her shirt, and the fabric loosened around her again. He placed the tips on his fingers on her waist, as if unsure of it, and whispered into her ear. "It's just too much fun to see you squirm."

An involuntary shiver ran down her spine. She prayed he didn't notice. "If we're accosted by fans, I'll hold you responsible for it."

"There are like five other shoppers here. We'll deal." He took his hands away and took a step back.

She didn't like it, but at least she could breathe better.

Two hours later they were surrounded by forest, and Liam drove them through a narrow road.

"The thing is," Ana said, in the middle of a story, "I'm not fluent in Spanish. I understand it, but I can't speak it. So the first time Ely's parents offered me some tintico, I was extremely confused. Did I get it right? But I was too young for wine... and I couldn't even ask! They wanted me to practice Spanish. Turns out that while tinto is a word for red wine in a lot of Latin American countries, it means black coffee in Colombia."

"So there you are, right after lunch with your parents and Ely's family..."

"And her parents are offering me red wine. Or so I thought."

He laughed. "And your parents didn't say anything? They knew about tinto versus coffee, right?"

"Yeah, they knew, because Ely's parents had pulled the same trick on them years before. But of course they didn't say anything. They wanted to laugh at my expense, too."

He chuckled and shook his head at the same time. "I think I'm not going to ask a lot about *that* right now."

"That's probably wise..."

Liam turned into a gravel side road, following the GPS indications on the car's screen. After ten minutes, they reached a closed wooden gate; Liam got out of the car and opened it. Driving into the property, Ana studied the minimalist-looking cabin in front of them: clean wooden lines and one large glass wall, where the floor of the cabin extended to a deck and the roof to a partially covered terraza. A decent-sized swimming pool glittered on the side, trees all around them.

"A great find. Mo's gonna get a bonus," Liam said, bringing the car to a stop.

They unpacked the car and chose rooms, settling into the new place. Liam offered to get drinks, and Ana waited for him sitting with her feet in the pool. A few minutes later, Liam gave her a glass of bubbly water with ice and lemon, and sat next to her by the pool.

"Thanks," she said.

He sighed. "No problem. I'm thirsty. A nice, refreshing drink seemed *Urgent*."

She stole a glance at him but said nothing, and took a sip of her drink instead.

"I guess you're a *Long, Long Way From Home*, aren't you? Are you missing home yet?" He faced the pool with a small curl to his lips.

She frowned and shook her head. Was he up to something? "Not yet. I travel often to film and my place is fine, but I'm not sure it's home, if you know what I mean?"

"I think so." He nodded again. Liam looked up and scratched his forehead. "I think I'm starting to sweat. I hope your drink is *Cold As Ice*?"

"Yeah, actually." She squinted at him. He was definitely up to something.

"I'm definitely getting *Hot Blooded*."

Catching on, she let out a delighted laugh. He was referencing Foreigner songs. He laughed with her, a deep, rumbly chuckle coming out of him. The vibrations grabbed her right behind her bellybutton, causing a tingling sensation.

"Okay, I get it. Very clever," she said, pointing at her shirt and ignoring her body's reaction.

"I think I'm going to get in the pool for a while. *Say You Will* too? Even better if we put some music on. I don't know, it can be anything you're inspired to listen to right now. You can be a *Juke Box Hero*."

"Har har. Sure. I'll put Foreigner on." She got up, and went into the cabin to change.

Liam leisurely floated in the cool water of the pool, eyes closed behind his sunglasses. He always felt at peace when suspended in the water like that, but didn't do it often despite having his own swimming pool back at home.

He shifted and stood on his feet once he heard the music start to play. His eyes found Ana; she walked about in her simple black bikini. She placed a wireless speaker on a table nearby, and he could easily imagine she did so in black underwear— but stopped. He shouldn't imagine such things.

He dunked his head underwater, sunglasses still on. His brain needed some cooling, stat.

He gazed at Ana again only when he thought he had himself in control. Foreigner sounded in the background at a low volume. When she positioned her camera at the edge of the pool he understood her reasoning: she wanted to record any conversations they might have.

"I saw you floating," she said as she approached the pool stairs. "I can't do that."

She stepped into the pool, two quick exhales escaping her at the contact with the cold water. He was close enough to see the goose bumps that appeared on her skin. It gave him a shiver, though he couldn't blame it on the pool's temperature. He created some space between them with a casual chest stroke in the opposite way.

"Pools aren't much better than the ocean for you?" he finally asked, turning to face her. She had put her hair on a high ponytail; he followed it down with his eyes, studying the width of her bikini strap, a freckle on her shoulder.

"As long as I can stand on the bottom if I need to, I can manage some strokes."

Protected by his sunglasses, he perused the sight of her some more. She held herself in the water, arms crossed and hands on opposite shoulders, perhaps still getting used to its coolness. The waterfall of her hair was long; the ends were floating in the water. Her neck was exposed, a few droplets resting on it.

"Where did you grow up?" he asked suddenly. "I hadn't thought to ask."

"Bloomington, Illinois," she said, finally opening her arms wide in the water and moving around. "Or thereabouts. What about you? Where did you grow up?"

"San Luis Obispo."

"So the ocean and swimming and perhaps pools were normal for you? No wonder you're so good in the water."

They ended up paddling and circling each other, as cowboys did in a Western movie.

"Yeah, but it was also my sport growing up. I was a competitive swimmer all throughout college. I got a scholarship for it, too."

She nodded, facing him, but her eyes seemed a bit unfocused. "What is your best memory growing up?"

"I don't know..." Flashes of different happy moments flooded his mind, too quick to grasp at a single one. "I don't think I could choose one single memory."

"Then tell me a random one."

It took him a minute to choose. He smiled. "I must have been ten or eleven. Alex and I— that's my brother— we decided we wanted to build a treehouse. We begged my dad all winter, hoping that in the spring time he would help us build one. My dad kept telling us it was impossible because A, we didn't have a tree in the backyard," Liam laughed, pleased that Ana did too. "B, he was used to our antics and knew we would get bored with it. We were the kind of kids that would rather wrestle in the basement or play basketball in the garage pad than be out in the backyard."

"Did you and Alex get what you wanted?"

"No," Liam replied, still smiling. "My dad made us a deal. He said that if we built a lean-to— you know, the kind you would see castaways building on a deserted island— if we built one and we used it, we could talk about making a more definitive structure."

"Okay, you got me. I want to know how this ends."

"Alex and I did our best with a tarp, cardboard boxes, plastic bags... anything we could find. It took us half an hour to be so frustrated that we started a fight. Dad came out to separate us and said we needed something to take our minds off the project. That evening, we had a small bonfire in the backyard, where we ceremoniously burnt the cardboard we had wanted to use for the lean-to. We cooked marshmallows on it."

She laughed as he finished his story, the sound full of delight. "That is an amazing story."

"Thank you." Though there was mirth in him, the memory also made him nostalgic.

"Based on that alone, your childhood sounds fun."

Through the water, he saw her lifting her legs to her chest. He imitated her.

"It was a good childhood, I think. Nothing extraordinary; my family was nice, I always felt cared for. We had enough money to cover our needs and to help a bit with our education. The extended family was good too, never too much drama during Thanksgiving or Christmas."

"It really sounds lovely."

"Yeah. I know I'm one of the lucky ones."

"What do your parents do?" she asked.

"Dad's a veterinarian, mom's an admin at the university. "

They treaded water for a short while, before she spoke again.

"What about a sad memory?" she asked, this time with a soft voice.

An event came to mind loud and clear, unrepentant. Heart-wrenching. His throat constricted and, to buy himself some time, he took slow steps to the edge of the pool. Resting his arms on the side of it, he stared at the trees across the yard. She came to his side and mirrored him.

"When my dog died," he finally replied. He could imagine himself back in that moment, when he knew his dog was gone. Almost feel again the tears stuck in his throat, the sob that escaped him. "I was sixteen and took it poorly."

She put a hand on his arm. "You don't have to tell me the details."

He put a hand on top of hers. "I don't want to tell you the details, to be honest."

They stayed there, only the sounds of the water and the smell of chlorine around them.

"Sounds like you had a lovely youth, Liam."

Her voice had been wistful. He smiled, not knowing how nostalgic he looked in turn.

Chapter 12

T HEY WENT ON AN extended trek the next day, and retired to their rooms after a long dinner. A couple of hours later, Ana sat on her bed talking on the phone with Ely. A knock on the door interrupted their conversation; Ana smiled at something her friend said and opened the door for Liam.

"Come in," she whispered, going back to sit at her bed. Liam didn't do as told, instead choosing to lean on the door jamb, arms crossed, a sideways grin on his face. He wore a sleeveless, white undershirt, which highlighted his shoulders and made them look wide and solid. Gray, thin lounge pants hung low from his waist.

"Give me a sec, Ely." Ana gulped and took her phone away from her ear. She asked Liam, "Everything okay?"

"I was going to ask the same," he replied. "I got up to get something to drink and saw the light coming from under the door. I thought maybe you couldn't sleep, but then I heard giggling—"

"Tell him I had a terrible date!" Ely's voice came from the phone, loud enough to sound clear in the middle of the night. "And that I process by making fun of it!"

"You heard her?" Ana tracked the amused angle that appeared on Liam's lips. "Sorry."

"Gimme." Pushing his hand forward, palm up, he asked for the phone. Ana's bed was close enough to the door that she only had to stretch her arm to reach him; she placed the phone in his hand.

"Hey, Ely," he said. After saying that, he put the phone on speaker.

Ana bit her lip not to laugh. This was the first time Ely and Liam had a conversation with each other.

"Hello, Liam."

Ely sounded confident, as she always did. Ana knew her well enough to know that, inside, she was squeeing.

"You're on speaker," Liam informed her.

"Perfect."

Ana burnt time as her best friend and her... and Liam talked on the phone. She forced her eyes off him and focused on herself instead. She straightened her pajama shorts down, suddenly wishing they were longer; she loosened up her sleeveless shirt around her breasts, trying to hide that she wasn't wearing a bra. Upon inspection, she learned the attempt had been unsuccessful.

"I'm sorry about your date," Liam said, eyes checking the result of her efforts.

Looking away, she lifted her arms to undo her messy ponytail, and used her fingers to rake her hair free of knots and braid it.

"Me too."

"Ana tells me you're amazing."

Unconsciously, she tried arranging her shirt again, stealing a glance at Liam. He leaned against the door frame with his shoulder; his hips were cocked to the side, one foot crossing over the other. He seemed to be paying attention to Ely's words, except for his eyes: they followed the movements of her hands, roaming over her torso and her legs.

The room had a warm atmosphere; she'd covered the lamp shade with one of her shirts, aiming for diffuse soft light. It reflected on him with a muted glow. He didn't seem to realize that she looked at him. Seemed he didn't even know he stared at her, too.

"She's right. Ana is just as amazing," Ely commented.

"Yeah, she's cool." He smiled at the general direction of her thighs. She stopped fussing around with her clothes and stared at the dark window, torn between wanting him to look at her that way, and scared of what it meant. He added, "but we're talking about you and the loser who's going to miss out on you. What did they do?"

"The whole thing doesn't bear repeating, but I'll give you the highlights: he texted to say he would be a few minutes late, turned out it was twenty minutes. He showed up with a friend. They talked about a business project they had and the lady that was blocking their venture, which is the polite version of what they were saying. I decided to leave after one drink; they'd been so busy ranting that we hadn't even ordered dinner yet. He insisted on walking me to my car. Once there, he tried to kiss me and after I refused, he asked what my problem was, that he'd paid for my drink after all."

"Oof, what an asshole."

"Right? He didn't even notice I had left a twenty on the table."

Liam chuckled. "You're better off without him. Ten minutes was more than enough to write him off and good riddance."

"Agreed. What a waste of my time and twenty dollars."

"I hope you blocked him. Just get ready to sleep, forget about him, and move on. Isn't it at least a couple of hours later over there?" He came to sit at the corner of Ana's bed.

"Yep, it was a really bad date, but I should go to sleep. I'll regret staying up so late. Some of us have to get up early tomorrow. Let me say bye to Ana?"

"I'm listening." Ana lifted her legs and rested her arms on her knees. "You need a private word?"

"No, it's fine. I just need you to remind me of what just happened next time I decide to give dating apps another chance. I love you and go to sleep soon."

"Love you too."

"I can't say that I love you, Liam," Ely said, "but sleep well."

He laughed. "You too."

They hung up; Liam gave the phone back to Ana. "She is a delight."

"She is."

"Lots of energy."

"Nuclear levels."

"What's all of this?" He looked around at the array of devices she had on her bed.

"I was doing some light editing. I also recorded some voiceovers and prepped a couple of posts for Social Media."

"Are you a night owl too, then? It's one a.m."

"Yes. Voiceovers flow much better when I'm just about ready for bed. You know how people say the best conversations happen late at night?"

"Yeah." He leaned back on his hands. The gentle light in the small room made for a cozy space. His powerful shoulders and sculpted arms made for a dangerous distraction. The soft smile on his face made for neutral, safe ground. She focused on that part of him.

"I once read that those good late night conversations happen because our filters come down when we're tired. I think it has something to do with that; it helps me look at the material with a different perspective."

"That makes sense."

Sitting back up, he reached for her camera. He played with it, moving it around in his hands. Turning it on, he shifted on the bed so that he faced her, one of his legs folded on the bed. It seemed to Ana that he centered her on the frame.

"Ana Lira."

"Yes?" Her braid fell over her shoulder.

"Are you tired?" he asked.

"Getting there."

"Are your walls coming down?"

"My walls?"

"Yeah. Your filters."

"Are filters the same as walls?"

"I'd say so, wouldn't you?"

She considered, her head dropping to the side. "I guess you could say that, yeah."

"If I asked you to tell me one of your fears, would you?"

She squinted at him, evaluating. "Maybe."

"Let's make this into a game. You tell me one fear, any random one, and I will tell you one as well. Prompts for a late night conversation, if you will."

She remained silent, her lips pursed in suspicion. She could see the mischief in his eyes.

Without an explanation, he balanced the camera in one hand as he stood. He approached her and signaled for her to move on the bed, making room for him. After she did so, he sat next to her, close together. Pivoting the camera's screen, he checked that they were now both in the frame.

"Okay, I'll start," he announced. "I'm afraid my make-up artist is going to scold me for getting so tan."

She laughed. "Not what I was expecting when you said we'd talk about fears. Fine, I'll play. What scares you about that?"

"He has a sharp tongue. It won't matter that I've used sunscreen every day. He'll be pissed at how I'm damaging my skin. Worse is, I know he's right."

"Yeah, but how often do you spend this much time in the sun?"

"Rarely." He smirked. "Okay, now tell me one of yours."

"I'm afraid of earthquakes."

"Oh?" He turned his face to look at her.

"Yeah, my parents have told me some pretty scary stories, but I've never really been in one myself."

"I see. I've felt a few here in California, but nothing major."

She shivered. "I hope nothing happens while I'm here."

"You don't have to worry. Everything is built to survive most earthquakes. And if there were a tsunami, we'd probably be okay up here."

"Probably?"

"Anyway," he interjected, stopping her train of thought; she suspected he did it on purpose. "It's my turn. I'm afraid of snakes. It's the silent, slithering cold."

"Understandable," she shrugged. "A living thing that's cold is so unnatural."

"Agreed." His eyes crinkled at the corners.

She searched for something to say during her turn and, seeing all the devices scattered on her bed, she voiced something she hadn't quite admitted out loud yet.

"I'm afraid dropping my part-time job was a mistake."

She noticed the small startle in him upon hearing her words. "How come?"

Ana gazed at her hands and the way she rubbed them together. He lifted a leg and balanced the camera on his knee, keeping it in place with a light touch of his fingers.

"I never made enough money making documentaries to afford to do it full time. I had a lot of hope that signing with TCA would make a difference, so I took a risk and quit. If I hadn't, I wouldn't have been able to spend a whole month with you doing this; I typically had to use vacation time to interview my people. If this doesn't work out, I'll be in debt and without much of an income."

"Shit, that sounds scary. But you're good at what you do and you're smart. I'm sure you'll figure it out and, if you'd like, I'd be happy to make some introductions, try to get some other projects going."

She bumped her shoulder with his, smiling at him. "Thank you, that's generous. I'd appreciate it."

He nodded his acknowledgement, perhaps dismissing how big of a deal it would be for her if he decided to help her. She chose not to say anything about that when he frowned.

"I think... I'm afraid this burnout feeling is never going to go away."

"Do you think Coulton is right and that it'll end soon? That once you're able to choose what you want to work on, the pace will slow down and it'll get better?"

"I have to believe it will, because I don't think I can keep going like this for much longer."

"It must be frustrating to have to wait until Coulton tells you it's okay."

"I kind of have to trust him— he's my agent. Also my manager. And like we said, I owe him."

"Doesn't mean he's always going to be right, or that his opinion is good for you."

He stared at her with a deep crease between his eyebrows. After a moment, he shook his head as if to dislodge a thought.

"Your turn," he reminded her.

Watching him consider her words about Coulton brought a fear to the surface. She hesitated. Pursing her lips, she ping-ponged between sharing and holding back, but this game was all about not censoring themselves. Perhaps because of the late hour, she made herself speak before she could overthink it.

"I'm afraid I'll be pushed to make films I don't like."

"Like Coulton does with me?"

"That's exactly it. I don't think I'd actually considered how much pressure I could get from my agent to do things their way. At least, not until I saw how Coulton tries to convince you to let him build your name even more. Until Diana started asking for updates and making suggestions."

"Well, like we said the other day... you're just starting. Maybe you can use my experience to push back as soon as she starts trying to make you do things you don't like."

"I'll have to do my best to nip it in the bud," Ana agreed. After a few seconds she told him, "How much more fame could Coulton want from you?"

He sighed but didn't respond. He shared another fear instead.

"I'm afraid I'm losing my good friends from before being famous."

She frowned. "Text them. Don't let too much time go by."

"How do I keep them, if I can't see them or talk to them often? With the kind of schedule I have..."

"I get that, but good friends would understand and make the effort to maintain the relationship even if 99% of the time it happens on a video call. You have to call them, include them... and they should, too."

He seemed to examine her words, before he slowly nodded his acceptance. "You're right. I'll text Logan tomorrow. Okay, your turn."

Ana contemplated telling him she worried Ely was more hurt than she'd let on during the call, that her date had been so bad... but that was about Ely and not Ana.

Without much thought this time, she blurted a fear she had noticed within her, after their conversation at sunset a few days ago.

"I'm afraid of my fear of pain."

He shifted again, to face her more fully.

"Tell me." His voice was soft, understanding. It reached her like a balm, probing at her walls and encouraging her to open up.

Letting her guard down was easy— too easy. She didn't let herself stop.

"I hate to say this, I really do, but I think that's the worst thing to come out of what happened with Dave—with my ex. I trusted him implicitly. Even after the first time I realized he hadn't respected our agreement of exclusivity, I decided to trust him. I hate that I did that."

He bumped his arm against her shoulder. "Maybe you can cut yourself some slack."

"I don't know. I made the wrong call. I was so sure of us and I couldn't have been more mistaken. And I was terrified of what my future would look like without him— I had so many plans that included him. But you're right. It's not fair that I am so worried about being lied to that I can't trust anyone. What kind of life would that be? The problem is, I know myself well enough that I know I might never want to take the risk at all again, because I can't imagine anything worse than feeling that kind of pain over and over."

He kept silent for a moment, processing her words. She bit her lips as she waited.

"I think I get it. You're afraid that if you can't go at it full of doubt but don't know quite how to trust, you might want to avoid putting yourself in that place at all."

Rather than answering, she sighed and rubbed her face with her hands. To her surprise, instead of continuing to talk about her fear, he shared one of his.

"I'm afraid that while fame gives me access to the kind of work I want to do, it also blocks me from having the kind of relationship I want."

She let her hands drop to her lap. With her eyes closed, she shook her head in frustration.

"That's messed up," she said.

"What do you mean?"

Taking a deep breath, she let herself lean sideways to rest her head on his shoulder. "You deserve so much love, Liam."

"We both do."

She nodded but said nothing, letting the deep rumble of faraway crushing waves fill the space. He rested his head on hers; she studied their image on the small screen of her camera. They were really close.

"I'm afraid of how much I'm going to miss you when filming is wrapped," he whispered, barely louder than a breath, his voice was so low. Like he said it just to her.

She closed her eyes again, her heart in her throat. The spark of her feelings for him roared to life, each heartbeat fanning it further and further away from her control.

She exhaled slowly this time, pressing her lips together, trying to reign in the torrent of emotions.

"It was my turn to tell you a fear," she finally said.

"Go on, then."

"Me, too."

The words barely made it out of her; silence stretched between them. Lifting a hand, he pressed the button to stop the recording. He left the camera on her bedside table.

"I guess it was true," he said. "Filters do come down."

Her head still on his shoulder, he surprised her by kissing the crown of her hair. She lifted her face to gaze at him, but he'd turned away. With slow movements, he got out of the bed and stood next to it. Her side felt cold and unsupported without him there.

"Try to sleep in tomorrow. I've been wanting to take you on an adventure, but we need to wait until it gets dark."

"Okay."

He got to the door. "Good night."

He closed the door with a small smile. It didn't reach his eyes.

———

"So what's the adventure?" Her eyebrow arched in suspicion. "Are you going to tell me now?"

Giddiness filled every cell in Liam's body at the night's prospect.

They'd spent a lazy day swimming in the pool. They had dinner outside, talking until the sun had disappeared behind the tree line. After cleaning up, he'd asked her if she was tired because, if not, he'd like to go out with her. Although he'd referenced their little quest during the day, he hadn't told her any details. He'd wanted to surprise her.

He collected a few items: a big flashlight, a blanket, a couple of water bottles.

"We're going stargazing." He'd kept his plan close to his heart and now he watched her reaction closely.

He'd brought these things with him hoping he'd get to use them; he'd hoped he'd go away one night by himself to look at the stars— or that had been the original plan. After these many days with Ana, he'd changed his mind. He couldn't imagine not sharing that with her, anymore.

"We are?" She exclaimed, voice full of joy. "What else do we need?"

He grinned at her reaction and did nothing to hide it. He put everything they needed in a backpack, and considered anything else they might want.

"Do you want us to take something to drink maybe? Not too much since we need to be sharp for the drive."

She nodded. "Yeah, I think it could help with the cold."

She went to the kitchen, getting a bottle and glasses. She wrapped them in kitchen towels for safety, before handing them to Liam.

"Alcohol doesn't really help," he said, taking the bottles and glasses from her. "That's an illusion caused by blood flowing to the periphery of the body, but alcohol doesn't actually help keep you warm."

"There's no need to get technical. I'm good with an illusion."

He snorted. "Okay, then."

They packed what they needed into the car and he drove them away from the property. They went back on the same road that they'd taken on the way in but, instead of taking the highway back to the city, they kept going on the small road inland.

They drove for close to two hours, chit chatting and laughing. He slowed down when he saw the sign for the regional park.

Going from memory, he made his way to a location he'd visited several times before.

After following some gravel roads, he turned one more time and followed a trail going upwards.

"Yes," he exclaimed when he saw he'd found the right spot. "Here we are."

Liam parked the car on a hilltop, rising above the tops of the trees surrounding it. She got out of the car and turned on the spot, studying the place. He copied her, knowing what she could see: a few spots of city lights twinkling in the horizon, far in the distance, and darkness around them extending for miles.

"This is amazing," she said. "It's like we're all alone, surrounded by nothing but darkness."

"It's why this is such a great place to look at the stars."

He took the blanket out of the bag, setting it on the ground as she admired the skies.

"Wow. It's amazing."

He couldn't get enough of the wonder in her voice. "C'mere."

He sat with crossed legs on the blanket and invited her to sit next to him. She did, and they regarded the dark vault above them together in awe.

Liam sighed, the comfort of the stars filling him with peace.

"I wish I had brought a telescope," he whispered.

"You have one?" She set up her camera on a short tripod, elevating it to frame them better. She'd mentioned it didn't have night vision per se, but that she hoped to get some good footage with editing magic. As usual, he let himself forget she was recording this.

He got the bottle of Scotch and two tumblers out of the bag. "Yeah, I have a couple."

"So you do this often?"

"I used to. That's how I knew about this place."

They sat at a slight angle; he gave her one of the tumblers with a serving of the golden liquid.

"Thanks," she said as she took the glass.

"Cheers."

They clinked the tumblers together and took a sip.

He lifted his knees and rested his forearms on them. He looked up again and, taking a deep breath, let his eyes roam over the dark skies.

"What's the story?" she asked in a soft voice. The quiet of the place, nothing more than the sound of crickets around them, made anything louder than murmured words unwelcome.

"What do you mean?"

"How come you have telescopes, know about this place, et cetera?"

"Wow." He shook his head while looking at Taurus, Orion, and the Pleiades. "You really didn't look me up online, did you?"

"I told you I hadn't."

"Not even before working together? Maybe back when I was just one of those far-away Hollywood actors?"

"Nope. Not even back then. I followed your social media but didn't really go beyond that."

"No news alerts, then?"

When she didn't reply but opened her eyes wide in an unbelieving look, he grinned.

"No, Liam," she said, "no news alerts."

"No notifications on your entertainment app?"

"There are entertainment apps that let you do that?"

"I don't know, actually, but it's fun to wind you up."

She flicked his arm; he chuckled.

"Anyway," she insisted, "answer my question."

He sipped his drink.

"I know of this place because I came here a few times during my undergrad. I still came during my Masters, and at least once when I began my PhD courses. I was on my way to becoming an astronomer."

He stole glances at her, tracking her reaction. She studied him in silence and squinted, sipping Scotch, before giving up whatever she was doing and looking up to the stars again.

"I don't think you're winding me up right now."

"No, I'm not. Acting was my artsy hobby. Then, one day, we're doing a play with Logan and our group and I didn't know it, but Julia Hunter, the actress? She was there, I'm not even sure why. Anyway, she saw me and called a friend, who called Coulton. A month later, I was signing with TCA and putting my PhD on hold."

She chuckled, shaking her head. After inspecting him for a minute, she looked up again, her neck long, open, and vulnerable as she did so. It was like she couldn't decide what she wanted to stare at the most— him or the skies.

"All I ever cared about was the artsy thing," she said. "I was very lucky that my parents didn't cause too much of a fuss about it."

"I liked school fine and I did well, but when Coulton's offer came along, I thought, well, I can always go back to study. I won't get an offer with TCA like that twice."

"That does make sense."

"I thought I would get to really give acting a go, see how it went, how good I could be and how far I could take it."

"I think you've done amazing," she said, gazing at him now. "I do think you're a good actor."

"Thank you."

"Teach me something about the stars," she sighed.

———

They'd ended up laying side by side, Liam telling her random things about space, about his Master's degree research, and pointing at some of the things they could see from their place on the hilltop. Ana liked the wistfulness in his voice when he talked about space.

"One of my favorite things to do when looking up like this, with the naked eye, is to simply lay down and let myself fall into space."

"What do you mean?" She did her best not to think too hard about how close she knew his hand rested, next to hers.

"In space there's no up or down. To us it feels like we're looking up, but we could very well be looking down. The only thing keeping our back to the ground is gravity. Without it, we'd be floating away and falling into space. Do you want to try?"

"Tell me what to do."

"Okay," he said, setting the tone by deepening his voice. He spoke slowly. "Look at the sky, at all the stars above us. Notice the space between them, and understand that there's thousands of lightyears of room between them. An infinity between one bright spot and the next. So much space between us and the stars, a vast open nothing below us."

She did as he instructed, silence around them, butterflies in her stomach.

He continued, "realize that we're really looking down and we could sink into space forever, not a single thing blocking our way. Feel gravity start to release you... and let your eyes unfocus a bit. See the infinity of the universe in front of you. Let yourself fall into it."

It was easy to do as he whispered, his voice so soft she could imagine she heard it in her mind. Hypnotic. His words guided her right to the place where gravity didn't exist, her stomach dropping as if she were jumping off a cliff.

"Woah."

He sighed. "I love it."

They were quiet for a while. Ana put both her hands on her stomach, still feeling some ungroundedness there, like she could fly away if the wind picked up around them. She took a few slow, deep breaths, before dropping her hands and placing them palm down on the blanket underneath.

Liam barely moved; she would have never known he had, except for the warmth of two of his fingers finding their way among hers.

It was her heart that soared high, and she threw an anchor down with all her might.

Liam had no idea what he'd just done. He didn't know he'd reached to half-hold her hand until he'd already done it. He laughed it off in his mind; it was such a silly thing, what his fingers had done of their own volition.

"I'm sorry to break the magic of the moment," she said next to him, her fingers still under his, a slight tremor to her voice, "but is there something I can use to warm up? The cold is starting to get to me."

"Oh, I'm sorry. I'll go grab something."

He got up and got an extra blanket from the back seat. He brought it back and, sitting next to her, accommodated it over her and himself. He laid back, making sure they were both well covered. He turned to his side and so did she. Face to face, he reached with his hand to rub her arm, helping her warm up. Her skin was cold under his hands and she shivered; he moved a bit closer to share heat.

"You'll be good in a minute," he said.

She didn't respond, but her tremors slowly dissolved as they warmed up together. Even as space quieted around them, between them, his hand continued to travel up and down, up and down her arm. Moving a tad slower as seconds ticked by, maybe not so much about friction, now, but a caress.

Fuck. What was he doing? He was definitely crossing the friends-only line. What did it say about him that he didn't want to stop? She'd just told him she wasn't ready to trust. He knew he needed to wait. The documentary was a professional arrangement. But his hands wanted more contact. He wanted to forget himself under the stars and take. Give. Share.

His eyes tried to catch hers, but she didn't look at him; her eyes were cast down. He frowned. Certainty filled his chest, bringing with it a clear vision of what it would be like if they lay in bed under the covers like this: she'd be looking at him and he'd be lost in her eyes.

He wanted her to look at him. He wanted to get lost in her eyes.

He wanted to be in bed with her, like this, side by side.

His attention sharpened. His hand stilled.

She gazed at him from under the ridge of her eyebrows and the connection grabbed him by the breastbone. Time slowed. Her eyes didn't waver; she stared at him with openness, her eyes so dark in the low light they looked black.

She didn't shiver anymore. The agitation in her breathing betrayed the effect the moment had on her. His own breathing quickened, responding to the fast rhythm of hers.

An electrical switch flipped inside of him, completing the circuit: where he'd felt comfort he now felt a pull, a longing to see his desire reflected in her eyes. What might her lips feel against his? The rough ground beneath them disappeared, even the infinite skies above escaped his mind. This feeling had been right beneath his skin, so familiar yet unknown; he'd been feeling it for days but had not, could not...

Her lips parted. They'd feel soft, he was sure, and warm. He found himself wetting his, the pull of his want going taut and yet he resisted it— pulled back against it just for tonight— until he could figure things out— make sure it was what he'd been waiting for— because once he tasted her mouth, he didn't think he'd ever stop.

"When we met," she said, her voice soft, "I was wearing a Queen shirt. You said you were partial to Brian."

"I did," he confirmed, tearing his eyes away from her mouth to gaze into her eyes again. He was sure now, her eyes shone with longing.

"I get it now. Brian is an astrophysicist."

Damn. She could see straight through him if she could make that connection.

His lips tingled for hers. His heart fluttered. His blood rushed in his ears.

He hesitated. He'd promised himself he'd live his life with intention. Especially in the case of love. With the way she could see into him, this thing between them deserved more than an impulsive kiss.

"We should head back," he said, before he let himself press his lips against hers and to hell with everything.

"It's getting late," she agreed.

Despite their words, neither moved. It took them several minutes to get going, as if she felt as torn as he did... but she was the first to pull away.

Putting a hand on his chest, she turned to her back and sat up; reaching back around her neck, she guided her long hair to cascade over one of her shoulders. From where he was on the ground, he thought she'd taken a deep breath.

"Thanks for this. It was lovely." She didn't look at him.

"Yeah, it was."

He couldn't look away.

Chapter 13

ANA STAYED IN BED late that morning, staring at the ceiling. She counted as she slowly breathed in and out, in and out. She couldn't close her eyes because, when she did, all she could see was Liam on his side in front of her, helping her warm up under the blankets and a boundless vault of stars.

She had wanted to kiss him, so badly. The look on his eyes had planted an ember right next to her heart, and now it scorched the edges of it.

Her phone rang; a quick glance at the screen revealed Diana wanted a talk.

"Hi, Diana." Ana begged the call to dampen the flame burning in her.

"Hello, Ana. Everything's good, I hope?"

"Yeah, everything's great." She gulped. "I'm getting some wonderful material. I think this documentary is shaping up to show the costs of fame, very well."

"Right, right, that sounds like a powerful piece! Do you think it'll have a bright side, too? Something to balance out the negativity?"

Ana frowned. The ember darkened as her brain teased Diana's words apart. "We've also talked about some of the perks, of course."

"Fabulous. Make sure to make it balanced, all right? It should appear more... objective, that way, don't you think? And hey, if you want some ideas, Magda at Coulton's office came up with a list of potential themes you can bring into the film. Here, I'm forwarding you the email." The line went silent except for a few clicks. Ana's mind worked at full speed. "You should have it now. What do you think?"

"I'll look at them later, and will see if they fit the story we're telling with this film. It'll be interesting," she added, hiding behind it her impulse to reject it all on principle.

"Yes, please do. Call me if you want to discuss anything. You have no other producers that can help guide you if you need that, so I'm happy to do that for you right now. You know, until you're bigger and have your own team. I'm sure we'll get you there!"

"Thanks, Diana. I hope so!"

"Talk to you later. Bye, Ana!"

Crap. Ana had been wrong to ask the gods to curb her longing for Liam through a conversation with Diana. Her agent's veiled pressure to follow TCA's suggestion dropped bitter into Ana's stomach. And though it helped curtail any impulse Ana may harbor to drop professionalism and kiss Liam already, it did not dissolve her feelings. It just doomed her to live with them, unanswered.

———

After breakfast, Ana and Liam had decided to stay in the cabin and rest. Ana hoped Liam was relaxing, because she was not.

She sat on the swimming pool stairs, enjoying the way cool water lapped against her shoulders. Liam sat on one of the tanning chairs, reading what looked like a script, and she couldn't take her eyes away from him for more than a minute.

She glanced at him, eyebrows wrinkled as he read, visible despite his sunglasses. His naked, sculpted torso glistened with sun lotion. The muscles were trim enough that she could see them ripple when he did something as simple as turn pages. His bathing shorts were short enough that his tanned legs were visible up to his mid-thigh. Tempting her to question what hid behind the strip of fabric.

She closed her eyes and scooped water from the pool, wetting her forehead to cool off.

How inopportune, to pine for Liam that way. She. Was. Working. Talking to Diana was all the reminder Ana needed. She would never, ever risk her professional reputation that way. She needed to cling to that, and never allow a fantasy to ruin the opportunity that this project had opened up for her.

She dipped her head back to submerge her hair, imagining that all these thoughts could just drip from her mind into the water.

"This is horrible writing," Liam said from the patio, flipping the script closed and flicking it carelessly to the side.

He got up and shook himself. He swung his arms wide to stretch, following a long arc from his back to his front. In the next fluid motion, he reached for her camera, resting on the other tanning chair.

"This thing is waterproof, right?"

"Yes— if you take the puff off."

"Good," he replied, before taking the puff off, turning it on, taking his sunglasses off, and jumping into the pool.

The resulting splash fell over her like rain. She swept away the excess of water from her face; he whipped his head once, hair spiking to the side, stubborn curls falling back on his forehead. He smiled mischievously at her, sparkling drops running down his face. Effortless beauty.

She cleared her throat. She wouldn't give him the satisfaction of being annoyed.

"If you could be just a bit more cautious with my bread and butter, I'd be really thankful," she said. A teasing smile stretched his lips but he said nothing. She rolled her eyes and changed topics. "So, why did you bring that script at all? Isn't that work?"

He played with the camera, filming around him in a full circle, to finally stop when the lens faced her. His smile had subdued, now apparent only as a small upwards bend on the corner of his mouth.

"I don't know. To justify to Coulton that I did indeed work?"

She stepped away from the stairs and further into the pool, lifting her knees to pretend like she could float. "I infer that you don't feel like you've been working much, over the past few weeks."

He didn't say anything right away. He checked the frame, submerging the lens halfway. She had been so focused on what he was doing with the camera that she didn't see him set up to splash her until water ran down her face again.

He laughed. She scoffed. She didn't care that she wasn't as adept in the water as he was, she jumped at him and tried to steal the camera.

"Give it to me," she said, wrestling with him— or trying to. Her fingers had no grasp on his slick skin, and he easily managed to keep her at a distance with his long arms. His hand held her shoulder, his arm fully outstretched.

His grin exuded confidence; it irritated her that he was likely right to feel self-assured. He was bigger and had tons more experience in the water than she had and he knew it. He evidently felt so sure he didn't think he needed to keep his eyes on her to keep her at bay; he currently focused more on submerging the camera to take an underwater shot of them than on her. Maybe she could use his cockiness to her advantage.

With her feet as firmly on the ground as she could afford in the water, she turned and slammed her back into him, stretching her arm to reach for the camera. She got as close as to touch it with the tip of her fingers, before he pulled it out of her reach again. The water slowed her down and he stopped her in time, and he had the gall to laugh at her attempt.

The arm that he'd been using to keep her away now curled firmly around her, holding her in place and deterring her from further attempts. His free arm kept the camera away from her and to their side; the reverberations of his slowing chuckle pressed against her back.

It did not escape her mind that it had been her doing, having his arm tight around her like this, muscle taut and warm over her clavicles. Her hands came to rest on his forearm, grasping him. Her heart beat fast. This hadn't been a part of her plan, but she fell prey to it, anyway.

He didn't laugh anymore. He barely moved; he stayed behind her, skin to skin. Some indefinite amount of time later, he moved his free arm in a wide arc, bringing the camera to their front but keeping it out of her reach. The preview screen faced them so they could both check the frame; their eyes met on the small display. The water reached his forearm and, except for the one visible strip of her black bikini, it would have been easy to imagine they were naked. She recognized the spark in his eyes— it was the same spark she'd been fighting for a while.

His chest expanded against her as he took a deep breath. Time froze despite the warmth in the air, but the spell broke when he created distance between them. The rush of water that replaced him at her back was cold, making her shiver.

"Here," he said, handing her the camera. "You tell me what happens next."

She bit her lip and took it. She tried the same angle he had and submerged the lens halfway. She let herself drop deeper too, until the water reached her jaw line. She circled him, filming him as he stood still.

Once she faced him again, she stood tall with him dead center on the frame.

He watched her, serious, with a certain intensity in his eyes.

"Liam McMillan," she said.

"Ana Lira."

"Teach me something."

"Pardon?"

"I always ask my people to teach me things. You've taught me about stars; what will you teach me in a pool?"

He considered her words. "Anything?"

"Yeah."

He studied her through hooded eyes.

"Any ideas?" His voice deepened further, daring her.

She shrugged, doing her best not to respond to his tone. "I want to see what you come up with."

She told herself she wasn't flirting with him.

His eyes changed and he squinted, before he extended his hand to her. "Okay. Give me the camera."

She did. He set it on the side of the pool, then he extended his hand to her again. This time, she put her hand on his.

"Come here," he said. She recognized the deep tone from some of her favorite movie scenes of his. "I'm going to teach you how to float."

"What?" Her lungs malfunctioned.

He pulled her closer to him. "Is it okay if I touch you?"

Her heart stopped. Her mouth opened to reply but nothing came out.

"I need to, to help you float," he said.

"Yes," she whispered. She hid a gulp.

He took a step closer to her, oh so slowly as if she might spook easily, and put his hands on her waist. He stood in front of her with his fingers clinging to the curve of her torso, eyes flickering over her face until her breathing picked up. With a firm touch, he turned her sideways and one of his arms wrapped around her back.

"Lift your legs," he instructed, his voice throaty yet commanding. "Put your feet on the side of the pool."

"Okay." Her movements were less graceful than she would have liked. Most of her weight, light as it was in the water, rested on his arm. Her lungs hadn't yet recovered from the force of his eyes on her.

"Nice." His other hand found a place low in her back. "Lift here."

"I'm trying." While her bewilderment might have had to do with how close they were and the novelty of the situation, his short, direct sentences made it seem like he was solely focused on leading her movements.

She stole a glance at him. He stared at her breasts, as if checking out the way they rose above the water, the surface tension line moving up and down the curve of them with each one of her breaths, nipples hard beneath the wet fabric.

He must have felt her eyes on him because he gazed at her then away, clearing his throat. He may have been somewhat affected as well, after all.

"You're breathing too fast," he indicated, his gaze back to her. "Too shallow. You need to hold air in your lungs, more than half-full."

She pushed her thoughts away and breathed in deeply— too deep. Her chest came up high, the tension in her neck and the angle of her back pushing her head down into near-submersion. The hand in her lower back stayed in place, but the other came to push her head above water.

"You're good," he said. "You're okay."

Flustered, she dropped her legs from the side of the pool. "This is tough."

"You're too tense." He let go of her. His lips were pressed together. "Is this the wrong thing? Should we try something else?"

"No, let's try again. Any other techniques?"

"Yeah, let's try this. Come close to the edge, here where the water reaches your chest, and put your feet against the wall. Try to get flush against it," he said, showing her what he meant; he looked like he planned to do a push up against the pool's side. "Then, keeping your feet in place, allow your chest to come away from the wall and let the water support you."

He modeled the strategy for her. As he released the push up position, his body moved away from the side of the pool as if an undercurrent pulled him towards its center. His chest and hips gained buoyancy by the second and, after a minute, his body leveled up to the surface. She studied his face, calm as if the water gave him instant peace. She came back to herself when he shifted and stood on the bottom of the pool again.

"Ready to try?" he asked. "I'll spot you."

"Okay, let's see."

She imitated what she'd seen him do; he stood close to her, paying attention to her movements. She did her best not to get self-conscious nor focus on his proximity— she failed.

"Keep your feet against the wall unless you're fully floating," he said. "Let the water hold you up."

"What if I sink?"

"I'll hold you up. Relax."

He pressed his hand on the space between her shoulder blades, fingers splayed on her skin. She shivered, but didn't think it had anything to do with the water's temperature.

"I'm here, you can let go," he insisted. Her body moved on its own like his body had, when he'd been showing her. "Yeah, like this. Just keep air in your lungs, that's essential."

Relax. Relax. Relax!

She worked hard at softening her body, fighting against her instinct to tighten up. Somehow, the looser her muscles, the more solid the water felt.

"There you go," he said, pride in his voice. He took his hand away from her back. "Just stay there."

Her body stayed diagonal to the wall, unlike Liam's which had been parallel to the water. Despite that, excitement built in her heart.

"I'm doing it, Liam! I'm floating!"

She laughed but it came to an abrupt stop— she'd let out too much air and, in the way of treacherous waters, she'd gone slightly underwater. Tensing up, she sank even faster and she kicked and flailed trying to find the bottom of the pool. As promised, Liam saved her from submersion; in a flurry of water and movement, he straightened her up and held her against him.

His laughter vibrated against her again. Her arms were trapped between them, barely allowing her to clear the water and wet hair from her face with trembling hands. She curled her fingers, knuckles rubbing against each other.

For all the embarrassment warming up her face at her difficulties, begging her to look away, her desire to glance up at him won. He already gazed at her, his green eyes earnest, the remnants of a smile on his face. As if her eyes had triggered the action, his hands followed a downward path, making their way from her shoulders, down her arms, and onto her waist. Her own hands fell to his chest, and the warmth of his skin glued them to him.

The distance between them grew smaller. Her chest pressed against him as her breathing quickened, and his hands squeezed where they rested, on the curve above her hips. His smile all but disappeared as his eyebrows furrowed, the barest signal that he was as enthralled as she was.

He moved slowly. She could imagine what his beard would feel like on her skin. How their kiss would taste like chlorine, and he'd grab her harder, and she'd bite his lip, and their hearts would beat loud and in sync... and wanted to test it. Prove it. Be able to say, *yes, Liam. Kissing you is exactly what I imagined.*

He gave her time to pull away; he stopped a breath away from her lips. He waited for her to make the final decision. He'd made his intentions clear, showing her with steady lips that hovered over hers. His fingers dug into her skin, the only sign of his impatience, but he waited. Like he knew she was the one that stood to lose the most.

A wave of fear released within her, fast, relentless, a tsunami making it clear that if they kissed, if she— they— let this happen, she might come to regret it. The flood took over everything she knew, replacing it with visions of a crumbling career.

Her heart sunk to the bottom of the water. She closed her eyes and pulled her face away, frowning and pressing her lips closed.

She lifted her hands off his skin and curled them into fists, lest she grabbed him again. His breath tickled her temple, a quick warm release against her.

"I can't..." she heard herself say. Hating herself a little bit. A lot.

His hands left her.

"Okay." He took a step back, cold water rushing in.

He turned without another word and, ignoring the stairs, walked straight to the edge of the pool and used his arms to get himself out. His steps were heavy as he went into the house, not caring about the water still streaming down from him. His leaving her there had taken less than five seconds, but it felt like time had scratched to a stop. She stayed where she was, her body growing cold in the water. Ana welcomed it, begging it to reach that hurting, breaking organ caged in her chest.

<hr>

Fuck.

Liam escaped into the bathroom, craving the privacy of the shower. He took off his wet shorts with sharp, brusque movements, the wet fabric clinging to his legs. He panted by the time he got under the hot stream of water, his hands on his hips, his head hanging low. Water dripped down his neck and shoulders.

Shaking his head to no one in particular, he straightened up and reached for the soap. He washed up as if the menial task had the power to clean the mess he'd made of things. He'd known he needed to move slow and be careful for both their sakes; she'd told him several times this project might be a big break for her, and he'd promised himself he'd be mindful about any relationships he chose to pursue. Trying to kiss her in the swimming pool was none of those things. It was mindless, it was careless, and it was rushed.

It also felt natural. Inevitable. Like his body had no other purpose. Like his brain could reach no other conclusion.

Lather now covered his body and, for the briefest moment, he considered letting out some of his frustration by using his hand.

"Fuck," he whispered. His hands slowed as he let his fingers drag soap over his chest and abs, while staying away from his growing erection. His mind had filled with awareness of her at the pool; all her softness and generous skin within reach, tempting his hands to wander every time they touched. His mind had filled with fantasies of all they could have done, had they been here for pleasure.

They weren't here for pleasure. Not technically. And she'd said she was scared to trust again.

With a growl, his will and his arousal fighting for attention, he recalled his frustration, the pain of rejection, and forbade himself from seeking release. If he wanted her— he did— and if he liked her— he did— then he couldn't rush or force anything. He had to be thoughtful and patient. If this were ever to become the relationship he'd begun to hope for, he had to be okay with the way things were and pace himself for the sake of his future.

He took deep, calming breaths, and willed the water to cleanse away the urgent void in his gut. He rinsed the suds on his skin and washed his hair, before getting out and drying off quickly. She still sat outside when he came out of the bathroom, with her eyes seemingly lost in the distance.

He cleaned the streak of water on the floor from his run inside, then sat on the sofa with a book he knew he wouldn't read. His thought had been to show her he was fine, that she didn't need to worry, but he reeled. Even though his eyes moved over the page and latched on random words, his brain hyperfocused on her and her *can't.*

He thought he got it— he couldn't assume she was wrong in fearing negative consequences if she got involved with him. Hollywood typically saw romances between colleagues as fodder for gossip, nothing more than a commodity they could sell to someone for money or status. But it *could* affect her professionally. He couldn't prevent that. And none of this even touched on her fears about trusting him as a partner.

Was there a way to move past all of this, and respect her fears? Maybe take them into a place where they could really give this thing between them a real try?

He didn't hear her come in, but realized she was in the cabin when he heard the shower run. He blocked the mental image from his head, and read a full sentence from his book instead. When that failed, he sprinted to his room and hid there; he couldn't take the tension, not when he had so many unanswered questions swarming his head.

Much later, he lay in bed awake, thoughts still swirling in his mind. When he finally checked his phone, he had a text from Ana.

Ana: I hope things are
okay between us. What
can I do?

She'd sent him that message over an hour ago. Crap, he hadn't meant to leave her steeping in worry.

What could she do?

Give us a chance.

He didn't even attempt to type that out. It hurt to think she may not trust him enough to risk it, but it made sense.

Maybe he could reframe and see this impasse as a gift. If he focused on understanding her better, then any choice he made—

whether to pursue or retreat— would align with all the work he'd done to prepare for a moment like this. And it would serve to accept her choices as well.

Liam: We are okay. I'll
need some space tonight
but we can move on. I'll
be fine tomorrow.

He'd waited a long time to find someone with whom to try anything. He'd met plenty of people, but no one had fit so seamlessly with him; no one's chemistry had ignited the right kind of alchemy. Rejection fucking *sucked*, but he didn't want to ruin their camaraderie with his frustration, and he did not want her to feel like he was punishing her for not wanting to kiss him.

He could be patient. For her.

Chapter 14

A NA'S INNER WORLD RIOTED, pulling her in two directions. How could someone be so cleanly split down the middle?

On one side, she was thankful that Liam appeared to let go of their almost-kiss right away. At least it seemed that way, as it had been two days since the pool incident and he had yet to bring it up. He seemed to have gone straight back to his usual, before-trying-to-kiss-her friendly self. On the other, she desperately wanted him to try to kiss her again. The intensity of that want fought for attention with such tenacity, she worried she might end up taking the matter in her own hands.

She, who had been the one to tell him no. She, who had all these good, rational reasons as to why it was a bad idea. She might end up wound up so tight that she could spring on him and kiss him until they'd lost their minds. And she. Could not. Should not.

Besides, who knew if he still wanted to, anyway. While it was clear to her why she'd said no— she panicked—on his side, it was almost impossible to guess the reasons for anything... and she couldn't just ask. Not about this, not after saying no. And she wasn't ready to hear the response. Maybe the almost kiss had been a spur of the moment thing, and not something that held as much significance for him as it did for her. Maybe he didn't care much either way, or maybe he was actually grateful it had gone nowhere.

The one clear thing was how okay he was with the way things had happened. He couldn't have moved on so quickly, otherwise.

"You seem restless," he told her, interrupting her thoughts. They were outside on the deck, having breakfast.

"Do I?"

"Yeah. You're wiggling in your chair and keep sighing. Everything okay?"

She hadn't noticed, she'd been so lost within herself.

She didn't look at him but to the piece of toast she was busy breaking into crumbs. How to answer his question? She often felt like she could tell him anything, but no way could she tell him she had a hard time accepting they were not kissing right at that moment.

"Yep. All's good," she lied. She heard the clipped way her words came out.

She gave him her eyes, hoping that it would help convince him of her words. It was a mistake; she didn't have to stare at him very long to see he didn't believe her. He didn't push it. She cleared her throat and looked away to trees surrounding their forest clearing.

"Do you want to go for a walk?" He asked after a while. "Mo gave me a map of some nearby trails, one of which leads to the water. According to his notes, it ends on a small, rocky beach. The only way to get there is from this place, so it should be private as well."

"Sounds good. Let's go do it."

They cleared the dishes from breakfast and set up for their walk. He put water bottles in a backpack; she took her camera and put a strap on it so that she could carry it on her neck, freeing her hands.

Once on their way, Liam guided her through the trees until they reached a gentle cliff. A roughed-in path opened at the edge and steered them down. He stepped into it and checked the incline and general state of the gravel for safety. He offered her his hand to help her down onto it and didn't let go once they started walking; she did her best to not let it fuel the commotion inside her. He held her hand until the track narrowed down so much that they had to walk single file.

They didn't talk. It was a good thing, because she still hadn't quieted her inner world. They followed the wandering path, bordering the cliffs rising from the rocks where waves crashed; as they got closer to the water, cold mist reached them once in a while. They trekked on rough terrain, surrounded by severe inclines; no construction could be made here and there were no houses overlooking the ocean. Just Liam and Ana, making their way along the edge of the continent.

The views set a contemplative mood, the infinite ocean finally allowing her the space she needed to set her turmoil free. She decided to use these takes for film imagery; the kind she would use for one of her voiceovers. She stayed behind on the path for a few minutes, taking a wide shot of him walking ahead of her. The line of his shoulders suggested deep thinking, and she wondered what occupied his mind.

After about an hour, they reached the tiny beach he had told her about. It was no more than a small indentation in the cliff, huge rocks at the bottom of it. They had to climb down from the path, jumping onto them. They sat on one of the rocks, watching the waves crashing against them. Brine had opened her heart, and she breathed in the respite she'd craved.

"Apparently, when the tide is low, there's a small patch of pebbles between these rocks and the water," he said.

Ana had turned the camera off a while ago; she now put it in the backpack. Liam tracked her movements, still seemingly lost in thought.

"I should probably reapply sunscreen," she said.

"Good call." He whipped his shirt off. He glanced at her with a glint in his eye. "You mind giving me a hand?"

If her face warmed up, she could blame it on the walk under the sun.

"I can help," she said, pretending nonchalance.

She rummaged in the bag for sunscreen and kneeled behind him.

Shit. Shit! C'mon. You should be used to these shoulders by now. Act chill!

She squirted cream on her palms, warming it up before putting her hands on his shoulders. She bit her lips as her fingers rubbed his sun-warmed skin, slippery with lotion. She didn't make a conscious decision to allow her thumbs to massage his neck in a wide arc. His resulting groan made her close her eyes, muscles tightening in her core. She sighed. He shivered.

"Sorry, didn't mean to do that." He reached for the sunscreen bottle and applied some of it to his chest and arms, while she finished with his back. "Thanks. Your turn."

She was sure it'd be easier to have his hands on her. He'd be at her back and she wouldn't have to see him; plus she didn't plan to take off her shirt. Liam moved behind her, and his hands were sure on her skin as he helped her. He lifted the combo of shirt and bikini strap to put lotion there, slowly rubbing sunscreen where she couldn't reach; when his hand continued to travel lower on her back under the edge of her clothes, she had to admit she'd been wrong.

"You don't have to answer this," he said, his hands shifting to the other strap. "But I was wondering. Why have you been single for so long?"

She didn't know what she'd expected he'd been thinking during this trek, but her reasons for being single were not part of the mix.

"Because Dave was an asshole and a liar and I don't want that again in my life." Bluntness erected a solid wall between what his hands did, what she felt, and what they were discussing. "I can wait."

"Right, waiting." He chuckled. "But it's been more than two years since you broke up with him. I'm sure you must have met someone at some point that caught your attention?"

She didn't dare wonder why he questioned her about this. One thing was to hold her hand, another to challenge her decision to be single. It was harder to look at both together and not hope that he asked out of his own interest.

"I am in no rush to meet someone," she said. "If it happens, that'd be great, but if it doesn't... that's fine, too."

"Not looking for happily ever afters, Ana?"

She shrugged. "People can have their happily ever afters without a partner, too."

"I suppose." One of his hands rested on her shoulder, unmoving. After a moment, it left her. He sat next to her.

"I just think we should be able to find contentment on our own, you know?" she continued. "Not only if we have someone to hold our—to share our lives with."

"Yes, of course."

They fell into a brief silence, the roaring of the waves and bird calls filling in the space.

"Are you looking for happily ever afters, Liam?"

He sighed. "Yes. I want someone in my life."

He didn't hesitate. It took her breath away.

"If you want someone in your life, why be single?" she asked. "If I remember correctly, you said you chose not to be involved with anyone until you figured out how to know if it was right."

He stole a glance at her. "Yes, that's what I said. I needed to give myself time to learn. I was afraid I'd simply fall back into how things were, otherwise. I knew myself well enough to know that I could easily repeat my mistakes, if I didn't learn better. I needed to stop clean, no casual sex and no casual relationships. I'm sure there are plenty of people I could click with and find something meaningful, but I didn't know how to find them. It felt important to make sure I got to know myself a lot better, and did some work to make sure I could get to know other people as well."

"Okay, I can see that. And does it still feel like that? 'Cause in my head, wanting someone in your life and staying single don't quite align."

"They do, in my head. Doing things as I had been, I was never going to find what I was looking for. Nothing would have changed. I would only know how to have shallow encounters, and that's not what I want. I'm not going to find what I want in casual relationships, so why bother?"

"So you haven't been with anyone since that time you told me about?"

"No, I haven't. Not even for a single night."

Her eyebrows shot up. "I kind of imagined you would have, just made no attempts to make it a stable relationship."

"Then you were mistaken. In my case, casual sex did nothing to help me get to know the person. It put things on the table that got in the way. So no sex for me."

"It's just..."

"Hard to believe? Why?" His tone was both curious and pressing at the same time. "Is it hard to believe you haven't given relationships a chance after Dave?"

"No," she tried, but saw the double standard in saying she expected him to have casual sex, when she hadn't.

"I don't have anything against casual sex," he added. "I quite enjoyed it before I got wrapped up in a toxic cycle. I think it was the right thing for me to stop, at least for a while, that's all."

"Okay, I'm sorry. You're right. There's nothing wrong with choosing to have casual sex, and there's nothing wrong with choosing not to."

"Thanks. I agree."

They were silent again. The waves kept on crashing against the rocks, setting a calm rhythm in her heart; more than she would have imagined she'd feel, having a conversation like this. The sound of the water soothed her, mist refreshing and cool on her skin.

"I suppose we can't swim here?" she wondered out loud.

At the same time, Liam asked, "If you haven't been with anyone, is it because you're afraid of heartbreak?"

Her head whipped to look at him in shock, but he gazed at her with amusement.

"No, we shouldn't swim here. It wouldn't be safe," he said, as if he hadn't just sliced a piece of her heart. "We could be crushed against the rocks and that would be bad."

"Why are you asking me all of this?"

"I want to understand your story."

"So you're asking me if I was having casual sex? No, I wasn't, if you must know, although I don't think I have to answer that question."

She heard the building defensiveness in her tone, and pressed her lips together to contain it.

"That's not what I'm asking you, and you could have declined to answer. I thought it was part of our agreement; we can ask and the other person chooses whether to respond."

He was right. That's not what he asked; she'd misunderstood on purpose, hoping irritation would protect her.

Forcing calming breaths through her nose, she made herself give him an honest answer.

"I'm sorry. Let me try again. I... well. I suppose you're right, in a way. While I honestly think you can have a happy life and be single, in my case, I'd be lying if I said that being single had nothing to do with being afraid of pain."

He thought about her answer. "I see."

"I know I sometimes get wrapped up in all the things that could go wrong if I make this or that choice, but there's no other way to prevent bad things from happening. I don't like that it's like that, but it's the truth. That includes whether I decide to risk getting involved with someone or not."

"Right. And what if bad things happen anyway?"

"Then I have to suck it up and learn from my mistakes; do my best to make different choices next time."

He nodded, his eyes getting lost on the horizon. She did not ask to know what was on his mind.

After a while, he sighed and took the water bottles from the backpack, offering her one. She took it and opened hers at the same time he opened his.

"Cheers," he said, holding his bottle towards her. "To intentional singlehood."

She touched her bottle to his, a plastic *thuck* taking the place of clinking glass.

Without any further conversations, they made their way back to the cabin. Liam again helped her climb up the trail opening near the cabin, but this time he didn't keep her hand in his.

That night, Ana did something she knew she would regret. In the security of her room, she rewatched the raw footage of their almost kiss in the pool. She allowed herself five minutes of torment: she slowed down the film to inspect each single frame, letting the wave of awe and yearning wash over her. Damn, she could feel the tension through the screen. Her nerves turned into sparklers. The ghost of his touch lit her skin up.

Okay. Done. The five minutes were up and she had to return to reality.

She closed the video player and opened her email. She'd avoided it since her last phone call with Diana, but reading the document she sent would be the bucket of cold water she needed.

Only there were two email follow ups in the chain, one of them from Magda. Asking for confirmation on Ana's plans regarding the documentary, and whether she agreed to include some of the questions greenlit by Liam's team. Ana suspected she'd receive an email from Coulton himself next.

She slammed closed her laptop, putting it away for the night. She spent the next few hours thinking of the film, the material she had recorded, and her guiding questions. She balanced her vision against the pressure from Diana and Coulton's office. It was time for difficult decisions.

The next day, Liam offered to make a simple lunch for Ana and him. He'd had a session with his therapist that morning, and he was still deep in thought from it. Maybe he and Ana needed a distraction. He cut up tomatoes for a sandwich, wondering where to go next.

He finished preparing the food and took the plates out to the deck, two cold water bottles held between elbows and torso. She sat on the stairs connecting the deck with sand, and he put the food next to her. She put her ebook reader aside upon hearing him approach.

"Here you go," he said.

She took her things from him. "Thanks, Liam."

It was hot under the sun. She wore jean shorts and her bikini top; he was in his swimming shorts. They were both half-leaning on the railings, angled toward each other as they ate in silence. They'd eaten most of the food by the time they talked again.

"I was thinking," he said. "Do you think we should go somewhere else?"

"If you'd like." She pushed her plate to the side. "We don't have much time left. My flight back is booked for Friday morning."

He took a sip of his drink, the gulp a little more forceful than he would have liked. "Five days."

She nodded, still not glancing at him. She played with her plastic water bottle, tearing the label apart. "What can we do in, say, three or four days? Or if you want some time by yourself, I could go home now. I should have enough material so we have flexibility. It's up to you."

An alarm blared in his mind. He put his plate and bottle away. "I'll have to think about it."

"Sure. Just let me know."

He didn't want her to go away. Not now, not in five days. But she'd go back, and he'd be left reeling. Crap.

He swallowed through the discomfort in his throat. "It's going to be strange, going back to normal. Is it always like that for you?"

"Yeah," she replied. She put her bottle aside and leaned back to rest on her stretched arms, hands flat on the rough surface of the deck. "I get a little hangover from it."

He smiled at the image, and let it relax him. He lifted his arms and stretched, before dropping them so that his hands held the back of his head, supporting it against the railing.

"I've never had a hangover from filming before. Something tells me it'll be different this time."

He glanced at her when she didn't respond right away.

"Yeah? What makes you say that?" She finally asked.

Her eyes were all over him, gazing at one of his arms, appearing to pay close attention to the point where his biceps met his shoulder. If he were to guess, he would say that she really liked what she saw. She looked like she wanted to eat him whole, and then put him in her pocket for safekeeping.

A flood of adrenaline twirled in his belly. She wanted him, right? She wouldn't be looking at him this way if she didn't. It was good, really good that she did... and it was so little, compared to what he really wanted.

He frowned. "Please don't look at me like that. It makes this harder for me."

She tore her eyes away, face whipping forward. "I'm sorry. I didn't mean... I know it must be hard to..."

He scoffed. "Do you really know?"

Her eyes shot to him again, her back straightening into a rigid line. "I know I was objectifying you."

Blood turned to fire in his veins. In that instant, it didn't matter that he had worked really hard at trying to be okay with her decision and had retreated. He was not going to ask her to change her mind, but he was ready to share a little bit of his.

"Is that what you were doing? 'Cause to me it looked like more than that."

She crossed her arms and glared at him. He wanted her like this, feisty, speaking her mind and matching his mood. If they were going to be in limbo, the least she could do was be there, suspended with him on the tightrope.

"Fine, yeah. I like how you look, Liam. I like who you are. None of that has anything to do with what could happen if we gave in to infatuation."

"I don't think I've pressured you, Ana. I haven't asked anything of you, except not to look at me with a damn glint in your eyes. It hurts to know you like what you see, may even like me more than that, but not enough to do something about it."

"C'mon. Does it hurt that much? This isn't about you or me. This is about my career. And you flirt with me then are totally casual about it all. That doesn't scream pain."

"Yeah, I've flirted in the past but— When I flirt, I know you won't do anything about it. If you can't kiss me, you won't risk doing anything about anything you might feel. If you do the same, if you show me you want me— it wouldn't work the same way, because you don't want me to respond."

"And you would respond?"

"I would."

The moment held. Seconds ticked by, their breathing fast. They leaned towards each other and his heart never slowed down, but the pattern of its beat switched, anger giving way to a heady mix of desire and angst. How dare she call it infatuation; she had to know this was more than that. Different. She'd leave in five days, and he had to use every bit of strength not to grab her head and kiss her, not to pull her to him to taste her lips, not to hug her and beg her to quiet her mind and check again if she'd be willing to give them a chance.

She shook her head, saying no to something— Liam wasn't sure what, exactly. It didn't matter. They were at a standstill, anyway.

"Thanks for lunch," she said. She got up and picked up their plates and bottles. "I'll clean up."

He watched her walk back into the cabin, escaping him and their feelings alike.

Night had fallen. Ana did her best to work, sitting at the kitchen table with the laptop powered on in front of her. She slowly prepared a video for her social media channels, trying hard to concentrate but mostly failing.

It took her an hour to give up the pretense. She flipped the screen closed and, with her elbows on the table, held her head in her hands. She needed to talk to Liam. She didn't like the tension that hung between them after their conversation over lunch. They'd avoided each other but, several hours later, distance had done nothing to soothe the strain.

With a big sigh of resignation, she got up, got two glasses, and poured a serving of whisky in each. Carrying her peacemaking gift, she made her way to Liam. She could be the one to build a bridge, this time.

He sat outside on one of the lounge chairs, arms crossed, eyes lost in the forest. He heard her approach and turned his head to her but, where he would have smiled at the sight of her before, he now remained serious.

She filled her lungs with pine and salt, begging her heart to calm down.

She offered him one of the glasses. "Truce?"

He pressed his lips together and stared at the liquor, as if he were amused but didn't want to be. He lost that battle, and let out a half laugh, half scoff.

He reached for the glass. "Truce."

Her breathing easier, she let herself drop to the ground, where she sat cross-legged.

"I don't like this tension between us," she said.

"I don't, either." He sipped from his glass.

Ana copied him. "Is there any way we can go back to how things were?"

He didn't look at her, but lifted his eyes to the half moon above them.

"Of course. We only have a few days left and I'd rather enjoy them with you, than be stuck in this feeling."

She nodded. He agreed with her, so why did it make her so sad?

"I'm sorry. All of this is a big deal to me, Liam. What this documentary can do for my career, my professionalism, as much as what I feel... what's happening... between us. I'm scared," she admitted, her breathing fast, her voice thin. "So please, let things be as they are."

"Okay." He looked down to his glass, resting on his lap. "I won't ask you to risk it with me."

She sighed. "I can... like I said earlier, I can leave. Go back home tomorrow. You'd get a few days by yourself, if that'd help."

He raised his knees and rested his arms on them, giving her a sideways glance. "Do you want to leave? Go home early?"

Her chest grew heavy. She'd thought of this for hours the night before, and her answer hadn't changed since.

"Not really. I'm enjoying this..."

"Despite the array of... frustrations?"

She chuckled. "Yes. I enjoy your company. But if I leave, I might have something to push back against TCA's pressure— it'll be too late for them to insist on things— and you could have a tiny break from everything."

He gazed at her and sighed. "I don't want you to go."

"Then I won't go." She gave him a small smile.

"Give me tonight. I'll let you know where we're going next in the morning."

They stayed outside, drinking Scotch slowly. Together, and in silence.

———

Ana didn't find Liam in the cabin the next morning. She found a note from him on the fridge; she lifted the watermelon magnet and read it: *Went for a run. Be back later.*

After taking a shower, she set up to make breakfast; she had almost finished when she caught Liam stretching on the deck. She didn't ogle.

"Hey," he said a while later, entering the cabin. "Good morning."

"Morning. Hungry? I made food."

"Thanks, yeah, starving. I'll take a quick shower and eat with you."

He disappeared through the hallway as she set up the table, and was back soon after.

"How was your run?" she asked as he poured coffee for them.

"Great. I'm almost high right now. Some of that is the exercise but a lot of it? The pine smell."

She chuckled.

"So." He reached for strawberries and added them to his plate. "I have an idea. I have a college friend who's working in an observatory a couple of hours from here. I thought we could go there and talk about astronomy a bit."

"That sounds amazing!" she exclaimed as she buttered toast. "It would be great to see you in that environment, seeing more of you on that side of things."

Liam checked his watch, then his phone. He frowned. "Ugh. Magda has been calling me all morning but I haven't answered. This time it's Coulton, though."

She was so busy imagining all the things they could talk about in their visit to the observatory that at first she didn't realize how strange this was. Liam had talked on the phone with people; sometimes his parents, sometimes a friend. At least once with his therapist. As far as she'd known, he hadn't talked with anyone at TCA since they'd gotten here.

"Did they leave a voicemail?" she asked.

"No, they never do. They know I might ignore what they say on a voicemail but, if they call a few times, I'll have to return the call to check with them."

"Smart but evil." Just as she made the comment, his phone lit up again with a call.

"Hello?" he said, answering the phone. He got up and went to his room, but soon she could hear his voice getting louder and more irritated by the minute.

"We had a deal," he said. "Right. Yeah, you said that already. No, you're right, I don't care."

Ana's nerves went up as she impatiently waited for his return. When he finally reappeared, irritation marred his handsome face.

"Bad news," he said. "There'll be no astronomical tour. We're going back to LA instead. TCA is hosting a party and we're invited.

Chapter 15

L IAM CLOSED HIS CAR door and put on the seatbelt, Ana mirroring him in her seat. He turned the key in the ignition with a sigh, the fresh air of the early morning still in his lungs.

"You know," Liam said, driving them out of the property and onto the gravel road, "I'm really disappointed that we're not going to visit my friend at the observatory. For all of the five minutes where that was the plan, I got really excited for it."

"Yeah, I know. I would have loved that, too, but I think this party will take up a lot of our time. I will have to go shopping, by the way. In the email Diana sent me with the invitation, she described a kind of dress code I'm not prepared for."

"So you didn't fit a fancy dress in one of your two bags?"

"Would you believe I did not?"

She went out shopping that same afternoon, after they arrived at his place in LA. Alone in his home for the first time in weeks, he entertained opening his laptop and getting into his emails, but didn't. He called Mo instead, and checked in with him that everything was in order for his flight on Saturday. Confirmed that he could take the next few days off in peace, too.

Once the call was over, Liam remained sitting on the couch, out of sorts with the silence around him. He tried calling Logan;

he didn't answer. Instead of leaving him a voicemail, Liam texted him.

Liam: Hey, just calling to chat. Wondering how you're doing. I'm going on a PR tour on Sat. What's up with you?

He thought of telling him about Ana but second-guessed it. Logan knew about the documentary, but Liam hadn't told him yet about the more complicated part of their relationship. How could he possibly tell him all of that over text?

Still holding the phone in his hand, Liam considered calling his brother. The screen locked and darkened as he imagined what would happen if he took the risk and dialed Alex; Liam let his phone fall to the sofa. As much as Liam wanted to find a way to mend fences with his brother, he knew he couldn't push.

Now what? How to fill the silence?

Ana came back in the evening. She let herself in using the keys he'd let her borrow, maneuvering a slim box in which he presumed she carried clothes. She held her phone between her shoulder and her ear, and laughed at whatever was happening in her call. A bag dangled from the wrist of the other hand.

"Hey," she called, closing the door behind her. He approached her and tried to take the box from her to help her, but she dismissed his help with a flip of her hand. She gave him his keys back instead. "Don't worry about it. I was going to ask, should we get dinner?"

"Is that Liam?" Ely's voice came from Ana's phone. "Is he shirtless?"

Liam pressed his lips together, barely holding in the laughter at Ely's question.

"Ely, stop," Ana said to the phone. "Please tell me you didn't hear that," she asked Liam. Her eyes were wide with embarrassment.

"But I did," he said, grinning.

"So are you?!" Ely insisted on the phone.

This time Liam did laugh.

Ana rolled her eyes. "Ugh. Okay. If you want to get food, I'm fine with whatever," she told him. "I'll be in my room. Let me know when the food is here?"

He nodded and she waved, leaving him standing alone in the entrance hall.

He put his hands in his pockets, letting his shoulders drop low. Coming back home and getting his first taste of not having Ana around, having her come back as if she lived there with him, seeing her retreat to her room and shutting him out— it left him swaying in his spot.

With a sigh, he made his way back to the living room, picking his phone up from where it lay on the couch, opening the take out app. As he took those few steps, he heard the echo of Ana's laughter from her room.

The unfamiliar pang of jealousy stabbed his gut. Ana shared herself so freely with Ely but, as much as he wanted her to do the same with him, she didn't. Before things had built up to their almost kiss, he had thought she let him see her unrestrictedly. He now knew that she reserved a part of herself away from him, and the awareness of it settled like a rock in his belly.

***

The next day, Ana retreated to get ready for the party a couple of hours before him. He didn't think much of it; he knew how long it took to do all of the things that were asked of women in the industry.

Mo arrived with Liam's suit and his hairdresser, who helped put Liam's curls into submission. They also decided to trim and shape his beard; it had grown quite wild the past few weeks. More than the convenience of it, sometimes it served as a disguise when out and about.

Tonight the purpose wasn't camouflage, though. Tonight he wanted to look good. He wanted to have the kind of night with Ana, where they would both be done up and look their best. The closest he'd likely get to going out on a date with her.

He studied himself in the full-length mirror in his room after Mo and the stylist left. Liam had chosen a sharp suit tailored to him, in a purple so dark it looked black— the perfect shade to play off the color of his eyes. A black shirt with cufflinks. An expensive watch and a couple of rings. Ana may prefer them not to take any steps further in their attraction to each other, but it didn't mean he didn't want her wanting him back. He wasn't vain enough to think that his looks alone would do the trick, but seeing her react to him patched tiny cracks in him.

He checked his watch and, upon realizing he was a couple of minutes late, he sprayed on some cologne and left his room, making his way to the front of the house.

He walked looking down, checking his cufflinks again, but lifted his eyes when he sensed her presence. His steps faltered when he saw her standing in the middle of the large room, waiting for him. He had to take a long, calming breath at the sight of her; it burnt him from within.

She wore a dark teal dress, almost an emerald color, with a deep V-neck. It was cinched at the waist and flowy around her thighs, with pleats that made her waist look narrow and her legs long. A simple, gold jewelry set complemented the look: a long necklace resting its pendant between her breasts, long, thin earrings, and a thin bracelet. Her clutch was a soft gold, her make up the same, and her hair fell long and straight.

He'd wanted to impress her, but he was the one at a loss.

He forced himself to complete his walk, taking the last few steps to her slowly.

"Wow," he said. "You look..."

She smiled as he struggled to find the right words. "It's the closest I could find to the color of your eyes on short notice."

His throat closed up. "That's... incredibly sweet."

She tilted her head. "You look amazing, but that's no surprise."

"People won't be looking at me tonight."

"Thank you," she said with a smile. She reached out to his arm. "The car is here. Shall we?"

Liam tried to stay close to Ana at the start of the party. For the first half hour, he made introductions and helped Ana acclimate to a networking event like TCA's. After that, Diana came to get Ana for what she called a spin of the room. He watched Ana walk away, her dress swinging around her hips.

"Nice score," Dan Reeves, another actor signed with TCA, said showing up at Liam's side. "Where'd you pick her up? She an aspiring actress?"

Liam took his eyes off Ana to glare at Dan. "Everything you just said missed the mark."

"So you're not hitting that? Why?"

"We're working together." He sipped his drink, forcing himself not to scowl. "She's a brilliant documentary director."

"Since when does that have anything to do with things?"

Liam shook his head and changed the subject. "So, what projects are you on?"

They continued their small talk, and Liam did his best not to steal too many glances at Ana. He mostly failed. A couple of times their eyes met across the room and, each time, her resulting smile made everyone else disappear.

He had to force himself to remember this was a professional function and had to work the room too.

Liam walked around the venue, saying hello to producers, directors, and actors. He chatted about past and future projects; he posed for pictures for the press. He sometimes talked about the documentary and the interesting process of working on an unscripted project.

"Yes, I heard we just signed with Ana Lira. Is that who's directing you on the documentary?"

"Yeah," he replied. He liked Leanne; she was an agent at TCA. There were two other people in their small group, new actresses that had signed with Leanne. "She's fantastic. Do you know her?"

"Are you talking about Ana Lira?" Margaret, Coulton's wife, said as she joined their small group.

"Yes," Leanne said to his other side. "Liam was telling us about working with her."

"Wonderful, I've been curious about that myself," Margaret said, turning to Liam. "I was so glad when John told me how it had all worked out. It was my idea to connect the two, you know? I told John it would be a great project."

He nodded. "It's been incredible so far. I'm really excited to see the final result."

"And after, what will you be doing?" Leanne asked.

"I have to go on a short press tour after we wrap up filming the documentary—"

"Oh, excuse me, are we talking about my client?" Diana said as she approached them. Liam searched for Ana, but she wasn't around.

"You've signed Ana?" Leanne asked. "Congratulations!"

"Yes! I'm so glad. She has so much potential, you know? Like a diamond in the rough."

"I'm glad she has you," Margaret added. "She needs a strong lead, if she's to become everything she can be. John always tells me that fame is fragile, and that it'll never last without a careful team to sustain it."

"I plan to be that team for her, of course," Diana assured everyone. "Documentaries don't make or break Hollywood, but they have their niche. And if I can convince her to direct fiction... I mean, to have a female director who is also a Latina? We could do amazing things."

"Where is she, anyway? I'd love to meet her," Leanne said. "If she might direct, I have these two lovely actresses who could use a break."

"I left her dancing with Joel Thornton," Diana told the group. It was clear she hoped to get the rumor mill going. When Liam gazed at Diana, he caught her looking at him with a spark of curiosity. "He seemed immediately taken by her, as soon as I made the introduction."

"If you'll excuse me." Liam put a smile on his face to appease them and stepped away. He needed out. He did not want to hear about Diana's machinations.

He did not want to think much about Ana dancing with Joel, either. It's not like he would go interrupt them and take Ana away.

He wasn't the jealous or possessive kind and, even if he were, Ana was her own person. He had no claim to anything with her. He knew she could do as she pleased. Joel Thornton would be lucky if she decided she wanted to see more of him.

He hated that his thoughts sounded like he was trying to convince himself of something. No, he really didn't have any right to any of those feelings, so why was he struggling with them?

Because you've never wanted like this, the voice of his therapist said in his mind. *And you don't know what to do with yourself. You hate that despite whatever she feels, she might still not choose you.*

"Shit," he mumbled under his breath, turning towards the bar. "Not now, Doctor."

After getting a new glass of Scotch, he strolled the room until he saw Joel and Ana dancing. The man was a good dancer, which made Ana's own moves shine. Her smile, by far his favorite thing about her, was wide and free; she seemed to be enjoying herself.

He stayed away, sipping his drink, a hand in his pocket, observing the situation. Eventually, Diana approached Ana. She seemed apologetic, putting her hand on Ana's shoulder as Diana talked to Joel. They appeared to exchange a few more words, before Joel took out his phone and Ana looked like she was dictating her number. They waved goodbye as Diana took Ana to another group of people. Liam shook his head at Diana's efforts, and walked away to find someone else to speak to.

He was talking with Karl, a producer with whom he'd been friendly, when he felt his phone vibrate.

Ana: where are you?

"I'm sorry, I need to take this," Liam said to Karl.

Liam: by the bar

Ana: I'm coming. Get
me a gin & tonic?

He excused himself from his conversation and did as she had asked. He received the drink just as she appeared next to him.

"I'm so happy to see you again," she said, taking her drink from him. "I've never been to a party that was such hard work."

"You've been doing great. You came up a few times in conversation and at least half of the people I talked to seemed to be smitten with you."

"Pfft." She flicked her hand. "Sure."

"No, really."

She glanced at him, but he couldn't read her eyes. "Anyway," she said as if she didn't want to talk about it. "Would you like to dance?"

"Dance?" he asked, his jaw locking up. "Not particularly. I'm not that good at it."

"Diana wanted me to dance with a couple of people; I think she thought, hey, I'm Latina, that's a thing I can do?" she shook her head and rolled her eyes.

"I saw you dancing with Joel, and it did look like you dance well."

Crap, he had not meant to mention that. He must have still been rattled by his earlier thoughts.

"That's besides the point," Ana argued, apparently not noticing his discomfort. "I also think Joel was fetishizing me a bit. I don't know."

Liam made himself remain silent.

She let a long breath out. "Would you dance with me if it's a slow song? Diana may throw me into someone else's arms if I don't find another dancing partner on my own. I'd much rather dance with you, if you're willing."

Of course he had to say yes to that. They ended up bribing the venue's music producer to put a few slow songs on, and they took to the floor among other guests.

He held one of her hands in his and put his other one on her lower back; she put her free hand on his shoulder. They found their rhythm, keeping their pace to the music. Liam had thought it would be innocuous enough, dancing with her surrounded by people, but he quickly realized he'd been mistaken. Dancing close to her like this on this fake work date brought all his wants back to focus. Why were they not together, again?

Right. Work. Fear.

"You sold yourself short." She looked up at him. "You're a good dancer."

"Slow dancing is different from actual dancing, though, wouldn't you say?"

"Yes, I would." Her smile was soft and her eyes didn't waver. The lights in the room shone like stars on her brown eyes in sparkles of gold.

"You look beautiful tonight," he said.

"Thank you. You smell amazing."

He grinned and arched an eyebrow. "If you keep talking sweet to me, I'll forget about all these people and dance with you like we're alone."

"I may be falling for the magic of the moment." Her smile was shy for once, but she kept it as she looked around the party hall. "No one is really paying attention to us."

He splayed his fingers on her lower back. "I'm sure some people are."

Her eyes came back to him and searched his face for a second, two, before she sighed. "If I didn't think it'd make me a huge hypocrite, I'd be happy to ignore them all. I'll be gone on Friday, anyway. What could they say after a simple dance? Even Diana thought dancing would be a good idea."

He brought their joined hands closer to him, placing them against his heart. "They could find something to say and... I wouldn't care. I'd give a lot, Ana, if we could have these two hours to dance together. Slow. With all these lights shining in your eyes."

"You're a romantic." Her smile grew, and faltered. "Tonight I could be, too. For this dance."

"Thank god."

In heels her temple reached his cheek; she leaned towards him and rested her face against his beard. He couldn't help himself, he pulled her closer.

They swayed to the slow music. She fit perfectly against him, and he willed himself to settle into the moment, trying to sear it into his memory: the warmth of their bodies together, the soft caress of the fabric of her dress under his fingers, the hope she could feel the beat of his heart under hers. This, this is how it should be, but not just for tonight. Not just because Ana thought she had Diana's permission. Not just for work.

Damn it all, but he couldn't let it go. He wanted to respect the answers she'd given him, and he still couldn't stop his brain from desperately searching every corner for possibilities.

"Do you think we'll stay in touch after filming is done?" He found himself asking.

"You do have a right to veto, so we'll see each other once a rough edit is done. Then if we premiere it on a festival—"

"No, not professionally. You and me."

A few lines of the song had gone by when she answered. "I would like that. I would love to stay in touch with you."

To hell, but he had to share his side. Tell her what he felt. Her choice didn't have to change, but he wanted her to know. Wanted, with fire in his belly.

"So that we're clear," he said, as conversationally as possible, "I'm not talking about friendly calls once in a while. I want something different than friendship with you."

"Liam..."

"Ana. When I tried to kiss you, you told me you couldn't. I think I understand what's stopping you. What if we could remove some of those barriers in the future? Would that make it better?"

She stirred in his arms but didn't pull away. Her temple still leaned against his beard, her hand still over his heart, but her back had hardened. "We shouldn't do this. No matter how much I want to forget about it— there are people around us. I have too much to prove. Too much at risk."

"You have nothing to prove— you've already shown the world how good you are. That's why they signed you up. They're not doing you a favor; they're looking to capitalize on your talent."

"Do you realize that if we did something about how we feel— about how we think we feel— they'll assume the worst of me? They'll think I'm looking for my fifteen minutes, or that I'm unprofessional, or..."

"Yes, they very well might do that. They could also decide I'm taking advantage of you, or conning you for my benefit. For the promotional factor."

"Pfft. You are adored by millions. Your posters decorate the walls of half the teens in my city. Who am I? I'm nobody! And I'm a woman. Of color. Somehow, we always get it worse."

He pulled her closer to him. "But what if this were real? How will we ever know?"

She shook her head.

"Ana, I think you're afraid of what we have, because you're scared of it going sideways."

"Yes, of course I am. At the most basic level, I'm scared we'll hurt each other." She pulled back enough that she could look him in the eye. He didn't loosen his hold on her. "But this is more than that. I've never been involved with someone in my films. That would be just poor boundaries. What will people think of my next documentary? How will they trust my professionalism?"

"You wouldn't be the first filmmaker that sleeps with their talent which, by the way, happens a lot. This is about you and me."

Her eyes searched his, matching the intensity of her feelings. "Even if other filmmakers do it, it doesn't mean I should, or want to."

"Not that it's right, but it's common. People don't really care about it much. It's just more fodder for the gossip mill."

"It's still a huge risk for me. Our agents have made it clear over the past few weeks. You heard Coulton the first time we met. My reputation is all I have."

"It isn't. It's all he has and all he likes to wield. No one can take what you've done so far away from you. You built that without anyone's help. Don't forget you also have your skill and hard work."

She shook her head again, her lips in a thin line.

He curled his fingers on her back, trying to grab her and keep her in place. He squeezed her hand to his chest. "If we wait, I won't be the subject of one of your documentaries, anymore."

"And you'd wait?"

"I would, if you told me you wanted me to."

"Liam, I... I'm afraid. I can't think clearly. Maybe we can—should talk about this another time."

"When? On Friday, when this project is officially over? The weekend, while I'm on a plane somewhere? Will we open up and talk, really talk about us then? This is all coming off wrong. I just— Ana, most of these problems will disappear if we wait a while. After some time has gone by, the only question you'll need to answer is whether you want to risk being with me, not knowing how it will end, but hoping it won't."

She didn't reply. Sadness and incredible longing filled her eyes.

He rested his forehead on hers. "Tell me what you think I'm doing. Am I forcing this, or am I fighting for us? If you ask me to stop trying, I will, Ana."

She remained silent. It did more for him than their arguing had.

She wasn't asking him to stop asking.

Ana tore her eyes away. "Maybe we should leave the party. I don't think I want to talk to anybody here anymore."

"Okay."

They walked out the venue without touching, and without talking. They didn't say goodbye to anyone, either.

They waited for their driver to come pick them up. The air was fresh, but frost filled the space between them. As they stood outside, side by side, he was shocked that she leaned into him and took his hand.

"I hope you know," she said, "if I'm conflicted it is because I do feel it, too."

She kissed his cheek and let go of his hand, going back to simply standing by his side. She looked up at him, the breeze moving a strand of her hair across her face.

With a sigh, he reached up to put the hair back behind her ear.

"Okay," he said.

He'd have to wait, then.

Chapter 16

A NA WOKE UP TO multiple texts from Ely.

Ely: what happened???
Did something happen???
#mcana is on fire

Ely's messages included a bunch of screenshots: a group of paparazzi had taken pictures of them while they waited for their car, with scandalous captions suggesting the very things she had been afraid of. One of them included her kissing his cheek while they held hands. Another screenshot showed higher quality pictures of them dancing at the party; these were official press releases, and they included the moment when he rested his forehead on hers. A final screenshot collected a few comments on the hashtag, where three out of five comments were negative towards her.

"Crap!"

One moment together in front of people. She'd weakened for just one dance, and it had been enough to push her into the mess. She thought they'd been alone while waiting for their car.

> **Ana**: I made a huge
> mistake. I thought it'd
> be fine. I was so focused
> on Liam and I didn't
> see anyone on the street.
> What am I going to do?

Just as she pressed *send*, her phone rang in her hand. Diana's direct number flashed on her screen.

"Crap. Crap. Crap." Ana pressed the green button on her screen and answered. "Hello, Diana."

"Hello, Ana. We need to talk."

"Sure." She sat up on the bed. "What's up?"

"I hope you know what's up. Did you see what's going on online?"

"You mean, the rumors about Liam and I?"

"Yes, I mean what they're saying about you and Mr. McMillan. I saw the picture of you and him outside and I warned you— people are going to think you two are together. You kissing his face isn't helping the situation."

Ana winced. "Yes, well. We're not together."

"Good!" Diana let out a small chuckle. "It's not that I don't get it. His level of fame may seem very alluring to you right now and, though these pics are good publicity, I promise you it won't last. I wouldn't risk a fling with McMillan. You'll pay the price, and who knows what Coulton will say. I'd rather you pursue Joel Thornton. He would still help you climb the ladder, help you network, and he's very handsome too... but poses a much more manageable risk for you."

"Right." Ana bit back a groan. "You're worried about this backfiring."

"It's my job to keep track of these things. I'm trying to mentor you and set you up for the career you deserve. The tabloids and blogs and Mr. McMillan's rabid fans will try to destroy you and, though it's a good thing to get your name out there... I don't know that we're at a place where you can withstand the storm."

"I hear that."

Yeah, she got where Diana was coming from. Ana had thought about that, too, hadn't she? She worried about the varied angles where things could go wrong. Still, hearing Diana name some of her fears out loud filled her blood with lead.

"Great. If Mr. Thornton calls, answer, okay? And I'll get a PR rep involved to see if there's anything we can do."

Ana doubted she'd answer the phone if Joel called, but she didn't think Diana would like to hear that. "Let me know what the PR rep says."

"For sure. Call me if you need to chat, okay?"

"Okay."

"Talk to you later."

Ana hung up, muttering a soft *fuck*. Her eyes filled with tears, but she didn't need her sight to navigate to Ely's number.

Her best friend answered on the first ring.

"This sucks," Ana said in the place of a hello, her face now wet.

"Tell me everything."

Comforted by the gentleness in her voice, Ana poured her heart out.

***

Ana laid in bed, the blankets a mess. She'd hung up her call with Ely just a few minutes ago and was now lost in her thoughts; the knock on the door made her jump.

Liam.

"Come in," she said, sitting up on the bed.

He opened the door, leaning on the door jamb. "Hey."

She looked at him, thin gray track suit and cut out shirt. He hadn't changed yet for the day, it seemed.

"Hey." She knew her voice sounded morose, but didn't try to change it.

His eyes surveyed the room; he cataloged the untidy sheets, her hair up in a knotty bun, and her impossibly crumpled pajamas.

"You look like you're a messy sleeper."

"I'm told it's not that bad, but you wouldn't know that because, despite what the tabloids are speculating, we are not sharing a bedroom."

"Ah," he said, coming to sit at the corner of her bed. "You saw already. I thought I might have to tell you what's going on."

"No, I saw."

"I heard you talking on the phone so I didn't want to interrupt. I was hoping it had nothing to do with this." He watched her, pensive. "How are you doing?"

"I'm overwhelmed, to be honest. They're saying some pretty nasty things."

"Please tell me you didn't go looking."

"I haven't. Ely sent me just a couple of screenshots. Then I asked her to check while we were on the phone. Not to read anything out loud to me, but to tell me the tone of what they were saying."

"Ana, try not to—"

"Yes, I know. Looking makes it worse."

He didn't say any more, but he crossed his arms and furrowed his eyebrows.

"You can say it," she told him.

"I'm not going to say anything."

"Then I'll say it: you told me it would be like this. And Diana... ugh. She's already giving me advice. Said she's going to get a PR rep involved."

"She thinks this needs to be managed?" His eyebrows formed a high arc at that.

She nodded. "She thinks it's good publicity but I should aim for Joel instead."

"What the hell does that mean?" Irritation had wormed its way to his tone.

"She thinks I'm trying to climb that ladder you've talked about, and that I'm aiming too high with you."

He stood again, hands on his hips and face cast down, severe eyes on hers.

"We're people. We're not fucking chess pieces."

"She said she's worried that my career will suffer if these rumors don't die down soon, and that's why I shouldn't be involved with you."

He turned away and took a few steps as if needing to pace but, not having enough room for it, he turned back to face her.

"That's not going to make a difference, is it?" He asked in a low, rumbly voice. "They already made up their minds. They already think we're together."

"Well, it makes a difference to me. I know I've acted professionally."

"They don't care about that," he insisted. "Co-workers sleep together all the time in this business. I had people at the party assuming we were having sex even before all of this happened. Flings are common in Hollywood."

She flinched. "They're not common to me! I have no interest in a fling."

"I'm not saying that I see anything that could happen between us as a fling. I'm saying they already assume we're having a fling. Diana wouldn't have called you, otherwise, and that's what Coulton is thinking too. For what it's worth, he thinks it's good PR; that it'll help with the documentary's promos."

She got out of bed, restless. Her hands trembled as she stood in front of him, and she crossed her arms to hide it.

There was something intimate about standing in front of Liam, both in their pajamas; despite the low cut of her shirt and the limited length of her shorts, she didn't feel exposed physically, per se. Vulnerability reached deep into her.

His eyes were steady on her. "I'd offer to say something on social media, deny the rumors, but that's not going to really change anyone's minds."

She shook her head. "No. Let's not respond to any of it."

"What did Ely say?"

You might as well sleep with him now.

Ana did not repeat that out loud, as clear as she had remembered. Ana had laughed at Ely's joke, but something told her that Liam wouldn't think it was as funny.

"She said that even though I had never planned to be in the flashier side of Hollywood, I was in it now by association and have to deal with it, at least for a while. That after the documentary is over, they'll forget about me when the next thing shows up in the tabloids."

"She's likely right. Although maybe not before they speculate we... that you couldn't take the pressure and that's why you left. Never mind that it was always part of the plan, for you to go away and edit." After a bit, he added, "I'm sorry."

She shook her head. At least her tears were spent; her eyes were dry as she stared at him. "It's not your fault."

"If it helps, you can put it in the documentary."

"What's that?"

Despondency surrounded him like a cloak, heavy on him. He wasn't crying, either, but she thought his eyes were glassy. His lips curled down at the corners, in any case.

"That anyone thinking of being with me will have to cope with this kind of bullshit. That it keeps people away." He lifted a hand to cup her face.

"This isn't about who you are," she tried to explain, unsure of her words, "or what a relationship with you could be like. This is about having the strength to cope with all the bullshit around it."

"It doesn't make a difference. It's difficult to accept that someone I want in my life might feel they can't be with me, because of things that have nothing to do with me; things I have no power over."

She hugged herself. He was right, and it was incredibly unfair. She wished she were stronger and that everything going on around them didn't matter to her; that she were more courageous because a relationship should be allowed to germinate and flourish because of its own nature. Truth was, sometimes seeds fell in the wrong soil.

"All this could go on after the documentary is done," he continued. "If it does, would you ever want to be with me?"

"I... maybe... if..." She frowned, angry at herself, stuck in place.

He nodded. "I understand."

His hand fell from her face. He leaned down and kissed her cheek; she shivered.

He didn't look at her as he left the room, leaving her standing alone.

———

Ana set up to pack her bags that Friday morning with a certain air of fatality.

She had barely seen Liam the day before. He'd only approached her to let her know there were paparazzi outside, in case she planned to go somewhere on her last day. Otherwise, their day had been empty of their friendship and conversations, and full of suspended farewells.

She put all her electronics on the bed, making sure she didn't miss any cables or connectors. She packed them in her carry-on with the same method and purpose she'd followed the first time she had traveled for filming. The last thing to go in the bag was the camera. She held it in her hand, thinking about the past few weeks and the many times Liam had taken charge of the filming. It would make for interesting edits for the documentary. It would also exist there to remind her of how much she had loved her time with him.

Chains of regret and grief twisted and coiled around her ankles. If she wasn't careful, the weight of them would be enough to make her sink.

Instead of getting her computer out and watching the recording of Liam trying to kiss her, again, she put her camera in its case and into her bag. She zipped it closed with a firm hand, as if the pieces latching together could give her a sense of closure as well.

She'd put the first batch of shirts into her other bag when Liam knocked on her door.

"Come in," she said.

As was his custom, he opened the door and leaned on the door jamb. The familiarity of it soothed her, creating a harsh contrast with the weight in her heart.

"Almost done?" He crossed his arms over his chest. He was clean shaven and wore jeans and a gray shirt with three words printed across his chest: Tears For Fears. She wore black jeans and her Duran Duran shirt. She wondered if he'd chosen his shirt on purpose.

"Yeah. It's the good thing about traveling light. My new dress will suffer the consequences though. It's scrunched up in there." She pointed at the puffed-up shopping bag on the floor.

He nodded but said nothing. Silence stretched between them.

"What time is the driver coming to pick you up?" he asked.

"I still have some time. Probably about an hour."

He nodded again. He sat on the corner of the bed, watching her pack. "Any final questions?"

"No more filming, if that's what you're thinking of. Camera's packed. That's done."

"You can still ask questions, if you have them."

Questions? She didn't have any, not until she was in the process of editing but, even if she did, she didn't want to ask anything to do with the documentary. Everything filling her mind had to do with hating going away and saying goodbye.

She didn't want to leave. She did not want to move on and grow far from him. She wasn't ready. She wanted him in her life.

"Well," she began but words got stuck in her throat. She was about to rebel against grief, the shackles of it rattling as she attempted to get free. Determined to find any ounce of courage she could muster, she made herself continue. "Well," she tried again, "I'd like to know if you think we can remain... friends."

Fuck. No. Not enough courage. Not the right kind of brave.

He lifted his eyes to her. "Friends. What kind of friends?"

"I want to... talk. What's— next?"

He frowned. "I have a press tour coming up for *Space Bureau III*. After that, I have a week of prep for principal filming of my next movie. Then, principal filming. After that, I have the premiere for

Space Bureau III and, after that, I'm working on an ad campaign for a deal they signed me on. The first of a bunch of things that got moved around for this documentary."

Fuck. Fuck! Think, Ana.

"Busy as expected. And after all of that?"

He lifted his eyebrows. "I could share my calendar with you."

"No." She half chuckled, half scoffed. She was wrecking this. "I mean, in life."

He sighed. "I think I want to produce; get involved in the decision making and the making it happen. Maybe direct one day. I have been smart with my money so maybe I could set up my own company. We'll see."

"So not only acting, not forever."

What do you want, Ana? This is not it.

Feel.

"Yeah, not forever. I don't know how long I can keep doing this, like this. Although if I get it my way, I might want to continue acting, but in roles I really want to do."

She nodded. "I'd love to see you achieve all of that, if you're okay with that."

He smiled, but it looked sad.

"Do you want to ask me anything?" she offered. She needed time to think. To feel.

Talk to him.

"Did you ever come up with your question? The one that you'll use to ground the editing," he asked.

"Yeah, a while ago. Before we left the beach, actually." She stopped packing, her hands were shaking.

"Can I know?"

"Of course. My question is going to be, how do you escape loneliness, when you're looked at but not seen?"

Her eyes had been fixed on the last shirt she'd put on her bag. When he didn't reply, she glanced at him and was surprised to see the raw emotion on his face.

"I want to have you in my life, Ana, but you're not a friend. You're something else to me." His voice was thin, his tone low. Like it was an effort to say it.

His words and his voice hit her like an arrow. She turned to him, the movement automatic, trying to tell him she was open to what he had to say. That perhaps his words would be the key to breaking her bonds.

"You know what I want," he added. His voice was no more than a breath. "If you want me as a friend, then that's what I'll be."

He stared at her with eyes full of longing. He reached for her hand, his fingertips gently coercing her hand to curl around his, his thumb caressing her knuckles.

She studied the way their fingers embraced, at the way they moved against each other. Liam and Ana could have that kind of closeness, if she got out of her own way for once.

He didn't want friendship and neither did she. Why on earth was she pretending? The filming was done. She'd been professional enough.

What the hell am I doing?

Don't think. Don't feel.

Act.

Her grounding question hit him like she'd reached into his chest and squeezed his heart with both hands. He craved being understood like that, but he wasn't prepared to hear her give a voice to the fear in his soul.

He watched their hands together, their fingers holding on to each other, and willed the contact to whisper his request, asking her to give him a chance. When her fingers changed the language of their touch, he had to wonder if perhaps magic like that was possible.

She took his hand and brought it to her lips, where she kissed the back of it. She guided it to rest against her face, holding it in place with one of her own.

"I'm afraid despite myself," she said, eyes closed.

"I understand."

Things could be so different, if she chose to risk it. As much as he wanted to convince her, he couldn't. Not about this. Her choice couldn't, shouldn't be coerced. It had to be hers, authentic, or they'd never have what he yearned for.

Her eyes found him. The connection squeezed his throat.

She let go of his hand to put both of hers around his face.

His hands flew to her hips. His heart tripled its pace, the rush of blood loud in his ears. Could it be, that she was going to make the jump? Did he dare to hope?

She bent closer to him, too slow if the timing of his heart had anything to say about it. He stilled, afraid to scare her off, hoping he'd show her whatever she needed to see. He only dug his fingers further into her hips and it must have been the right thing, because her lips softened into a small grin. His throat burned with the words he didn't let himself say; his brain yelled and called and begged.

The first contact of her lips on his was minimal, tingles bursting on his lips. Desperate, he angled his head for a deeper kiss. He skimmed his bottom lip against hers, a sort of challenge. The warm air of her sigh brushed his face, before she gave in and pressed her mouth against his.

It was like diving into the deep end, with no rush to make it out for air anytime soon.

He'd happily let himself sink into this forever, let himself drown in her.

The kiss was both tentative and intense, bursts of passion and hesitation burning through their skin. She was the one to use her tongue to make a path on his lips, asking him to open his mouth and let her in. He did, taking as much as she took.

It wasn't enough. Her kiss opened the dam of need within. Aching for more, he twisted from the waist to bring Ana onto the bed. The movement was swift; she let out a huff of shocked air. He had to stand for a moment to turn his body to lay down; as he did that, she scooted back on the bed— she'd recovered quickly from the surprise and her eyes told him, finally, that they were on the same page.

The smile stretching his lips may have been slightly feral, he wasn't sure, and didn't care. It matched the fire in her eyes. He followed her on the bed but didn't rest fully on top of her; he laid down on his side, as close as he could get without being on top of her. He kissed her again even as they continued to shift with each other's body.

Kissing her was everything.

"I want you, Liam," she said as his lips explored her jaw, the tender skin where it met her neck. "I don't want to think of anything else."

He followed a lazy path down the column of her throat, painfully aware that as much as he'd wanted to hear those words from her, her wanting him wasn't going to be enough.

He needed her to crave him, to care about him, to make her way into his heart, and to let him fall into hers. He sought more than a simple release, and as he nibbled on the concave hollow between her clavicles, he knew he wouldn't get that from sex alone.

Her hands found their way to his waist and pulled at the bottom of his shirt, trying to undress him. He lifted his torso to make it easier for her; when his shirt had landed somewhere on the floor, she pushed him back to the bed and climbed on top of him. She settled on his cock, hard as a rock against his jeans. Her hands wandered across his chest and abs, her fingertips pressing hard enough to make grooves on his muscles as they moved.

"Fuck," he said, his eyes darting to her ruffled long hair, her parted lips. He despaired at the lust in her eyes.

He needed to know if he could have her heart.

He grabbed her hands and pulled them above his head, forcing her to come to him for a kiss. He twisted and rolled them so that she'd be on the bottom. For a moment he let the weight of his body crush her, but he broke their ongoing kiss by pulling on her bottom lip and shifting his weight back to his knees. His hands moved from hers to her forearms, where his long arms still kept them above her head even as they roamed down to her biceps.

"Liam," she whimpered, as he kissed her neck again, the swell of her breasts, and ended his journey by gently biting a hardened peak through her clothes. She moaned.

"I want you to want me," he said, now letting his fingertips make their way down the soft skin above her breasts and around them, until they reached the bottom of her shirt. He lifted it only enough that he could caress her belly. He kneeled between her legs, their weight resting on his thighs. "But that's not going to be enough."

She sat up to come close to him. His hands moved to her thighs, rubbing them up and down. Her hands came to his shoulders, one of them falling to his naked chest as the other climbed to grab his nape. She pulled him to her for another kiss: their tongues clashed and their teeth nipped, as if they were already arguing about his words.

"I want all of you," she whispered against his lips, eyes on his, searching. "I'm gonna risk it."

"I don't want us to jump without a parachute. We need to build a good founda—"

She kissed him again, this time falling to her back and bringing him down with her. He let her guide him to lay on her, and rested his weight on his elbows. Unwittingly, he moved his hips against hers, causing the tension to build in his lower back.

"Sex can be a cornerstone," she argued against his ear, nibbling on his earlobe. He groaned. He was going to explode if he wasn't careful.

"I need more than fifteen rushed minutes," he said as she explored his neck, kissing his Adam's apple. "I don't want sex clouding your judgment— or mine. Not when we talk about our relationship. When we have sex, I'm going to be all in."

He angled his head so that he could kiss her again, shifting his weight to rest three-quarters on top of her. He pillowed her head with an arm around her neck. He created a small distance between them, only enough so that he could look into her eyes and see every sign of her willingness.

"Sure," she breathed. "Makes sense."

"But I'd like to give you a taste of what we can have. Let you know how good I'll make you feel."

Her lips parted. He brought his free hand down to knead her breast. When his thumb teased her nipple, her eyes closed and a soft whimper escaped her. With his lips in front of hers, he breathed in her sighs. He smiled and guided his hand down to her waistband.

"This okay?" He asked as he unbuttoned her jeans.

They stared at each other, green studying brown. She nodded. He pulled her zipper down and bit his lip as he found the line of her underwear.

"I want to touch you," he said. He caressed the soft fabric of her panties, gentle fingertips over satin. "Tell me you want me to touch you."

"Touch me, Liam."

He pushed his fingers under the edge of her underwear and beyond, curving them around her mound. He slipped one, two fingers into the warm, slick folds, reaching for the bundle of nerves there.

One of her hands touched him over his jeans and he hissed.

He jerked his hips back. "No. I want this to be about you."

"It's not enough." She writhed under him, adding friction against his fingers, her eyes still locked with his.

"Then we'll want more, until we know what's next."

He moved his fingers slowly, exploring the new territory and learning what made her wild. He let the momentum build, focusing his movements on the raised, hardened nub, or giving her time to catch her breath by allowing his fingers to tease her entrance.

Her eyes were half closed now, her breathing ragged, her mouth open. He rubbed his nose against her temple, keeping his arousal under control. He was so hard that his hips wanted to jerk and move out of their own volition, but he held back.

"C'mon, Ana, let me see you. Let me have this before you go," he said, his voice hoarse to his own ears. "I don't want to miss a thing."

The fingers against his shoulder scratched his skin. The undulation of her body picked up the pace; she rode his fingers and he stroked her faster, her moans catching in her throat, driving him out of his mind with the need to see her climax.

"Liam—"

Whatever she said died in her throat as she came undone under him. He dropped his forehead to her temple, only then becoming aware of his own labored breathing. He smiled despite the throbbing hardness in his pants, trying with his half-aware brain to subdue it.

When she opened her eyes again, he let himself fall into their warmth.

Her body still shaking from her orgasm, she opened her eyes to search his.

His eyes crinkled at the corners, shining with amazement. She'd been looking for a demand, for a request that she returned the favor, but saw none of it. He seemed wholly content with the state of things.

She rubbed her forehead with a hand. She sighed and squirmed as he took his hand away from her tender flesh. She wiggled and shifted to her side, feeling him still hard against her hip in the process. He moaned.

She spied on his jeans and saw more confirmation that he was still aroused. She moved her hand towards that hardness trapped beneath denim, but he intercepted it by wrapping his fingers around her wrist. He brought it to his chest instead.

"Not today," he said. "Think about it while we're apart."

"Liam..."

"You need to catch your flight home, I need to go on this PR tour. We'll text, call, all that. We'll talk about what's next. We'll figure it out."

She nodded, accepting his words. The only options were to further antagonize TCA by rescheduling the flight they were paying for, or to go away as planned. And Liam would be gone in less than 24 hours anyway.

"Okay. We'll figure it out," she said, holding on to the possibility.

"What if I drop you at the airport? We'd have a bit longer."

She put her hand on his face; she ran her thumb against his shaven skin.

"My flight is departing from LAX, not from a private airport. TCA may be paying for my flight but it's the cheapest ticket. No chartered flights for the runt. I actually think they're doing this only because of this project with you, not because they treat us the same as you A-listers. Anyway, chances are people would recognize you and bother you. I don't think it's a good idea. "

"The runt, huh?" He smirked at her sass and kissed her again. They would have gotten lost in it, passion quickly escalating, had her phone not dinged.

Cursing, she stretched back to reach her phone. She checked the notification; it was an automated message reminding her that her driver would be there in ten minutes.

"Shit," she said, pulling away from him. "I still have to finish packing."

She got up from the bed. Liam stood as well, reaching for his shirt on the floor. She jumped to the dresser, to stuff her bag with the few clothes still there.

"I'll take over," he said, a proud smirk on his face as he reached into a drawer. "You might want to fix your hair."

She lifted a hand to self-consciously pat at her head. "Thanks."

She stepped into the bathroom to check herself in the mirror, raking her fingers through her hair to put it back in order. She couldn't help the butterflies taking flight at seeing the twisted shirt, messy hair that had resulted from their kissing. She straightened her clothes, belatedly buttoning and zipping up her jeans.

When she came out of the bathroom she aimed for her bag, hoping to check that everything was packed, but he grabbed her from the waist and brought her to him for a kiss.

"Your bags are ready," he said. Kissed her again. "If anything stays behind, I'll keep it safe. And I'm keeping your dress, so it doesn't get ruined. I can mail it to you at another time, if you like."

"Thanks." She let herself surround his neck with her arms. Kissed him. Like they needed to make sure this was really happening, despite her leaving in a few minutes.

Her phone dinged again, just as the gate's doorbell rang in Liam's phone. He grabbed his cell from his back pocket and opened the gate for the driver. She attempted to take her bags, but he took them from her before she could.

"I'll do it," he said.

They walked to the main door and out. Liam put Ana's bags in the already-opened trunk before closing it.

She stood by the car's door. He came to her and, with hands around her face, kissed her deeply.

"Is this it?" She asked, putting her hands over his on her face. "Our month together is over?"

"Just this month is but... we'll make more time. This is really the beginning."

Her smile was fueled by the warmth in her heart.

"I'll miss you," he said.

"Me too. We'll talk soon."

"Yeah, there's a lot we need to discuss."

He opened the door for her and closed it after she'd settled down. He stood next to the car and stayed as the car drove away.

"Really the beginning," she whispered to herself.

Chapter 17

"MY FRIEND," ELY SAID as she hugged Ana. "I'm so glad you're back."

Ana bit her lip so as to not let it slip yet that she'd done something unexpected. They made their way to the parking lot and found Ely's car; they quickly drove out of the small airport that served their city.

"So, did you leave Liam sad and desolate over your departure?" Ely joked.

"No, I think he was fine."

"Can't believe it— so no tears, desperate cries to get you to stay?"

"No. We agreed to talk on the phone, text. We need to discuss some things. And we need to get together for a round of rough editing, at least. I might see him before that, though, I hope."

"Ah," she said as if she understood but was disappointed. "Always the professional."

"I think we'll have to be professional at times, yes."

Ana stole a glance at Ely, taking joy out of her frown. Ana pressed her lips together not to laugh.

"Friends, then? That's good. Like with the other people you've worked with. A check in email twice a year or something like that."

"It'll probably be different. Or I hope so, anyway. None of the other documentary people kissed me or used their fingers on me 'till I saw stars, after all. Well, I kissed him, but. Same results. It kind of changed things."

Silence. It stretched for one second, two, before it broke with her friend's scream.

"What? What?! I thought you meant— but then— When?!"

Ana laughed with delight. Ely had shot those questions in rapid succession, her tone shrill. It was a minor miracle that she hadn't lost control of the car, as Ely expressed some of her shock by shaking the wheel back and forth. It echoed the movement of Ely shaking someone— Ana— by the shoulders.

"Ana María Lira Gutiérrez," Ely said. "What the hell happened?"

"I think Liam and I decided to give our rel— a potential relationship— to give this thing a chance."

"When the fuck did that happen? We talked early today and you didn't say anything!"

"Okay, first of all, we don't always talk about that stuff and rarely in detail. Second of all—" Ana began, but she got distracted by a text notification.

She checked it right away and butterflies took flight in her stomach at seeing Liam as the sender.

Liam: According to my calcs, you made it home already. Hope it was a good flight. Call later?

Ana: Yes to all :) Ely
is driving me home.

Liam: Say hi from me.
Did you tell her yet?

Ana: Yes. She's freaking
out

Liam: good

"Was that Liam? Did he send an *I miss you already* text? Please tell me he's cheesy."

Ana laughed. "I don't think he's that cheesy, I'm afraid. But yeah, it was him. I'll talk to him later. He says hi, by the way."

"Cute. So?" Ely insisted. "What happened? What made you change your mind?"

"A mix of things, I guess," Ana shrugged. "I was packing and we were talking. I was panicking because I was leaving and didn't want to lose him— I almost messed up, Ely, but he said he didn't think of me as a friend; that I was something else to him. Then I lost it. And did something about it."

"That you're something else to him? What does that even mean?"

"I don't know. We didn't talk much after—" Ely snickered. Ana grinned and wrinkled her nose. "It was so... he took my hand with such tenderness, like he wanted more but he wasn't going to ask for it. I couldn't lie and tell him we should be friends, not when I also wanted something different."

"So you kissed him."

Ana bit her lip, flashes of the moment going through her mind: the feeling of his lips on hers, his warm breath against her skin, the intensity in his eyes. The way he had taken the lead after she kissed him, as if he'd just been waiting for permission and knew exactly what he wanted; how to get it.

"I did."

"Oh my God, Ana. You kissed Liam McMillan."

"Do you think I shouldn't have? Do you think that maybe I should have had the actual conversation we still need to have, ask how exactly are we supposed to make this work—"

"No. All you did that month you were together was talk and it took you nowhere. Also I know how your mind works; if you'd stopped to think you'd've fallen into a trap of your own thoughts. It's what you do, isn't it? Overthink things and avoid actually doing until it's gone. So kissing is way better than words in this case. It's a clear sign of where things could go— nothing platonic. Besides, letting Liam McMillan give you an orgasm with his fingers is a good idea in every scenario."

Ana laughed. "Stop using his full name."

"I'm using it for effect. Remember when we went to see *Love, Never* in the theater?"

Scenes from the movie came to her: Liam's smile and green eyes in a close up, his toned up body as he undressed for the protagonist.

"Yes," Ana sighed.

"Okay. That's the guy we're talking about."

"How did this even happen," Ana asked in wonder.

"There must be good gods out there, and they're smiling down on you."

She sighed. "What the hell are we going to do? I don't even know when I'm seeing Liam next."

"Is that what's worrying you, then? You're not going to see each other for a while. Long distance is tough, especially in the beginning."

Ana mulled over Ely's words, fighting the nerves settling in her stomach. Out of all of her worries, she hadn't considered that one yet. He had often said how his schedule made it difficult to stay in touch with people. Would they overcome that very basic challenge? On top of everything else?

"I'm sorry, I don't mean to make you worry," Ely added, her tone softening, matching the change in mood.

"No, it's fine. I think I need to trust that he meant it when he said we'll figure it out. That he meant that he wants something with me."

"Yes, you should. There are no flags here for you to doubt him."

"Diana doesn't want this. Coulton doesn't seem to care," Ana said. "So not as bad professionally as I feared, but still something to think about. I don't know how future projects could be affected."

"Why does Diana get a say? Or Coulton?"

"She's my agent. She thinks this can go badly for me."

"What do you think?"

"I can see it happening— way too clearly. The paps, we know they're bad. Also, if anything happens, it'd be easier to erase me from the industry than erasing Liam. Not to mention the fans. It's really scary."

"Talk to Liam. It's him you should be discussing this all with. Besides me, of course."

"I know."

"And don't you dare look for news online. I'll monitor things and let you know only on a must-know basis. Better to wipe your memory clean of their existence, okay?"

———

After Ely left her at home, Ana set up her traveling equipment in her editing room. She made copies of all the audiovisual files, starting with the video of them in the swimming pool when he'd tried to teach her to float. When they'd almost kissed.

She watched the scene for the tenth time. She'd probably do it again and again, studying his face closely each time, trying to find the moment he decided to try to kiss her. She got shivers each time.

> **Ana**: I'm at home now
> but I have to go get
> groceries and stuff.
> After that I'll be home
> for the rest of the evening,
> if you want to call

She was at the grocery store when she got a reply.

> **Liam**: Sounds good.
> I'll call you when I'm
> packing

Was it strange that she felt relief at the menial exchange?

Evening fell. She sat at the editing table watching some of her other favorite scenes— their late night conversation about fears, stargazing and almost-cuddling under the blanket— when Liam's call lit up her phone.

"Hey," she said, accepting his video call, not bothering to try to look cool and unaffected. She smiled at him with every ounce of the excitement she felt.

"Hey. Wow, do I like your smile."

She laughed. "I like yours, too."

"Can you talk?"

Ana didn't recognize the background behind him; it was his bedroom, which was the only place in his house she had never seen.

"Yeah. I was organizing some of the video files from the last few weeks."

He arched an eyebrow. "When do you think you're going to have something to show me? I do have to check for any scenes I may need to veto."

She pursed her lips and pulled them to the side, but a flutter of amusement softened her eyes. "Depends on whether you're willing to veto scenes based on a rough draft, or advanced draft."

"What gets us in the same place the soonest?"

Yep, butterflies were a common occurrence now. "Are you flirting with me?"

"Yes. I hope it's obvious." He sat on his bed, its big headboard framed by dark wood, with a deep blue, tufted fabric body. "It's really bugging me that you're not here."

"I want to be there. I keep looking around and having a hard time recognizing my apartment."

"We'll make it happen. We'll be together again. And until then, all I'm going to be thinking about is how different things might have been, had you let me kiss you in the pool that day. We'd've had a lot more time... we could have done so much more."

"Sure, that could have been great but... then we wouldn't have had today. I liked surprising you."

His eyes wrinkled at the corners. "I need to ask... what made you change your mind?"

He wasn't teasing her, this time. His voice was soft and tinted with amazement, as if he was still trying to put the pieces together.

Holding the phone at eye level, she looked out of her window into the parking space below, the concrete wet. She hadn't realized it was raining.

"I guess... the way you looked, what you said, the way you held my hand... I had to stop lying to myself. I knew that if I didn't do something about it I'd regret it."

His voice dropped low. "God. I'm really, really upset that we're far right now," he said, his voice husky. "I want to kiss you again."

"I want to kiss you, too. It was a good kiss."

"Oh? Tell me more." He dropped back to lay on the bed, holding the phone above him.

She chortled. "I will not." She got up from her chair and went to the kitchen, getting a glass of water. "When do you think we'll see each other?"

"How soon 'till you have the rough draft?"

"A month if I really rush." Glass in hand, she sat on her couch. "Typically the rough-rough version of editing is six weeks to two months. But whatever I show you then is far from final, and it'll definitely be crap."

"A month? Two? I don't want to wait that long."

"Me neither, if we can see each other earlier than that at all. When are you back from the press tour?"

"I fly out tomorrow. One week in the US and Toronto, Vancouver. One week in Europe: London, Edinburgh, Paris, Berlin. I think I'm going to Rome, too."

She shook her head. "That sounds intense."

"It's actually a short one," he said, lifting a shoulder.

"Will we have time to chat while you're traveling?"

"I'll find time. I want to see you. Talk to you." He turned to his side. She could see a window behind him, looking out to the gym on his patio.

She nodded. "Me, too. How often do you think we'll be able to? You said that your schedule makes it impossible to stay in touch with people."

A corner of his lips turned down. "I want to think this is different. I can't justify calling Logan or my parents for five minutes here and there, or a couple of times a day, or even every other day. I can't say, *hey, Logan, just eating a sandwich and thinking of you. What's going on over there?*"

She laughed. "I mean, you could. I say that to Ely all the time."

"Right. I guess Logan and I never quite got to that level."

"But you're hoping to with me?"

"Exactly. The way I see it, if you're okay with quick catch ups while I'm away, I think that'll be doable even with my ridiculous schedule. And we can text a lot, as if we just kept our conversation going. I've never really tried something like that, but... we can see what happens."

"And seeing each other?"

He sighed. "I'm counting on managing with a couple of days at a time in between projects. It's not ideal, but until my contracts slow down, I don't know what else to do."

She nodded, biting her lips. "You've been thinking about it."

"Of course. Every minute since you left. I want to do everything I can."

She nodded again.

"Maybe after I'm back from the tour I can escape for a weekend," he added. "We can meet somewhere."

"Yeah, that sounds good."

"So are we on the same page? You want to see where this goes? You and me?" His voice had been clear and open, comfortable with the vulnerable conversation. She admired that of him, how often he could unlock and say what he felt.

"Yes. I want that, too."

"Then this can work." He frowned. "One more thing. Are you worried about what they're going to say?"

"Who?"

"The paps. Fans. TCA."

"Yes."

"Is there any way I can make this easier on you?"

"I don't know, but I'd like us to work it out together."

"Deal."

———

Over the next several days, Ana found a comforting rhythm of communication with Liam. They texted and sent pictures to each other and, if Liam could find any 5 minutes all to himself, he called her. They'd decided that since his schedule held the most strain, packed with being dragged around for interviews, he would be the one to try to reach out whenever he could. Whenever Ana was free to answer, she would.

Perhaps because they had spent a month talking before doing anything about their feelings, it had been effortless to switch from face-to-face to phone. They talked about anything and everything, as if they were still at the cabin at the beach, and often their calls ended with one of them saying that they wished they were together, again.

Liam called her one night when she went out for dinner with Ely, Christina, and Maggie. She went out to the street and took the call. They laughed about how he'd been so tired he'd almost tripped on his way to his hotel room, how he had lost track of time and space after countless junket interviews, but he thought he was in Edinburgh because he really liked the view from his window. His brain had stopped working properly, too fried and too bored to know for sure. They held the call while he prepared for bed after a party he hadn't wanted to attend and she kept him company until he fell asleep, all of 15 minutes after starting the call.

She returned to her table with a smile on her face.

"Someone's smitten," Maggie said. "That had to be the call of someone you're seeing. Those heart eyes are broadcasting it."

"It was… someone I'm kinda seeing, yes." Ana's breath quickened; she wasn't prepared to tell anyone else but Ely about Liam yet.

"Give us details," Christina demanded. "First you fail to let us know you'll be working with Liam Mc-Frigging-Millan— thank you for that, *again*—

"— I didn't tell you on purpose because of the privacy clauses in the contract—"

Christina continued without acknowledging Ana's words. "—then you ask us to make no comment and to ask no questions about him or the project when you returned—"

"— but then I was posting about the project on my social media so I decided to text you—"

"— you owe us some juicy news and I guess your dating life counts."

Ely snickered to her side. Ana did not look her way. The waiter came with a big plate of loaded nachos and they all waited until he left.

"How did you meet him?" Maggie sipped from her drink. "The guy you're dating, not Liam Mc-Frigging-Millan. It must have just happened; you were on this latest project for a while and you were single before that, right?"

"Why do you have to call Liam that?" Ana complained.

"Because he's one of the top actors of the world, looks as amazing as a love-fool as he does in a space suit catching bad guys in zero gravity; because you *worked* with him and have shared nothing. The shock will come out somehow." Christina cheered with her glass as if her explanation had been bullet proof.

"Not all of us are friends with him, you know," Maggie added.

"You should share more about the experience." Ely arched an eyebrow and Ana fought the temptation to kick her leg under the table. "Maybe then they wouldn't call him anything other than Liam."

Ana shook her head, ignoring her best friend.

"Or," Christina insisted, "you could take our extremely generous offer and tell us about this person you're dating instead."

"Right." Ana gulped. "To be honest we haven't labeled it yet so I'm technically in limbo, I guess?"

"I don't think so," Ely argued. "I'd say you're closer to labels than limbo. You're trying even if you're long distance and I think that's a sign of actually making an effort. Although if you haven't talked about exclusivity, maybe you should. Define the structure you two want, so you know what to expect."

Ana cringed. Ely didn't give anything identifiable away, but still managed to challenge her. So very typical of her best friend.

"Oooh." Maggie's eyes opened wide. "Long distance? Did you meet him while away, then?"

"Yes."

Christina got a serving of nachos onto her plate. "Long distance can be romantic or it can be the death of a romance. How's it working?"

"It's tough. He's traveling a lot right now so even if we lived in the same city, we'd have to contend with that."

"Where was he calling you from, now?" Maggie took some nachos for herself as well.

"Edinburgh."

"It's really late there. It must be love, then," Maggie added.

"Do you have any pictures of him?" Christina sipped from her drink before digging into her food.

Ana froze. She should have expected the question. Somehow she had forgotten quite how curious her friends were.

"We could find some," Ely said and Ana, knowing her friend well, knew she meant it as a tease. Ana glared at Ely with a minor scowl.

"Does he have an Instagram?" Maggie asked.

"I don't know about that." Ana reached out for her glass. Her gin and tonic cooled her throat, even as warmth rushed to her face. "I'm not sure how he'd feel about me showing you pictures of him."

"Is he super private then? Or is he hiding the relationship? That's such a red flag."

"Look, all we've said is that we want to see where this goes. That's it. I don't think it means we're in a serious relationship—"

"But you're in a relationship of some kind. Don't treat it otherwise or it's destined to fail," Ely insisted.

"You're acting weird, Ana," Christina said. "Are you embarrassed by him? Is that it?"

Ely laughed hard and Ana couldn't help but chuckle. She couldn't imagine who'd be embarrassed by dating Liam. She could hate all the risks involved, but shame over Liam was not the problem.

"Can I tell them? Please, Ana." Ely put her hand on Ana's forearm. "It's not possible to keep this a secret. You know I'm right."

Ana's stomach swirled with indecision. She trusted Christina and Maggie, but what if Liam preferred to keep it private? Would that be the red flag that Maggie had talked about? Whatever her relationship with Liam, it would always be different from other relationships. It would be scrutinized, written about. She couldn't treat it casually. It had to involve a lot of intentionality and this was perhaps one of those times.

Ana could see Maggie's and Christina's eyes shifting between her and Ely, back and forth, wide open.

"If the relationship works, they'll have to know," Ely said. "Are you hesitating in case it doesn't work? Is that the problem?"

"Is he someone famous?" Maggie said, making a wild guess. "You were in LA, you signed with a big representation agency. You were out and about with someone everyone knows, so you might have brushed shoulders with other celebrities. You must have met him there, either at the agency and he's famous or works with famous people, which would make it harder for us to find him... but not impossible."

"Okay, I need to know now." Christina grabbed her phone but didn't unlock it yet. "There's something big here."

"I can't pretend I'm not going to do a quick search online before bed tonight, I'm sorry," Maggie said. "I'm not gonna look too hard but—"

Ana stared at Ely with panicked eyes, asking for help without words.

"We should be thankful none of us are interested in tabloids," Ely said. "I think it's better if you tell them. They'll eventually find out, anyway. Would you rather they hear it from you or find out from a grocery store magazine cover?"

Ely was right but Ana's vocal cords refused to activate. Recognizing the problem, Ely sighed and talked directly to Christina and Maggie.

"Go to Twitter. Check the hashtag, mcana. M-C-A-N-A."

"Is that how you're going to tell them?!" Ana exclaimed, putting her elbows on the table and covering her face with her hands. Christina and Maggie were probably already reading tweets about her and Liam, and they would likely—

"Oh my God!" Maggie almost screamed, catching the attention of other people in the restaurant.

"Shh!" Ely commanded.

"You're dating *him*?!" Christina managed in a half-whisper, half-screech.

"And he just called you from Edinburgh?!" Maggie added, voice shrill. "*Liam and Ana will make such cute babies #mcana. Another, I wonder what #mcana are up to right now. I can't, Ana. I can't.*"

"There's also some horrible ones." Christina's voice came back to normal. "Wow. People can be mean."

"Yeah, don't read those out loud," Ely said.

"In fact, don't read any of it out loud, please," Ana begged. "It's too weird. And please, please don't tell anyone."

"Like that'd go well," Maggie said. "Hi, did you know my college friend is dating Liam McMillan? Yes, the Hollywood actor. The one that is in that movie franchise, yes. The one on your daughter's poster, yes."

"Ugh." Ana took her face away from the mask of her hands, but let her head hang back from her shoulders, her eyes closed. "Please, don't."

"I can't believe it," Christina said. "It wasn't just work between you two, apparently."

"So no one else knows?" Maggie continued to look at her phone from time to time, continuing to scroll and read.

"Well, you two and Ely. A section of the internet, of course. And our agents suspect."

"This is so weird," Christina said. "You're dating Liam McMillan."

"She lived with him for almost a month, too." Ely brought her fingers to her mouth in a chef's kiss. "Epic."

"You *lived* with him? For the documentary?" Christina asked. "Not just interviews? I have so many questions."

"Not just interviews. We were together 24/7," Ana confirmed while throwing daggers at Ely. Ely only smirked and winked. "I currently have over a hundred hours of never-seen footage of Liam in my home."

"And if any of it disappears, we know who to blame," Ely joked. Maggie flapped at Ely's arm.

"If you went from not knowing each other to living together for a month and it went well, then there's a high chance this can work out." Christina finally locked her phone and put it back on the table, screen down. "Unless it's just lust. And long distance is a big problem."

"And paparazzi," Maggie added, evidently finding some of that on Twitter. "This is terrible. They're so nasty."

"Don't fill her head with anxiety, c'mon," Ely said. "Let her enjoy what's happening with Liam. He seems like a cool guy and he seems to be crushing hard on our friend here."

"And if his rom-coms are any indication, he's a great kisser and has the bod of a god," Maggie said as she put her phone on the table. "So she really should get to enjoy it."

"I'm sure we all agree that Ana, here, is a goddess herself, and I don't mean only her looks," Ely argued. "He's lucky she likes him like that."

"How are you feeling?" Maggie asked. "This is… huge. I can't imagine, with the tabloids and stuff…"

"I am trying to ignore that for now. Things with Liam are good and I don't want to think about what they're saying about us. I want to pretend we're just two people who like each other, for as long as I can."

"Totally!" Christina said. "That's smart. Better not to look."

"I'm helping her with that." Ely finally put food on her plate. "She's under strict instructions— no social media scrolling."

"We have your back," Maggie said. "We're rooting for you."

Chapter 18

DUE TO LIAM'S SCHEDULE, they continued to limit communications to texts and one or two short video calls a day. It took four days to find the time to have a conversation that went beyond discussing their day.

"Where are you tonight?" Ana tracked the little changes in his expression on the screen, the way his green eyes sparkled, or his lips stretched on a smile.

"I really should share my calendar with you."

"Maybe one day, but I like having you tell me."

"I like that you want to know." He changed the camera to the front lenses, showing her a view out of his window. "I'm back in London. I have a couple last-minute things here then we'll be flying back to North America."

"When's that?"

He changed the camera back to him. "A couple of days."

"Any big plans once you're back in LA?"

"Mostly I want to catch up on sleep," he laughed. His face softened as he added, "Figure out when I can go see you."

"Yes, please." She smiled. "I can't wait until we're in the same room again. We could be cuddling right now."

He sighed. "That would be great. I could be catching up on sleep using you as a pillow."

"Is that what you fantasize about?"

"Among other things."

She laughed. "Well, let's really think about how to make that happen, then."

"On it."

"Also, I've been meaning to tell you. When I went out with my friends the other night?"

"Yeah?"

"Thing is, we talked a bit about you."

He arched an eyebrow. "In what way?"

"It unfolded quite unexpectedly, really. They assumed— correctly— that the call I answered from you that day was from someone I'm seeing. Why else would I interrupt a night out with friends? They asked me about it and I didn't want to lie. I tried to be vague, too, but that didn't work very well. At the end I ended up telling them it was you. They know about us— from me, not from rumors on social media. I'm sorry."

"Why are you sorry?"

"I... well, good question. I guess it's because we haven't really talked about where we're at, how private we're keeping things, if we're looking into something open or exclusive or..."

"Right." Even through the reduced size of her phone screen she could see him rub the back of his neck. "I suppose we should talk about that. I thought I might wait until we were together in-person again, but maybe best to do it now."

"Yeah, it probably is. Questions are already coming up and I'd like us to know where exactly we stand, so that when my friends or my parents ask, I know what to say. Mom and Dad ask me periodically if I have a boyfriend, so I want to be prepared."

"Boyfriend?" The spark in his eyes had humor and something else.

She half-cringed, half-smiled. "God, I don't remember what the cool way to do this is. I've been out of the dating pool for too long."

"How about we keep it simple? Let's share what we want and see where we're at. No games, just honesty."

"Okay." She took a calming breath. "I'll start with something I think we have in common: even though it's hard to know where this is going, I'd like to give it a chance. I'm in it. I jumped in, and I'm not going to quit until I've given it a fair chance."

He grinned. "Yes, I'm there with you. If this seems to be working out— and it is— then I'm not interested in a fling."

"Same." Lightness filled up her chest. "If it feels good between us— and it does— then this is meant to be a real start to something that matters to us."

"I like how you said that."

"Okay, another thing. What do you think about keeping it private?" She watched his eyes, seeking as much of his truth as she could gather.

"Private in what way? I don't want to hide it but, well, I half-expected you would." He frowned.

"Me? From my friends?"

"No, in general. I thought that maybe you wouldn't want people knowing we're seeing each other, because of your worries over your professional reputation."

His words trickled down her consciousness, clinking against different walls in her body and mind. While that fear hadn't changed, choosing to be with Liam couldn't be reduced to that one question.

"But what's the alternative?" she asked. "I already made up my mind. I want to be with you. Really, the only thing I can do is keep working and creating, and try not to think about what could happen if someone judges me for being with you. I'll keep fighting to do what I love."

"I hope you know, even if it doesn't work out— if we discover we're not good together— I would still do what I can to help you. I know I'm the safest one here. So, if you want to keep it private, I think I can live with it, for now, until you feel safer."

Her heart skipped a beat at his offer, but she shook her head. "I don't want that kind of privacy. I don't want to make it a secret. I want to be able to tell my parents, my friends, and anyone else who might believe me." She chuckled. "That's different than publicizing it, right?"

"I'm all for that. I'd like to go out with you, be together... but we don't have to discuss it with anyone else. We won't let it be used for PR. I just want it to be about you and me."

"I'm good with that. Let's ignore the noise."

He smiled, slow. "Sounds great."

Her grin echoed his. Words spilled out of her. "I want to kiss you right now. We haven't kissed enough."

"Exclusively?" he asked, a spark in his eyes, a slight curve to his eyebrow. After a bit, he added, "You said you also wanted to talk about exclusivity."

She nodded, her stomach tensing. "When we see each other... well, I expect us to have sex... if you want."

"If I want it? If?" he scoffed. "I get hard every time we talk."

She laughed.

"If you don't mind me saying that," he added.

"I don't, of course I don't. I guess I'm surprised— you didn't let me touch you that time. You seemed okay with just touching me."

His smile grew devious. "I'm glad to see you've thought about me touching you."

A heavy pull appeared in her lower belly. The fine hair in her arms stood on end at the rawness in his voice.

"So you meant it," she said. "It's not that you don't want it, but that you didn't want to rush it."

"I want it, Ana. I want all of you. I want it so much that I'm having a hard time not losing myself into the fantasy of us together in bed. All the blood is gone from my brain and I can't focus on much else."

Her breath came fast and shallow. She was ready to lose herself in the moment, too.

"Damn, you're beautiful," he said.

She didn't know what he saw that made him say that, but it made gravity heighten its pull within her. She bit her lip, heart drumming fast in her chest.

He groaned. His eyes looked hungry. "I've waited a long time to find someone I really, really wanted to get into bed with. I'm going to take my time with you."

"Take your time... but don't make me wait."

"I'll tear your clothes off, if you let me."

"Liam..."

"I want you. Just you. I've been celibate for over a year because I didn't want more of the same. I don't want to do it for fun, for the release. I want something different. Exclusivity is good for me, if it's good for you."

"Monogamy is good with me," she said. Her voice sounded thin in her ears, the intensity of her feelings getting stuck in her throat. "I haven't had sex with anyone since Dave. I don't need to start finding random partners now."

"Then it's you and me, Ana. I'll show you just what that means to me as soon as I can be with you again."

———

The next day, Ana woke up to an email from Diana. It included a link to a video.

Hi Ana,

Watch this. Liam McMillan talked about you in an interview.
You said you're not involved with him, and neither this interview nor the pictures we previously discussed are enough to assume things have changed, but I will speak as if they have.
If you two are together in any romantic capacity, whether he tells you this is casual or he's telling you he wants commitment, I want you to know I understand where you're coming from in taking a chance with him. He's one of the hottest actors in Hollywood right now— both in looks and in success. From the little he did say about you and the documentary, especially considering how he said it, he may have taken an interest in you. It doesn't change the fact that I still believe it's best if you let this go. It's likely not going to work; few relationships last long in this industry. What happens then? You'll easily be treated as a pariah. Women are the ones to be treated unfairly, trust me on this. I'm trying to look out for you.

Ana's chest darkened as she read the email; she had to breathe in slow, deliberate breaths to clear her mind from the surge of nerves wanting to take hold of her thoughts. She pushed every worry away and clicked the link in the email.

The interview kicked off with a shot of Liam, an easy smile on his face, charisma exuding from every pore. How amazing, that the man on the screen had a real life, a real personality different from this show persona. And she knew it well enough to know the difference.

"Thanks so much for chatting with us today," the interviewer said.

"Of course. Glad to be here."

"I wanted to start with a small tangent. I heard that you've just wrapped up the filming of a different kind of project, haven't you? A documentary."

"Yes, I did. It turned out to be one of the best projects I've been involved with."

"Tell us more. How different was it from filming *Space Bureau III*?"

"Where do I begin?" he joked, his best professional smile.

"No shirtless scenes?"

They both laughed.

"Actually, yes, some shirtlessness as a lot of it happened at the beach."

"Well, that'll be great publicity right there. Do you think the director did it on purpose?"

She saw it— the slightest shift of his body, a subtle change in his smile. Tingling traveled through her chest. This felt so much better than the tightness she'd experienced while reading Diana's email.

"Now that you say that, she may have," Liam said on the video, with that teasing smirk she'd learned to enjoy.

"You two have been rumored to be a couple. Do you think it impacted how the documentary was filmed? It must have been difficult to avoid influencing the material."

"We became friends while recording but never got involved romantically, so things remained professional for the film." Liam seemed serious on the screen but Ana smiled, because he spoke the truth even if they were involved now. "The type of documentaries that Ana— the director— creates require so much intimacy that growing close is almost inevitable— and it's necessary, really, to create a film like this. I think Ana is honestly amazing, and this film is going to give a raw look into some of the hardest things about being an actor in Hollywood. That's the material, and I'm really looking forward to seeing the final cut."

"That sounds great! Have you watched *Space Bureau III*'s final cut yet?"

"I haven't, no. The script was fun, though, and the director was great to work with. *Space Bureau III* is a great sequel," Liam said, easily following the change in topic.

Ana finished watching the interview and closed her laptop. She wasn't sure when he'd recorded this interview, but it fit perfectly with what they'd discussed the night before. He'd handled that like a pro— which he was.

She grabbed her phone and texted Liam.

> **Ana**: call me when you can? I saw an interview where you talked about me.

He returned the call by video an hour later.

"Hey. What interview did you see?" he asked, jumping straight into the conversation as if they'd been talking about it already.

"The one where you talked about the documentary and me directing you to be shirtless."

He smiled. "Yeah. I think I did pretty good? Even though I couldn't help getting a bit flirty just saying your name."

She chuckled. "God. You're a terrible flirt."

"C'mon. The interviewer suggested you wanted me to be shirtless. I know for a fact you enjoyed it. Just thinking about that got me going."

"Liam," she laughed. "The beach was your idea."

It was his turn to laugh. "So did you finally get those news alerts for me? How come you saw that?"

"I did no such thing. Diana sent me the link."

"Oh," he said, his tone changing. "What did Diana say?"

"She's insisting we shouldn't see each other."

"Don't listen to her. Fuck, she's really grating on my nerves."

"I'm not listening to her. I won't engage with her when she talks about us."

"Good. This is about you and me. So maybe don't tell her I'm trying to go see you this weekend."

She gasped. "What?"

He grinned. "Yeah. I had a lightbulb moment earlier. What would you say if I bribed the pilot tomorrow and got him to drop me off at your airport? I know it's short notice but I got the itinerary for the flight and I realized—"

"Yes," she said, without thinking twice.

He released a gust of air. "Good. That's great. I'll see you tomorrow, then. I'll bribe as many people as I need to."

"Let me know as soon as you can what time I need to be at the airport."

"I will. But I suppose that means..." He frowned. "Ana, I think I need to ruin the mood a bit. I want to talk about Dave."

Her eyes opened wide. "Why?!"

"'Cause you trusted him, and I need you to trust me, too."

"I... I do."

"No, listen. I remember what you told me. That you'd trusted Dave and he lied. Told you that he had no other partners though he did. Well, I'm going to ask you to trust me on something. I got an exam done a while ago. Everything's fine, I don't have anything, but the test's old— I didn't get one again since I wasn't having sex. I haven't had time to go to the doctor, so... you're going to have to believe me that nothing has changed since that time. And that I really haven't slept with anyone since then."

"Right." Her breathing changed, her lungs working faster.

"Even if we use condoms, they don't protect against everything."

She pressed her lips together. He was right, it was a lot of trust. If he was lying about that, this could backfire pretty quickly... for either or both of them. She wasn't the only one taking a risk on this.

"Liam... you're trusting me as much. I haven't gotten a recent test either, and I can't prove I have an IUD."

His frown remained. "But I... I'm okay with that. My therapist said— when I talked to her about trust— she said that trust comes from being met where we are with honesty, acceptance, and consistency over time. I've known you for a little less than two months, I know that, but— I'm there, Ana. I trust you— I think I want you this badly because I trust you. I want it all with you because I do. So take your time to get there, I can wait. I know it's different for you. But if we don't want to wait to have sex, you're going to have to trust me in this. I know it's a lot."

Despite the fast pace of her heart, her lips curled up. "Liam, the fact that you're talking about this... that you're thinking about this, for me... I wouldn't have dared getting into this relationship with you if I didn't trust you, too."

His face relaxed. He gave her a soft smile. "Glad to hear that. Means a lot to me."

"I know it's not the most responsible thing, but if the trust is there and there is consistency in our stories and we're having this conversation so openly... maybe it's okay."

"I'm good with this. I've spent a lot of time wondering how I'd know I trust someone. Now that I'm here... it's new, and wonderful... and so clear." He laughed. "I'm going to have to tell that to Dr. Linda."

She smiled. "How far do we want to take this? Because, since I have an IUD..."

She saw the exact moment he got what she meant. He gulped. "We don't need condoms."

Later, when she responded to Diana's email, she made sure to word it in such a way that she appeared appreciative, but made no commitment to listen to her advice.

Chapter 19

F RIDAY

Ana parked at the airport with a heady mix of anxiety and anticipation gripping her gut, fifteen minutes ahead of schedule. She rushed her steps; she didn't want him to wait for her and end up being recognized by random people. Not to mention how badly she wanted to take him home as fast as possible. There were clothes that needed to be torn away.

She stood within clear sight of the arrivals gate and watched people trickle out. One p.m. came and went and, for a little while, she didn't think much of the fact he hadn't shown up yet. At one-twenty, she lost her cool.

Ana: have you landed yet?

Another five minutes and she hadn't heard from him. She navigated her phone again, double checking the strength of her signal and refreshing notifications. Hyperalert, she lifted her eyes upon hearing the arrivals doors open one more time. After almost half an hour of checking the doors automatically, she hadn't expected him to be there— but there he was, wearing a baseball cap and sunglasses, carrying a bag. Somehow taller than she remembered, wearing a The Police shirt and faded jeans, and melting all tension from her with his mere presence.

He must have seen her, because he made his way to her without hesitation, smiling in her direction.

She walked to him with slow steps. Once they were within reach of each other, she meant to say hello but didn't get to; he put a hand behind her head and brought her in for a kiss. A really good kiss.

She softened further, taking a step closer to him and leaning against him, letting his very real, very solid body support her. She stayed in place once he broke the kiss, eyes closed and almost dizzy. He kissed the tip of her nose; the gesture made her smile, and she opened her eyes.

"Hey," he said in a breath. "Sorry about the delay. We had to wait around for permission to land and taxi and the pilot had already asked for no phone communications. It happens when itineraries change like this."

"Okay. Nice shirt."

He grinned. "Thank you. I bought it in England. Made me think of you."

The back of her neck tingled. Glancing around them, she found someone in a nearby airport shop that stared at them. "We should go."

She grabbed his hand and they walked out of the building. Once in her car, she took the long road home, including a long stretch of Veterans Parkway. She pointed at the endless mixture of shops and chain restaurants lining it, spanning the entire twin cities area. She told him about the lively night scene of her city, where bars got flooded with college students every night.

"It's a pity we won't get to go out much," he said. "I'll have to take your word for it."

She kept quiet, unsure whether he meant they had to stay inside because of his fame... or because of how busy they would be with each other.

"I can't believe I didn't ask, but... when are you flying back to LA?" she said instead. Much safer to discuss that while her attention divided between him and driving.

"Monday morning. I have meetings on Monday afternoon."

A brief silence filled her car, which he soon broke.

"You should have seen their faces," Liam told her with a chuckle. "They were so confused when we stopped here for fuel, only I actually went off the plane and said goodbye."

"I'm just glad we have the weekend together. We needed this."

They parked at her place and made their way up the three flights of stairs. She took her keys out of her pocket, nerves coming back to her stomach, but for altogether different reasons.

***

Liam didn't remember the last time he felt so eager to see someone. It was an old, unfamiliar, but welcomed feeling.

They made it to her place, an indistinct beige building; a wide structure no more than 5 stories high. Her apartment was on the third floor; she opened the door and went in, standing to the side to let him in. She closed the door behind him, toeing off her shoes. He copied her. Taking two steps into the middle of the room, he dropped the bag at his side and studied the small living room. He took off his baseball cap and sunglasses, dropping them on top of his bag.

He finally turned to face her. "So do I get a tour or—"

He didn't get to finish the sentence. She had taken two steps to him, hooked her arms around his neck, and kissed him.

He responded in an instant. He wrapped his arms around her and held her close. Letting himself drown in the moment, he lifted her off her feet.

"Okay?" she said, almost nonsensically, but he knew what she meant.

"Okay," he nodded, before kissing her again.

Her smile— striking— hit him right in the gut. She put her hands on his shoulders and got him to drop her on the floor. She took his hand and pulled to guide him, he was sure, to her bedroom. He wet his lips, slowly. She bit hers.

The darkness in the short hallway gave way to her bright room. His quick glance around picked only a few details: a big, colorful painting above the bed, some functional furniture, and not much more. His eyes sought hers again as she stopped a step away from her neatly made bed.

He stood in front of her. She pulled at his shirt to bring him to her lips and kiss him; her hands eager, they ran up his chest to his neck, then to his hair, then under his shirt. She dragged her fingers through the ridges of his abs and pecs, and he stopped the kissing only so that he could take off his shirt— he wanted more of her hands on him. As soon as he was free of it, she kissed the center of his chest, lips above his heart, which skipped a beat in response. She looked up at him again with a flame in her eyes, and raised up to the balls of her feet, wanting to find his lips with hers again. He obliged her, and saw her smile as they kissed, before he closed his eyes.

———

Liam's heart beat fast under her fingers and it made her breathless. She bit his bottom lip and pulled, needing to distract herself from the lack of air, to gain some leverage. He wrapped his arms around her again, before dropping his hands to take hold of her ass. He pulled her hips flush against him; she could feel his erection on her lower belly. Her lungs melted with the heat it sparked inside of her.

She let her hands drop to his pants and hooked her fingers around the waistband. She tugged and took a step back, until she felt the mattress against her knees.

"You're way overdressed," he complained in a rumbly voice, as his hands found the bottom of her shirt and pulled it up. She lifted her arms for him to get rid of it; from the corner of her eye, she saw him throw it somewhere, she didn't know or care where. He grabbed the naked flesh of her waist with strong hands but it didn't seem enough for him. He slid his hands under her jeans to take hold of her skin.

He turned them in place and sat on the bed, bringing her closer to him. Guiding her to stand in between his legs, he kissed the center of her chest, then her breasts over the thin fabric of her bra. Her hands continued to swim in his hair, messing it up, her eyes drawn to every one of his movements. Never stopping his kissing, he unbuttoned her jeans and pulled them down her legs; she kicked them away, took away her socks, and came back to standing up in front of him.

He stared at her, eyes roaming all over her body. He grabbed her at the waist but held her slightly back— only enough distance for his lips to trail down the sensitive skin of her torso, down the center of chest, lower. He bit at the edge of her underwear and pulled, before letting go of it. It hit her with a soft slap. She gasped at the sensation.

"I've wanted to do this for weeks," he said, his hand following a path down the back of her thighs. "I'm glad you're wearing black.

I can pretend I'm finally peeling off that damn bikini. It's haunted my dreams."

She would have laughed, had she had the capacity for it.

His hands came up to unhook her bra; she helped him get rid of it. He cupped her breasts and, with apparent reverence, flicked at a nipple with his tongue. Her breathing hitched, he closed his lips and sucked around the puckered tip. As he switched sides, his eyes sought hers. The jade of them seemed to be lit from within, a kind of power that reached for something deep inside her and challenged her. She bit her lips in response, a feeble attempt to pace things and grab at control, to modulate the rising intensity of feeling. Arousal pooled at her core.

"Get on the bed," he asked in that deep, rumbly voice. With a shiver, she obliged.

He stood. She watched him unbutton and unzip his pants slowly, teasing her or prolonging the moment, she didn't know. He lowered them down, taking his underwear in the same movement, and getting rid of his socks.

He straightened and let her have her fill of him. He was magnificent, standing naked in front of her. From the look of him, he knew it.

"Come here," she said. He approached her slowly, prowling, a glint in his eye.

She rested on her elbows, waiting for him, captivated by his feral look. He climbed on the bed and crawled closer to her but, right before kissing her, he turned away. He nipped at her neck, nibbled on her collarbone. Her muscles seemed to fail her and she fell on the bed, his lips following her.

Her hands explored his body, fueled by greed, getting acquainted with his muscled shoulders, the curves of his arms and chest, the ridges of his toned waist. He made his way down her front, open kisses on her skin. He left soft bites at the base of her breasts. He continued on his downward path until he found the only piece of clothing between them. He kissed the lace and the triangle of fabric, and her body bucked. The warm breath of his low chuckle tickled her skin.

He sat back on bent knees. He hooked his fingers in her underwear and pulled it down her legs. With a hungry smile, he tossed it over his shoulder.

"I want you on me," she breathed. "In me."

He didn't move to her. Instead, he reached for one of her legs; he guided it to his shoulder, where he kissed the inside of her ankle.

"I've waited a long time to do this," he said, his voice rough. His lips traveled down her leg, slowly.

"In general, or with me?" she asked.

He kept her ankle on his shoulder; he braced her leg with an arm as he came down to her and devoured her mouth.

"Yes," he said, almost nonsensically, but somehow she understood his meaning. She wrapped his neck with her arms to keep him close as he bit her lip and soothed the spot with his tongue.

Her thoughts disappeared as he positioned himself between her legs, still not entering her, length to clit.

"Fuck, Liam," she moaned, hooking her free leg behind his thigh. "I need you."

"Not quite yet," he said with a rumbling, strained laugh, as he ground his erection against her tender, sensitive flesh.

A faint sound seized her throat at the intensity of sensation. His movement began slow, making sure to wake up every single nerve ending at her core. He gained momentum until his rhythm became unrelenting, constant, making her arousal climb up to unbearable. Their breath caught, their moans filled the room in unison. His head dropped to her neck, where his breathing teased the fine hairs with every exhale.

Ana had never been one to beg, but a desperate part of her brain said fuck it.

"Liam— I— just—" She didn't care that her voice had come out in a whimper. "Please."

He slowed down his movement again, bringing his lips to kiss the line of her jaw, nibble on her clavicles.

He shifted his weight to brace his legs on the bed, her leg still hooked around an elbow.

He changed the angle of his hips to get the tip of his length close to her opening. She didn't know she had closed her eyes until he brought her attention to it.

"Open your eyes," he said, soft command in his voice. She complied.

When their eyes locked, he pushed into her in a swift, long flex of his hips. She gasped. He whimpered. She willed her body to adapt to the size of him, he gave her the time. He must have felt her body relaxing, because he moved out and in again not a moment too soon, right when she had needed him to.

She brought her hands to his waist, her fingers asking for more with digging nails. His body knew hers already— he responded without hesitation. He thrust deeper, faster, completely letting go. His expression at once fierce and glazed with pleasure, their eyes never wavered as she approached the crest building inside of her.

An explosion of tension and sensation rocketed through her body, her climax catching her by surprise. A gasp caught in her throat; her back tensed into a sharp curve at his persistent pounding. Waves of pleasure rolled through her and she fell into him, around him.

"Fuck," he said as her trembling body slowed him down. "Ana."

When she returned to herself he rolled his hips in a measured rhythm, his head hanging in between his shoulders as if yielding to something. He shifted again; he hooked her free leg over his other arm, fully tilting her hips and opening her to him. He built speed again. Aftershocks still coursed through her, but her body and her heart had softened; his continuing, determined effort welcomed into her body, even as nerve endings awakened again, their hypersensitivity making her writhe.

His chest hovered close enough to hers that her breasts rubbed against his pecs, her nipples puckering up at the contact. His ragged breath filled the room; her own quickened again. Her hands came up to his biceps, then his shoulders, then his neck, then to the bed in a desperate move— she lifted her torso, needing to kiss him. She licked his bottom lip, thrust her tongue into his mouth, and moaned into him— he came with a shuddering force, a groan escaping him. One, two more thrusts and he released her legs, crumbling down onto her.

She smiled against his temple, his heavy presence on top of her, his arms around her, the hard and sweet sounds of him making their way into her soul.

———

Ana turned her head to gaze at Liam, now laying on his back next to her. His face was in a soft smile as he caught his breath. She reached with the back of her hand to rub the skin around his navel, and a grin took over his features.

He let out a satisfied sigh. "Worth waiting for." He turned to his side, holding his head on his bent arm. "I'd say that you enjoyed it, too."

She grinned. "Oh, yeah? What tells you that?"

"Oh, you know." With his free hand, he ran the tips of his fingers back and forth on the sensitive skin of her belly. "The way you said *please*. How you moaned into my mouth."

"I'd say you enjoyed that, too."

"Yeah, I did." His fingers went up and down, up and down her torso. She shivered. "And it's kinda refreshing that you're not telling me it was mind-blowing, bone-shattering, best sex you've ever had—"

She laughed. "Not saying it wasn't."

"So it was?" His eyes twinkled, crinkling at the corners.

"Can't believe you're fishing for compliments."

"Is that what I'm doing?"

"Evidently," she replied, before using her hand to bring him to her for a slow, exploring kiss. "But I think it's healthy to make you guess a bit. It'll motivate you to try to do even better next time."

He laughed; the bed shook with the force of it. "Even better next time? Wow."

"That's the plan."

He leaned to kiss her neck. His breath titillated her skin as he followed a path down her body.

"I'm okay with the challenge." He settled between her legs and licked the tender, still-swollen flesh there. "It's only Friday."

"Show me what you can do," she replied before they tried again.

They kept it simple that night and ordered pizza.

"Thank god. I'm starving," he said.

"You exerted yourself, huh?"

He gave her a cheeky look as he reached for a slice. "Not really. I'm always hungry because I'm forced to starve all the time. And it takes a lot of energy to fuel my muscle mass."

They sat on her sofa, facing each other. Comfort wrapped the space in warmth, relief settling further within her. Two weeks apart had not changed a thing.

She rolled her eyes. "Sure. But in terms of starvation... I've never felt sorrier for you than I do right now."

Ana bit on a chunk of cheesy heaven.

"I'm sure you like the results, don't you?" He ate half of the slice in one bite, his eyes teasing. "Tell me what you think."

She wore yoga pants and a cut out shirt, no bra. He wore a thin tracksuit and a gray shirt; many of his clothes were currently in her washing machine.

"I do. But I'm sure I'd also enjoy some padding. I fully expect to find bruises on my inner thighs tomorrow."

"I'll take better care of your thighs, I promise." He grinned. "I like them too much to mistreat them, you know? And one day I won't have to push my body to its limits, but today is not the day. Principal photography is coming and my diet starts on Monday."

"Here, have another slice." She added one to his plate and he winked at her, his mouth full with the second half of his first slice. "One day, you won't have to diet and the only cardio you'll do is sex."

He laughed. "Oh, I might swim, too."

Before she could say anything, they were interrupted by the notification of an incoming message on Ana's phone. He checked his own as she unlocked hers and read her texts.

"It's Ely," Ana announced. "She's wondering if you're settling in nicely."

"That's nice. Say thanks from me, please."

"How do you feel about meeting her?" she asked as she typed a message back to Ely.

"I'd like that. She's close to you, and I think she'd be fun to spend time with."

"Maybe we could invite her over for brunch tomorrow."

Ana tossed her phone and reached for another slice of pizza. She glanced up at Liam, who had a deep wrinkle between his eyebrows. He stared at her but his eyes seemed glazed over, and he held his phone against his chest. Whatever was on his mind, it appeared to worry him.

"Are you really fine with seeing Ely?"

His eyes refocused on her and cleared up. His eyebrows relaxed.

"Yeah, brunch sounds really good."

She squinted at him. "I'll text her later."

He must have still been half-thinking of whatever nagged his brain, because he only nodded.

"What's going on?" she insisted.

He glanced at her again with furrowed eyebrows. "I want to tell you something."

"Sounds serious."

"I hope it isn't, but I'd feel better if I share this with you."

"Okay..." She chewed on her food slowly, waiting for him to speak.

He reached for another slice of pizza but left it on the plate next to him. His other hand scratched his eyebrow.

"Uh oh, you're scratching your eyebrow. Out with it," she said.

He let a chuckle out. "I don't know how to begin without sounding like an asshole."

"Just say it."

"I sometimes get suggestive pictures from people, inviting me to, you know... go out with them or just do as I please with them."

She had to force the mouthful of food down her throat. "What?!"

He unlocked his phone, scrolled and tapped on it, before giving it to Ana.

A picture of a blonde, gorgeous woman filled the screen. She lay naked in bed, prone, her breasts half-hidden by white sheets. The camera angle overlooked the coy curve of her shoulder, providing a clear view of her ass. She looked at the lens with sparkly, mischievous eyes. The text underneath simply read, *at your disposal.*

"Who is this?" She aimed for a curious tone rather than accusatory, but she doubted she'd been successful. She hadn't been able to erase a certain shrill from it.

"I don't know. I don't know how they got my number, either."

"How often does this happen?" The timestamp on the text read only half an hour ago.

"Less and less since I stopped dating, but often enough that it's still an issue. I usually just block them, but I really wouldn't want you to come across one of them one day and think I welcome them."

"Usually?" she asked despite herself.

He let out a soft laugh. "I always erase them. To be honest, I didn't use to block them, before… but I never took anyone up on their offer, either. Even before the last person I dated; I've never responded to one of these texts."

Her breathing tightened up; she had to purposefully loosen it. She believed him. She didn't like it, but she believed him.

"For the benefit of complete disclosure," he said, "I kept some pictures for a while, which I used when celibacy was particularly difficult. I've deleted them all already."

"You did?"

He nodded.

"Why is that?" she asked him with a knowing smile.

"I can't think of anyone else but you, Ana Lira."

—

SATURDAY

Liam had the first long, well-rested night he'd had in weeks. He woke up slowly the next morning, the warmth of the bed soothing him into a pleasant half-awareness. He didn't know how much time had passed when he felt Ana stir next to him; his brain didn't fully engage with reality until she kissed his shoulder, then his arm. It was a reality worth waking up for. With no words, kissing turned into more, until they were ravenous and spent once again.

They had agreed that Ely would come at 11; Ana and Liam showered and got ready, making coffee, setting things up. Ely arrived only fifteen minutes late, which Ana said fit the standard. When Ana opened the door, all he saw was a flurry of movement as arms surrounded Ana's neck.

"Sorry I'm late." Ely's voice sounded muffled against Ana's shoulder. "I had to stop to buy some stuff."

Liam stood in the middle of the living room, hands in his pockets, more nervous than he'd like to admit. Ely was an important person in Ana's life, and it felt like her approval would be critical for Ana's and his relationship.

Ely finally let go of Ana, who grabbed the bags from Ely's hands and took them to the kitchen. At the same time, Ely gazed around the room until her eyes fixed on him. He smiled to hide his nerves. She toed her shoes off and approached him.

"Hey, you!" she said.

She was pretty. Her gorgeous, almost-black eyes shone as they studied him. Her hair had a slight wave to it and fell to right above her shoulders; aside from that and her darker skin tone, she could be Ana's shorter sister. She wore a blouse with a flowery print and black jeans, and mischief seemed to sparkle all over.

"Hi, Ely. It's nice to finally meet you."

She bumped his shoulder with a fist. "You, too. Can't believe you're real, to be honest."

He laughed. "I'm sorry I'm not shirtless."

"You could fix that if you really wanted," Ely replied, her smile growing wider. The glint in her eye intensified.

"Stop it, you two," Ana said, coming out of the kitchen. "No one's going to be shirtless today for breakfast."

Liam crossed his arms and dropped his head to the side, stealing a long glance at Ana, before returning to Ely.

"Is she possessive, then?" he asked Ely.

"Nah, she just really wants me to stop objectifying you."

"That would make sense. She's had opportunities to be really jealous and she just... hasn't been." He shrugged with only one shoulder.

"She knows what she's worth, that's all."

"Guys. I'm right here," Ana said. "I need food in my stomach before I can cope with the two of you teasing me at the same time."

Ely winked at Liam before turning to the kitchen, much more familiar than him with Ana's place.

"I'll feed you first, then. I'll tease you later."

"I'll make you a deal," Ana said to Liam. "Ely and I will cook, you can do the dishes. All three of us won't fit in my kitchen."

"That's fine," he said. "I'll get some coffee and sit at the breakfast bar."

"I'll get it for you," she replied, before lifting to the balls of her feet to kiss his cheek.

He sat on one of the bar stools. Her space was a lot smaller than his; it didn't have a proper dining area, just the island-slash-breakfast bar and a living room. He watched Ana and

Ely as they worked in complete harmony, the kind of ease of movement that came from knowing each other for so long.

"So, tell me, Liam," Ely said. "What's your favorite thing about Ana?"

"Ely..." Ana warned, handing him a mug.

"C'mon. I have to play the best friend role. I'm not going to threaten him or anything— maybe just a little— and I do want to hear him gush about you."

"You can go ahead, Ely. I expected this." He sighed and took a sip of his coffee, eyes fixed on Ana's best friend. "My favorite thing is the long conversations we have. How introspective she is. That I feel I can open up to her and that that's gonna be okay."

Ely's eyes softened and she smiled for an instant, before the teasing gleam returned to her eyes. "Fair. I like that you had such an immediate answer. She's amazing that way."

Liam checked in on Ana, who bit her lip as she stole glances at him and her best friend, but returned to Ely when she continued with her questions.

"What about that ass, though?"

Liam laughed and Ana groaned. She put down her head and focused on shredding cheese.

"That too," he said. "Her thighs make me weak. And I live for her smile."

Ely grinned at him. She grabbed a red pepper with one hand and a big knife with the other. She cut the top of the fruit in one swift motion.

"Ana, I think he's going to do just fine." Ely casually pointed the knife in his direction for a few seconds, before cutting the pepper in two. "Aren't you?"

"I'm going to do my best."

"And you're doing your worst, Ely," Ana added. Ana filled her mug with coffee and drank half of it at once.

"Oh, stop it. This is all pretty standard best friend behavior."

"Are you actually uncomfortable?" Liam asked Ana.

"Yeah, she is," Ely answered. Ana cracked some eggs into a bowl as Ely finished chopping the pepper. "So I will only say one more thing. For all of your good looks, for what it's worth, I'm sure that's not her favorite thing about you."

To his surprise, it was Ana that said, "What do *you* think is my favorite thing about him?"

She added milk, spices, cheese, and the results of Ely's work to the bowl, and mixed it all together.

"Part of me wants to joke and say his clear stamina," Ely replied, cleaning the knife slowly and putting it away. Ana and Liam laughed. "But I'll answer the question. I think your favorite thing about him is that you can talk to him for hours, and that he's somehow getting you to try new things, take some risks."

Ana gazed at him, studying him, a sweet smile confirming Ely's words. He smiled in response, before the curve on Ana's lips turned playful.

"And his stamina," Ana joked.

Both Ana and Ely continued to work on the food, Ana focusing on the omelet and Ely on the arepas, creating a short silence.

"I'm sure you have an opinion about me already," Liam said. "I know it's going to matter to Ana a lot, so I have to admit that I'm hoping to make a good enough impression."

"I trust you're a good guy. Ana wouldn't like you if you weren't. Just keep at it and I'll like you well enough. I do have a question for you, though."

"Hit me."

"You have a brother. Would I like him?"

Ana's laughter exploded, before she slapped Ely's shoulder.

Liam sniggered. "Physically, or as a person?"

"Uh oh, this doesn't bode well," Ely said, absentmindedly rubbing her shoulder.

"Physically, we're brothers and that's clear enough from looking at us. Personality wise... let's say you're bubbly and fun, while he's not."

"So he's an asshole."

"You were an asshole when I first met you," Ana commented in Liam's direction.

Liam squinted his eyes at Ana. "Not as bad as that, was I? And it was one time, and I apologized for it. I'd like to think I haven't been an ass since then."

She nodded and lifted her palms in acknowledgement. "You're a delight, Liam."

"But your brother is an ass full time?" Ely asked.

Liam scrunched his face. "I don't want to be unfair to Alex. He's a decent guy, just a bit of a grump. Mind you we don't exactly have the best relationship. We're short on patience with each other."

Ely sighed. "I guess it is doomed, then. It would never work if his name is Alex and mine is Ely. Too much of a tongue-twister."

Liam opened his mouth to make a joke but closed it right back. He'd been about to say it'd be hilarious if Ely and Alex ended up together, because it would make them all a big, happy family. The scary thing was, he didn't think of it as a joke. He could see it way too easily, not so much her brother and Ely... but Ana and him. In a future together that was as idyllic as it was too soon to contemplate.

"Did you know Liam gets propositioned all the time?" Ana asked Ely out of nowhere. "Random people send him pictures offering themselves up to him."

Ely turned in place to inspect him, her smile turning feline.

It seemed that he'd have to wait to analyze the truth of his feelings, and whether he could trust himself with them. It was his turn to get teased.

They said goodbye to Ely at the door. Brunch had been fun and he'd been right: spending time with Ely had been great. She was a powerhouse and she liked him; what else could he ask for?

After hugging Ana, Ely hugged him.

"Hey," Ely said before stepping out of the door, talking to both of them. "Will you go to Christina's tonight?"

"I'm not sure," Ana replied, stealing a glimpse at Liam. "We haven't discussed it yet."

"What's that?" Liam asked.

"Christina is our friend and it's her birthday tonight. She invited me, before you and I knew you'd be here. We need to talk about that."

Liam nodded.

"Does she know it's your birthday on Monday?" Ely said to Liam.

Liam glanced at Ely, and he mirrored her mischievous smile. Ana looked between the two, back and forth.

"I don't think she does, no," Liam said.

"Monday?!" Ana exclaimed.

"Bye," Ely trilled. "Text and let me know whether you're going to Christina's tonight or not!"

She closed the door behind her. Ana stayed where she stood, hands on her hips, watching him with an incredulous look.

"Why didn't you tell me it's your birthday on Monday?"

"Am I in trouble?" he asked, crossing his arms, cocking his head to the side.

She lowered her chin and looked at him from under the ridge of her eyebrows, one of which curled high on her forehead.

"How was I supposed to broach the subject? Hey, my birthday is on Monday, but I don't need a gift or celebration, so I'm just telling you for no reason?"

Ana's posture relaxed as she sighed. She shook her head and took a step toward him, kissing him softly.

"I'm sorry I didn't remember. You mentioned your birthday was coming soon, once in passing, and I totally forgot."

"It's fine. I'm more disappointed that I have to leave at all, to be honest."

She nodded. She went for their mugs of coffee, gave him his, took his free hand in hers, and led him to the sofa.

"Why didn't you tell me about the birthday party today?" he asked.

She shrugged. "I kept getting distracted. I imagine it's going to take some planning to figure out."

"How come?"

"I don't know... the group shouldn't be that big, but it's probably more people than you'd be comfortable with. I don't know how they're going to react to you, I mean."

"I see."

"I think my friends are pretty cool and would be okay, but then Christina also invited a few other people, and at least some of them are coming with their partners. I don't know them all. I don't know."

"What are you afraid could happen?"

"That they'd accost you— ruin the fun for you somehow. I know I have to share you, in a way, with the fans," she said. "But maybe not this weekend."

"Do you think they would? If it's a small group, I would like to think they'd just be a bit awkward, take some pictures... but maybe it being a casual get-together will act as a cushion."

"I hope that's how it's going to be, but I'm not sure and that's the scary thing."

He frowned. "I'd like to know your friends, you know. I don't want to be hidden—"

"Oh, no, I'm sorry— that's not how I mean it—"

"—and be separate from your life."

"I don't want you to feel that way," she said, squeezing his hand in hers.

"If we're invested in our relationship, then it makes sense for me to meet your people."

"Of course. I want you to be a part of my life."

He remained silent. "I don't know what a situation like that is going to be like— it's new for me, too."

"And you're willing to go for it? As an adventure?"

While she was surprised that he would consider it, he seemed surprised that she thought he wouldn't.

"Yeah. Whatever happens, we'll deal with it."

She blinked at him. She needed to rewire this doubt of hers, and learn what Liam had shown her so clearly over the past few weeks: once he knew what he wanted, he made it known and, even if he never asked, he always went for it.

"Let's try it out, then. It'll be fun."

Ana texted Ely and then Christina to confirm she could bring a plus one to the party. Instead of name-dropping Liam, Ana sent a gif from one of his movies. Christina said yes and sent her a gif back to show her excitement, followed by the statement that she wouldn't tell anyone; that she wanted to shock them all.

Ely opened the door for them at Christina's house. Ely hugged Ana, then Liam. "It's nice to see you both again!"

Hand in hand, Liam and Ana entered Christina's townhouse and stood in front of her scattered friends. Ana's stomach rolled with nerves.

"Hi guys," Ana exclaimed to the room. "This is Liam. My— My boyfriend."

Liam squeezed her hand, as if approving of his title. The gathering fell into silence in stages.

"Hi, nice to meet you all," Liam said to her side. Ana glanced at him; his smile was wide and spectacular as he greeted everyone, and he looked amazing in a forest green shirt and dark wash jeans. He looked exactly like the star he was.

Ana watched the room at large, noting the amount of people staring at them, immobile.

"Who's Christina?" Liam asked the room.

Christina, her eyes wide, stood and waved.

"Hi, I'm Christina." She approached Ana and Liam. "It's nice to meet you."

"You too. Thanks for having us." Liam shook her hand and offered her a bottle of Scotch. "Here, we brought this. I was just in Edinburgh and loved this one."

"Thank you," she replied, taking the bottle from him and leading them to the kitchen. "Here, let's go pour you some."

As soon as they'd turned the corner into the kitchen, the room behind them exploded in excited chatting. Liam and Ana snickered at each other.

"That went well," he said, winking at Ana, grabbing her hand again.

———

An hour and a half later, Ana sat next to Liam on the couch after chatting with almost everyone in the room. Maggie and her girlfriend had let Liam know he was one of the patron actors for women who love women and had asked him for several pictures; after that, he'd taken pictures with almost each party guest. Ana got included on most photos but, when she didn't, people invariably took her to the side to express either shock or awe that she was dating Liam, and asked her a thousand questions about how she ended up with him. When not taking pictures, people got curious about the film industry, but Liam had seemed comfortable enough talking to them about it. Ana had been the one to get tired of it first, it seemed.

Now, sitting but still surrounded by people, she needed a break. It took a while longer for a lull to occur but, as soon as one happened, she leaned closer to him and spoke to his ear.

"I'm going to run to the washroom. Are you okay staying, or do you want to come with me?"

He glanced at her with a blank look.

"I'll go with you," he said.

She got up and led him to Christina's room, appreciating that she knew her and her house well enough that she could take that kind of liberty. Now that she had escaped the noise and attention, she leaned against the dresser and sighed, tugging Liam at the waist to bring him close. She rested her head on his chest.

"I don't know how you do this," she told him.

"Do what?"

She lifted her head to gaze at him. "Deal with the attention."

"Oh. I thought there was something completely different in your mind."

"What do you mean?"

He didn't respond, but gave her a sly smile. She would have asked for clarification but he held her head with both hands, lifting it to him, and kissed her hard.

She was slow to catch up with him, shocked. He insisted, his thumbs moving on her face in an arc. Her hands came to rest on his big arms.

"Yes?" she said, as if he'd just said her name.

His chuckle vibrated low. "Was the need to use the washroom an excuse?"

The twinkle in his eye told her enough. "You thought I wanted to escape for a quickie?"

"I thought it was a ruse to seduce me and get me to have sex with you again."

"I did not think of that. And I would not use Christina's bed for that— ever."

Still holding her, fingers entwined with her hair, he led her backwards and then towards the bathroom. "Agreed. I wouldn't disrespect her bed like that." Once they were inside, he closed the door with his foot.

"But the washroom is okay?"

"C'mon. It's a party quickie staple." He pushed her against the vanity and placed small kisses on her temple, then her cheek, then her jaw.

"I've never done it in the bathroom at a party."

He stopped kissing her to give her a look. "Never?"

"No, never," she said, eyebrows high. "Not all of us have had partners desperate to have sex with us in any and all situations, throughout the years. Enough to risk offense and embarrassment if we'd been caught."

Instead of deterring him, her comment made him smile. By now she recognized it as his wolfish grin.

"I am desperate to have sex with you in any and all situations. Including right now."

"Liam..."

"What would you say," he began, kissing her cheekbones, "if I tried to seduce you."

"Liam..." her tone had changed, even to her ears.

He kept his eyes open as he closed the distance between them, only to lick her bottom lip. She opened her mouth despite herself and with a small grunt, he kissed her deeply. He pressed his hips against her, pushing the proof of how into this plan he was. A shiver ran down her spine, and her hesitation went down several notches.

"Can I seduce you?" he asked, his voice raw.

"You already have."

"Is that a yes or a no or..."

"We can't take long." She accompanied her answer by making a quick job of unbuttoning his shirt.

"Don't worry." His hands left her hair to make their way down her back, where they dipped under her pants and underwear to grab her ass. "I won't last long, when I take you rough and hard."

Her heart fluttered at being wanted like this. Her knees weakened and he must have felt the way her legs had almost failed her, because he freed his hands to grab her legs and pull her up to sit on the vanity.

He stood between her legs. His hands roamed, hungry, his mouth insistent. He unbuttoned her blouse and pulled down at the thin fabric of her bra, freeing her breasts. His fingers found her nipples, teasing her, rubbing, gently pinching. He then lowered his head to use his tongue on them, sucking, flicking.

Her body answered quickly, shocking her with the intensity of her response. She would have never thought it possible that she'd say yes, and yet she despaired for him. He certainly seemed greedy, wanting more of her, and quickly. The risk of being caught filled her with an intoxicating rush of adrenaline, and the wave of desire built intense inside of her.

His hands held her hips and brought her down from the vanity again, to stand on her feet. Without words, he kneeled in front of her as he unbuttoned her jeans. He looked into her eyes as he pulled the zipper down, his lips hitching at the corners in lust.

He pulled at her jeans and underwear, bringing them down, frantic. She didn't mind. He didn't break eye contact until her clothes were pooled at her ankles; he licked his lips and stared forward. Her lungs froze in anticipation when she felt his warm breath on her. She trembled at the first touch of his tongue on the seam of her sex, at its confident stroke parting her lips and tasting her arousal.

He brought his hands to run his fingertips on her legs, up and down her thighs, teasing the back of her knees— they almost buckled again. Her hands came to his hair; for support, to guide him, encourage him. She had to bite her lips not to moan at the sight of his powerful shoulders in surrender as he kneeled, the bobbing of his head as he licked her and teased her. The sound escaped her anyway, when he moaned against her.

It seemed to undo him, unravel something within him. After one long, demanding pass of his tongue over her swollen flesh, he stood and unbuttoned his pants.

"I want to take you," he said, "hard against the counter."

"Do it," she replied, not recognizing her own voice.

"Fuck." He pulled down his pants and underwear to somewhere in the middle of his thighs, turned her around, and pressed a hand on the middle of her back to lower it. She braced her hands on either side of the mirror over the sink, preparing for him. She looked at his reflection, at how he stood behind her, eyes cast down, as his hands secured her hips. Her eyes closed of their own volition when she felt him against her, the push of him into her. He thrust in one long, effortless move, stealing a low whimper from her. His fingers twitched on her hips as he took a moment there, deeply sheathed in her, before charging into her in a relentless rhythm.

She could hear his frantic breathing, and could feel the quick beating of her heart, loud in her ears. She had to bite her lips hard to keep herself from making sounds as he pounded into her. She suspected she'd have new bruises from where her body hit the counter with each lunge— and she didn't care. She'd never been had like this.

She ventured a look at his reflection, to find him looking at her, eyebrows furrowed in concentration, his lips loose, jaw hanging open, a ravenous look in his eyes.

"Look at us," he said. "Look at us in the mirror."

She did. She saw her open blouse hanging loose, her bra twisted, her breasts wobbling back and forth with the force of him. He seemed to have gotten caught on that as well, for one hand reached to knead a breast, pinch a nipple.

"I have to... we have to..." she tried.

She didn't know what she had meant to say, or what he understood from it, but he left her chest and leaned forward, guiding his fingers to her clit. He rubbed on it as he continued his powerful thrusts.

It didn't take long for her to climax— hard— the waves of pleasure matching the intensity of their fucking. Her arms buckled, a leg twitched.

"Ana—" he spilled himself in her, both hands keeping her in place by the hips.

Time suspended, they both recovered slowly, their rapid breathing filling the small room. She was the first to hold back a laugh and he echoed her, chuckling.

He pulled back and they cleaned up, quickly fixing their clothes.

"Can't wait to do this again with you," Liam said. "Somewhere else."

"It was so hot," she admitted, checking her reflection for signs of their tryst. "How long have we been away? Do you think anyone noticed?"

He grinned. "That's half the fun!"

They came out of the bathroom, hand in hand and giggly.

"So do I have to expect quickies everytime we attend a party together?"

"Only if you enjoyed it as much as it seemed—"

As they approached the bedroom door, they startled as it opened and Maggie appeared behind it.

The mirth Liam and Ana shared died in an instant. They all stood still upon seeing each other, Maggie's eyes jumping between the two of them, mouth slack. Her eyes studied the bed, still spotless, then the bathroom.

"It's not what you think," Ana said, aiming for damage control.

"It's exactly what you think," Liam said next to her. Ana slapped his arm. He laughed. "What, like she will believe you!"

"I... don't know what to say," Maggie said.

"Don't say anything... to anybody... please?" Ana asked.

"Of course I won't but— I— I don't think I can use this bathroom now," she said with a chuckle and a shake of her head, turning away and walking out of the bedroom.

———

Ana's notifications multiplied exponentially by the time they were ready to say goodbye to Christina. When she glanced at the varied icons and dots and numbers as she plugged her phone on her bedside table, they had reached numbers she had never seen without posting something herself.

"I think some people posted their pictures and tagged me," she said, leaving her cell face down on the flat surface. "Are you sure you're okay with this?"

He shrugged as he unbuttoned his shirt. "This is normal for me. It's either something like this in San Luis Obispo, or away while filming, or at snobby industry parties. I have all notifications off, all the time, if you want to do that too."

"I think I might."

"How do you feel?"

She undressed to her underwear.

"I don't know what I'm supposed to feel."

"You're not supposed to feel any one way. What do you actually feel?"

He discarded his shirt and got rid of his pants, just as she put on her pajama bottoms.

"Dread," she said. "I don't know how big this can get and it scares me. Could this become a second wave of opportunistic tabloid bullshit, or stay contained?"

"I get it," he told her as he threw his pants and socks in the same general direction as his shirt. He stood in his boxer briefs. "You want to know what you're contending with."

"Yeah. More than anything, I want to keep it in check."

She studied him when he didn't say anything. He looked really sad, vulnerable in only his underwear, despite the powerful body. He took a couple of steps to her and held her.

"I'm sorry."

"Why are you sorry?" she asked.

"This is happening because of who I am."

"No, it's happening because of the industry and how they treat people who do what you do."

The line of his shoulders relaxed, the tension in his back under her hands softened.

"Then I'm sorry because there's nothing I can do to fix it," he added.

"I suppose it means there's nothing I can do to control it, either."

"No, there's nothing. Even the absence of an attempt is fuel for someone on the internet to say mean things."

She shook her head in frustration.

"How did you learn to cope? What can I do? I mean, I should like the publicity, right? But I'm not sure this counts and I'm kind of hating it."

"I do my best to ignore what's going on, to remember it's all a mirage. That I know what's true and that it has to be enough, if the people I care about believe me. I sometimes tweet or put things on social media but I don't really interact with anyone. And I never, ever read comments if I can avoid it."

"That's so counterintuitive," she said, putting her head on his shoulder. "I built my small platform by doing the opposite."

"Just remember, the mean people are loud, the big fans too. The people you need to reach and for whom you work are the ones in the middle. And they're the quietest. You won't see them in your notifications the same way."

"So I stay out of it," she said.

"You stay out of it," he confirmed, kissing the crown of her head.

SUNDAY

Upon opening her eyes, Ana found Liam already awake. He sat up, his back to the bedrest, the sheets down to his waist. He held his phone in his hands, his eyebrows furrowed.

She leaned sideways to kiss his arm.

"Morning," she said. "Everything okay?"

"Coulton is freaking out," he replied without looking at her, typing fast on his phone. "He didn't know I didn't go back to LA and he's angry nobody thought to let him know."

"Geez, the guy isn't your guardian."

"I don't think he knows tat," Liam said as he continued to tap, thumbs furious on the device. "I'm writing an email to remind him."

She stretched in bed.

"He also said some of the pictures from last night were used by a tabloid— he was pretty upset that that's how he learned of me being here."

She lay quiet for a while. "Did you see the pictures? Or what the tabloid said?"

"No."

"Okay. I'll go make us breakfast," she told him, getting up and putting on pants— discarded after they'd had sex again before sleep— leaving him to write the email in bed.

While they were eating at the breakfast bar, he got a new email from Coulton. Liam checked it as they had coffee.

"Sorry I'm distracted. I just want to get rid of him. I'll send this email and be done."

Liam typed a response email while she checked her social media accounts. She had hundreds of messages unread. She scrolled through them, tracing it all back to posts made by friends and friends of friends; she also had many messages from random people reaching out upon seeing those stories, hoping to get in touch with her and, potentially, Liam.

It was a good thing that her general group of friends weren't the kind to have great reach online. If they had, she'd probably had a lot more to deal with. Yet someone had had a public profile, and the pictures had been used elsewhere… with or without their permission.

She also had a few emails from reporters for small local newspapers, asking for an interview. One of them assured Ana the interview aimed to discuss her work; the others only mentioned Liam. She stared at the emails and did nothing, just like she had done nothing with the messages on social media.

"Done," he said, putting his phone to the side. "He wanted to know when I'm going back, because *Lethal Whispers*— the new movie— is starting in a few days and that I have to prep before that."

She put her phone away as well. "Does he think you'd disappear and not fulfill your contracts?"

"I think he's terrified one day I might. It doesn't help that I shocked him by coming here."

"You're still leaving tomorrow, right?"

"Yeah. Early in the morning, as I have to meet with Brad— my trainer— in the afternoon."

"Where are you filming?"

"Vancouver for exteriors, LA sets for everything else. It's the good thing about how much CGI goes into a movie like this."

She nodded. "Do you have any decent breaks during filming? Any number of days where we could visit?"

"I was thinking about that." He took a sip of his coffee. "Shooting can take so long each day that a lot of the time I prefer to sleep in my trailer. If I'm filming in LA, though, I like to go home on the weekends. I was thinking you could come stay with me for as many weekends as you can."

She smiled. Calm settled within her, at learning that he'd been thinking about it too and, while his idea made sense, she wasn't sure she could make it happen. It had nothing to do with how exhausting it could be to travel so much, which she was willing to do for this relationship. For quality time with Liam. No, the problem was her bank account.

"That's a lot of flying," she finally said.

"I hope that doesn't mean you're okay with not seeing me much," he half joked, "because I want to see you as much as I can."

She squeezed his hand. "No, that's not it. Of course I want to see you as much as I can. This weekend has been..."

"Wonderful."

"Wonderful," she agreed. "I just don't have the money to cover all those flights."

"Oh." He scratched his eyebrow. "That should be fine. I have the money."

"I don't know. I don't want you to feel like you have to pay to get us together every time. I also want to contribute... but we can keep it proportional."

"I don't mind, Ana. I don't care about the differences between our bank accounts, unless you do?"

"Not in itself, but I don't like the idea of you being the only one using your money. "

"I care a lot more about seeing you sooner rather than later. I would rather use the money and give us a real chance at being together— really together. We have a lot of challenges as it is— my fame, our agents— distance is something we can do something about."

"Is there any sort of middle ground? You can pay for most of it, but I'd like us to see if there's a way to minimize distance and money spent."

She stared at Liam's eyes and he did the same, trying to come up with ideas.

"What about this," he said. "Maybe you can come stay in my place for a while. You can live there while I'm away, doing your editing and such. I'll come see you on the weekends. You can come back home and back to LA as often as you'd like. And I'll help pay for the tickets. That would minimize the amount of travel while giving us a few weekends."

She remained silent for a beat, her stomach fluttering at what he implied with his generous offer.

"Would you really be open to that?" she asked, breathless. "Giving me access to your home that way."

"Sure. Why not? The house will be empty otherwise. You can see it as your LA base, for when you want to be there. You'd have weekdays all by yourself, and I'd come stay with you most weekends."

"That's not what I mean. You'd be giving me the keys to your place and though I wouldn't be moving in, it's still a big step for only two months of knowing each other—"

"I know what you mean," he said, his tone careful. "And I think it works. I don't really care what you want to call it. If you say it's a practical solution to making sure we have time together, I like that. If you want to say it's a key moment in the development of a relationship, I'm fine with that too. It's just you having my key and spending some time in my house. You'll still have your own place, go back and forth... All that matters to me is that we'll be together when we're both in LA."

"Liam," she tried, but no words came out. Her heartbeat drummed against her chest.

"I know it's eager of me and I know people say we should play it cool," he argued. "That it's not modern to show real interest. I say fuck that. I don't care. I haven't felt this good in so long; I've waited a long time to feel this way. I don't want to risk it with more distance and instability than we have to. I'm feeling butterflies again, Ana."

She smiled. "I do, too, but not everyone would want to risk as much after only knowing each other for so little."

"These weren't just two months. We dove into getting to know each other and— I like— I think we both liked what we found. I think it's worth choosing it, over and over again. So yeah, maybe others wouldn't want to risk it, but I would."

"I love your openness to life; to feeling." She sighed.

"You know, I don't think I ever told you all my reasons to get into the documentary. I didn't tell you everything I discussed with Dr. Linda."

"What's that?"

"I told you she encouraged me to think of what the documentary could do for me, remember?"

"Yes."

"One of the things I took into consideration was how it gave me the opportunity to get to know someone. You let me know you, Ana, and it showed me what was possible. When I knew you... I didn't expect to like you quite so much but— here I am. Trying to convince you to take my offer, because I want you in my life this badly."

"I want you in my life, too."

"So will you do it?" he insisted. "I'm not asking you to leave everything behind, and I'm not asking for more than you want. I'm just hoping you'll want what I want."

"I want to give it a chance," she said, standing next to him and giving him a sweet, long kiss. "I'm taking your offer."

"Then think of me as your LA roommate, and my house as your LA base. I'd be that roommate that visits on the weekend and you share a bed with. Because we're trying to make it work."

—

They spent the rest of their Sunday in quiet companionship. After a lazy afternoon, Ana coordinated with Ely for the latter to bring her a cake and candles while Liam took a shower.

Ely's face didn't have the teasing smile Ana had expected.

"Ana... there are a couple of people outside and... they have cameras. Just so you know."

Her heart sank. Her stomach flipped. "I won't go out. Thanks, Ely."

Ely gave Ana a hug and left. Ana hid the cake in the fridge silent- ly, and sat on the sofa to temper her reaction to Ely's warning. She mostly failed, and Liam noticed right away.

"What's up?" Whatever he'd seen on her face, he instinctively reached for her, cuddling her on the sofa.

"Ely dropped by for a minute," she explained. "She told me there are paparazzi outside."

He squeezed her against him but said nothing. They didn't move or talk much until they were ready for dinner. Ana thawed in Liam's arms until she could grin from within, and it was then that she brought the cake with its single candle. Liam seemed genuinely charmed by the gesture and, after eating some off a plate, insisted on eating some off her belly, too.

They spent the evening in bed, with light touches and whispered words. They came up with a plan: she would take a couple of weeks to prepare things, then she'd fly to stay at his place for a month. She would edit the documentary there while he did principal photography for the new movie, and they'd have the weekends to spend time together. After that month, they would see how they both felt; whether she needed to come back for a while or stay a bit longer. It was a hell of an adventure for both of them but they were both willing to take the leap, as long as they did so holding hands.

Ana and Liam were able to escape her building undetected the next morning, taking advantage of the private parking lot. A few paparazzi swarmed the front entrance but her car left the backlot without much notice. Once in the small airport, they didn't escape notice for long. Ana got much needed coffee from a convenience store, desperate for it since she and Liam hadn't had breakfast and had opted for more sex instead. People whispered around them.

Ana stole a glance at Liam. He wore a baseball cap but not his sunglasses. Probably not enough to keep him mostly anonymous, and people had noticed.

"Word must have gotten out through social media," he said.

She caught someone taking a picture of them with their phone.

"Let's go talk to the airport people," he suggested. "Maybe they can get us in some office or some place else that's private, before my plane gets here."

"Good idea."

She walked away from the coffee place with as much aplomb as she could muster, one of her hands in Liam's.

They managed to find staff that would help them. On the way to the private area, a couple of people had built up the courage to come ask for selfies and autographs. Liam was polite and friendly, but Ana did her best to keep things moving and get through to privacy.

When they finally made it to an empty administrative office, he let out a big sigh. She hugged him tight, unsure if she did it to provide comfort or obtain it. They held, kissed, and stood in silence for several minutes, arms around each other.

"I know you said you didn't need a gift or celebration," she said onto his shoulder, "but it's really bumming me out that you have to leave on your birthday... that we need to hide in this drab office to say goodbye."

"It's not goodbye. It's see you later."

She closed her eyes, daring to believe him, letting his surety settle in her blood.

A knock on the door interrupted them. An office assistant entered the room, accompanied by a flight attendant.

"We're ready for you to board, Mr. McMillan."

"One more minute," he said to them. With a nod, they left the room without closing the door.

His arms tightened around Ana, before he created distance between them. He sought her hands and guided them to his waist, before putting his hands on her face. He kissed her once more, reverently, sweetly.

"I'm quickly falling for you, Ana Lira," he whispered against her lips. "It makes all of this worth it."

"It's worth it," she said, before they kissed one last time.

Chapter 20

I T DIDN'T TAKE A full two hours for things to go wild on the Internet. Liam and Ana weren't trending; wild was a subjective term online but, for Ana, the amount of talk about herself and her relationship with Liam seemed riotous. And terrifying.

Ana uploaded a short tease of the documentary to her YouTube page and comments flooded in. The video was of the technical type, in which she talked about the editing process; she had even used a neutral bit of footage, a wide shot of the ocean and the cabin. Despite the dry content, within minutes of it going online, messages and comments filled the page. Most of them had nothing to do with the process or the project, but were about her and Liam. Some were excited, *did Liam take you there? Amazing!*; others were nosy, *were you there with Liam all alone?* And yet others were downright mean.

You shouldn't use him for publicity. You're disgusting!

Ana left her computer processing footage and took a shower, hoping the warm water would help her regain her calm. It didn't work. A wrecking ball swung chaotically in her mind, the *woosh* of it as it flew back and forth creating havoc, and insisting that people would never see her work for what it was ever again, that Liam's fame would overshadow everything Ana tried to accomplish. By the time she'd gotten dressed, her stomach ached and her chest constricted her lungs into shallow breaths.

While she would have typically walked to the grocery store, she drove there just in case there were still photographers lurking around. She thought that'd be enough to evade them, so she wasn't prepared to feel so closely watched at the grocery store, nor to have her cashier inform her they'd been to high school together and had seen her pictures online.

Her hands were trembling by the time she got home.

Liam called her a short while after that, having made it home. She smiled as she answered his video call, trying to hide her distress. She didn't want to worry him.

He smiled on the phone when the video came on, but it quickly disappeared.

"What's wrong?" he asked.

She sighed. "I didn't want you to worry."

"If we're together, I'm supposed to help when something's going on."

"You have very lofty ideas about relationships."

He lifted an eyebrow. "You don't?"

"I do, I just never thought— and I should be able to—"

"Well, let me prove you wrong," he said, a challenging smile breaking over his face.

She scoffed, but nodded. This time, her features softened authentically.

"I'm getting bad comments on social media and the cashier at the grocery store recognized me." She scoffed again, this time at herself. "I'm sorry. It's ridiculous. I'm just overwhelmed."

Liam could have laughed, but didn't.

"It's not ridiculous. I remember the first time I was recognized on the street. It felt like it all happened at once. This weekend— this was your *all at once*."

She nodded. "Even with what happened after the TCA party, that was another world— I can expect that of Los Angeles, even here when I'm with you but— somehow— if it happens when you're not around, if it's online, if it's the paps outside of my building— then it's about me, not you. I'm being looked at, too."

"Try not to get sucked into it, okay?" he said. "Remember, the comments are not the true sample of your fans, only the most extreme ones."

"Okay. I'll do my best."

"Did any paparazzi get close? Did they harass you?"

"No one harassed me, I just— it felt like I was in a fishbowl. It was uncomfortable."

"Has Diana said anything?"

"Nothing yet, but it's still early in LA," she tried to joke.

He smiled. It faded. "I hope these two weeks go by in a flash."

"Yeah, it'd do me well to hide in your house and edit until I can't think of anything else."

"Hide for a little while, if it'll help, but come out for air, okay? The paparazzi will tire, and you'll have space again. Then you pack and come to LA."

"Thanks, Liam. You're... you are..."

"Far, and I hate it."

She laughed. "You're amazing."

"We'll survive this, okay?"

"Okay."

Ana heard from Diana that evening. It probably signaled trouble, when her agent called her on the phone instead of sending another email.

"Hello?"

"Hi, Ana. I need to check in with you."

"Sure. What's up?"

"It's the Liam McMillan thing. My team has let me know there's still a lot of content out there about you and him. He visited you, didn't he?"

"He did."

"Are we still pretending that I believe you when you say you're not involved with him?"

Diana's words were stern on the line and they hit her like a punch. One thing was to hear the disapproval, and another to be seen as a liar. Ana didn't appreciate any of it.

"I don't think that's fair. I understand why you advised against starting a relationship with him; you've been clear about that, but I'm not a liar. When I told you we weren't together, it was the truth. Things changed after you and I had that conversation."

"Okay, okay. I'm sorry about assuming you had lied, but that also means that you ignored my recommendation and got together with him anyway."

Ana winced, but hid the reaction from her voice. "Is this really happening? Do you really have an opinion on my private life?"

"I don't have an opinion on your private life. I have an opinion on your public life and it's going to be impossible to keep your relationship with Liam McMillan private. That is, it will be seen as public. That's what I have an opinion on, because it will impact your career."

Ana didn't have an answer to that.

Diana continued, "Look, this is a difficult thing to talk about but it's really important. For one, I like you. And I want you to be successful."

"I know."

"Do you want to be successful?"

"Of course I do."

"Then you'll have to learn to trust my guidance."

Ana couldn't help but compare Diana's words with Coulton's to Liam, not that long ago. Would her life in this industry always be like this?

"I've already tried to give you good advice," Diana insisted. "I've had my doubts about getting involved with Mr. McMillan from the start. I for sure did not want you to flaunt this thing you have with him, whatever it is."

"Noted."

"I am still very much concerned with the consequences you—and, by extension, me and my team— might have to go through when it fizzles out, or if it reaches much more presence online than it has now. At the moment, I think you're still at a place where you will benefit more than you will suffer from this fling; at least some of these people searching for you online will actually watch your films and like them. Whether that's going to be enough to compensate for the many, many fans of McMillan's that hate you right now, that's up for debate. And what happens when it ends?"

Ana's throat closed up. She fought the tears.

"What we have is real," Ana whispered more to herself than Diana, but the latter reacted to it nevertheless.

"Oh, Ana. Of course he's going to tell you that you're special and make you feel like a queen... and of course you want to believe him. We're talking about Liam McMillan! Your feelings probably feel very real. But I've seen this happen— I've had to help a number of people through the storm— and I've seen what happens when things fall apart. Few careers survive the fall. His will, no doubt, but I'm trying to protect yours."

When Ana didn't respond, Diana continued.

"Okay, let's imagine it's real. That he does feel for you what he's telling you he feels. It still doesn't mean this relationship will last for a long time. Few relationships last under the pressures of Hollywood. He travels a lot, his career will always eclipse yours, and you will be scrutinized. Constantly. At some point, whether it's a week or a year, your heart will be broken, and it will break publicly. If you end it now, it's still in your control. I'm trying to help you, here."

"Are you?" Ana's stomach had progressively twisted into a worried knot. "Because it feels as if you're trying to make me break my own heart."

"I need you to understand, you haven't been around enough to know what I know. You'll need thicker skin to go as far as you could go. Especially as a woman. A Latina. And you're... uhm... plus size for Hollywood. I'm sorry, but you'll have to make tough choices."

"So you called me to tell me breaking up with Liam is one of those tough choices that will protect me? Are you aware that Coulton is okay with us dating?"

"I am aware Coulton is not against it at the moment, but don't think he can't change his mind. One day soon he may have this same conversation with McMillan. After the documentary is done and the publicity isn't necessary anymore, he might decide you're not helpful to him and his client any longer. That's up to them; my goal is to think of you. I am here to protect you and your career. You believe that, don't you?"

"I can believe you think that that's what you're doing."

"Okay. I can see that we're not in agreement on this yet. I hope you understand I need to keep insisting." Ana didn't answer. "Think it over. When you come to realize I'm right, let me know. I can help you break things off with Mr. McMillan. The team will be there to help you handle it. Otherwise, focus on only interacting with the positive comments, and continue to do your work as discussed."

"I will. My work will never suffer."

"I hope that you're right about that. I really do want you to do well."

"Thanks. I do believe you in that.

"Goodbye."

"Bye."

Ana threw her phone on the bed, her heart in her throat. She paced in her apartment, the need to figure it all out coiling inside of her. When her restlessness made her want to go for a walk, and when she realized she couldn't go out, not when people might not leave her alone— that's when she felt tears building up. She didn't want to feel trapped, but she did.

She went back to her room, grabbed her phone, and quickly navigated to her calendar. Liam had ended up sharing his with her, and she checked it to see if he was free. He wasn't.

She squeezed her eyes shut for a moment and, forcing herself to take a deep breath, she called Ely instead.

"What's up?" Ely said as a greeting.

"Diana wants me to break up with Liam," Ana responded without preamble.

"That harpy! Don't listen to her."

"I'm not! I don't want to break up with him."

"Then tell her to get out of your business."

"That's the problem, though, isn't it? Shit. She's my agent. She is right about how this can affect my career. And I don't want to break up with Liam. I don't know where to draw the line with her, when my relationship with Liam influences my career and Diana is in charge of that."

"No, you're in charge of your career," Ely argued. "She's like your administrative assistant, the person that represents you in business meetings and negotiates for you and runs interference."

"She's more than that. She's a network— an easier entry to film festivals, to funding..."

"Well, yeah, that's her job, not managing your life."

"That's true. This feels... imbalanced. I don't feel I have as much power as she has and that's messed up."

"Liam has that power, though. Maybe ask for his advice?"

When she finally got to talk to Liam, he didn't like what Diana had to say.

"Listen to Ely, please, she's right," he told her. His voice sounded strained, as if holding back. "Diana is supposed to make things easier for you and multiply your opportunities, and that's it."

"I won't listen to Diana about you, of course not! Whether Ely had agreed or not, being with you isn't for others to decide. But professionally... don't you think Diana's right? That if something goes wrong between us, it'll hurt me not only personally, but professionally?"

His lips pressed together, his eyes turning fiery.

"I am not planning on our relationship going wrong," he said, his voice stern. "I don't think it's fair for us to plan around the possibility that it'll fail."

"You're right. I don't want to start preparing for the possibility that things may go sideways."

"So what do you want?"

"I want to believe nothing bad will happen," she admitted. She rubbed her forehead with a hand and sighed.

"I wish I could tell you that for sure, but I can't. Bad things might happen. But we can't let it break us. We need to help each other."

"How can you help me with my career? With Diana. You know how hard it is, you have the same problem with Coulton."

"I don't have all the answers yet but— dammit, we can figure it out."

She watched him on the screen, a deep wrinkle between his eyebrows, his mouth in a hard line. She knew her face echoed his gesture.

"Yeah. I need a plan."

"What are you going to tell Diana?" he asked.

"I think I'm going to tell her that I don't need her help in regard to my relationship with you. I'm afraid it'll make her angry, but... I just can't have her think she gets a say in this."

"Good. I'm glad. On that note," he said, and he visibly took a deep breath before continuing, "I really think we shouldn't be apart right now. We should be together to figure these things out. If we're apart... that's scary. Makes me feel like we're teetering at the edge of a cliff but we're not there to keep each other upright. Maybe you should come sooner. That way we can withstand this initial storm together."

She sighed. "Maybe you're right. It's only been one day, but..."

"Think about it, okay? I'll be happy to have you as soon as you're ready."

Ely called her early the next morning with a severity in her tone Ana had never heard before.

"You're going to delete all your social media apps right now," Ely said. "You're not to visit any websites or read anything about yourself or Liam online."

Ana's blood left her skin and found its way to the ground. "What happened?"

"Don't worry about it. Just delete the apps, okay? And don't go and read anything online."

"Ely, I need to know." Her voice shook. "What are they saying?"

"You don't need to know, believe me."

"Is it me? Or Liam? Are they attacking my career?"

"They're saying shitty things. That's it, okay? Now delete the apps, please."

"Fine. I'll delete the apps." Her hands shook.

"Good. Come stay with me? You can hide here. I'll wrap you up in a blanket until it's all gone."

A small smile appeared on her face despite the chaos within. "You're the best, Ely, but I'll stay here. You're already risking being dragged into it by coming here—"

"— you couldn't stop me if you tried—"

"— and I love you for it, but I'm not going to risk your home. Or my parents' home."

"Fine. But I have my eye on you. Text me if you need anything or you hear anything— hell, call me if you just need to talk in order not to panic. And I'll take dinner to your place tonight and we'll have a nice time. Maybe we'll watch *Love, Never* again and be like, can you believe you're dating him?! Until we're blue in the face. And please, please go to LA to stay with Liam ASAP, okay?"

That afternoon, Ana bought a plane ticket to LA, departing in a week. She hoped it would give her enough time to pack her equipment appropriately and close up her apartment again, leaving it empty for as long as she ended up staying with Liam.

"I think you made the right choice," Ely said. They were sitting together on Ana's sofa, after having a quick dinner together. They hadn't watched the movie yet.

"I hope so. I can't lose sight of the goal. I need to come up with a plan to deal with all of this, pack my shit, and go to Liam in LA."

"I'm glad that TCA fields a lot of the publicity stuff, too. Can you imagine how it'd be if you were also trying to manage calls from journalists and stuff?"

"I don't want to think about it, honestly."

Ana's phone rang. "It's Liam. Give me a minute?"

"Sure," Ely responded, grabbing her own phone for a distraction.

"Hey," Ana said to Liam. "Did you get my email with the flight details?"

"Yes. I'll be sure to go home that night," he replied.

"I'd love for you to be there when I get to your house." She had this image in her head of him opening the door like the first time but, instead of awkwardness, this time he kissed her and welcomed her to his home for a while, not for interviews, but just for them.

"Then I'll do my best to make it happen and be home when you arrive. I'll just have to get up early for my call time the next day."

"How early?"

"I don't know yet what time they'll want me there, but I usually get up around 4 or 5."

"4?!"

"Fuck," Ely muttered under her breath.

Ana left the screen to stare at her best friend. "Everything okay?"

She frowned but flicked a hand in Ana's direction. "Forget about it. You can go back to romancing Liam."

"What's up?" Liam asked.

"I don't know," Ana said. "Ely doesn't want to say."

"It's for the best," Ely insisted. "Forget about it, I didn't mean to say anything."

"You know it makes me think it's bad news, right?"

"Then let it go," Liam said.

Ana turned her eyes back to her boyfriend, and caught a notification as it came in. A text from an unknown number.

(Unknown): Your ex spilled
the beans. Search
Ana Lira is a liar

A deep chill ran through her veins. Her bones turned to icicles.

"Ana?" Liam said. "What's wrong?"

"I... someone... I just got..."

"Hey, hey— shit, Ana, shh." Ely put an arm around Ana's shoulder. "It's gonna be okay."

Ana's throat seemed blocked by a cold, rough cannon ball. She spoke around it, her voice thin. "Someone reached out to Dave."

"What?!" Liam exclaimed on the phone.

"It was all lies, Ana María. Forget about him."

"You read the article?!" Ana had a slight ringing in her ears.

"I skimmed it."

"Do you have an alert or something?" Liam asked. His tone was harsh but Ana could barely take note of it; she'd gone numb.

"Don't judge," Ely said. "Someone has to keep an eye out here for my best friend, see what I need to protect her from."

"There's nothing you can do. C'mon, Ely, she doesn't need this stuff."

"I didn't plan for her to know! But I need to know. It's about feeling protective of her."

"How is this protecting her?"

"Because anything they say about her could affect her. She's worked so hard to get here—"

"What did Dave say?" Ana asked, ignoring them both.

"Fuck this," Liam exclaimed from Ana's phone again. "It shouldn't matter what he said."

"What did he say?" Ana asked again.

Ely pursed her lips tight, fighting Ana quietly, but gave in. "Nonsense. Attacked your professionalism, called you a cheater. Please, don't let it affect you. Block that number—"

"Change your number," Liam added.

"— and ignore that shithead."

"I didn't cheat on Dave, Liam." Her voice wavered.

"I know."

"I told you the truth."

"Ana, I know."

Ana took a long, deep breath. Ely and Liam were quiet now, the weight of their attention heavy on her shoulders. "I think I need to sleep this off. I'm sorry, Ely."

"Are you sure? I can stay."

"I know you would. Thanks, but I'm sure, Ely. I want to get in bed and go to sleep."

"Okay." Ely hugged Ana for a long minute, holding her tight. "We'll talk tomorrow. Bye, Liam. Take care of my friend."

Ely left the apartment and Ana closed the door behind her. She turned off the light and went straight into bed, leaving the dinner mess untouched and not bothering to change her clothes. Pulling up the covers, she lay on her side, holding the screen in front of her as if Liam were there in bed with her.

"Thanks for believing me," she said. "Who knows how many people would."

"I've never had any reason to doubt you. I've been with you for a couple of months and I know it's not too long, but unless you're a consummate actress with evil plans, I don't see how you could have lied about it all."

"So you found a way to trust people you've gotten to know."

"I'm confident I know you. I trust you. That hasn't changed in the past few days."

She took a deep breath. "What is this going to do to me? This bad press?"

"I don't know," he said, his voice sorrowful. "I worry, too."

"I don't want this." She rubbed her skin to wipe away a rebel tear.

"Ana..."

"I'm sorry, I don't mean you," she reassured him, still trying to dry her tears. They seemed to be multiplying. "I mean the tabloid stuff. I don't want any of that."

"I wish I could leave it behind. Not bring it around me like a curse."

"It's not you, Liam. You... I want you."

He loosened a deep sigh. "I'm glad."

"I wish you were here."

"I should be there."

A while later, she fell asleep with the phone on, Liam still on the screen.

Chapter 21

FIRST THING ON WEDNESDAY morning, Ana escaped through the parking lot again and got a new phone. She gave her new number only to her inner circle, and added no social media apps to it.

From the moment she stepped out of her apartment and until she made it to her parents' for lunch, she had to fight against the constant impulse to check over her shoulder.

She parked outside her childhood home and vowed to keep this time with her parents a safe place. If she could keep lunch comforting and familiar, it would be a much needed balm to her frayed nerves. She hugged them and kissed their faces like she always would, and let their warmth soothe her.

As soon as they sat down to eat the seco de pollo, her parents asked her if she was seeing anyone.

"Uhm... yes, actually." Ana half-smiled, half-bit her lip.

"¿Qué? ¡Hija!" her mom said. "And you didn't tell us? How long has it been?"

"I'm telling you now, Mami."

"¿Cómo se llama el muchacho?" her dad asked.

"His name is Liam. "

"You should invite him for dinner." Mami added, cutting into her chicken. "It's been a long time since you've dated anyone."

Ana took a long, deep breath. She hadn't had a chance to prepare for this conversation, and all she knew was that she didn't want her parents to worry. She clung to the fact they didn't follow celebrity gossip, and she prayed that nobody would tell them what was going on.

"He's amazing, but it's hard right now because he travels a lot and he's not from here."

"So he can't come for dinner yet?" her mom asked.

Ana smiled. "No, not yet."

They had coffee after their meal, continuing to casually chat. When her parents asked about work, she managed to talk about the latest documentary and Liam as if they were two separate things, nervously navigating the fine line where omission became a lie. At some point, Ana's parents would learn the whole truth and she'd be in trouble anyway, but the way things were right now, this was the best she could do.

Later, she quietly took a picture of the three of them and, asking for silent forgiveness, Ana sent it to Liam without letting her parents know. She didn't want to put the idea in their head that they could ask for pictures of Liam; she'd been there before and it had ended in a big reveal. She waited on her phone just in case he replied right away and, as she didn't have social media apps on her phone anymore, Ana made the mistake of checking her emails. She had one from Diana.

Ana,

I need to share bad news. You may not know, but there's currently a campaign to downvote your previous work.

People are leaving bad reviews everywhere to lower your ratings— and your previous documentary participants are being harassed. We're doing our best to help them field questions and direct people our way.
This is precisely the kind of situation I wanted to avoid. At this point all we can do is focus on damage control. On your side, we will send you a draft of a statement to read. As per our agreement, you get to give your opinion on what we say in any public communications. Once it's approved, we'll ask that you say something to the same effect on your social media and then pretend it's all in the past. We hope for your helpfulness in this process. Finally, this may be the final push you needed to break things off with Mr. McMillan, if you haven't already. You really need to stop living in a dream world and focus on your career. Let me make it what we both know it can be.

The email lit a fire in her belly. Liam wasn't easily discarded. There had to be a way to keep him and her career, too. She just needed to hunker down and figure it out.

The conviction lasted only until a flash temporarily blinded her while waiting for the gate to open at her building's parking lot. Someone took a picture through her side window, making it clear that her safe exit wasn't safe anymore.

"Oh my god," she mumbled, trying to cover her face as she drove past them.

Later that night, one got into the building and knocked at her door.

Being with Liam would be like this. There was so much more to it than simply how much Liam and Ana cared for one another.

Ana's blood boiled at people, at the industry, and everyone who thought they had an opinion on the matter. For the first time, she thought she could truly understand Liam's bitterness when she first met him. Underneath her anger, dread caved a hole in her.

She wanted to be with him, she knew that, but how was she supposed to deal with all the chaos and pain?

Ana: Diana is really angry.
I think I'm in trouble
with her. There's a
campaign to bring down
my ratings, my documentary
people are being harassed.

Ana: Paps have been
harassing me today.
I hate this

Liam: I'm sorry. None
of this should be happening.
I wish we could talk
right now.

Liam had been in meetings all day and now he was about to go into training with Brad again. Ana lay in bed, drained from a long day of frustration and fear. Immobile, eyes open yet unseeing, she shut down, thoughts leaving her one by one, emotions going away for once. It won her over, the quiet of being numb for a while, and she embraced it with open arms.

She fell asleep before she could talk to Liam that night. She woke up the next day to a few missed calls and a text from him.

Liam: you must have
fallen asleep. It's even
later there and I'm
sure you're tired. This
shit is exhausting.

Liam: Talk tomorrow

———

Liam woke up with a tension headache. He had had a difficult time falling asleep, anger and confusion pumping adrenaline into his bloodstream.

How unfair that this was happening to Ana. How difficult to keep hope, to trust that this wouldn't tear their budding relationship apart. How ironic, that it was in the middle of this that he'd shocked himself with the words he'd almost typed out the night before. Words he hadn't expected, but that had wanted to come out of him as naturally as he breathed.

It had almost slipped from his fingers, a ready conclusion to the last text he'd sent the night before: *I love you.*

It felt grounded, real. Scary. New and predictable. He'd never gotten to this place this fast, nor this deeply. He'd loved someone before— or so he'd thought at the time. Even so, this thing building between Ana and him, the feeling burning inside him, it was different. It was solid, and rich, and it felt like certainty.

What was he supposed to do with it now?

Such an inconvenient time to be shocked with the revelation of it. He wasn't ready to tell her, especially not now that tension had appeared between them— scratch that, around them. He understood that she needed time to feel impervious to the mess surrounding them, and he wanted to respect it, as scared as it made him. All in all, this was not the time to share this bit of news with her. He didn't want to scare *her*.

Maybe he needed to call Dr. Linda and get an appointment. When he'd come to the conclusion that he felt lonely and that he needed friends and wanted a partner, he'd failed to realize that making sure he became the right person for the people he wanted amounted to only half of it. That not only he had to overcome the impact this industry had had on him, but he'd have to witness his people do the same. And that their survival wasn't a sure thing.

A fist squeezed his stomach into a tight ball of nerves. He could do nothing but be the right person for her, and pray that showing her how invested he was would be enough.

After some deliberation, he asked Mo to make a copy of his home key and send it to Ana. He wrote a note and gave it to him to add to the envelope.

After Mo left, Liam took his phone and typed quickly.

Liam: I'm hopping
into a mtg right now,
but can I call in ab
an hr? I want to hear
your voice.

He checked her text in the middle of the meeting with Kyle, the director of *Lethal Whispers*.

Ana: Yes, let's talk

For the sake of professionalism, he ignored the instinct of calling her right away. He had to settle for continuing the conversation with Kyle with a rock on his chest.

He called her as soon as he'd hung up on the meeting.

"Hey," she said, her voice teary. Her eyes were red on the screen.

"Hey. You okay? Holding up?"

"I think so." After a wet chuckle, she continued, "Well, somewhat. There are still a few paps swarming the public parking lot like flies. What are they even waiting for? Don't they have to return to their much-bigger, much-more interesting cities? Where actual celebrities live? And a couple of my documentary people texted me. Diana told me they were being harassed and that she's trying to help them, but... I feel horrible that I can't do anything for them. I've been chatting with them but... it's too much. And I still need to reach out to my other people, check in on them."

Her voice broke, her lips pressing into a helpless line.

"What is Diana planning to do?" he asked. His free hand itched with the need to touch her, comfort her. His fingers dug into his thigh instead.

"She told me she'd send me a draft for a public statement, and that she wanted me to make a post about it. After that's done, she wants me to pretend nothing happened."

"That's kind of standard."

"She also said to stop living in a dream world and to finish things off with you."

"Fuck that," he said. It escaped him through a scoff. It made her chuckle.

"I happen to share your sentiment. This is all a mind fuck, but I don't appreciate her thinking that part of managing the situation is telling me whether I should be with you or not. That's not what this is about. This is about whether I can handle the bullshit around us."

"I'm so sorry this is happening, Ana. I wish I was there. Maybe I can fly there tomorrow for the weekend? I could be there by midnight or so."

"You don't have to do that. You'd be here Saturday morning and having to leave Sunday afternoon at the latest to be there for your call to set on Monday morning. And my flight is two days later."

"I don't care. I really don't. All I care about is being together right now. I think being apart can really confuse things for us."

"But if you come, things can get worse. They're on high alert here, I'm sure. They must have traveled to keep an eye on me, right? I don't imagine there are a lot of paps in Bloomington most of the time. I don't want to give them any more stuff for them to put through their news mill. They need to leave."

"Then will you come to me? You could change your ticket. We'll hire people to pack what you need and send it to us."

He saw the hesitation in her eyes before she spoke. It fell on him like a big bucket of ice water.

"I'm not sure about that," she whispered. "I think I need a bit of time."

"Why? Ana, please— let's not be apart."

"I need to think."

"Then think. With me."

"Liam..."

"C'mon. I'm trying here. I'm showing up for us, for this."

"Me too! In my own way. I need to figure out how to cope, how to create a bubble for myself in all of this where I can feel safe. I need to think of how to frame this, how to respond to all of it beyond what you've told me worked for you. Who am I in this mess? How do I let go of everything else?"

"I know you're scared and uncomfortable and that it makes you want to pull back, but—"

"It's not the same," she interrupted. "This is not about Dave hurting me and worrying about what it would do to me if you and I break up. Being with you is much bigger than that! I was afraid of taking risks, Liam, before I met you. That was the fear I overcame when I kissed you in LA. This? It's a whole 'nother level. This is not me being afraid of normal things happening in my life. Now I'm *also* afraid of things happening to me, to people around me, for what's going on with my career to get even worse— one thing is to be lied about, but I could also be exposed, exploited. Attacked online."

"That's not what I was implying. Don't forget I understand how it is, too, maybe even better than you think because I've been surrounded by it for years. I knew this would get in the way, of course I did! But I didn't know— I didn't realize— I'm powerless in this and seeing you go through this so far from me, I just—"

Tears fell down her face and she rubbed them dry. "You travel for more than half the year, Liam. Being with you means being apart a lot. I need to learn. I have to find a way to protect myself from this mess."

His chest caved in. "Ana, please. You can't let this matter more than what we want."

She shook her head; his heart skipped a bit and resumed at a heightened pace.

"Don't you see that we're saying the same thing?" she said. "I want to make it not matter. These past few weeks, especially the past few days, are making it clear what I'm getting into. All these people putting us under a microscope and saying the worst things they can come up with... it risks so much of what I've worked for. I only know you because I was trying to get closer to my professional goals but I could end up with nothing. I need time to sit in my shower, cry, and hate them all until I don't care about any of them. I need time to organize my head and write to Diana and tell her to not fire me but to kindly fuck off. I need time to... to think, dammit. To stop feeling devastated. To make a plan on how to protect my people. Make all the right decisions."

There had been a time when he believed that asking for what he wanted meant that he couldn't get an authentic commitment from her. He'd always imagined that finding someone to love would feel like a click so unique, a chain reaction so powerful that everything would fall into place. That having all elements in place would be enough and asking for it would change its very chemistry.

He'd been wrong. He couldn't be passive about this. He needed her to know what he wanted, what he felt; give her all the information she needed to make this decision to stay in Bloomington longer or fly to him. This wasn't only about keeping her career and people she worked with safe. This was about them. This was about what he wanted to offer her, as a partner, a person in love... and about what he wanted from her. She had to know.

"There's a lot of crap around us, things we can't control. But we can control what influences our relationship and what doesn't. Together, I can hold you and help you in all of this. I want it. I want it all with you," he tried. He shook his head; he was speaking his truth, but it felt incomplete. Not enough. "You talk about making decisions— if you're going to make a choice, choose me. Please.

Don't let them win. I didn't want to say this on the phone and, sure, you could say it's early but I don't— I know it's true. It's true. I lo—"

"Don't," she interrupted him, anguish on her face. "Don't say that right now. It's unfair. If you feel it, wait until I can be there with you to take it in. If you say it..."

"You're making my heart ache, Ana. Don't do this."

"I'm not doing anything, Liam. I'm not breaking up with you."

"Then what is this? You say you need time. So you're putting us in limbo?"

"No!"

"Then what are you asking? That I leave you alone for a while?"

Her silence stabbed him in the gut.

"You said it yourself," she finally mumbled. "You've had years to get used to this. I've had three days. I need to let things settle inside of me and reset. Get a grip on what I'm supposed to do about it all."

"Is that what you need? Time?" he asked. His voice sounded incredulous, hurt, even to his own ears.

"Just a little bit of time. Give me a few days to breathe. I'm not canceling my flight; I'll go to LA soon."

He had no words. His fight had dried up when she'd asked him to say nothing, to step aside.

"Just a few days, okay?" Ana said, her voice small.

"Okay," he said, defeated. He scoffed. "I sent you my key earlier today. I did not expect this to happen."

"Your key?"

"To my house. I thought it'd be a romantic gesture. A sign of how much I want this."

"Liam, I want it too. I'm going to take the key. I'm not saying I'm not going to use it."

"I still hope you do."

"Me, too."

He believed her and, yet, as he hung up the call, he felt like fog had fallen around him.

Chapter 22

A NA CRIED FOR A long time after their call. After her tears had dried up, she texted Ely and asked her to come spend time with her after work. In the hours before Ely arrived, Ana searched online for stories of people who had fallen in love with someone famous. Some had worked out, some hadn't. Just like any other relationship. It helped her hold on to hope it could work for Liam and her, if only she learned to handle the attention.

Ely came to Ana's place with aguardiente and their favorite take out. They sat on the floor and used the coffee table for their food and glasses. It felt more intimate that way, as Ana told Ely of her conversation with Liam, her fears, and Diana's email.

"Have you heard from Liam?" Ely asked, a slight arch to her eyebrow.

"No. He's giving me time, like I asked."

"Is it everything you wanted? Is time helpful?"

Ana knew Ely's tone: a challenge to admit she'd been mistaken. That she'd messed up.

"It's only been a few hours. I need more time to settle, don't I?"

Ely shook her head.

"Tell me what you really think," Ana said with sarcasm. Ely's directness was one of Ana's favorite things about her friend, but it didn't make it easier when she had difficult things to say.

"I think time isn't what's going to make a difference. You need to get clear about what you want and how to make it work."

"And I need time to do that."

"Sure, but alone? That's not letting Liam into your thinking. That's not very relationship-y of you. He's also the one with the most experience here about what it's like to deal with B.S. like this all the time. You know, you can let him give you advice."

"He told me to ignore it, but isn't it easy for him to say? He can ignore it and it won't affect his career. Ignoring it could hurt me."

"Ana, you know I love you, so I'll tell you this: letting this get in the way of what you feel for him will also hurt you."

"So I'm doomed. I'll be hurt anyway."

"Yes."

Ana put her box of takeaway on the center table, finding it hard to eat. "Great."

"You know it's true."

"It's true, but shouldn't I do my best to plan how to manage it? Minimize the pain? See if there's a way to avoid it? There must be a way where what people say doesn't matter and my career survives and I keep Liam."

"I'm sure there is, but it's not something you can predict. You can't control the future that way."

"So what do I do?"

Ely left her food on the table and surrounded Ana's shoulders with an arm. "You learn to be okay with it and let the people who love you hold you while you weep. That should include Liam, by the way."

Ana sighed. "I don't want my career to collapse. To break."

"I don't think all the tabloid nonsense will ruin it; at worst it might slow it down for a bit, but you won't lose it all, and not permanently. You've worked hard and your films will stand the test of this crap. Especially if you let Liam help you balance things out with his influence."

Ana shook her head. "Isn't that using him?"

"It's not using him if he honestly wants to help you. Isn't that like allyship? Using his power to help you use your voice. I'd expect that from my partner."

Before Ana could reply, the doorbell rang and she got up to open the door— not before taking a look through the peephole. It looked like a mailman. The memory came back to her: Liam had sent her his key.

"Shit," she mumbled, a spear to her heart, before opening the door and signing off on the certified delivery.

"What's that?" Ely said, curious, as Ana returned to sit on the floor.

"I think I know."

Ana opened the envelope and peered inside; upon confirmation, she angled the package to let the keys inside slip onto her hand.

Ana sighed, and her heart flew up to her throat. "These are the keys to Liam's house in LA."

"What?! I thought— well— wasn't he giving you space?"

"He told me he sent them before we had the phone call."

Ana took a note from the envelope.

Ana,

As much as I feel like I want to do a grand gesture, I don't think it's what you need from me at the moment. So please let me show you in this small way instead how much I believe in us.

- Liam

Ana couldn't help it, her eyes filled with tears. Ely leaned toward her and read the note in her hands. Without saying anything, she hugged her.

"You haven't asked," Ely finally said, letting go. "But I think Liam might be it for you."

"I think so, too."

"And you messed up."

Ana sniffled. "I did."

"If this weren't Liam McMillan, if he weren't the hottest actor in Hollywood and had more money in his bank account than our whole town put together," Ana chuckled at this with her, "even if he were a random Liam in the world... this is someone who clearly wants you in their life. Isn't that what this should really be about?"

Ana didn't reply, but not because she disagreed— she didn't reply because Ely was right.

"The question is, do you want him in your life?" Ely added.

"That's never been the question," Ana said. "I know I do."

"It is the right question, my friend. All this stuff around you two— that's going to die down. After you're together for a while, people will get bored because there will be no news."

"Do you really think it'll die down?"

"Okay, maybe there's always going to be a bit of that, so I oversold it," Ely joked and Ana laughed. "But I'm sure it'll go down to something you won't even think about much. Even if it didn't, though— Liam is worth that mess, and I know you know it."

"Thank you for being awesome."

"I can't help it."

"I need to talk to him." Ana sighed. "Tell him how I feel. Let him help me and hold me and not run away until I rationalize it somehow."

"At the very least. Find a grand gesture maybe. The poor guy must be dying."

"It's been three hours, Ely. Four days since he was here."

"So?"

She laughed. "I want to do it."

"Meanwhile, I'll keep my alerts for you two. You don't have to worry about a thing. I'll always have your back."

───

Ana woke up with resolve in every cell of her body: she would show Liam she chose him. That, more than quiet, more than a plan, more than anything, she wanted him.

She packed some of the things she'd like to take with her to LA, fantasizing about the moment she'd see him and cling to him, holding him close until he believed her. She tried to reschedule her trip to Sunday but wasn't successful. She tried to find Mo's number, too, hoping he'd be able to help her. She wasn't lucky with that, either.

Deciding to call again later, she watched her favorite recorded moments, then got a couple of hours of work done. She caught herself checking her phone often, wanting to see a text from Liam, missing him. No texts came through. Of course, he didn't know she was done needing time and, after less than a day since their last talk, he respected her request and didn't push. It only made her want to show up with a grand gesture herself even more.

She tried calling the airline again. While on hold, she posted a clip to social media which got flooded with comments within minutes. With lava in her veins, she read a few despite everyone's advice, testing herself. Proving that she could take it and it would not make her change her mind: she wouldn't be afraid, and she wouldn't hide. Hiding in fear could hurt her career more than anything anyone said about her could. Fear could ruin the magical thing she'd found with Liam, and she would not take that risk, anymore.

While still waiting for the airline to pick up, she received an email from Diana with an attachment titled *Statement Draft*. Ana ignored it; she was done with that, too. Instead, she announced a live stream for an hour after.

Forty-five minutes later, Ana still had not been connected to someone on the phone, and she had to hang up and lose her place in the queue again, forced to set up for the live video. After one last look at her notes, she had barely enough time to ignore one more email from Diana, one asking her to confirm approval of the draft she'd sent before the stream started. Clicking the notification away, she took a deep breath and pressed *go live.*

At first she kept to her notes. She talked about how this latest project got set up and the importance of being genuine but, not five minutes into it, the amount of live reactions and comments overwhelmed her. They were too loud to ignore: most of them asked her about Liam and a few were about Dave; some were messages for her, fans expressing their feelings about her and her work. She tried to keep chatting with fans, to keep the rhythm going, but this stream was different than the ones before. Her pace broke.

She turned silent, unaware. At least two minutes went by— a century on a live stream— where her eyes focused on the words inundating her screen. So many of those insulted her, insulted Liam, aimed to poison what they were to each other. Accusing her of terrible things, making her see red.

Ignoring the trolls wouldn't be enough, this time.

"You know what?" She finally said, looking straight to the camera. "There's no version out there of the truth. You're going to make up things about us anyway, but count yourself lucky if you're watching: this is what I want you to know about Liam and me."

Liam thanked the powers that be that he was on a break when Ana would do her live stream. How could he miss her so much after only a day?

He signed up to social media with his anonymous profile, ready to watch. He wasn't sure what to make of her choice to work despite everything going on, but at least it allowed him to check in with her in a way. God, but he hated this waiting limbo.

She came online and greeted everyone. She looked happier than he expected, both gratefulness and pain flourished inside of him. He watched her describe what the goals for this stream were and, although it all referred to work, comments were going wild. He read some of them: the fans with their *I love yous*, the trolls with their venom. Biting the inside of his lips, he typed *I love you* and sent it in. It got lost among the comments, just like he expected.

Ana got progressively flustered from reading people's words on her screen; she went silent and his ears perked up, sensing something was about to happen. She got a fiery spark in her eyes.

"You know what?" she finally said, looking straight to the camera. "There's no version out there of the truth. You're going to make up things about us anyway, but count yourself lucky if you're watching: this is what I want you to know about Liam and me."

Time stopped. He didn't breathe, lest it blocked him from hearing every single thing she said.

"Liam is an amazing man," she continued. "What we have matters more to me than all this noise some of you are making. Way more than any of the lies doing the rounds out there. He's everything, the show around us is nothing. You want the next fix in your need for drama and I don't want to give it to you. I told Liam I needed to figure out how to cope with all of you. Well, this is the first thing I'm going to do. I'm going to cope with you all. I'm here to do my work, to connect with the people who really want to connect with me. I'm going to ignore those of you who are here for a spectacle, who twist what we are out of morbid hunger for— for *dirt*— and I'm going to focus on Liam, me, and my work. That's all that matters. So I'm moving on from the crap. Sorry, folks. No Q&A after all. See some of you around! And keep an eye out for more content of my latest documentary."

She signed off. Thankfully, she had set up the stream to continue to be available for rewatching— or had forgotten to delete it. Either way, he watched it again, twice, smiling at her Depeche Mode shirt, taking everything in, burning time before he had to go into the next meeting.

Locking his phone, he made his way back to the office where he'd chat with the director and producers for *Lethal Whispers*, a new spring in his step. Seemed Ana was finally getting into a place where she didn't let things affect her.

While on his next break, Liam got into Twitter. He tended to be a bit more active on the platform while filming. His optimistic mood gave him enough energy to engage with some fans himself.

@liammcisacting
I'm doing well, thanks for asking!

He tweeted a bit nonsensically. As always, replies flooded his account almost instantaneously. He ignored them for a second, writing another tweet and sending it into the void.

@liammcisacting
Prepping to film Lethal Whispers. Not the allegory that best fits my life right now but filming action's gonna feel good.

He skimmed through the replies tab, focusing on positive ones. He wasn't surprised to see a bunch of them now talked about Ana. He read a few, until he found a couple he could reply to.

@iloveuliammc
Hey @liammcisacting, Lethal Whispers COULD be an analogy for $hitty tabloids and still be an action movie #perfectscript #mcana
@liammcisacting
.@iloveuliammc the marketing strategy would be difficult but it could work

@mcana4eva
With your help we could get #stopthenoise trending @liammcisacting #dontneedadramafix #leavethemalone
@liammcisacting
.@mcana4eva thanks for your support, but we don't need anything trending. You heard her, she wants peace.

@hollywoodfan34
@liammcisacting Any thoughts on Ana's stream?
@liammcisacting

.@hollywoodfan34 I'm wondering why I haven't lis-
tened to @depechemode in a while

Satisfied with his work, he closed his phone just as the meeting began.

Hope came to life inside of him like a nebula giving birth to a star. Though his fingers tingled with his desire to text Ana, he let himself believe there was comfort in watching her live stream. If she felt strong enough to share thoughts like those with a faceless crowd, he could trust she'd be ready to tell him those things soon, too.

Maybe it was contagious. If there was one place where he could be brave, he should. There were things of which he was tired; things that needed to stop. He finally had the resolve to do something about it. He wasn't willing to wait for his wishes to fit someone else's schedule, not anymore.

———

Ely: he watched your
live stream

Beneath the text, a screenshot of his Twitter profile. Ana read the tweets, a flutter in her stomach.

Ana: I also wonder why
he doesn't listen to
Depeche Mode more
often

Ely: What are you going to do?

Ana: Go to him asap.
I've been trying to get
the airline to reschedule
my flight but I can't get
through to them. Once
I do that, I only
have to finish packing
and go to him. Oh,
and, you know, figure
out the best way to declare
my undying love

Ely: You love him.
He clearly loves you.
This is the kind of situation
where ad libbing is best

Ana: I LOVE LIAM MCMILLAN

Ely: I think he's the
only one who doesn't
know it yet, poor guy

Ana: I will let you know
as soon as I get through
with the airline

Ely: I'll fucking drive
you if I have to

Ana: I love you too

Chapter 23

ANA DIDN'T HAVE ANY luck with the airline. She lay in bed until late that night, brainstorming ways to get to Liam, including driving to LA herself. Tempted as she was to call him, she held back; she knew she'd spill out her heart over the phone if she called him, and he deserved better than a declaration over the line while so far away.

On the other hand, she didn't want to keep him waiting. Hell, she didn't want to wait, either. Even though she'd asked him for time, which gave her a couple of days to figure things out, waiting could hurt them. Would hurt him.

She was done playing it safe. If she couldn't get the airline to reschedule her flight for the next day, she'd get further into debt and get to him, no matter what it cost her.

Her heart jumped to her throat when she woke up past eight the next morning, and saw three missed calls and two voicemails. She ignored them when she saw they weren't from Liam but from Diana, who'd called well past one in the morning for Ana's time. She'd also sent Ana an email, which she decided to read instead.

Ana,

I can't believe we've gotten to this point. You didn't

respond re: draft, you did a live stream without our input, you have yet to make it clear you and Liam are not involved, you're not answering my calls and emails. You're very lucky that things seem to be still balancing towards all of this being publicity for you, or this could be a career-killing disaster. Please, don't count this as good news. We're definitely not out of the hole yet.

A big problem right now is that Mr. Coulton is really angry and has demanded a meeting with you tomorrow. I don't know the particulars but something has happened with Liam McMillan that Mr. Coulton may be blaming you for. I have a meeting with Mr. Coulton first thing in the morning and then one with you and him. I'm confident I don't need to tell you how detrimental to your career it would be to have Mr. Coulton against you in this industry. So be at the airport at 9:00 am (documents attached) and a car will take you straight into the TCA offices.

I trust you will be on your best behavior.

- Diana.

A short string of curses went through her mind. She ran to the bathroom and showered in record time, then called Ely as she went through her clean clothes.

"Ely, I need your help."

"Sure, what's up?"

"I'm in trouble with TCA."

"Uh oh."

"They're flying me to LA. I have to be in the airport before 9 and I haven't even packed yet. I'll take a cab to the airport but—

will you come to my place tonight and clean out the fridge, check everything will be safe while I'm gone? I may need you to pack my editing equipment, I'm not sure yet."

"Sure! Does this mean you're planning to stay in LA for a while?"

"If Liam will have me, yes."

———

Ana didn't have time to worry about paparazzi when she left her building. She ignored the people calling questions and invading her space as she climbed on the taxi, and made it on time to the airport— barely. Things calmed down while flying to LA on a chartered plane and, once landed, someone took her to the build- ing and someone else up to the 23rd floor again. There, Alexis met her once more, this time cold more than professional. Magda also seemed displeased with her, a judgmental slant to her lips as she took Ana directly to the boardroom.

Okay, she was getting the treatment of a scolded child, then. Ana couldn't find it in her to care. Not her fault that they were working on a Saturday. Instead of worrying, her thoughts filled with the fact that she was in LA and, if everything went according to plan, she would see Liam that night.

She'd had time to think during the flight. All she'd thought about was him.

Coulton and Diana waited for her, sitting at the big meeting table. She studied them both, noting Diana's mouth pressing in a severe, tight line; Coulton's frown and dark eyes.

"Hello, Ana," Diana said. Coulton said nothing.

"Hello, Diana. Mr. Coulton," she greeted, thinking that it might be best to go back to formalities.

Diana indicated Ana could take a seat. She did. She waited, eyes assessing.

Silence stretched, a heavy cloak in the room. Diana checked in with Coulton, who continued to silently fume in his chair. Perhaps seeing something Ana missed, Diana turned back to Ana and stared at her with a severe frown.

She cleared her throat. "Ana, we called you in here today because we need to discuss matters of the utmost importance."

"I'm listening," Ana replied.

"As I described to Mr. Coulton, you and I have been communicating extensively over the situation between you and Mr. McMillan. I've advised you again and again that whatever it is that the two of you think you're doing, my professional opinion is that it is not to your advantage to continue your involvement with him beyond what results directly from the documentary project."

"You have," Ana confirmed.

"I do not appreciate you putting ideas in my client's head," Coulton said on the other side. His voice echoed a growl.

Ana's blood went on a slow simmer at his words. "I've done no such thing."

"Careful, Ana—" Diana seemed to want to add more, but Coulton interrupted her.

"Last night, I received an email from Liam." Coulton's tone attempted coldness, but it failed at hiding the fire beneath.

Coulton gave a printed copy of the email to Ana, who read it.

Coulton,

Since we began working together, I've been doing things your way. Lately I've come to realize that it isn't how I want to do things anymore. I asked you for time to rest, cope with the demands of my schedule, and I didn't get what I needed— not that I could ever regret what did happen. But it wasn't what I asked of you, and I don't want that to happen again.

I'm moving on from projects that don't mean anything to me. I want to do my work and connect with the people who love what I do— both in terms of fans and people I work with. I want to ignore those who only care about the spectacle and I'm going to focus on what matters to me. The decision will be mine. I hope I can count on your support.

I expect you will want to talk about this. I can move some things around and see you tomorrow. Set the time and I'll be there.

- Liam

Ana didn't think her imagination played tricks with her: his email and her speech on the stream shared some similarities. A small smile creeped on her face.

Coulton confirmed her impression.

"As you can see, he seems to have been *inspired*—" the word held a hint of irony as he said it— "by your little rant from yesterday. Diana has confirmed that this sounds like what you've said."

"I do think so, yes," Ana agreed, butterflies in her stomach.

"You're so new, Ana." Diana frowned next to Coulton. "You may not have realized yet you're not only putting your career at risk, but his too."

"You think I'm ruining his career?" While Ana did her best to hide the scoff building in her, it escaped her through a tight throat.

"You're feeding him lines!" Coulton exclaimed to her other side.

"He's been telling you he wanted a break since before I came into the picture. You wanted to use me to not let him take a break."

"Ana," Diana warned.

"Use you?" Coulton continued, ignoring the other agent. "I gave you the opportunity of a lifetime and this is how you repay me? Now he's fighting me, thinking he can do what he wants. You convinced him he can do what he wants. You will ruin his career."

Ana allowed some of her frustration to fuel the volume of her voice. "I would never presume to know what's best for him. I've never as much as implied what I think he should or shouldn't do regarding his career and, even if, for some strange reason I did want to do that, he wouldn't just fall for it. He has a stronger character than you give him credit for."

"Yes, and I've had to challenge that, train him, hone him into the star he is." Coulton's voice now truly held a sharp edge. "I see his timelessness, the potential in his future, but you— oh, you, pretentious nobody, you quickly underestimated Diana's advice and made your own choices. It'll be your downfall."

Ana stared at him in disbelief, then at Diana, hoping her agent would have a word in her defense. She didn't. The betrayal twisted a knife in her gut. Her agent showed her clearly what Ana could expect from her.

"Liam is making a mistake," Coulton added. "After all I've done— but somehow he'd rather listen to you. So if you really don't want to jeopardize his career, then you'll have to help us change his mind, and guide him back into course."

"I'm not following." Ana didn't glance at Diana again. She would not try to engage her agent anymore.

"We are here to represent the best in the business. Liam has proven his star quality, but you have a ways to go." Coulton rested his elbows on the table, stapling his hands.

"We will meet with Mr. McMillan to discuss the situation," Diana finally added. Ana's stomach flipped. "As your manager, Ana, you have to know I want the best for you. My advice is always based on the experience I have in the business, which you don't have, and the connections we have as TCA, which you also lack. I know you signed with us because you understood what we can do for you. What I can do for you. I can only do that if you trust and follow my guidance."

"What are you really saying?" Ana's attention narrowed to the threats clouding the room. She'd have to prepare for that meeting— for seeing Liam— later.

"Prove that you can do your part to follow TCA's representation of your work by following our guidance," Diana further explained. "Do as we ask."

"What do you want me to do?"

"If you care about your and Liam's career," Coulton said, "then you won't mind helping us convince him that we know what's best for both of you."

"Don't break up with Mr. McMillan yet." Diana glanced at Coulton once more. "Use your connection to him for a little while— help him see reason. Once things calm down, I'll help you slowly create distance from Mr. McMillan. If we can, we'll end it before the premiere... but we can wait until after. Mr. Coulton believes it can serve as good publicity for the film. To... support you, Mr. Coulton has graciously offered to help us use his connections to plant positive articles in your name, helping you come victorious out of everything, as well as to help you film your next project— whatever you can dream of, he'll help us."

"Anything," Coulton added. "I'll help Diana make it happen, if you do as we say. But if you feel you know better than we do, despite our experience... then perhaps TCA is not the best place for you."

Ana's eyes jumped back and forth between the two people in front of her, unbelieving. She would have laughed in her disdain, but the door opened behind her.

"Mr. Coulton, Mr. McMillan," Magda announced.

Ana's laughter died in her throat, surprise squeezing her vocal cords. She turned in her seat to stare at him, her hands trembling as they fell to the arms of her chair. When their eyes locked, he startled; it seemed Ana wasn't the only one in shock at this encounter.

Ana never imagined that the meeting Diana mentioned would happen within the next ten minutes. She didn't have time to prepare! To coach her heart to be calm, to show him with her eyes that she was on his side, to push her feelings to her skin so he would see it all, and understand. Instead, she got lost in him, in the sudden tension in the line of his shoulders, in his tight lips, and her want to kiss him hard. To soothe him— to soothe them both.

She opened her mouth to talk but no words came out. While on the plane, she'd imagined something completely different, an intimate moment in his home. She had imagined that she would be at his place when he made it home from meetings— his calendar had one big block scheduled until 5:00pm— and that when he looked at her, he would know: she'd chosen him. She would confirm everything with her words, telling him that she was ready, she knew how to make it work. That she was in LA to be with him, despite all the noise.

Instead, they were meeting in Coulton's office and their witnesses wanted to play them like marionettes.

Liam slowed down upon seeing her, but took the final steps to the empty chair next to Ana with casual aplomb. He glanced around the room, going from Ana, to Diana, and finally to Coulton.

"Thanks for coming, Liam," the man said in a much more conciliatory voice than he had used for Ana.

"I didn't know we'd have company," Liam replied, his eyes stealing another glance at Ana.

"We thought we could all help you think things through," Coulton said. "I invited Diana because she represents Ana, and Ana because, well, because I think she might get through to you."

"You mean you staged an intervention." Liam crossed his fingers over his navel, elbows on the chair's arms.

Coulton laughed but there wasn't a lot of mirth in it. "Do I have to?"

Liam shrugged. "I don't think so, no."

"I need to be honest, Liam. I'm worried." Coulton frowned, and Ana wondered if maybe he'd missed his calling as an actor himself.

Liam's mouth turned down at the corner in a dismissive gesture. "I'm not."

"You don't understand. If you start getting choosy then you won't be the top choice anymore."

"I don't need to be at the top of the a-list. I only need to work on things I personally like. Do fewer projects a year."

"That's not as easy as you think. You still are at a place where you work to be chosen. Only after you've reached the point of having more offers than you can handle, can you pick and choose."

"I think I'm there. I already have more offers than I can possibly take. I think I can start choosing what I want to work on and still remain relevant."

"You're nowhere near as big as you could get!"

"And what is that going to get me?"

"Freedom! Money, power. Anything you want."

Liam stole another peek at Ana. "I don't think I want much more than I already have."

"Ana," Diana said, her eyes glancing at Coulton, who glared at Ana. "Would you like to chime in?"

Liam studied the agents in front of them for a second or two, before setting his eyes on Ana.

"Did they coach you on what to say?" He asked.

"Not quite," Ana replied. "They dangled bait and told me what they want— they think they're making me choose between you and my career."

She'd expected her voice to tremble, her gut to twist at the words she chose. Instead, she'd found the calm she'd wanted.

"How dare you!" Coulton raised his voice.

"Ana!" Diana called at the same time.

"What are you going to choose?" Liam asked, his voice soft despite Coulton and Diana's energy. His eyes were steady on her, ignoring their agents, waiting for Ana's reply.

Ana put her hand on his arm. "It's not a real choice. The answer is very simple."

"Out! I'll deal with you later!" Coulton tried, reading into her tone, the way her fingers grabbed at Liam. Ana ignored him.

"I love you, Liam. I'm proud of what you're doing, setting boundaries." Liam allowed a short, quick inhale, maybe it had escaped him. His eyes widened and softened an instant later. "I've been trying to get to LA since yesterday morning—

His lips opened into a soft smile. But Diana interrupted anything else they might have said.

"Ana, let's go to my office," Diana commanded.

Ana looked away from Liam to challenge her agent.

"So that you can fire me as a client? No, thank you."

Liam took her hand from his arm, interlocking their fingers together.

"You can't seriously think this is going to last!" Diana told Ana.

At the same time, Coulton talked to Liam. He stood, hands on the table. "You're making a huge mistake. After all I've done? I want us to be the best! I want you to be the very best. Don't throw that away for something as temporary as a romance!"

Liam got up, still holding Ana's hand. Squeezing it tight.

"We'll talk to resolve the pending contracts and discuss an exit strategy," Liam said. "Now I'm leaving with Ana."

"Liam, we have to talk," Coulton tried again.

"Yes, we do, but not now."

"Exit strategy is the wrong term as that's used for—"

"I know what it's used for," Liam said, pulling Ana out of the office. "You're fired, Coulton."

Ana's heart rioted in her chest. She let Liam guide her out of the boardroom, not before Ana took a last glance at their agents—ex-agents. Bubbling joy filled her lungs at the pure shock on their faces, and she smiled— a wide grin in goodbye.

She held on to Liam's arm, whose hand kept on crushing hers. They raced through the office with fast, heavy steps, quickly gaining ground towards the elevator. Liam pressed the button several times with his free hand.

Coulton power-walked to them while they waited for the lift.

"Liam, listen, we can discuss further—"

The doors opened and Ana and Liam stepped in.

"Sure, yeah. We can talk more if you want, but not now. Talk to you on Monday," he added as the doors closed.

It took Ana a second to truly believe they were alone now, another second to breathe again, and one more to look up at Liam. It took no time for them to jump at each other.

He grabbed her head, angling it for an earth-shattering kiss, and she kissed him with the same desperation. He walked her back and pushed her against the elevator wall; her arms went over his shoulders and around his neck, holding him tight. His hands were rough where they roamed over her body, fingers clasping and grabbing as they moved. As if he tried to make sure she was real, and stood with him. Fireworks exploded in her chest and in her brain almost to the point of dizziness.

The elevator stopped a few stories below, the ding of it barely making it into Ana's awareness. Liam took a step back and Ana had to shake her head to re-orient herself to the mirrored car. Two people were joining them in the elevator, and their eyes studied Liam and Ana with a spark of recognition, and a smile that made it clear they'd gotten a bit of a show.

"Good morning," Liam said. He cleared his throat and reached for Ana's hand again; the elevator continued its journey down the building.

"I love your movies," one of them said. The other one gave Ana a curious look.

"Thank you."

"Do you mind if we take a picture?"

Ana watched Liam with panic freezing her brain and, even though his wide-open green eyes reflected similar feelings, he recovered quickly.

"Uhm— sure—"

"C'mon," their companion hissed. "Don't you see that... didn't you see how... we're *interrupting*."

Liam laughed, loosening a chuckle from Ana herself. The elevator made it to the parking level.

"We can take a picture, if you like." Liam checked Ana with mirth in his eyes.

They stepped out of the elevator into the slightly humid, cold air of the parking lot.

"I'll take the picture," she offered, letting go of Liam's hand after a brief squeeze.

Pained by the horrible lighting, Ana did her best to take a good picture of the three of them. When the owner of the phone came closer to take it back, they whispered to Ana, *you queen.*

They said a quick goodbye and Liam guided Ana to his car. At first she thought he took her to the passenger door as a show of gallantry, but got it right when he pressed her against it and kissed her once more. Her arms crossed around his neck again, and they settled into slow kisses in the parking garage, his hands mostly settling on her waist, enjoying the moment as if they were alone like they were back in the cabin. Like they were surrounded by ocean and rocky cliffs, instead of drab columns of concrete and wire.

Liam peeled off her with evident effort, breaking the kiss, but keeping his face close to hers. She could feel his breath on her lips. "Let's go to my place."

Heart fluttery, she got into his car and he drove them off the building and towards his house. He drove with one hand, the other hot on her thigh. As if he still had trouble believing she was there.

At their first red light, he gazed at her with starry emerald eyes.

"I didn't know you'd be in the meeting," Liam said. "I thought I'd have to wait a few more days to talk to you again."

"I flew in this morning. I was hoping to see you tonight. I had big plans."

"You did?"

"Well... I went as far as imagining showing up to your house and surprising you somehow. I had so much trouble getting through to the airline; I wanted to reschedule my flight to come this weekend but I couldn't and then... then TCA brought me here." The light went green and Liam looked out to the road again, and she held his hand on her thigh between her palms. "I've improvised everything since arriving this morning but I had one goal: find you and—and—"

"We have a lot to talk about," Liam said, entwining his fingers with hers on her leg. "I want to see you telling me these things and not miss a thing. I can't do that while driving in LA traffic."

"I get it, of course."

"Let me call Mo and plan a couple of things, okay? I need to reschedule my meetings today and also—"

"My stuff!"

"What?"

"I left my bag in the office! I was too— and I didn't realize—"

"It's fine. Let me call Mo and we'll figure it out, okay?" He brought their joined hands to his lips. "We're together now."

———

Liam rescheduled a few things over the speakerphone, including a plan for Mo to come to Liam's place in a couple of hours to drop off Ana's bag and food for dinner. Once he hung up, Liam and Ana chatted about the production for *Lethal Whispers*, keeping away from personal matters while he drove.

Ely texted Ana as they got to his house. It included the screen-shot of a blurry picture of them someone had taken in the parking garage, and which was doing the rounds.

Ely: I'm happy for you
guys! You'll have to tell
me the deets after you're
done tearing each other's
clothes off. Don't hurry,
I can wait!

Ana chuckled. "Seems the couple you took pictures with spied on us and posted it on social media."

"Mh?" Liam put the car in Park and opened his car's door.

He came around to find Ana, who'd gotten out of the car as well and now showed him the picture.

"Worth it," was all he said.

She followed him inside. She kicked off her shoes automatically and, with a chuckle, he did too.

"I wonder why I kept my shoes the first time I came here," she said.

He took her hands and walked backwards, leading her further into the house. "I thought maybe you taking them off now meant that you're entering my home feeling more comfortable... like this could be a home to you, too."

"Huh." She smiled, a response to his grin.

She assumed he'd lead her to the living room but he didn't, he turned towards his bedroom. She arched her eyebrow, her smile in place.

The decor echoed the same style as the rest of his house: dark tones, broken up by warm wood and light gray bedspread and linens. The headboard served as a focal point in the middle of the neutrality, its blue so intense it reminded her of the ocean. In the same vein, there were more paintings here, like in the rest of his house. Her eyes rested briefly on a family picture on top of his dresser.

A small, curious part of her wanted to study the photo, but she didn't. She'd have time for that later. Now all that mattered was the gleam in his eyes.

He pulled her to him. He placed her hands on his back and then put his own on her face, holding her with thumbs on her jawline.

"There is something you need to know," he said.

"What's that?"

He smoothed back her hair, fingers running through her loose hair until they cradled the back of her neck. "I love you, too."

Warmth exploded in the middle of her chest, the spark she'd tried to stomp out the first day at the beach bursting into a constellation.

She filled her hands with his shirt and stole a kiss from him.

"I love you, Liam. Everything I was most worried about happened—" she let out an exasperated chuckle— "my career was threatened, I'm in the tabloids. I was so scared of getting hurt again, and I did get hurt, and yet all that stuff doesn't seem so bad now. Not because it wasn't awful, it was. But because it was worth it to get to this place, with you."

"I feel at home with you too." He kissed her again. "Let's do this together. It's all I ever wanted."

Chapter 24

T HEY HAD A MEAL together with Mo, who left in the early evening. Liam and Ana made drinks and took them outside, where Liam insisted that they sit on the same lounge chair. Ana rested against his chest and between his legs.

She sighed, burrowing into him.

"Comfortable?"

"Very."

"I imagined this many times, when we were at the beach." He surrounded her with his arms.

"It was a good time, wasn't it."

"Ready to talk?"

"Yes. There are a few things we could use chatting about."

"I'll start. I want to know how the hell you ended up in that meeting with Coulton and Diana."

"First off, I want you to know, I had already planned to come as soon as possible. A few hours after we talked on Thursday, I decided I couldn't risk our relationship because of everyone else's opinions. Trying to cope alone made no sense. I tried to change my flight but failed so I did the live stream— well, you saw that."

"It gave me hope, but I didn't realize you had already decided."

"I was trying to figure out how to do a romantic gesture. I wanted to show you how committed I am."

He squeezed her tight, his hands on her belly. "I didn't need more than your words and your presence next to me, but you declaring your love for me in front of our agents did quite well."

"That was not planned."

"It worked. You were so certain; no hesitation. Like you didn't care about the nonsense anymore and were willing to tell them to stuff it."

"Maybe Ely was right, then. Being spontaneous— ad libbing, she called it— works best for this kind of thing."

He grinned. "Have I told you how much I like Ely?"

"I like her too. She's probably at my place now, making sure things are okay there. I had to leave so quickly this morning to make it in time that I had to basically abandon everything. I think I forgot a couple of things so I may need to go shopping soon, but I'll figure it out. I'm here now and that's what matters. In a way, Coulton and Diana did me a favor by calling me in for that meeting."

A bird called from somewhere, disrupting the quiet sounds of the lapping water in the pool.

He sighed. "So what do we do now?"

"Are you really going to fire Coulton?"

"Probably. How can I trust him? He staged an intervention and tried to use you to get what he wanted."

"He'll blame me for it. It was the whole point of having me there; they thought I was telling you to stop listening to Coulton. That if I said something about your career you'd listen."

She put her hands on top of his, running her nails against his fingers.

"I mean, I would." Liam's words caressed her ear. "Of course I'd listen to your opinion. But not in the way he expected. If we're a couple, I would want to think about our careers in terms of how we plan our lives together. Wouldn't you?"

"I would, of course. Our careers will have an impact on how we live our lives, so, yeah."

"I think we need to talk through some things, here." He took a hand away to reach for his drink. Ana did the same. The evening remained warm, but a gentle sea breeze danced around them.

"What do you mean?"

"I think you're right, Coulton is going to blame you. Did they really threaten to fire you?"

"Yes. I guess I need to figure out now what to do about that."

"Your contract with Diana was for representation and management, right? My contract for the documentary was with your own production company."

"Yes. The documentary is a deal between you and me, facilitated by Coulton and Diana as our representatives."

"Perfect. That means you can continue with that project as usual. It's yours."

"Yes, which is an enormous relief. I basically have to go back to what I was doing before. Distribution is going to be difficult again, as my reach got cut back to what it was six months ago. At least your involvement will likely open a few doors."

"Okay. That works."

"How?" she asked, frowning, turning on the chair to gaze at him. Close like this, she could see each thick lash around his eyes, and even the furrows within his impossibly green irises.

He gave her a small kiss. "I'd like to invest in your production company."

"Wait— What?!" She reared back.

He laughed. "I thought about it last night, before sending the email to Coulton."

"You've been thinking about this?"

"Yeah. Remember your last day here the first time? You asked me what I wanted to do."

"You said you want to produce, direct, act."

"I think it makes sense. If I invest in your production company, I can use my connections and resources to set up the things I'm interested in... while I help minimize the ways things are impacting you."

She took the words in, silent; her heart tender, her breathing deep and fast. She leaned her forehead to his chin.

"You've said you're the one who stands to lose the most in our relationship," he added. "I'm afraid you're right. I thought this is a way in which I can help change that. Use what I've built to help you and, in that way, help us. If we set up something together, we both can grow closer to where we wanna be."

"Career wise, that's an amazing idea but... don't you think it'll make things complicated for us? Mixing business with our relationship?"

"Only if we break up and if it's up to me, that's not gonna happen. Still, I think we need to have a contract to make things clear. Written by a lawyer and all. Something that draws clear lines between pleasure and work."

She reached for his hand. "I agree with that."

"I think one of the rules we should have as a couple may not fit there in the contract."

"What's that?"

"We should put our relationship first. We invest in our relationship first and foremost."

"I'd like that. It's what I'm trying to do with being here for a while."

He kissed her temple. "We can see what happens in the next couple of months. We can start planning and setting up the company, and build that up."

"And next?"

"We make it work. Maybe you'll find you want to go back to Bloomington for a bit, maybe stay back and forth for a while. Maybe you travel with me sometimes, and we go on like that."

"And next?"

"Next never ends."

⸻

"Get in the pool with me." He uttered the words directly into her ear, stealing a nibble from the shell of it.

Light had faded, the sun hiding behind the Pacific.

She shivered and he squeezed her tight. "I didn't bring my bikini. Packing in a panic, remember?"

"There's no one around. We can keep the lights off and swim in our underwear. I'd prefer it that way, anyway."

His eyes sparkled. She smiled.

"Maybe you can teach me to float again, and I can fall into space from the weightlessness of the water."

"We could do the floating but there's too much light from the city for the other part to work. We could still try."

"Let's try."

They undressed, flirting by the pool.

He got into the water and when she stood close enough, he took her hand and brought her close to him.

Her arms around his shoulders, she wrapped her legs around his hips. His hands held her from the curve of her lower back, almost her behind.

He sighed. "This is how it should be, every time we're in the water."

"You make it sound like this has been in your mind."

"It has."

"How badly did you want to kiss me? When you tried in the pool."

"I wanted it so badly that I tried even when I knew I shouldn't. That I should wait."

"I've watched that clip a hundred times while editing, trying to guess, imagining what would have happened."

He submerged them in the water until it reached their neck. He took a few awkward steps with her still clinging to him.

"Do you plan to let go of me?" he asked.

She shook her head. "This is too good, and the weekend is only so long, before you have to return to your ridiculous schedule." She gave him a soft kiss, another. "I plan to be as close to you as I can."

He grinned, reaching the deeper end of the pool so he could stand almost upright, Ana still holding on to him. "What about floating?"

"I changed my mind. I want to stay like this forever."

He chuckled. "Okay. Teaching you how to float will be part of our long-term plan. And if my eyes and hands wander a bit while practicing in the future, at least it won't be too bad, from now on."

"What do you think would have happened if I'd let you kiss me, that day in the pool?"

"I'd argue I didn't try to kiss you, per se. I made it so you would have to kiss me. I made it clear I was inviting you to."

"Sure. Okay. Then, what do you think would have happened if I'd kissed you?"

"I would have kissed you back. I would have held you and kissed you some more. We would have spent the next several days kissing on the sand and in the ocean..."

She laughed, squeezing his neck with her arms and kissing his jaw. "There's a lot of making out in this alternate universe."

"And sex. And cuddling. And talks."

He walked her back to the side of the pool, where he pressed his body against her. She grunted a bit and kissed his neck, then gazed at him full of adoration.

"Well, I'm glad to hear there would have been *some* conversation. I had a documentary to film, after all."

"But we did more than that, didn't we? More than filming a documentary."

She nodded. "And I'm pretty sure it'll show through on the film."

"You know, Coulton is many things but, out of everything I'll be grateful to him for— getting us into this project is number one.

"I don't know what's going to happen. How people will react to my documentary, or to what happened with our agents, everything that's going on in the media... but one thing I know."

"What's that?"

"I'm going to do it with you."

He smiled, giving her another kiss, this one slow and lazy and full of enduring promise.

"For light years to come."

Chapter 25

Epilogue

FOR THIS PROMO TOUR, Liam's team had scheduled a round of interviews for late night talk shows. Today he was a guest on their favorite show in New York, and Ana had flown there to spend a few days together. She waited for him in the green room, watching him on the small screen for the live stream.

She didn't think she'd ever get tired of staring at him. He was easy on the eyes, for sure. Her lip curled at imagining his reaction, if he knew her current thoughts admiring his looks. He'd get those flirty eyes that used to worry her, only now she'd welcome them. She'd flirt right back.

The show's host directed the conversation. "You're here promoting your latest movie, *Burnt Falcon.* It's a thriller where you are a lawyer that gets involved with criminals against his will, and you end up having to do some dark things to get out of it alive."

"Yes. The story is really about pushing my character's morals to the limit. He has to ask himself the question, what am I really doing this for? And then we see him struggle with the answer."

"And it was fascinating to watch! That scene where you have to–"

"Don't spoil it for people!"

The audience laughed, ready to go wherever Liam took them with his charisma.

She was so, so lucky.

"Right, right," the host conceded. "Okay, let's say it's the scene in the woods."

"Sure."

"It broke me, man."

"This is going to sound weird, but... thank you."

"There are rumors you'll get a nomination for it."

"We'll see. It would be great but, as long as people enjoy it, I'll be happy."

"And recently you started a new project, right? Directed by Ana Lira, again, I understand?"

"Ana is directing me, yeah. It'll be a new thing for both of us. It's fiction, which is new for her, and being directed by someone so close to me..."

He didn't finish the sentence, but the sparkle in his eyes showed clear through the screen. She smirked and shook her head at the TV.

"It'll be interesting?" The host suggested.

"Yeah. *Interesting.* That's the word."

Everyone laughed again.

"Now, let's talk about that for a minute. There have been some reports saying that you and Ana have indeed gotten married and that you've been married for a while. Some people on the internet—" the host showed a picture of a Twitter thread— "are convinced that you and Ana Lira eloped. One of them found this." The host dropped the first picture, revealing a second one behind it: a picture of a marriage certificate, with the names of witnesses and parents blacked out but leaving Liam and Ana's name clearly visible.

He played with the ring on his pinky finger. She did the same with hers, which she wore on her index finger. They both wore simple bands permanently, with their wedding set worn occasionally.

Liam nodded at the picture. Ana wondered if he also thought of their wedding, like her, or if he only focused on how to handle the conversation. Ana had talked with Liam about what he planned to say; they had had a discussion with the show producers about how far this conversation could go. They had chosen to talk about this development for the first time on this show, and actually commenting on their relationship publicly was new for both of them.

"Did someone fake this?" the host joked.

Liam chuckled. "No. We did get married a few months ago."

"You eloped?!"

"If you want to call it that."

"Congratulations!" The audience applauded, and the band played a quick rendition of the wedding march.

Liam smiled, and the grin was one of his real ones. "Thank you."

"Neither of you ever talk about the relationship, so forgive me if I'm a bit out of sorts."

"It's all good. Yeah, we don't talk about us with people."

"You only make documentaries that show you falling in love with each other."

Liam laughed alongside the audience.

"That's right. Although it wasn't the official theme of the film, we stopped arguing with people when they tell us it also shows the start of our relationship."

"You also have a successful indie production company together."

"Yes. We're pretty proud of what we've built together with Jump Cannon Productions."

"It's a family business, I understand?"

Liam nodded. "My brother and Ana's best friend are part of it. The four of us make a great team together."

"But it hasn't always been easy."

"No. We've had some ups and downs with the tabloids but, luckily, besides the random fake scandal or pictures of us living our life, we're just not that interesting to them anymore."

"You're just an old married couple. Boring."

Liam laughed. "Exactly. It's what I wanted. Being an old, married man."

"I'm just going to warn the network that they're going to have to bleep part of this but— Liam, you clearly got what you wanted. You look happy as fuck!

Liam laughed. It warmed Ana's heart.

"Congratulations again, Liam. Thank you so much for coming here today. Liam McMillan, everybody!"

The show on the screen continued, going to commercials. Ana leaned back on the sofa, expecting Liam to come into the room any time now. When he did, she jumped out of the couch and into his arms.

"Sorry it took me a bit," he said. "I ended up chatting with people up there."

"It went great!"

"Now we can be rid of the speculation. Ely can retire from trying to keep up with the tabloids."

"Ready to do this, then?"

He smiled and, without words, reached for her neck. Getting under the collar of her blouse, he found the chain around it and pulled it out from between her breasts. She took the rings he'd held in front of her, warm from the heat of her body.

She took them with one hand and took the chain off with the other. After untangling it all, they put their rings on.

They were going to wear both sets, moving forward.

She got on the balls of her feet and reached up to kiss him.

"Three years and counting. Doesn't feel like that long, does it?"

"Doesn't feel like enough."

She put her arms over his shoulders leaning on him. "Will it ever?"

"I doubt it, and I'm good with that."

"Well, old married man. Let's go be an old married couple in the world."

He gave her one of his bright smiles, green eyes shining. "Until the stars burn out."

The End

Would you like to see Ana and Liam's half-elopement wedding? You might recognize the location ;)

Go to <u>leonorsoliz.com/ss2ndep</u> or use the QR Code below.

Thank you

WHEN I TELL PEOPLE that I moved to Canada for a man, I usually get a shocked response of some sort. If they knew this man like I do, they would understand exactly why that was the best choice I ever made. Thank you, Mr. Leonor, for believing in me and in my dreams, and for editing this book for me. You know how prepositions like to play tricks on me.

I want to thank Janelle, Sara, and my Coven for their support and encouragement. I want to thank my Discord friends, whose advice and cheerleading and feedback helped me make this book into what it is today. I want to thank every person who read this story before it was published and helped me make it into a safer read for all of us.

And I want to thank you, my reader, for giving this baby author a chance. I have so many books planned, and I can't wait to share them with you all!

About the Author

LEONOR WROTE HER FIRST Meet Cute at eight years old and never really stopped. After many years of practicing and dreaming, she took the plunge and wrote a full-length romance novel. Then she wrote some more.

Her stories are written for comfort: love as it can be. Writing love for today means diverse characters with emotional depth and wisdom. Her characters are doing the work, folks.

Leonor is a Latina living in Canada, working as a therapist during the day and fitting as much writing to her life as she can. She's also a multi-crafter, trying her hand at watercolor, jewelry, and anything else that strikes her fancy.

YOU CAN CONNECT WITH ME ON
leonorsoliz.com
hello@leonorsoliz.com
TikTok: https://www.tiktok.com/@leonor.soliz.author
Facebook: https://www.facebook.com/leonorsolizz
Instagram: https://www.instagram.com/leonor.soliz/
Twitter: https://twitter.com/leonorsolizz

Next in Series

Upcoming Series by the Author

Build My Love

The story of two Latine siblings and their best friends, and all four of them find their person.

Laguna Island

Several interconnected stories with one thing in common: their love for this slice of heaven by the sea.

Upcoming Standalones by the Author

DEAR MR. BEANPOLE

Modern retelling of Daddy Long Legs.

NO PLACE LIKE YOU

Alejandro and Jess.